# THE TYCOON WHO HEALED HER HEART

BY
MELISSA JAMES

AND

# DARING TO DATE THE BOSS

BY
BARBARA WALLACE

MILLS & BOON

Dear Reader,

This is a book about new beginnings. Life forces changes on us all. What we do with those changes and how we grow with them is what makes us the people we are. And sometimes a very special person comes along and the journey becomes beautiful.

I hope you enjoy Rachel and Armand's journey.

*Melissa*

# THE TYCOON WHO HEALED HER HEART

BY
MELISSA JAMES

All the characters in this book have no existence outside the imagination of the author, and have no relation whatsoever to anyone bearing the same name or names. They are not even distantly inspired by any individual known or unknown to the author, and all the incidents are pure invention.

All Rights Reserved including the right of reproduction in whole or in part in any form. This edition is published by arrangement with Harlequin Enterprises II B.V./S.à.r.l. The text of this publication or any part thereof may not be reproduced or transmitted in any form or by any means, electronic or mechanical, including photocopying, recording, storage in an information retrieval system, or otherwise, without the written permission of the publisher.

This book is sold subject to the condition that it shall not, by way of trade or otherwise, be lent, resold, hired out or otherwise circulated without the prior consent of the publisher in any form of binding or cover other than that in which it is published and without a similar condition including this condition being imposed on the subsequent purchaser.

® and ™ are trademarks owned and used by the trademark owner and/or its licensee. Trademarks marked with ® are registered with the United Kingdom Patent Office and/or the Office for Harmonisation in the Internal Market and in other countries.

First published in Great Britain 2012
by Mills & Boon, an imprint of Harlequin (UK) Limited,
Eton House, 18-24 Paradise Road, Richmond, Surrey TW9 1SR

© Melissa James 2011

ISBN: 978 0 263 89397 7

23-0112

Harlequin (UK) policy is to use papers that are natural, renewable and recyclable products and made from wood grown in sustainable forests. The logging and manufacturing processes conform to the legal environmental regulations of the country of origin.

Printed and bound in Spain
by Blackprint CPI, Barcelona

**Melissa James** is a born-and-bred Sydneysider who swapped the beaches of the New South Wales Central Coast for the Alps of Switzerland a few years ago. Wife and mother of three, a former nurse, she fell into writing when her husband brought home an article about romance writers and suggested she should try it—and she became hooked. Switching from romantic espionage to the family stories of Mills & Boon® was the best move she ever made. Melissa loves to hear from readers—you can e-mail her at: authormelissajames@yahoo.com.

To my lovely sister CP and confidante Mia.

We've always been there for each other, through all the ups and downs of life.

# CHAPTER ONE

*Graubünden Region, Swiss Alps*

'YOU'RE doing much better,' Rachel Chase's ski instructor said as he performed a smooth cross-country sliding ski across the final slope towards the Bollinger Alpine Resort.

'It's not true, Matt, but thank you for persisting with me.' With a grateful smile, Rachel filled her lungs with crisp, clean mountain air, set her jaw, turned her face and kept sliding across the baby slope. It was humiliating, but she constantly had to grab hold of his hand.

Probably she just didn't have the confidence to ski, but in every other way the Bollinger Alpine Resort had been the perfect hideout. The staff took excellent care of her in this lake-filled valley nestled beneath the Alps, and with complete discretion. When Max, the manager, had offered her refuge in a hideaway cabin at the back of the resort, she'd grabbed the chance.

For a week she'd refused to unpack, remaining ready to run again. The peace felt too good to be true after the nightmare of ringing phones and flashing cameras she'd endured in LA after Pete's lies had hit the headlines. She shuddered to think what it was like now 'Dr Pete' had discovered he could only fix his failing ratings, and hang onto the fame and adulation he craved, by publicly reuniting with the wife he'd denounced as a cheater.

Rachel rubbed her wrist. It had long since healed, but it was symbolic. An hour after she'd seen a doctor privately and alone to have the broken limb put in a cast, she'd had the locks changed and filed for a temporary restraining-order. She hadn't pressed charges—it would have destroyed Pete— but she'd go to court if he touched her again. Her lawyer had made that crystal clear.

Her phone had been off for weeks. He couldn't use tracking, charm, love, guilt or even her mother and sister to get his way. She had enough to deal with learning how to survive alone, without the constant knowledge that her family loved Pete more than they'd ever loved her.

A soft voice asked from behind her, 'Rachel, are you okay? Does the key not work?'

She started. Though Pete had only hit her twice before she'd left him, it had left its mark in a nervous reaction she hadn't learned to control yet. After a deep breath she turned to the pretty brunette with the hint of willowy figure that Rachel had once had to starve herself to maintain. Apart from her second cousin Suzie—who'd arranged her new name, two new passports with different names and had given her thousands of dollars Pete couldn't trace—the members of staff at Bollinger Alpine Resort were the only people she could trust.

She apologised in German and entered the cabin. 'I'm fine, thank you, Monika.' She unclipped and with both hands pulled off her snow boots and damp, tight ski socks.

Monika had brought her lunch. Jami and Max joined her soon after to listen to her stories about life as a celebrity wife in Tinsel Town. She dredged another story from the depths of all she wanted to forget for the sake of those who were risking their livelihoods to protect her.

* * *

From the corner of the *terrasse* he watched the woman hold-ing court, three members of staff watching her in adoring awe, as if she was an affable duchess. He'd watched her try-ing to ski before, pretending to stumble so she could hold the hand of a young, handsome ski instructor.

He'd known women like her before and he despised them—using wiles and fame to get their way. She charmed people into falling into her hand. Obviously she revelled in being the centre of attention. And she was good at it: the sweet, rue-ful manner combined with her fawn-like eyes and her 'big as Texas, big as her heart' smile was a lethal cocktail for the uninitiated.

What a shame for Mrs Rachel Rinaldi—the now-infamous 'Mrs Dr Pete' of chat-show legend—that he'd been initiated into how far one could fall when the fame bubble burst. He wasn't naïve or stupid. He'd been taken, burned, lied to and left broken before she even left grade school—and he'd never let anyone do it to him since.

Mrs Rinaldi was about to discover just how far her charm would get her.

'And so He That Shall Not Be Named insisted those ten sec-onds of footage be cut from the interview. Apparently a top-action hero's being human enough to trip on a step and fall flat on his face could ruin his entire career and cause his wife to divorce him—quote, unquote.'

'I assume my invitation to this party was lost in the post.'

The giggles and snorts of her friends died. Brow furrowed, Rachel turned to see what was wrong, but with one look her breath caught in her lungs.

A man of dark, dangerous male beauty stood in the door-way. His tight, brooding sensuality hit her in the solar plexus like a drive-by shot. His features weren't quite classic, but his stormy eyes and sensuous mouth more than made up for the lack of perfection. His bearing had a loose-limbed elegance and his lean, strong body was encased in a dove-grey suit that complemented his eyes. She blinked hard once or twice. It felt as if the room was spinning around her—but this had happened to her once before…

*I am not that girl now.* She forced her eyes to remain open, focused on him. No man would ever make her close her eyes or fall to her knees again, physically or emotionally.

She held his gaze, returning it with an openness most men found unnerving. Yes, the man knew how to dress, to impress a woman with a glance, but it was probably all for show.

Definitely 'been there, done that'—and she'd thrown out the T-shirt.

'A shame, since it seems I'm the host.' The new arrival spoke quietly, but small flickers of restrained lightning showed in each word. His dark-grey eyes rested upon the occupants of the cabin one by one. And she'd thought *she* knew how to unnerve others…

'Herr Bollinger, uh, welcome back. We were not aware of your arrival.' Max spoke in German, with a nervous twitch in his left eye. Monika squirmed, and Jami gazed at the door as if it held the secrets of life.

*Bollinger.* So this was the resort's owner, the son of a French multi-millionaire and a French-Swiss movie star. She'd seen pictures of him from about twelve years ago, when he'd been in the top ten of the World's Beautiful People, but she'd never seen him in the flesh. Armand Bollinger—the man nicknamed 'the Wolf' for his brilliance in business circles as well as in his love life. And, now she had seen him, she knew why. The leashed storm in him took Rachel's breath anew.

He stepped inside the room, filling it with an air of absolute command, even as he spoke with exquisite courtesy. 'I'd like to speak with our guest alone, thank you.' He glanced at each of his staff in turn. Without a word, Jami, Max and Monika fled, and she couldn't blame them.

The man turned to her with a smile that was perfect, welcoming and professional. 'Ms Chase, I am Armand Bollinger.' He didn't waste words he didn't need, such as 'I am the owner of the resort'. His voice sounded like chocolate brandy ought to taste. In a suit whispering Savile Row, and a linen shirt two shades darker than the trousers, he was the epitome of European elegance.

So why did she sense such a dark cloud hovering inside him? He seemed the consummate beautiful stranger. Yet, looking just beneath the surface, she felt not the hunter but the wounded wolf, pushing ancient scars out of existence by force of sheer will. 'Are all your needs being met? Is there anything you need?'

*That's not why you came.*

Her years of psychology training and practice had kicked in at first sight of him, without consciously trying. The owners of resorts did not commonly knock on doors to check on service levels; that was left to the managers. The resort owners she'd met might come to visit her if they discovered who she was, but they wouldn't have the haunted look of Armand Bollinger's eyes. Beneath the exquisite manners he wore with the same comfort as his excellent clothing, whatever it was he'd come to say sat ill on him.

*He knows who I am.*

The thought panicked her—but she would *not* show any weakness. She would never give in to any man's demands again.

'Every need has been met, Herr Bollinger, thank you.' She lifted her chin, kept her eyes fully on his. 'Have you come to ask me to leave?'

Armand stared at the diminutive woman before him, her warm curves encased in jeans, a fluffy pink pullover and hotel slippers. Very different from the tiny angles, designer outfits and high heels he'd seen when she was TV's Mrs Dr Pete, the Texan sweetheart who'd made Dr Pete's show the hit it was—or the hit it had been until he'd tossed her off the show. He'd heard it had been canned in the past few weeks.

He'd always been told the camera added ten pounds. It seemed real life did that to Rachel Rinaldi. In fact, if he hadn't seen those fawn-like brown eyes, or her famous smile dazzling his staff through the *terrasse* windows, or heard her pretty, sing-song southern accent telling her story, he wouldn't have recognised her at all. Gone were her trade-mark mahogany waist-length locks, the flawless make-up, the four-inch heels and the jewellery. In their place were a light-brown pixie haircut and clear, creamy skin with a light dusting of freckles...not to mention the bristling stance and the challenging flash in her eyes as she squared up to him. She was expecting him to throw her out, but she'd go down swinging. But surely she knew why he was here?

She hadn't played the fame card yet to get what she wanted, or to railroad him with their respective positions. *But she will*, he thought cynically. Sooner or later they all did, which was part of the reason he'd left that world years ago. The world his parents had once dominated; oh yes, the Bollingers had been 'beautiful people'.

Then their world had fallen apart, and no one knew it but them. Even now, no one knew the truth of his father's death, or the things he'd done, the family shame.

'If you're going to ask me to leave, Herr Bollinger, I'd appreciate it if you'd get it over with rather than stringing it out this way.'

The aggressive tone seemed off-kilter in her pretty southern accent. Armand didn't start at the somewhat acid return to the present; even his mental shake was unseen. *Give nothing away, don't hand your power to anyone.* He'd learned that lesson long before he'd been kicked out of home at the age of twelve and he'd never forget it.

'You are a paying guest, Ms Chase,' he replied with all the practised smoothness of years, the acting training from young childhood. His father had called them 'deportment classes', but Armand knew them for what they were. *Put on a show, look pretty, display perfect behaviour at all times. No anger, no sorrow, no remorse. And don't ever be yourself.* So he'd play the game she'd set up and see where it led. 'We have just met. Why should you think I wish you to go?'

'Well, you're furious at me for some reason,' she returned, notably less hostile, but with her famed perception.

This time it was harder not to physically react. Damn it, she *knew* what he wanted! Surely she'd known he'd come the moment he found out where she was hiding out? 'Another assumption, given that I've only asked if you need anything,' he said softly.

'You're lying.' With an almost triumphant expression, she pointed at his eyes. 'See, there it is again. It's like lightning behind clouds, the look of fury hiding behind good manners. You're mad at me for some reason, so why not just say so? The sooner you get it off your chest, the sooner I can get back to my lunch.'

Dissected and dismissed within three sentences. Armand wasn't used to either happening to him. Rudeness from guests he could tolerate; stupidity he could ignore, certainly, though it irritated him. The superciliousness and constant demands of the super-rich were every-day life to him, his bread and butter. He'd been unfailingly polite, the perfect gentleman in all the years he'd spent rebuilding the resort and his reputation. The Wolf led the pack. Nobody got the best of him; nobody got *to* him.

How could this total stranger hop the barriers he'd erected twenty years ago with such ease? Damn it, she was laughing at him. Nobody had seen through him since he'd been sent to boarding school at the age of twelve. The day after he'd broken his father's nose.

The night his fairy-tale world had risen up to the light, exposed for the ugly lie it was. The night his sisters had lost their innocence. The night they'd all lost each other. Though they'd gained some closeness since his father had died, somehow it was never the same again.

He caught himself rubbing his finger.

*Shut down, turn off.* He forced a smile. He was damned if he wouldn't turn the tables. 'All right, then, Ms Chase—or should I say, Mrs Rinaldi?'

Not a muscle moved in her face, but something flickered in her eyes—a fleeting expression he'd seen on a woman's face before, and never wanted to see again. But she spoke calmly, almost bored. 'I realised you'd recognised me the moment you broke into my cabin and heard me speak, Herr Bollinger. Would you mind getting to the point of your visit? My lettuce is wilting as we speak.'

His moment of perception fled beneath the sheer gall of the woman. Now he was less important than lettuce. If Rachel Rinaldi was famed for her loving empathy with strangers, he surely wasn't seeing a sign of it. But, by God, he wouldn't let her get to him—or, more accurately, *keep* getting to him. 'By all means, Ms Chase, return to your lunch. It seems that you need it. Would you mind if I join you?'

The hesitation was so long it was almost as visible as the look in her eyes. She didn't want him here. Never once in his life had a woman refused his company, or even hesitated; always it had been women inviting him, women watching *him* hesitate. Women always had to watch as he walked through his invisible exit sign and never looked back.

He shrugged off the momentary irritation and waited for her to speak. What did he care? This woman was far from his type, and he wasn't looking. He had more than enough to fill his life without coping with a weak, tearful woman's sensitivity, or the ego-filled demands of self-proclaimed strong women hitting him like an axe to the head.

That was the way it always went. His last relationship— if it could be called that—had put him off for a long time to come. Behind her dark, sinuous beauty, Selina had used tantrums, tears, other men and sexual manipulation, all aimed at one thing: to gain the fame of being the woman to tame the Wolf and wear his ring. She'd nearly scratched his eyes out when he'd said only one thing to her as he'd packed his things: 'I don't do cheating women.'

'Certainly, Herr Bollinger,' Rachel Chase said after what seemed an inordinately long time. 'I'm getting a crick in my neck from looking up at you, anyway. Do come in.'

'Thank you,' he said, holding onto his courtesy, seething beneath. This woman wanted him to leave. She didn't feel his famed charm, and his manners only seemed to bring out an irritated acerbity in her he'd never seen on TV.

He didn't care—of course he didn't—but he couldn't help asking himself *why*.

Thrusting the thought away, he called the chef and asked for his lunch to be delivered to the cabin. He held out the dining chair in front of the salad Nicoise which was, indeed, wilting. Once he'd seated her, he called the chef again and ordered a new one despite her protests that it was fine to eat. She sighed and waved a hand around, vaguely indicating all five of the other chairs at the table, as if she didn't care where he sat. 'Please sit, Herr Bollinger.' Inviting him to sit at his own table; he felt the cold fury rack up a notch.

He took the plate of salad away, placing it on the kitchen counter before returning to her, deliberately sitting opposite her. 'The salad was sub-standard, Ms Chase. Of course I must replace it with a fresh one. We never serve stale salad in the restaurants, or in the actual hotel rooms.'

'Well, since it was…' And her sentence trailed off. She stared at him, her brow furrowed. 'What do you mean by "actual hotel rooms"? Isn't this cabin reserved for guests?'

He frowned. 'I assumed my manager would have told you—this cabin is only for my private guests, as it's my home.'

If there was one thing he hadn't counted would discompose her, it was that. But there was no way she could fake a face pale to the point of whiteness. No way to darken those big, wistful eyes until they were pure black, pupils dilated with unadulterated fear and horror. 'Oh… Oh, no, no. I didn't… Um, I—I'm so sorry!' she stammered.

No, she couldn't be that good an actress. 'You mean Max didn't tell you when you asked to move in here?' he asked, feeling the inadequacy of the words.

Now it was panic flaring in those easy-to-read eyes. 'I—I must have forgotten. It wasn't Max's fault! He would have told me, certainly. I—I bullied him into it.'

She was babbling. Armand's eyes narrowed as he kept his gaze fixed on her. He'd often found waiting an effective way to make women talk.

She was waiting in her turn, but not to unsettle him. She watched him with the air of one awaiting the guillotine. After a long pause, she whispered, 'Please don't blame your staff, Herr Bollinger. It—it was my fault. I saw the cabin, and—and I wanted more privacy, so I…'

'You bullied Max into it. I see,' he said, trying not to laugh. Half an hour ago, he might have believed it, but now he could no more see her bullying anyone than he could see her drowning a kitten. He didn't have a psychology degree, but his profession required an ability to read people, and something disturbed him about Rachel Chase-Rinaldi.

'And are you aware that other guests are complaining of neglect while at least three members of my staff come here at a time to be regaled with your amusing tales of the life and times of a Hollywood wife?'

Now she looked like a hunted deer, trapped in the headlights of his interrogation. She licked her lips; her eyes darted around the room, obviously finding no ready answer. At least ten seconds too late, she said, 'It was me, all me. I've… been lonely and, um, they've been doing what your brochure says—taking excellent care of me.'

Every word came out with the fumbling of an honest woman trying to find an excuse. She couldn't meet his eyes as she had so easily while she'd been fighting only for herself.

This was not the woman on the TV who always had the right words to hand, who always knew how to comfort others. So which of the two was the real woman and which was the fake?

'I'll have to commend them, then—but the arrangements will have to change, Ms Chase,' he said quietly. 'The current situation is unacceptable to me, and to my guests and, now I'm here, it will draw the kind of attention I think you wish least.'

The chair opposite him scraped back hard. She got to her feet, sickly pale but with determination in those speaking eyes. 'Of course, I understand. I'll leave on the first train. Do you know if there's one leaving tonight?'

Armand had to fight the urge to blink. Nothing had happened the way he'd thought it would. There was no triumph in running off a woman who looked like a shot fawn.

'You don't need to leave, Ms Chase. If we move you into a suite late tonight, when no one will see, the woman here disappears and you return to being just another guest.'

She shook her head. 'I think it's best if I just go. I've caused enough trouble for you and your people.'

He'd never know later what changed his mind, unless it was the hunted look on her face, the fear she was trying to hide beneath defiance and determination: a sham of strength beneath her pride. The wall surrounding her was crumbling, and she was falling apart behind it. *I have nowhere to go,* her eyes said. Just as his mother had looked the day his father had sent Armand to boarding school. Just as she'd looked the night before he'd left, as she'd watched him taking the blows for her.

'You don't need to leave, Ms Chase,' he said abruptly, wondering what the hell he was saying even as he spoke. 'I have a proposition for you.'

## CHAPTER TWO

RACHEL's jaw dropped. '*What* did you just say?' she demanded when she found her voice. 'No, you couldn't have meant— it's a language miscommunication, right? I'm sure you didn't mean that to sound like...' *You're babbling*. Abruptly she shut her mouth.

For the first time, Armand Bollinger's eyes gleamed with amusement. 'I should have said a *business* proposition. I beg your pardon for the confusion, Ms Chase.'

Though the words were smoothly said, his tone was filled with mirth. He was laughing at her for even thinking he could be attracted to her.

She felt her cheeks heat. 'No, I'm sorry I thought that you could... I realise I'm not...' Once more she broke off. The turbulent confusion inside her had grown to mammoth proportions in the space of seconds. 'Forget I said it,' she muttered, and closed her mouth.

'The word *proposition* is a *double entendre* in itself,' he said, and ended on that odd note. It felt to her as if he wanted to say more, but thought better of it.

The silences were becoming awkward, but she'd only make a mess of it if she spoke.

A knock sounded, and they both jumped to their feet. 'It's all right, I'm closer.' She ran for the door before he could.

His voice came from behind her as she opened the door.

'There are two trays.' He took the heavier one from one of the two staff members at the door, neither of whom were her usual friends. Rachel took the other tray, and with a brief thanks closed the door. Much as she wanted to have a buffer, she was not asking any of his staff to come in. She'd put them all in enough trouble as it was. Disturbed by something, but not sure by what, she returned to the dining room.

'I ordered a white wine. Will you take some?' he asked in a European way as he poured a glass. Looking up with a smile, he held it out to her.

As she took the glass—she loved a good Chardonnay— it occurred to her what she'd seen behind the waiter holding her tray. 'There were people watching us from the restaurant terrace.'

Herr Bollinger nodded as he sat again. 'Naturally, Ms Chase. My regular visitors have worked out that some VIP must have taken over my cabin in my absence—but I saw no one with a telephoto lens, so I doubt they saw you clearly. The cabin's over three-hundred metres from the main resort.' He began eating, seeming unperturbed. 'And that leads me to my original subject. We have a mutual problem, and we need to work out a solution that works for both of us.'

Rachel tilted her head. 'Why is my presence such a problem for you?'

He looked up. 'I don't bring lovers to my home, Ms Chase,' he said, cool as the snow outside. He didn't elaborate. He didn't need to. The lone wolf didn't want to deal with the complications that arose from this: the expectations from the women he dated. 'I expect it will be worse for you, with your husband publicly claiming your reconciliation. The pictures showing you together are obviously a mock-up, since he's in LA and you're here.'

If there was a question in his words, she wasn't answering. She picked up her fork and began spearing lettuce and tuna.

'Rebuke accepted, Ms Chase,' he said dryly, 'But you can't just hide from the issue this time. We share this problem. I can't sort it out without some sort of communication.'

'Mutual confidences, you mean?' she retorted. 'No thanks. You decide what you want to do. You own the place.' She popped the food in her mouth before she said too much.

After a little silence, he asked quietly, 'Are you always so impetuous? You don't know me. My solution might not suit you at all.'

'You have almost as much to lose as I do,' she said when she'd swallowed her food. She took a gulp of wine—a crime, really, given that it was true Burgundian Chardonnay. 'We both need this resolved with discretion. It's not as if you're going to ask me to be your mistress.'

'Is that so impossible?' he asked with an elliptical smile that set her nerves on edge.

'Given your anger over keeping this as your private hideaway without your future lovers invading? Yes, of course it is.' She shoved a forkful in her mouth, letting him deal with her insights. She was curious to know if he'd be as sarcastic as Pete when she'd out-talked him.

*At least I know he won't hit me. I'm a paying guest, and he wants discretion as much as I do. He can't afford to antagonise me.*

And the truth of it gave her the courage to speak her mind. She need not fear this man, and that was so liberating, she wanted to laugh with the joy of it. She barely remembered the last time she hadn't been afraid of someone's disapproval.

'I don't know whether to say *touché* or *en garde*,' he murmured, his voice rich with enjoyment. Was he enjoying this crazy seesaw of a conversation?

It was almost a revelation to her—or a revolution; she wasn't sure. Because she discovered, on thinking about it, that she was enjoying it too.

'Feel free to use either,' she said, waving a hand around, mock sword-fighting. She smiled at him.

It felt like a sock in the stomach, seeing that mega-watt, big-as-her-heart smile tossed his way. Armand stopped in his tracks, abruptly lost in it. She wasn't flirting or trying to make a connection. There was no agenda, no personal gain; she was smiling just because she wanted to. And it was like seeing a blazing blue sky after a long, dull winter. The absolute lift of his spirits started low down and finished with a light, silvery feeling in his head, as if he could fly.

Why her effect on him amazed him so much, he wasn't sure, when he'd met a thousand beautiful women—but he definitely didn't want to explore the issue. 'Can we work out stratagems before we duel?' he asked with deliberate lightness. Any kind of probing sent her into tight-lipped silence. He could think of far better uses for that gorgeously smiling mouth the colour of a pink rose.

'Where's the fun in that?' she mock-complained, her eyes shining like sunlight in dark wine.

Damn it, he had to watch his thoughts or he'd be in trouble. The last thing he'd ever do was start up a flirtation with a guest. It led to a hundred different routes, all marked 'danger'.

'You prefer to wing it?' he asked, a deliberate probe. If nothing else, it would cut her friendliness, make her keep her distance again.

And it did. One shoulder lifted in a careless shrug. 'Too many plans ruin the fun. Believe me, I know.' Her voice was wry, and her smile slipped a little.

Armand didn't bother asking the next question he was sure she wouldn't answer. Besides, something about this woman lit places inside him that had been dark for too long. Though it scared the living daylights out of him, he had to know if it would work more than once. 'Can we at least finish lunch before we begin our riposte?'

She blinked and chuckled. And that damned smile sent warmth and light into him so bright it hurt, little rainbow prism-shots. 'I'm always braver after a glass.' She lifted the wine glass but drank before he could raise his, make a toast or say anything remotely personal.

Why did so much about this woman seem to catch him out? Right now he only knew one thing: he barely knew her. So if he showed any sign of what she was capable of doing to him with a simple smile she'd bolt on the first train. Damn it, she wasn't his type, so why was his body reacting so strongly?

'This wine is heavenly. May I have more?'

Recalled by her abrupt words, Armand realised she'd caught him staring at her; she was blushing, biting her lip. Had his face shown what he'd been thinking? He poured the wine, drank his off and then refilled. 'The vineyard is eight-hundred years old,' he said to fill the silence. 'The grapevines are almost as old.'

'Amazing… Where I come from, anything a hundred years old is historic.' She gulped the entire glass of wine down so fast Armand doubted it touched the edges before she looked at him with hard-earned resolve. 'Look, can you please say what you came to say? The suspense is putting me off my lunch.'

How did she manage it, putting him in his place and making him want to smile at once, so dramatic over a salad? Not to mention the other parts of him that were breaking into an unwanted 'hallelujah' chorus whenever she looked at him or smiled.

Somehow he couldn't dismiss it as a normal male reaction. Probably because this strange connection felt too intimate for just an hour's acquaintance. With her stubborn courage and her willingness to shoulder her own burdens, Rachel Chase touched him somewhere he hadn't felt before. It wasn't normal for him. Usually when he felt something like this it was simple attraction. He'd ask them to dinner, enjoy hearing about the woman's life, take it further at his leisure if she was willing, become bored in weeks and then give the nice kiss-off.

Rachel wasn't anything like the usual women he was attracted to. Yet he was hurting, remembering, thinking—and, yes, he was enjoying himself, merely sitting here talking to her. Within half an hour she'd made him feel more than he had since he'd been twelve.

It only added piquant spice, knowing Rachel didn't seem aware. No feminine antennae were on at all, looking for a man to fill the blank time in her life. She didn't want him at all, barely thought of him as a man.

Then there was the flash he'd seen in her eyes, unmistakable, almost horrifying. For a single moment she'd been afraid of him; she'd been willing to run rather than be near him.

He had to tread lightly here. Just by crossing his own threshold he'd been dragged into undercurrents he wasn't prepared to swim.

'As I said, I know you're Mrs Pete,' he said. 'Given what the media's printed about your personal life, your need for privacy at this time is perfectly understandable.'

One by one, Rachel's vertebrae relaxed. It seemed she wouldn't have to find a new place to go—at least, not yet. 'Thank you,' she said quietly.

'But I need to make some amendments to the current arrangements.' His voice was smooth and even but she almost heard his heartbeat picking up, felt that unknown but strong emotion vibrating through him. 'I have assigned Monika to make up your room and bring your meals while you stay with us.'

Rachel felt the blush stain her cheeks. 'Have there been many complaints against the staff spending time with me?'

Armand Bollinger nodded curtly, and she knew they'd reached the heart of his problem. From what she'd read of him on the plane coming over to Europe, he had rebuilt this place from the ground up after a fire had destroyed almost everything about eighteen years ago—the same fire that had taken the life of his father. The enormous amount of high-flying Guillaume Bollinger's debt only became clear after his death, and speculation was rife on whether his death had been deliberate. Armand Bollinger had just turned seventeen at the time, but he'd taken control of his family finances. With years of hard work and dedication, he'd paid his father's debts before he recreated this five-star resort. He obviously didn't take his success for granted.

Thanks to her, his professional prestige had taken a hit. She knew too well how that felt.

'This situation is my fault.' She gazed at him in determined apology, trying to ignore that odd thrill racing through her body, just by looking into those dark-lashed, storm-grey eyes. An article from about a decade ago floated into her memory: the hypnotic eyes of the Wolf... 'Please don't fire anyone, Herr Bollinger. It wasn't their fault. It was mine.'

'I have no need or desire to fire anyone, Ms Chase. All my staff have given me complete satisfaction until now. I believe everyone deserves a second chance.'

'Oh, yes,' she agreed fervently, though he'd spoken in a voice almost as cold as the snow outside. 'They do. And it really was my fault.'

'So you've now said three times.' As slow as the nod he'd given her moments before, a smile was born. Not the perfunctory stretching of lips she'd seen on rare pictures of him during the past decade, but a real, warm smile. The silly little thrill became outright shivers racing through her as fast as a Daytona driver. She'd seen loads of pretty boys in LA: models, actors and the rest. But she'd never seen such true, strong masculine beauty close up before. When he smiled, Armand Bollinger was *devastating*.

'Moreover, I understand their fascination.' Either not noticing her reaction, or not caring, he lifted the painted china coffee-pot sitting on a matching stand with a candle to keep it warm and offered it to her. Trying her best not to stare at him, she nodded and he poured it into her cup. 'Having a real Hollywood star hiding out in our quiet resort is a scandal too delicious not to take part in.' He held out the coffee cup to her.

She stiffened. 'I thought you of all people would know the truth, Herr Bollinger, given your brief stint as both a French and international *noir* actor, years ago though it was. Stars belong in the sky.' She took the cup and put it down fast; her hands were trembling. 'But I agree that the whole world knows about my life.'

'Or think they do,' he said with a wryness that seemed to come from the heart. 'But, as you know nothing about my real life, I know nothing of yours, Ms Chase. I merely made a generalisation on how average people feel about meeting the rich and famous.'

Startled, she looked up, but his concentration was on his refilled coffee, watching the steam rise. She opened her mouth and then shut it hard. Something about Armand Bollinger was dangerous...and seductive. Oh, he was good, if he could make her yearn to unburden herself within an hour of meeting.

'I guess nobody knows anyone's true story but those involved, unless their publicist gives a quote,' she said lightly. 'But you know the first rule of the media: never let truth get in the way of good sales for the tabloids.' From staring at the curls of steam from her coffee, she looked up with a smile that was its own barrier, daring him to ask.

'So I've heard.' His tone sounded half a million miles away, a lifetime ago.

She found herself staring at him again against her will and even her need. It was as if he'd put her under hypnosis. He had a knack of being able to say so much with a few words, leaving her with the feeling of things unfinished, wanting more. It was as if an asteroid was flying by her, dragging her into its orbit as it passed.

This was the last thing she needed. All she'd wanted was her privacy, to pay her bills when she'd found the strength to face her life. He'd been the one to barge in here, expose her and then say everything and nothing at once. And she *still* didn't know why he was here.

'I think I've asked enough times, Herr Bollinger.' She put down her cutlery and pushed the rest of the salad away from her. More trembling little thrills, more resolute denial. She said calmly enough, 'What is it you're asking of me?'

# CHAPTER THREE

AFTER a long moment Armand leaned forward, looking into her face. Those eyes had a power he couldn't define—unless it lay in their utter guilelessness. He'd played the game of love so long with other players, being straightforward with a strange woman felt almost unfamiliar. He followed her suit, pushing his half-eaten lunch away. This discussion was too important to blur with food. 'It's obvious that the past few months have been harder on you than most people know.'

He waited for an answer but, as if refusing to hand her power over even in confirmation or denial, she kept her chin high and said nothing but merely waited.

When it was obvious she wasn't going to answer his unspoken question, to make his task any easier, he decided to plunge ahead. 'You need a place to stay with discreet staff, without needing to go out in public, or do your own shopping, et cetera. My resort is the right place for you. We offer you all the services you need.'

After what seemed like minutes of waiting, she bowed her head, stiff and cold. Just as he'd have done—in fact it was what he had done when he'd been barely seventeen, a rising star in the art-house industry and the secrets surrounding his father's death had been resurrected in the name of public entertainment. 'Go on.'

'But this cabin is my home. If I don't stay in it while I'm

here, it will cause the kind of remark and speculation you need least at the moment—but, again, if anyone sees you here and recognises you, you end up with the same problem.'

He saw the flash of fear cross her face before it disappeared. There was something deeper here she was worried about than just her public reputation. 'I don't know whether I caused your problem, you caused mine, or both,' she said, with a slow kind of horror.

'Both,' he replied dryly. 'Mine is but a minor nuisance, Ms Chase. I believe your problem to be more serious.' He left the air filled with the question unspoken. The women he'd known usually rushed to fill a conversational gap if he made it intriguing enough.

This woman didn't even look up, or seem to notice he'd left a half-question dangling there. 'But I caused it. If I hadn't left my room…' Frowning hard, she shook her head.

If he was reading the look in her half-fallen eyes correctly, she felt as guilty as she did fearful—and he had her right where he wanted her. The future of his resorts could be smooth, and her life set back on the right course, with just a little manipulation.

But he'd been hurt and manipulated when he was a boy. Long ago, he'd sworn he would never inflict his will on another, no matter what benefits it could bring him. Yet here he was, playing the worst kind of game, being his father's son. Was history repeating itself—the one thing he'd believed would never happen?

He refused to give in to the guilt coursing through him. *Damn it, this time it's right.*

'All the regular guests will wonder if I don't stay here,' he said, drowning the guilt beneath the weight of arguments he thought would convince her. Yes, he wanted something from her, but he was giving as much as he got, relatively speaking. He might gain financial rewards, but she got what she seemed to need desperately—peace and quiet. 'Apart from family, I've never had any woman here so your presence has already caused speculation.'

Another look crossed her face, similar to when she'd asked about the complaints against the staff. 'I didn't realise...' Her eyes squeezed shut. Her mouth opened, made soundless motions, and then she said faintly, 'Again, I can only apologise for the trouble I've caused you.'

Her embarrassment was too genuine to deny. Armand felt a crazy urge to run out of the cabin, get some fresh air to clear his head. The spoiled-brat media darling he'd assumed her to be an hour ago might have railroaded his staff into bowing to her will, but this woman's conscience seemed even more radiant than her smile. She reminded him of a clawless kitten. Whatever the truth was inside Dr Pete's press releases, a Delilah this woman definitely was not.

This could be almost too easy, except that Armand refused to stoop to stealing candy from babies. Or use another person's conscience against them, to make them sing his tune.

'Since you've made the name change, and with the subtle amendments you've made to your appearance, you could probably take another room without issue,' he said, giving her a last get-out if she wanted to take it. A sap to his conscience, even if he was sure she wouldn't.

'Your staff recognised me within a day, looking just like this,' she replied, with a despairing rather than pugnacious note. 'Apparently, my accent and voice give me away. I've been trying to learn Swiss German, but I'm about as good with accents as I am on skis.'

Armand felt an unusual urge to grin. Rachel Chase seemed almost disastrously honest—a definite downer for hiding in this electronic-media world, but it was a trait he strongly respected. 'Then we go with my plan. I'll stay here with you.

I'll go about my business through the day as usual. Monika will—'

'You want me to stay here with you?'

The squeak in her voice wasn't feigned. For all the stories Dr Pete had put out about her, she didn't seem the kind to fall into the arms of a rich man when he showed up on her doorstep—even if it was his doorstep. 'In another bedroom, Ms Chase,' he said in cool amusement. 'The cabin has four of them. You obviously took the word "proposition" to heart.'

A flare of pink touched her cheeks, but her eyes flashed. Though he waited a full minute, she made no retort, didn't try to defend herself. 'Go on,' she said eventually, sounding as angry as she looked.

'It's a necessary evil,' he said, fighting the renewed guilt of knowing he'd backed her into a corner, but torn between anger and amusement at the fact that he'd finally found a woman who not only didn't leap at the idea of staying with him, but fought it all the way. 'My staff's coming and going to the cabin throughout the day while I was gone has already caused curiosity. My regular guests have asked who the VIP is that's staying in my cabin, since I only arrived this morning.'

Again, he saw the riotous flush fill her cheeks. She looked quite pretty like that, in a country-girl fashion. Natural and pure. 'You seem to have learned a lot in a few hours. What did you do, take a general survey?'

She was quick-minded, he'd give her that. 'It's my job to know what's going on in my resort, Ms Chase.'

'You do it well,' she muttered, but it wasn't a compliment.

He didn't thank her; it would only inflame her anger at suddenly finding herself helpless in a situation that had felt safe until he'd invaded her sanctuary an hour ago. 'As you do your job well, from what I've seen.'

She only shrugged in reply.

Goaded, he said in a silky-smooth voice, 'I asked nothing of my guests, nor did I say anything. I didn't need to. Your total avoidance of the other guests has caused curiosity amongst those who come here hoping for a certain kind of company. My staff has been avoiding all the guests' questions, but you don't want them putting the pieces of your puzzle together. In other words, you need a good cover story, Ms Chase.'

She sighed and nodded. 'Call me Rachel,' was all she said.

'Rachel, then.' In saying her name, Armand took a step into unknown territory. It didn't feel as casual as it had in the past, probably because she'd offered the intimacy with such reluctance. 'I am Armand.'

She only nodded, frowning, serious.

'The assumption is that you must be famous or someone special to me, since my cabin's always been off-limits. The first causes the kind of speculation you need least and, as to the second, my sisters are well known here. I could pass you off as a cousin, but it gives you no reason why you wouldn't mingle with the guests. So either you leave on that train tonight, or become my lover in the eyes of anyone who asks when I refuse to explain who you are.'

He stopped when he saw her pale, a reaction no person could fake. With those enormous eyes, she looked like Bambi after his mother had been shot. 'I think it's best if I leave,' she said quietly, rubbing her wrist with an absent yet anxious movement which was horribly familiar.

Armand's gaze narrowed. He used to do that with his finger in the years before his father had died and he took control of his life.

He went on as if he'd seen nothing. 'But if it got about that you needed to run from here, it would ruin the reputation of my resort—and it has too many potential hazards for you.'

'Such as?' In her clear-to-read expression, there was a mix-

ture of wariness to trust and an almost desperate hope that
he had an answer to her problem.

'People already know you're in the run, Rachel—your
pictures are on magazines every week. The accent, not to
mention the eyes and smile, will give you away. If you leave
now and go elsewhere, someone will recognise you, no matter what name you use,' he said quietly.

She let out a tiny sigh. 'That's what I'm afraid of. I thought
of using coloured contact-lenses, but over brown eyes it never
really works. They end up looking muddy or weird.'

'Disguises aren't the answer. You need to stay out of the
public eye for now.' He made the assumption a matter of fact
and, as she nodded, he felt the anticipation soaring. 'You're
safe here, Rachel.'

The frozen look on her face relaxed. Slowly, the dazzling
smile that was as endearing as it was puzzling was turned
his way. 'In the time I've been here, every member of your
staff has worked hard to protect my identity.'

That smile, not to mention the fear crouching beneath it,
left Armand more confused by the moment; all his assump-
tions had been torn away. From the moment he'd seen her
start at the sound of his voice, the fear in her eyes too genuine to deny, the pieces had fallen apart. The rubbing of her
wrist left Armand to re-form a puzzle he didn't want to put
back together. More than most people, he knew that fame and
wealth did not guarantee a happy, trouble-free life.

Rachel wasn't hiding in his resort just to build suspense
to the right pitch before granting an exclusive interview to
some glossy magazine for the requisite six or seven figures.

'Your need for privacy exactly tallies with my own wishes.
I'm about to purchase land for my third resort. Like my first
one, it's on the French side of the Swiss Alps. The local au-
thorities investigate all new building projects thoroughly;
complaints from my current guests are the last thing I need

until the deal goes through. So, by solving both our problems this way, the work on my new resort will go ahead smoothly—if you'll agree to my deal.'

He'd hoped to have her hooked by this time, but she half-tilted her head away from him, her gaze riveted to something about four inches from his face. 'I'm listening,' was all she said, but with the air of waiting for the axe to fall on her.

He leaned forward, hands on the table. 'I stay here as usual, and will order a whole range of groceries to be delivered here, whatever you need. That won't cause remark, as I often cook for myself. Some lunches and dinners I will spend in the resort with the guests, but I'll be here the rest of the time. That's my normal routine and we don't need to break it. If by any chance someone sees you or us together, it's easy for me to pretend to be indulging in a private romance with a mystery woman. Your name will never be mentioned. I'll deal with inquisitive people.' He lifted his brow with a cool, imperious air.

She bit her lip over that stunning, alive smile that filled her face. It made her look like a naughty conspirator. 'I can see how that would work. I certainly wouldn't ask, if you looked at me like that.'

He held in the grin; her mercurial moods were as infectious as they were baffling. 'No member of the press can come unannounced through the gates onto the resort land, since the resort is solidly booked for months in advance. The only way in is through the dated key-card we send guests, and everyone that comes here wants the same level of privacy you need. If you stay here, you'll have the luxury of being able to say nothing. If you cover yourself when you go out, and don't talk to anyone but my staff, there is no reason that anyone should recognise you.'

'You did,' she pointed out. 'Your staff did.'

He gave her a wry smile. 'I heard your voice before I saw

your face. It's the voice that gives you away. Your show is on several channels here, dubbed into Italian, French or German for three of them, but the English cable-channel uses your face and voice for an advertisement for the show.'

She frowned and sighed. 'I thought I'd be anonymous here.'

'You are what you are, Rachel, but only for as long as you choose to stay famous. If you want to walk away from the life, people begin to forget soon enough and you can get on with whatever it is you want to do with your future.'

He'd spoken almost harshly, yet she smiled at him as if he'd handed her the key to the door of freedom. 'Thank you,' she said very softly, her eyes alight with relief, her entire face wreathed in the brilliance of her smile.

He had to wrench his gaze from her. When she came alive like that, it almost hurt him to look. 'We can keep the pretence up for as long as you need.'

'Oh, Armand… You don't know what you just said, do you?'

Jerked back by her first use of his name, by the wonder in her tone, he saw the whole room had come alight with the force of that marvellous smile. It was so bright he fought the urge to blink and turn away. 'What?' he asked, fighting to keep his tone even and smooth. For years, he'd kept the façade seamless. How did she pull apart the edges of his control like that and look inside his soul without trying?

'I might want a year, two years—and then you'd be stuck with me,' she quipped, but wryly, so self-mockingly, he wondered if she had any plans to return to her public life. He noticed that she'd neatly sidestepped his subtle query on how much time she'd need with the lame joke.

His brows lifted. 'I doubt it,' he said, just as dryly. 'There's just one personal question I must ask: is there a prospective Mr Chase on the horizon to upset our plans?'

That subtle stiffening of her shoulders spread across her

face and body. With deliberate grace, she sipped at coffee that must be nearly cold by now. 'No.'

Though there was an invisible sign screaming 'back off' in neon letters, he forged on. 'And there's no chance of your reconciling with Dr Pete?'

She stilled for a few ticks of the clock, a few moments that seemed for ever. Her fingers rubbed absently at her right wrist again. It was an unconscious movement, a picture that told a million words he didn't want to read. It was almost a full minute before she spoke. 'No.'

Again, it was all she said. Though he waited another full minute for her to continue, she merely lifted her brows and turned her face to the big French cross-beamed doors leading to the balcony. She stared out over the *terrasse* to the Alpine peaks soaring above them with so much absent absorption, it bordered on rudeness.

In Armand's experience, the less he said, the more a woman rushed to fill the silence. But Rachel sat silently, with a half-defiant smile that told him she didn't care what he thought. No details given, not even an explanation as to why there was emphatically no man to fill the void Dr Pete had left.

When she remained stubbornly silent, he tossed a bomb to make her speak. 'Don't you want to know what I wish in return?'

Without looking at him, she said without expression, 'You've already told me, I think. You want me to endorse the new resort for you, to extol the privacy and luxury of this one too, perhaps. You want me to bring other celebrities to your new resort when it's built. You want me to advertise your resorts.'

By now he wasn't taken aback by her perceptive guess—but he noticed that she didn't even ask if she was right. 'Yes, that is what I want,' he said with a similar lack of animation, hiding how damned important it was to him. Someone as loved around the world as Rachel Rinaldi could help him crack the lucrative upper-end of the American market, and she'd fallen right into his lap. He could make the deal without months of negotiations and the endless hassle of speaking through lawyers and agents. He studied her face for a reaction. 'Is it a deal?'

She shrugged with that slow elegance that felt like a wall being erected brick by brick. 'I'm willing to do it, if you're satisfied with such a poor bargain.'

He almost laughed in her face. Getting a woman as world-renowned as Mrs Pete to endorse his resorts was a coup of marvellous proportions for him, and she had to know it. 'A poor bargain?' he asked, tilting his head in clear enquiry. 'Come on, Ms Chase, stop fishing for compliments. The whole world knows you were the one who caused the ratings jump in your husband's show when it began failing. I've heard about the offer made to you since your split with Dr Pete. Your fans demanded you have your own chat show, taking Dr Pete's place.'

'That's no surprise. Thanks to my, eh, husband's public announcements about his love life and mine, half the world has heard about the offer.'

'It's all over the Internet and the news. People want to know where you are, what you're up to.'

'Trending now,' she retorted in a self-mocking tone. She turned to him at last, but those big eyes were filled with an odd blend of self-deprecating humour and challenge. 'But did you see that I'd accepted the offer? Is your *idea* contingent on my signing up for the show? You may be destined for disappointment.'

'I wasn't thinking of having my resort endorsed by a has-been, despite being one of the ilk myself,' he said curtly.

'I doubt anyone would call you a *has-been*. From what I

hear, you chose to walk away from acting at the peak of your career—and this resort is truly beautiful without being overly opulent or flashy.'

He said, touched by the genuine praise, 'Thank you, Rachel.'

She made a thoughtful face. 'You know, when you think about it, loads of products get excellent endorsement returns from the average has-been.' When he least expected it, she grinned. 'I guess the regular Joe on the street will be able to identify with someone like me. My work has always been among the normal people. You're quite perceptive, Herr Bollinger. It may turn out to be a sound business plan, if only your average schmuck could afford to stay here.'

She'd given away more than she knew. 'So Dr Pete lied about the reconciliation and leaving you for the other woman in the first place? You're not taking the job, either?'

Her cheerful demeanour vanished in an instant. 'No comment.'

He squared his shoulders and sat back, only then realising he'd leaned forward, his hand almost touching hers across the table. What the hell had he been thinking to ask? He'd always prided himself on his discretion. So why had he asked?

*Because, until now, women have told me their life story without my needing to make an effort. Rachel is my first failure since I was a teenager.*

In an attempt to lighten the suddenly charged atmosphere, he said, 'By the way, this is not the place to say "schmuck" to mean a person. People won't understand. The original word means jewellery, mostly used, but it's a general term.'

Her brows lifted, her darkness vanished in an instant. 'My, how words change meaning in other languages!' And she laughed, a rippling sound, loud and free. When she laughed, Rachel Chase laughed from the heart, and it made him want to laugh with her.

She was a constant surprise to him. Learning the little he knew about her had felt like he'd been pulling teeth, yet it left him feeling oddly fascinated, with a desire to know more.

Rachel was far from his usual type of woman. There was a sense that she'd left the most delicious parts of her conversation unspoken. Perhaps that was the source of his interest? 'Maybe the meaning is not so different,' he suggested, to discover what she'd say. Learning a single fact about this woman took more digging than he'd ever needed before. 'It's still something used, something tossed aside because someone no longer wanted it.'

She pulled a thoughtful face, looking like a pensive pixie. 'That makes sense. We Americans merely made the leap from thing to person. Poor schmuck,' she said again, and laughed. As if the sun had come out from behind clouds, the room seemed to light up with her face.

Armand had to drag his gaze away and get back to the business at hand. 'So are you agreeable to my idea? If so, I'll bring my suitcase in. Which bedroom are you using?'

She pointed to a door.

'Ah, my mother's old room.' Before she could do more than briefly look horrified, he put up a hand. 'Maman lives in her own house a few hours' flight from here. She visits a few times a year. She's not coming until summer now. She would be the first to say you're welcome, Rachel.' The name kept slipping so naturally from his lips, he barely noticed. 'I'll keep my room. The third is now a study, if you've noticed, with wireless Internet and computer. I can work in the hotel for a few hours a day, and if you need to work—' he saw her stiffen again and added '—or need to keep up your communications, feel free.'

'Thank you.' Her voice was subdued, but she neither confirmed nor denied the subtle probe. It seemed he'd finally met the woman who didn't want or need to defend herself against the accusations her ex had levelled at her. Whatever the truth was inside the story of Dr and Mrs Pete's break-up, Rachel Chase obviously did not want or need to unburden herself to a stranger about her life, no matter how much he was helping her.

He didn't care if she wanted to keep to herself—actually, it was quite refreshing. So from now on she would have what she wanted from him: peace and quiet.

'I need to work for a couple of hours. I'll be back before dinner.' He gathered the lunch plates and coffee paraphernalia on one tray and stacked the other beneath. 'There's no point in hiding that I have a guest stying with me when people saw you take the tray. Do you mind if I order dinner for us? Is there anything you don't like? What do you like to drink—wine, water, soft drinks?'

'I don't eat really spicy food, it burns my stomach,' she confessed with a fledgling smile.

Strange, the way her smile hit him every time. Every time she did it, something or someone new seemed to peep out from behind the confident, caring persona of the woman he'd seen on TV—neither the frightened kitten nor the cool, defensive rebel he'd dealt with today. 'And what is your drink of choice?'

'I tend to stick to water at night, though I love the hot chocolate they make here.'

'Consider it done; I'll order both.' He picked up the tray. 'I'll see you later.'

'Um, Herr Bollinger?'

He turned at the door, looking over his shoulder. 'My name is Armand.'

'Armand…' The name rolled off her tongue with that gorgeous southern accent of hers. It sent the oddest feeling through him, a sense of waiting fulfilled. 'Thank you. I'll try not to be too much trouble.'

He almost said *a paying guest is never trouble*, but he held it in. Seeing the smothered anxiety beneath her calm façade, he wondered what had happened to make her feel unworthy of even the most basic help—but he was afraid he already knew.

'I am doing very little,' he said coolly. 'A few weeks sharing my cabin, and I get an endorsement of my resort in return.'

When he saw her shoulders finally relax, he felt the tension disappear from his body, but when he left the cabin his mind was racing. If a woman as loved by her fans as Rachel Rinaldi could feel that she was a bother just by sharing his cabin, there had to be a damned good reason.

There must also be a reason why she wasn't giving her side of the story to the world. Surely she must know that, given her intense popularity, she'd be believed?

There were definite, unexpected depths to this woman, layers she didn't want him to see, things he didn't want to know.

He'd failed *Maman*—he'd left her to the abuse he couldn't stop until his father's death. He didn't know what the hell he could do to help Rachel. Anything he tried would probably make things worse. But he was committed to spending the next few weeks with her.

So what could he do to ensure it wasn't a disaster that would send her running from here before he got his endorsement?

# CHAPTER FOUR

'WHAT is this?'

Rachel looked at the electrical apparatus sitting in the centre of the table with vague suspicion. It looked like some sort of grill, with small-handled pots beneath the heating bars. A wonderful smell permeated the air: cheesy, but like no cheese she'd ever eaten. Bowls of food sat around the grill and a range of foods was sizzling on the rectangular grill-plate above.

'You haven't had this before?' Armand asked, looking surprised. 'You've been in Switzerland for weeks. Surely Max recommended it at least once?'

When she shook her head, he smiled with what looked like genuine pleasure. 'Then I shall be the first to share this experience with you. This is *raclette*, a traditional Swiss food for winter—but usually it's only served with potatoes and pickles. I like to switch it up a bit, add more to the menu.'

'It smells divine.'

He used little wooden spade-like objects to flip the food over. 'I order this for my first dinner whenever I return from being away.'

For a moment the impulse to ask where he'd been rose in her throat, but she forced it down. It wasn't as if they were friends. They were strangers sharing a cabin and an agreement, no more. He'd respected her secrets; she would be showing the worst form of ingratitude if she didn't do the same for him.

The trouble was that his patter, and the new food, had begun to relax her from the feeling of trepidation at his return tonight—that, and the jeans and sweatshirt he wore, both old but comfortable, by the looks of it. Everything felt informal, especially Armand himself—as if it was a deliberate ploy. She couldn't help but wonder if there was something else he wanted from her.

But the way he moved in those clothes was so fluid, with such natural grace, she felt a surge of envy—and another emotion she didn't want to identify. But she was a functioning woman, and any woman still breathing had to appreciate a man this masculine and this beautiful.

Although she'd showered this evening, she was still wearing a simple jeans and pullover. It was all she'd brought with her when she'd fled LA. She'd left everything behind: her name, her trademarks, any and all memories of Pete and her TV persona. And every day that she pulled on her comfy clothes, saw her natural brown hair, ring-free left hand, no make-up and didn't have to endure another day of hunger to remain svelte for the camera was another happy day.

There was no way she'd play the perfect doll again. Not for any man.

But her half-hearted attempt at defiance died with her first sight of him in his jeans. Without that little surge of rebellion to protect her emotions, she felt naked. She'd never been happy without having some form of barrier. Her mother had taught her that. Her mother's ladylike behaviour had been her protection from the hurt from her daddy's careless philandering.

But no form of refined protest Rachel tried had ever stopped Pete from railroading her. Nor did it seem to work with Armand. She guessed she just didn't have the way of it.

'Please, come and sit down,' he said with a smile, as if he hadn't noticed her silence. 'It's ready to eat.'

'Full points to Monika for the setting,' she murmured as she sat down, anxious to give her new friends all the praise she could.

Armand moved her chair in. 'Monika is finished for the day, but I will pass on thanks to the appropriate place.'

'Thanks,' she sighed, reflecting on Armand's courtesy with a slightly uncomfortable feeling. Probably his good manners were ingrained in him, but it had the feel of subtle undercurrents, as seductive as they were dangerous. She felt as if she'd fallen into unfamiliar waters from the moment he'd come into her life, pulling her with gentle insistence out to sea.

*Don't think about it. Don't look at him.* Frowning, she looked beneath the grill plate and saw cheese bubbling in the little flat pans. 'This looks delicious.'

'It is, and so easy. Just cook what you like to eat, and when it's ready pick what you want to eat, put it on your plate and pour the cheese over.'

The flavour burst on her tongue with the first mouthful. 'Oh, this is superb, Armand,' she murmured when her mouth was empty. 'No wonder it's a national dish—I'd eat it—'

'Rachel?'

Her eyes snapped open at his tone of voice which, though quiet, held inexplicable warning. A tiny shiver ran through her spine and she forgot about the food. 'What is it?'

He was looking only at his plate, seeming to enjoy the smell of his food. 'Someone's watching us through the *terrasse* door. She's looking right at you.'

She heard one of her vertebrae snap into place as she straightened, but she didn't look around. 'You said *she*?'

'Try to relax, Rachel,' he said softly, still not looking at her. 'It's okay. I recognise her. It's Amelia Heffernan, a regular visitor to the resort—she's a widow, an incurable romantic, and also incurably nosy. She only arrived today. She must have heard the rumours of a woman staying here and came to check for herself.'

One by one, her vertebrae relaxed again. She drew in a breath, her first in almost a minute. She looked at him, trying not to show her fear. 'Does she watch TV?'

'She's elderly—of course she does. And, yes, she loves the chat shows.'

Rachel turned cold all over. 'Armand, if she recognises me and tells anyone…'

She couldn't quite interpret his smile. 'From where she's standing, she can't see your face. Stand up and come to me.' He rose to his feet, moving to her. '*Smile* at me. Our ruse won't work if you look like you'd rather walk into an iron maiden than into my arms.'

She looked down, shaking her head. 'I can't do it. I just can't.'

He reached her chair, but didn't touch it, only her shoulder. 'Rachel,' he murmured, 'You don't know me. You have no reason to trust me. But right now I'm all you have.'

Slowly she lifted her face, turning her neck so she looked into his eyes. In them she saw not the predatory male after dominance, not even tenderness, but a reluctant understanding. It made her breath catch.

'Sometimes you have to leap,' he said quietly. 'It's your choice.'

He was right. It had to be now or never.

Her heart beat a hard tattoo as she rose to shaky feet and he turned her body so she was in his arms. The look on his face was confident, a man sure of his welcome. Suddenly she couldn't breathe…

'It's just like those days when the last thing you wanted was to be in front of the camera, Rachel. Remember? I'm smiling for her. If I must, I'll kiss you for her. But none of it's real.

It's all rehearsed. It's not who we are. This man is not who I am. I'm helping you, nothing more.'

Rachel gulped, and nodded. Somehow his words made it easier to snuggle in. 'It's not real,' she whispered to herself as she wrapped her arms around his neck. 'It's not real.'

'This is the only way she won't be able to see your face from any angle,' Armand whispered, holding her against his body, her cheek against his heart.

Despite the tender reassurance, she suddenly rocketed back a few months in time, standing in Pete's arms, waving to the audience the day after he'd first hit her. 'Smile, Rachel,' he'd muttered. 'They all love us. Smile for them.' He'd squeezed her waist, right where he'd hit her the night before after seeing that her fan rating was higher than his. He had been reminding her of who was in control, both in the show and in life.

'Rachel?'

Her vision cleared, and she saw Armand looking down at her, tender and troubled. He wasn't Pete, and she felt safer with this stranger than she had with anyone in a long time.

That gave her the courage to try. 'Smile at me,' she muttered through gritted teeth. 'She'll never believe it if you look at me like you're scared I might break any second.'

He gave a soft chuckle and lowered his face to hers. Rachel jerked back before she could stop herself. 'Make the leap, Rachel,' he whispered, moving close again. 'Trust me.'

She bit her lip, saw that look again, the sadness and the pain beneath the confident hunter—the wounded wolf. She gave permission in a tiny nod. 'Do it.'

His lips barely touched one side of her mouth, and then the other side, in sweet mimickry of the real thing, leaving her heart banging like a jackhammer right up as high as her throat. Then he drew her closer still but, though it looked loving—seductive even—she was in his arms in a hold more gentle and protective than any she'd ever known. 'I'm not him,' Armand whispered into her hair.

Slowly, still trying to take air into lungs that wouldn't behave and fill, she nodded. Not real? It was all too real, and something buried deep inside her came shimmering back to life. She could hardly remember the last time anyone had held her, unless it was for an audience. Though they had an audience of one now, Armand's tender hold made her feel as if they were alone, that he was holding her because he wanted to…

He bent down to murmur against her ear. 'Frau Heffernan has been coming to the resort since its reopening, and is very loyal. She just wants to know what's going on. So, for now pretend to dance with me. She'll interpret it as a private romance. She'll love having the power of knowledge no one else has and, beyond teasing me about it in quiet moments, nothing will be said, certainly not in public.'

With a tender hand he moved her head so her face was buried against his chest as he hummed a song. He moved her in a slow shuffle, always keeping her face from the clear *terrasse* doors, protecting her with every movement he made.

She felt so safe. She felt his heart beating against her cheek, heard the swishing of his breath in and out as they danced. He wound his fingers through hers, held her waist with a light, reassuring clasp. How he managed to give her personal space when he held her like a lover, she couldn't understand—but he did. Somehow he knew she couldn't bear any form of male dominance.

He'd given her the choice in everything since he'd invaded her life.

It was a revelation to her as new and wondrous to her as a bud unfurling. Armand had walked away from the life Pete craved like a drug. Armand allowed her to hold her power without punishing her for it. And, yes, he let her know who was in control—*she* was.

His arms were so gentle, his hands so tender. She wanted to melt into him, to fall into this safe, beautiful place and never leave...

*No.* She'd been alone too long, that was all. Even on her wedding day part of her had felt lonely and lost. At nineteen she hadn't known why; at thirty-two, she understood. Though Pete had always been extravagant with compliments and the words 'I love you', his self-love was all-absorbing, and allowed for nothing but the shallowest of affection for anyone else. The day she'd rebelled against his wishes, he'd shown her who was boss in punishing blows.

But now Armand had come into her life with his tender arms and his kindness, and he was a greater threat to her well-being than if he had been holding a sub-machine gun to her head.

And yet she couldn't move from this hold, more seductive than any practiced caress could be. No wonder they called him the Wolf. He knew how to charm her into a state of hypnotic compliance, trusting him within hours of meeting him.

'Is she gone?' she whispered after what seemed like hours, minutes, seconds—she couldn't work it out but, while it seemed too long, it wasn't long enough.

*He's a stranger.* She needed space now.

'Not yet,' he said quietly. 'She's got her heavy-weather gear on. She's there until we notice her.'

Her fingertips were quivering as she fought against running, against holding on with all the strength she had. 'What do you think?'

'It's your call, Rachel. I can look at her, embarrass her into leaving.'

About to assent, she thought of what it might cost him as

the owner and hesitated. 'Would you do that if I were a woman you—you…?'

'Wanted to make love with?' His voice sounded smoky now, and a hot shudder touched her skin with slow, sensuous fingertips. 'No, I probably wouldn't have noticed her at all. By now I'd have carried you to the bedroom.'

Gulp, gulp… The lump in her throat just wouldn't go away. 'I…Herr Bollinger…'

'It's Armand—and if I carry you to the bedroom tonight it will only be for show. I don't abuse women, or persuade them against their will, Rachel Chase. Remember that.'

At that, she stilled so totally she felt her pulse in her throat—and then from somewhere inside her, the fighter came back. 'Then don't speak to me so intimately. We're strangers sharing a cabin, no more than that—and, please remember, I'm still a paying guest.'

'*Touché*, Ms Chase. That's very good.' A rumbling laugh rippled through his body and, though she fought against his power, he still infected her with his mirth. 'And I will *not* point out that the fact that we're in this situation is totally your own fault because you moved in on my private domain. My mother raised me to be a gentleman.'

She grinned against the windcheater he wore, which was as warm as his teasing comment. 'And my mama raised me to be a southern lady. So don't touch me without permission, Armand Bollinger. You might be a wolf, but I can become a she-bear without warning.'

'Consider me appropriately chastened.'

The laughing tone made her feel absurdly happy. 'How weird is this conversation, given our current circumstances?' she whispered, feeling his skin touching hers. They were only hand to hand, cheek to cheek, but it moved with invisible fingertips into her soul.

'That's just what I was thinking.' He relaxed his arms and looked down at her, smiling.

Oh, those silly hot shivers! 'So, is she still there?'

He checked briefly without seeming to. 'She is, in a covered corner of the *terrasse*, and watching us avidly. Time to implement plan B—the wolf must dare the she-bear and we'll see who wins.' He lifted her in his arms, his eyes twinkling as he smiled down at her. Slowly, he rubbed his cheek against hers with absolute gentleness. 'You're a very little bear. I can *bear*ly feel you.'

Warm, safe and beautiful all at once—oh, this man was too seductive for his own good in making her feel this way, even when he was trying to reassure her with his teasing. 'Ha ha. That's because I'm fading away from hunger,' she complained, trying to joke her way into a normal breathing pattern and heartbeat.

He sniffed and his face darkened. 'The cheese is burning.' He put her back down in her chair, turned back and strode over to the *terrasse* doors. After flashing a dark look at the elderly lady, he wound the built-in blinds down. He kept going even after the startled Frau Heffernan had scuttled away. 'Good, now we can eat. I'll clean the pans and be right back.'

Rachel was glad she was sitting down. Her knees really didn't want to be straight at this point.

Armand's knees seemed just fine. After he picked up the collection of little trays, he headed for the kitchen with a clean, confident stride. 'Can you turn the heat down on the grill and take the food off the top while I clean these, please, Rachel? I'll be back in a few minutes. Hopefully everything won't get too cold.'

He spoke in his ordinary voice, as though nothing had happened.

Perhaps to him it hadn't.

'Okay, consider it done.' After speaking as calmly as possible, Rachel drew a deep, slow breath, wondering how the world could turn upside down in a few hours. From feeling safely hidden away, she was out of her depth in waters as sweet as they were turbulent, and all because of one tycoon in shining armour...

Feeling a fervent kinship with the elderly woman—she wanted to scuttle away from Armand too, never come back and definitely never see him again—she made a noncommittal noise of assent and began moving the food from the grill.

'Don't think about it, just don't think about it,' she chanted beneath her breath. She shoved a crispy piece of bacon on her tongue and chewed on it despite the fact that it tasted like ashes in her mouth.

*What just happened in there?*

Armand leaned against the sink for a moment, just breathing. He tossed the *raclette* trays in the sink and ran warm, soapy water over them. Even as he cleaned out the hard cheese and washed them he was conscious of the crazy feeling that had sent him running in here. It hadn't lessened, despite the space between them.

So stupid, to lose his temper over something as simple as burning cheese! He supposed he'd had to do something—and it was either take out his sudden anger on the *raclette* grill and Frau Heffernan, a rich widow without a life of her own, or give in to the consuming need to touch Rachel again.

How idiotic was it to touch a woman in his own home? And yet it felt so right.

He'd never brought a woman here, apart from Maman, Johanna and Carla. It was their home as much as his, since Papa had left it to them all equally. It had been almost all he'd had left to give after the fire destroyed the first resort, and he'd gambled away everything else. To Armand, this cabin was his home, a sacred place of refuge. He'd never brought a woman here until now.

At first, he'd thought it was simple pity. She was alone in a world turned against her, and her jerk of a husband had betrayed her publicly.

Then he'd seen the way she rubbed at her left wrist almost absently, as if in reminder. Maman had done the same thing, long after the breaks had healed from his father's repeated beatings. When Rachel had caught him looking, she'd tried to hide it far too quickly, just as Maman had.

Armand seethed and burned still, just thinking about the shame and embarrassment on Rachel's face. If that damned 'doc with empathy' had been here right now…

It came down to this: Rachel Chase needed protection from Rinaldi, and he could give it.

*And you have to do it, because you didn't protect your own mother.*

There was the crux of it. More than twenty years ago, Armand had woken one night to see the truth he'd probably always known—his father had beaten Maman two shades too hard to hide the bruises; he'd broken her arm.

Armand couldn't change the damage done to his family, but he'd stop Rinaldi from damaging Rachel any further. If Rinaldi showed up, he'd be here waiting.

Despite her spunk and her volatile changes, her inner strength and perception, Rachel was no she-bear. She couldn't protect herself physically against the likes of Dr Pete, let alone stand against the media onslaught. Armand had the skills, the wealth and the place to protect her—and the reputation didn't hurt. If Rinaldi showed his face here, he'd meet with the Wolf, all right—a wolf in protective mode. He didn't care what it took right now, he'd keep Rachel safe.

But he could not and would not hold her again. It was too dangerous to the calm demeanour she needed from him. She needed to heal, not have her protector fantasising about making her his lover. And to make sure she was safe, he had to be in control of his emotions.

*Damn it, when has touching a woman ever been this emotional for me?*

'So stop looking at her. Stop thinking about it,' he growled to himself.

*Stop remembering how it felt to hold her.*

He had to remember instead that she'd called him Herr Bollinger, putting space between them the moment he'd shown her that his male imagination was running riot. *She's been through enough. She doesn't want you for anything but protection. She needs a friend.*

So a friend he'd be. Nothing had happened, really—just a new kind of male reaction to a sweet, curvy bundle of woman in his arms. End of story.

But every single one of the cheese trays had grooves in them from the steel wool he'd gouged into them with his cleaning efforts when he carried them back into the dining table.

When he glanced at her, she was sitting in her place with seeming calm, but her fingers were laced so tightly together they had white patches. Looking up, he saw the apprehension in those shimmering, far-too-expressive eyes, and the paleness of her cheeks.

Had he frightened her with his emotions? He smiled in rueful apology, but it felt as if he'd gouged his smile in place too. Reassure her; be gentle. A friend, only a friend.

This was going to be a very long few weeks.

# CHAPTER FIVE

IT was almost nine the next morning when Armand—who'd risen at six, had showered, enjoyed breakfast and was currently working from the cabin office—heard the door of the other bedroom squeak slightly as if being opened. 'Good morning, Rachel,' he called.

He received only a grunt in reply. From the open door, he saw a pyjama-clad form holding a bundle of clothes dash past him to the bathroom. The door slammed behind her.

With raised brows, he kept working. Somebody, it seemed, was not a morning person—or, like most women he'd met, Rachel didn't like appearing before others while she was looking her worst.

Not that she did. The brief flash past him had been candy-pink, all tousled hair, rumpled clothes, curvaceousness and, altogether, rather delicious.

*Stop it.* With a determined growl, he pushed the vision of her from his thoughts and kept working on the latest round of paperwork from the local officials for the new land.

Somebody obviously also liked long showers. It was almost half an hour later when she finally emerged. Her curvy shape was encased in similar jeans to last night, and a long-sleeved T-shirt with 'sometimes your knight in shining armour is just a jerk in tin foil' emblazoned on it. Clear-painted toes peeped from the open-ended hotel slippers. Her hair was shining, cheeks flushed and her skin glowed with health. Again, her face was free of make-up, but she still managed to look radiant. It was her eyes, her smile. With those weapons at her disposal, she'd never need the rest.

'Now I'm human enough to say hi,' she announced gaily as she shuffled towards him, the slippers making a soft swish-swish on the wooden floors. 'Good morning, Armand. Did you sleep well?'

About to ask the same thing, he nodded, surprised anew that 'Mrs Pete' would be the one to ask first. 'Thank you. And you?'

She nodded in return. 'The beds here are very comfortable.'

'You've been here a few weeks now, I believe. Do you have any thoughts on ways to improve the standard of the resort?'

Her smile slipped a touch. A wary kind of nervousness entered her eyes. He didn't know what was going on. Such an innocuous question shouldn't send her running for cover. 'I only asked because I wish to attract all kinds of international guests.' he said gently. 'I've catered in the European style. You're American—your honest opinion is the kind of feedback I need.'

'Oh.' She relaxed so visibly he could almost see her muscles uncoiling. 'Well, while the rooms are wonderful, for people that want real privacy, or for family vacations or reunions, cabins like this would be in demand, I think.'

He frowned. 'The suites aren't enough?'

'Oh, they're wonderful,' she rushed to say. 'I—I was just thinking—you know, forget it. What do I know? I never stayed at a place like this until I was an adult. Your guests probably don't want kids and noisy families here. It was a stupid thought.'

'Rachel.' With a hand on hers, he stopped the babbling. 'I did cater this first resort for adults, and the second in

Chamonix, but I want to extend for the third, make it more family-friendly. I loved it when we stayed here when I was a boy. Providing cabins helps the resort to compete with the sport hotels and bed and breakfasts.' He typed the information quickly into the email he was composing to his architect and sent it. 'Done.'

Then he turned to her and smiled again. 'Thank you for that, Rachel. The more ideas I provide for the third resort, the better chance I have of acquiring the land. Laws for building resorts can be rather stringent here.'

'You're welcome,' was all she said, but the look of shy delight on her face both moved and puzzled him. This level of insecurity surely went deeper than his suspicions. How could a woman so famous for giving good advice not be jaded by people's thanks?

*You're getting in too deep here. She isn't Maman. You can't balance your debt to Maman and the girls by helping this woman.*

He knew nothing of her outside the tabloids, such as why she had the name 'Rhonda Braithwaite' on her suitcases and 'Rachel Chase' on the passport she'd given at the reception desk. He didn't know if she was a good person or...

Yes, he did know that, by the way she'd shouldered the blame instead of letting a single member of his staff be reprimanded. He knew it by the horror on her face when he had told her this was his cabin. He knew it by the way she hadn't tried to bargain with him over his deal, though she had to know who was getting the better end of it.

And, damn it, he knew how good it felt to hold her in his arms—and he knew she'd felt it too, even if she didn't want to be there.

Whether he wanted to get involved or not, he was already in way over his head here.

'You never answered me yesterday, when I asked how long you thought you'd need my help here.' He kept the question gentle, masking the intense need to show the turbulence inside. His anger wasn't aimed at her, but at the men of the world who felt it was their right to abuse a woman or a child. Anger, because it seemed impossible to change one man's way of thinking and behaviour, let alone the world's. *It will never happen again,* they always said, until they lost their temper again.

'Is time an issue for you? If so, I can go any time, really.'

Armand heard the undoubted tone of fear beneath the projected calm in her voice. She was using every trick in her psychologist's book, not to charm him or pry into his life, but to hide her deepest emotions from him.

'Well, it could be an issue if you were planning on staying here for the next five years,' he said, angling for a laugh, or at least to make her relax a bit. 'I do have three resorts to manage—at least once this next one's built.'

'And you ought to be there to oversee the project.' The words were sympathetic now the psychologist's persona she slipped into without a problem. He thought it was because then she could hide her real self—the woman she was ashamed of being. 'As I said, there's really no issue if you have to go at any time. If you don't mind me staying, I'll be fine here alone.'

Yet it *was* a problem for her. He knew that, but he had no right to ask. Even being her temporary protector didn't cancel out the fact that he'd known her less than twenty-four hours. He couldn't butt in on her private world.

So he tried the one way that seemed to work for her. 'And still she doesn't tell me her time frame. Rachel Chase, international woman of mystery... You didn't tell me you worked for MI6. Or the CIA, since you're American. Or are you?' he riposted with a grin.

Her face relaxed. She bit her lip, but laughed anyway. She laughed like a child every time, laughed as though she meant it. It lit up the room. It lit up his safe, predictable world, and filled it with warmth, colour and enchantment.

'Is two weeks okay with you, maybe three?'

The words broke into uncomfortable conclusions, giving the rainbow light and myriad warmth a time-limit. He was relieved; of course he was. It was best this way, short and sweet. He'd had small infatuations before with unattainable women and he'd recovered. Yes, he liked Rachel—found her adorable, damn it—and he definitely liked the way she felt in his arms. But it wouldn't be a tragedy if she left tomorrow or the next day. Or in two weeks or three. He was stronger than that, had survived a lot worse disasters than a woman leaving his life after a few weeks. *Facile venir, facile aller*— easy come, easy go—that was his motto.

'Good,' he replied at last, with a cheerfulness that seemed overdone, even to his paranoid ears. 'Two weeks is definitely doable—or even three or four.'

'Really? I can stay? It's not an issue for you?' she asked, her eyes wide and her smile bouncing off those unseen prisms in the room. Rainbow reflections were everywhere…

He felt his eyes blink in astonishment at having made an offer she hadn't asked for. What was wrong with him lately? 'Yes, of course,' he said smoothly. 'You are a paying guest, after all.'

Something came and went in her face, a frisson of apprehension. Her smile faded to something weak and half-hearted. 'Well, then, we both know where we are. The day I run out of funds, I'll be out of your hair for good, Herr Bollinger.'

Brave words, but her fingers trembled. And he could have kicked himself. No doubt Dr Pete had frozen the accounts, hoping that sooner or later his newly renamed wife would be forced to come into the open and use electronic funds to survive. Then he could find her, and bring her to heel. She might already have run out of money.

It was only when she'd left the room, still clutching at her pyjamas—cute pink things with little cats on the telephone—that he realised she hadn't called him Armand since he'd brought up the subject of her stay. She knew he was trying to manipulate her, however subtle he'd been in his effort. He'd tried to dig into her life, and again she'd given nothing away.

Two, maybe three weeks was all he had to get her out of danger—that was, if she didn't run out of funds first. And, given his complete failure in getting a single personal concession from her, three weeks wouldn't be nearly enough.

Without needing to think it through, he emailed Max again.

*Nobody is to mention funds to Ms Chase. She is our honoured guest, for as long as she needs to be here.*

He said nothing else, but he knew Max wouldn't ask. It was Armand's practise to allow respected clients some space and time to pay their bills. He'd always judged this by instinct alone and he'd never been wrong. They always came through sooner or later, and they'd all become numbered among his most loyal returning guests or even investors.

Now all he needed was to think of a reasonable excuse that would allow her to stay and still satisfy her pride. He just knew that, if he couldn't come up with something really good, she'd leave with her head high, refusing his charity. He couldn't let her vanish without trace, not when he was sure that sooner or later, she'd run into more trouble than she could handle alone.

*That afternoon*

'It's a simple contract, Rachel. You stay here until I've se-
cured the new resort and I have the architect's plans. Then
I'll take you there, and you can endorse at least two of my
resorts with honesty.'

Rachel frowned at Armand, sensing something deeper
than he was showing with this perfect courtesy. 'Why do you
need me to sign a contract? I've said I'll do it.'

His eyes darkened to stormy grey, the hidden lightning
beneath the handsome diplomat's face. He only looked like
that when he was hiding something. 'Because then, if you
change your mind and sign on for that show, or pursue other
avenues with your career, you're legally bound to this venture first.'

'I've never broken a contract in my life,' she replied, aiming for calm, but knowing her voice shook a little. 'Whatever
you've heard about me…'

His facial muscles didn't shift; he looked calm, but she
sensed the tempest buried deep inside his emotions, like black
clouds on the edge of a summer-blue sky. 'I've heard nothing
to your detriment, Rachel. I don't buy tabloids for entertainment. I'm merely used to conducting my business on more
than a handshake or verbal agreement. I've found it's safer
that way—for both of us.'

'I see.' Now she couldn't keep the stiffness from her tone.
No matter how he couched it, it was obvious that he didn't
trust her. 'Then I'll fax a copy to my lawyer and have him
read over it before I sign.'

A short pause, then he said, 'Are you certain it's wise to
contact someone from home?'

No matter how tactfully he'd said it, the unspoken knowledge hovered between them. Silence had become her bul-
wark and shield, but with a few tactful words he'd given her

a timely reminder. Yes, Pete *would* lean on her lawyer to divulge her whereabouts, should she contact him. She already knew he'd done the same with her parents and her sister, Sara. Until she'd turned off her phone, all their calls had been reproaches about abandoning 'poor Pete' in his time of need.

That Armand hadn't spoken about Pete directly showed she was right. He already knew or suspected far too much.

'Then I'll find a lawyer in Zürich. One that speaks English,' she added defiantly, before he could say it. 'There must be loads of them.'

'There are, and that's your right, certainly. You don't know me, and I don't know you. It's best we keep this entire matter as a business arrangement.' His tone was as withdrawn as hers. Though she knew it was stupid, she wondered what she'd said or done to put distance between them when just last night, they'd been so close.

*Don't think about it.*

Like it or not, separated or not—even though Pete had cheated on her at least twice—she was still a married woman for another few weeks. She had no right to think about how much Armand's holding her last night had affected her, let alone keep reliving how safe she'd felt How warm and tender his arms and hands had been. And the look in his eyes…

*No.* She had to remember, this arrangement was all just business: *keep Rachel happy, keep her here, let her think you might be interested until the resort's endorsed. And, if the ads fail, drop her like a hot potato.*

*That's why he's called the Wolf, right? He'll do whatever it takes to make his ideas work. It's said he hasn't failed at anything he's taken on since he was seventeen.*

And yet, impatient with this wary reserve, sick of trusting no one, she picked up the five-page contract and read it through. It was exactly as he'd said: straightforward, no hidden clauses. She was to stay here free of charge until the deal went through for the resort on the Swiss side of the French border. Then she would appear on a series of endorsements for the Bollinger resorts, and that would be that.

'You're right, it's very simple.' Drawing a fast breath, she grabbed the pen and signed it. 'There you are, Herr Bollinger, it's all done. Now you can get back to work.' Bundling the sheaf of papers in her hands, she shoved it at him as if palming off a grenade. Some instinct was screaming at her, *you'll regret this*.

Expecting further withdrawal on his part, or cold satisfaction at his victory however he won it, she was taken aback by the brief flash she saw in his eyes—it almost looked like relief. And that sent a spurt of confusion and worry through her. He *did* know too much. 'Thank you, *Rachel*.' And, if there was a slight emphasis on her given name, the crispness of his voice and the way he signed the papers, straightened them and put them in a folder was all business. 'I have a meeting with the staff for the rest of the afternoon. I'll be back in time for dinner.'

Rachel watched him leave the cabin, torn between indignation and aching wistfulness: a spurt of loneliness that hurt her heart but had little to do with being alone. She tried to shake it off, but it persisted through a two-hour session of reading, writing in her journal and listening to music. It continued even through an hour-long tramp along one of the marked nature-trails. Sweating through the layers she had to wear for her anonymity hadn't bothered her until today.

But there were three things she didn't and wouldn't do: check email, check her SMS's or watch TV. The first two were easily traceable if Pete paid an expert enough, and watching TV was a reminder of the woman she used to be. The longer she stayed here, the more she wondered if she should ever have been that person at all.

So who was she now, and what did she want from life?

For someone who'd lived her entire life on aspiration, always going forward to the next goal, this inactivity, this waiting—and especially this temporary dependence on a man she didn't know—felt as if she'd said goodbye to her most trusted instincts and even her brain cells. She didn't know who this alien being was that opened her mouth and said yes to everything Armand proposed, but she didn't trust her an inch.

# CHAPTER SIX

'I'M NOT coordinated. I'll fall and hurt myself. I can't do this, Armand, and especially not in the dark!'

The absolute panic in Rachel's voice was more than the natural trepidation at trying something new. Holding her close, steadying both their snowboards by keeping his at a ninety-degree angle to hers, Armand kept his voice low and soothing. 'You can't know that. We haven't even gone ten feet yet.'

'I can't even ski. How can I do this? I have no stocks. I'm going to fall. I know I will. Don't you understand? I can't go to hospital!'

He looked at her in the deep night, lit by the warmth of bagged fires on poles reflecting off the new fall of snow in small, glittering jewels. But she hadn't noticed either the night's beauty or even the fact that he'd had his arm around her waist for ten minutes. If she felt the same kind of half-amazed awakening of body and soul he experienced every time he touched her, especially since their dance and half-kiss, she wasn't showing it. She was staring down at her booted feet on a snowboard and was literally shaking.

'Have you had a bad experience in hospital as a child?' he asked gently.

She didn't even make an acid comment about his trying to psycho-analyse her, which told him her fear was very real. 'I can't be found until the divorce is final and made public. If it happens, he'll find a way to blackmail me into coming back to the show. The restraining order won't stop him. He's been losing ratings hand over fist since I left. The public now knows it was me that gave him his empathy, and that I was feeding him the answers people needed to hear. I know him—he'll be desperate by now. But he'll have a plan to win me back into his life. He's addicted to fame, and he'll do whatever it takes to make me come back.'

Now, at last, Armand got it. Really, he didn't have much choice but to understand. She was babbling her secrets in fear, secrets she'd kept chained inside her heart like a hated treasure. They'd been housemates nearly ten days now, and all this time he'd tried to get her to talk, with no success.

His arousal faded in a fit of protectiveness like a lightning-bolt, all but knocking him off his feet. His suspicions had been confirmed in a flash, and he wanted to knock Rinaldi flying—flying right off the damned planet.

*Stop it. You'll terrify her.* He knew that from bitter experience. He'd seen the terror on his sisters' faces on the rare times he'd been allowed home from boarding school and his father had walked in with that look on his face…

Aching to ask if she'd contacted her parents in the past few weeks, he forced himself not to reply to her secrets at all—she'd only hate him later if he did. Instead he asked, softly but in clear challenge, 'What would you say to a patient that refused to try a new experience before even attempting it?'

At that, she stilled. Slowly, she mumbled something he couldn't hear.

'I have you safe with me,' he went on, still gentle, persuasive. 'I won't let go.'

She gave a little, almost plaintive sigh. It was answer enough, since he could feel her disbelief beating from her, as strong and sure as her racing pulse.

Armand wondered if anyone had ever stayed the distance,

not with her but *for* her. Had anyone ever put Rachel's needs first?

'Look around, Rachel,' he murmured to distract her. 'See how beautiful it all is.'

A small quiver ran through her. 'I can't. My eyes...'

With tenderness foreign to him until now, Armand lifted her face from the terrified contemplation of the snowboard and saw her goggles were totally fogged. 'Are you so cold?' Or worse, he thought to himself, had he frightened her into crying and not even noticed?

'I'm from Texas. It reaches freezing there in winter.'

Her semi-defiant tone, and the way she pulled her face from his hold, filled him with relief. She was a fighter, all right. 'And how long has it been since you visited in winter? LA's climate hasn't reached freezing probably since the last ice age.'

She turned away. 'Good point,' she said lightly enough, but something in her voice disturbed him.

'How long has it been since you visited Texas at all?' he asked quietly.

For a moment she neither moved nor spoke. Then she said, 'How long has it been since you visited your father's grave?'

She'd hit him with the carelessness of a drive-by shot into a crowd. How could he possibly have expected a wound so sudden and deep from a woman that until now had seemed as empathetic as she was helpless? And how could she possibly know?

Answer: she couldn't. Just as he didn't know anything about her. They were two people forced into a strange proximity, knowing only what they saw—strangers in the night, each giving the other something they needed. And that was how it had to stay. He should have known the 'defenceless kitten' thing was only part of her woman's repertoire. Her segment of the Dr Pete show proved she had far too much perception for any man's comfort.

'Interesting question,' he said, his voice calm and steady, not even a tremor to betray him. 'Now, shall we continue, or are you going to let your fears win…Dr Rinaldi?'

Her back tightened, notch by notch, even in the heavy ski jacket. 'My name,' she said with slow, deliberate disgust, 'Is Chase.'

'Oh, I'm sorry, I wasn't certain which of your current names to call you,' he retorted in the blandest tone he'd ever used, injury added to insult. 'So has Rinaldi served its purpose? You can throw it away without regret?'

She wobbled on the snowboard as she turned fully back to him, hanging onto him for balance. Yet it didn't seem funny at all. 'The name Rhonda Braithwaite got me out of LA without his PI finding me. From Paris, I changed to Rachel Chase.' With a heavily gloved hand she pulled the goggles from her face. Her eyes were red-rimmed, watery, but she faced him from her ten-inch disadvantage with quaint dignity. 'If you'd ever had your wrist and ribs broken by someone you'd once trusted and loved, you'd know why I want to leave his name behind me—why it hurts so much to hear it. But believe me when I say I will never forget, no matter how many names I take on, or how many times I reinvent myself.'

It was a battle-axe blow to his sword-thrust—and a knock-out punch for honesty. And, though he was looking into her eyes, he saw three pairs of phantom eyes beside her, behind her. Because he'd seen that look before: with Maman, Johanna and Carla when they had waved goodbye to him, the day he'd started boarding school. They'd been left alone with a husband and father who drank and gambled too much and took out his anger on his family, without their big brother to protect them.

He cursed himself in silence, then said, 'Rachel, I—'

She put up a hand. 'I've heard enough apologies lately to last me a while. Now are you going to cure me of one of my less rational fears or not, Dr Bollinger? You said something about not letting me go, I believe?'

Her eyes were twinkling now. Even though he knew it was a thin blanket covering the pain beneath, it was taking them from dangerous waters to the safer ebb-tide. So he smiled back. 'So I did, Mademoiselle Chase,' he acknowledged with mock gravity, bowing his head, sweeping a hand around them to their very private night-ski-run he'd arranged. 'But not until you have at least appreciated all the trouble I went to for you. All this beauty surrounds us, and so far you've only looked at the snowboard.'

As he spoke, he pulled out a clean tissue—when skiing, he always kept a packet on hand—gently wiped her eyes and the goggles hanging around her neck.

'Would you like to wipe my nose as well, Papa Bear?' she retorted with a loud, theatrical sniff, and he laughed. He laughed because it was cute; laughed because no woman had sniffed with him before unless it was in rage or for effect, using tears to get her way. No matter how badly he ached to take this a step further, Rachel wanted nothing from him but a skiing lesson. Despite the disappointment, it was a liberating feeling: no expectation, no neediness, just two sort-of-friends having a night-snowboarding session.

With gravity, he put the tissue to her nose and with laughing eyes she made a loud raspberry sound with her mouth, pretending to blow. They both laughed.

'Oh…'

Looking at her—what was it about her that made it so hard to look away?—he saw she was looking into the night. There was wonder in those big eyes as she took in the scattered cloud in the star-filled night, the poles with the burning bags lighting up the night, the soft-dancing snowflakes and the white-laden fir trees along the slope. And, though it was all she said, she'd made all the trouble to surprise her more than worthwhile.

'You're welcome,' he said, resisting the urge to touch that cold, snowy cheek or to bend and kiss those bitten pink lips, half-open as she drank in the night.

Had his voice sounded as hoarse as it felt to him? Did she know how much he longed to just taste her mouth once, to move his hands over her skin and see those beautiful eyes come alive for him?

*Stop it. The last thing she needs right now is to start something I've never wanted to finish. I'm her emotional umbrella, nothing more. In a few weeks she'll be moving on.*

For the first time, a woman would be walking away from him and he would have no choice but to let her. So, struggling to ignore the stupid physical ache to touch that was part and parcel of being a man, he swirled his snowboard around, facing down the slope with her body fitting into his, sweet and snug. He ached again and again. It felt as if the ache would never end.

*Rachel; this is for Rachel. She deserves to know there's one man she can turn to without his demands, without regrets.* He had to be a better man than he'd ever been. For Rachel.

'Trust me?' he asked softly.

After the briefest of hesitations, and a tiny wobble, she whispered, 'I'm trying to.'

'I won't hurt you, Rachel.' Why did the light, teasing tone he'd employed to such effect in the past suddenly sound like a solemn vow? 'I won't let you fall.'

Her expression turned sad for a moment, even as she kept hanging onto him for the balance that seemed so elusive for her. 'There are some falls nobody can control, some hurts that can't be prevented.' Then she grinned again. 'But if I end up in hospital in traction you are *so* dead, Bollinger.'

Relieved she'd jumped back on the light, playful path, he winked at her. 'Ah, but you'd have to catch me first. Rather hard to manage from that position.'

And before she could retort in kind he moved the lower half of his body so they began sliding down the baby slope together on private, non-resort land far from the fun, romantic night-skiing he'd established years ago for his regular clients. He held her so that when she wobbled he could steady her; he moved them in as close to perfect sync as he could, slowly enough so that she wouldn't feel loss of control.

And when she was moving on her own, with her inexpressibly kissable mouth stretched in a wide smile of discovered poise and the simple joy of living, he had to move. He had no choice, really. It was move or kiss her, because if there was ever a kissing moment it was this one.

So he pulled away far enough to hold her hand. 'It's time to see what you're capable of.' After a few panicked wobbles, he said encouragingly, 'You're a natural at this. You're a snow queen. You can do this, Rachel. I know you can.'

Her astonishment, so clear even behind her goggles, and obvious in her open mouth, almost made him lose balance. 'I— Thank you. Nobody ever…' She gulped, gulped again. 'Nobody,' she whispered, and shook her head.

*Nobody ever said that to me before.*

And, instead of the wrong parts hurting, now it was his heart that ached for her—ached for the sweet, real 'doc with empathy' who seemed so overcome by a few words of faith. And he wished he hadn't used words he'd said before to a hundred female guests.

'It's true,' he said just loud enough for her to hear. 'Rachel, look at where you are. You *are* doing it.'

She looked down at her twisting body, at the tiny slope she was conquering. 'Oh,' she whispered, and her whole face grew alight with radiance. 'Armand, I'm *doing* it. I'm skiing.'

It wasn't the moment to correct her, or even to say that snowboarding was thought to be the harder discipline. He smiled. He smiled because he couldn't help it. His life had been dark and complicated for eighteen years and yet this woman, who was on the run from her life—a woman who'd suffered probably far more than he'd ever know—filled him with light and made him feel heartfelt bliss in this simple achievement. 'Yes, you are.'

'I feel like Lois Lane,' she said as they passed his 'start' line, making small S-slides down the slope. 'You know that scene when Superman let her fly just by holding her hand?'

'Yes,' he said, resisting the impulse to break the moment by asking if that made him Superman. She'd certainly made him feel that way.

'I feel like I'm flying, Armand.' She held onto his gloved hand as if she was about to drop off a cliff, not even realising she was all but doing everything she needed to on her own. 'You make me feel as if I can do anything.' She glanced at him; he knew because he couldn't keep his eyes from her muffled form. He felt as if he was imbibing her sparkling happiness, clear as new wine, just by being with her. 'Thank you, Armand, thank you.' Her voice was choked.

He didn't say it was nothing, because it wasn't, not to her. 'It's my privilege to be here with you, Rachel.'

'Darn, my goggles are fogging up again,' she mock-complained, trying to smile. 'Let me ski, will you?'

He laughed and said no more. It was enough for both of them.

But as they took his private cable-car back up the slope and snowboarded back down, he kept hold of her hand. He'd promised not to let her fall and she'd had enough of broken promises. And falls.

*There are some falls nobody can control.*

Even as he steadied her and taught her to find her natural rhythm and ability on the slopes, the words continued to whisper to him—because she wasn't talking about physical injury.

The words haunted him because he knew she was right. Rachel wasn't fair game, and he didn't know how to be the kind of man she needed. He didn't even know if he'd want to when these few weeks were over. He was cynical, jaded, had never known how to believe in any woman outside of his family, always looking for the 'exit' sign from the night he met any woman. This awakening faith, this need to be with Rachel, was too new for either of them to trust in.

Being near her felt like touching heaven, but he couldn't let this go beyond the odd half-friendship it was now. The thought of never seeing her again, never having another night like tonight, didn't work for him. He wanted to keep her in his life. But Rachel deserved love, babies and 'for ever', and a man who could go the distance.

She deserved a man who wouldn't lash out when times got hard. Could he do that? Damn it, he just didn't know—and risking it would destroy her.

What he wanted was to be Rachel's friend—to grow older, still exchange calls, emails and cards with her—a friendship that lasted the distance. Always to have her remember him and their time together with a smile. To have her want to see him again without pain, without complications.

So he'd do his level best to stop them both from falling.

'It's simple attraction, nothing more. I am not falling for Armand. I am *so* not falling for him. I refuse to fall for him!'

Satisfied, Rachel turned from the bathroom mirror where she'd wiped a clear bit in the shower-misted glass with a wet hand. She peered at herself every morning with almost anxious paranoia, but so far she was still doing well. There were no signs of that sickly-love face she'd had during those first months with Pete. She looked happy, sure, but why not? If she still wasn't trying to get pretty for Armand—trying to lose weight or impress him with flirty banter that would never work, because she wasn't one of those waiflike models he was usually seen with—then she was safe. Safe from infatuation, nothing more.

She wasn't about to make a fool of herself over a man who was merely being kind to her. Armand deserved better than the infatuation of a needy woman he was helping out. So she wouldn't do it. Simple as that.

'Good, done. That's the way, Rachel,' she told herself, looking back for a last glimpse. No sickly-face... Oh, the relief every time she looked!

Minutes later she skipped out of the bathroom in jeans and a long-sleeved T-shirt, her hair damp and tangled. Nope, she didn't care what he thought of her looks at all. 'If you can't compete, stay out of the race', Daddy had always said.

After putting away her bathroom essentials and pyjamas— no way was she going to exasperate him by taking over his bathroom with her products or clothes!—she found him in the kitchen tossing eggs, tomatoes and mushrooms in a skillet. 'Good morning, Rachel.' He smiled at her. 'Great T-shirt,' he commented, looking at the logo. 'Where do you get your shirts?'

'I get all my T-shirts custom made.' She smiled back, convinced she'd remained cool and calm, even if he was like something from a magazine matchmaker-ad in those casual trousers and woollen pullover, cooking with supreme ease. *Let me find you the perfect man...*

'Could you butter the toast, please, and just take the coffee pot off the stove? Thanks.'

The words were so prosaic, yet so intimate. Sharing daily tasks gave a pretty illusion of togetherness. But even after that amazing night-skiing, where she'd found she could actually stay upright while she was in his hold, she refused to believe in it. Any woman would find Armand attractive, and it was no more than that.

As far as she was concerned, love was an invention of men to trap women into cooking and cleaning for them and warming their bed while they did whatever they wanted. It was a truth she'd known for a long time. If her father hadn't totally destroyed her faith in happily-ever-after, with his casual affairs and insistence on lies even when he'd been found out again, Pete had knocked all belief in fairy-tale endings from her. And he'd done it long before he'd broken her wrist. His self-absorbed use of her skills to promote his own agenda without a thought for her needs and had put her heart and her confidence in a hiding-place she'd only rediscovered since leaving him. She'd let it happen without even really noticing until it was far too late.

That wouldn't happen again. But there was no reason not to enjoy an uncomplicated friendship with Armand—especially when he'd given far more than he wanted from her.

'Butter toast and take coffee pot off the heat. Sure,' she agreed cheerfully, and pulled the toast out of the slots with careful fingers. 'Want hot milk for the coffee today?'

'I could do latte today, definitely. And there's some caramel syrup in the cupboard if you like that. I sometimes do, but usually at night.'

She gave him a quizzical grin. 'I've never met a man before that drinks all different kinds of coffee. Usually they only like one, or maybe two.'

He laughed and raised his hands, palm up. 'What can I say? I guess I'm not the faithful type, even to coffee.'

He'd been saying things like that for a few days now, hence her mirror-mantra. Though he said it too lightly to be an insult, the inference was obvious: *don't get interested*. He wasn't, and she wasn't either. Part of her wanted to blurt out that he and all men could go live and love without her caring a bit. But to put it out there would mean 'the lady doth protest overmuch'. Saying it meant she *did* care, somehow. And of course she didn't care if he found her desirable or not.

*Oh, come on, who are you kidding? All people want to be attractive to everyone else. Nobody wants to be seen as unattractive. That's all it is.*

With the slight discomfort of wondering if she was in denial, she found herself laughing, with a slight defiance to it. 'So you're a "serial poly-coffee-ist". It's the latest syndrome in our sad world. I'll get right onto researching it, in case you ever decide you need help.'

'Thank you,' he retorted with that grave face and laughing eyes, the hint of relief that was always there when she played his game. 'But for now I'd appreciate that hot milk more.'

She bowed and, trying to sound like a genie, said, 'Your wish is my command.'

She'd hoped to make him laugh, but as she turned away to get the milk out of the fridge, there was a bare moment when she could have sworn she saw something...

Then the moment passed, leaving her unsure if she'd seen the flash in his eyes or not. Unsure if she wanted to know. Proximity—that was all it was. It was totally natural that, if he was holed up with a woman for a few weeks, even a man like Armand would feel a passing attraction.

'Any port in a storm,' she muttered as she laid the table—and faint nausea touched her at the thought. She was no man's storm-port. She had something to give the world that had nothing to do with being a man's pretty doll, cook, housekeeper, waitress, sounding-board a child-bearer. Or career-giver and dream-provider at the cost of her own dreams. Never again.

Her endorsement deal was not the same thing. Armand

was making certain her needs were being met. In return she'd give him what he wanted. Then she'd be out of here, heart and self-confidence intact.

# CHAPTER SEVEN

'A *CHILL-OUT* night?' Rachel was looking at him as though he'd suddenly gained an extra chromosome instead of proposing the simplest of recreations.

Armand wasn't sure what was going on, but he went with it. 'Yes, chilling out. You ought to know the term. Americans invented it, didn't they?'

'Well, sure, of course I've *heard* of it,' she replied, sounding vaguely doubtful.

'You mean you've never done it?'

She blushed hotly, as if he'd made an intentional *double entendre*. 'I've recommended it to my patients, of course.' But the words were half-defiant, almost a question. The uncertainty was palpable in the bitten lip, the way her gaze fell to her twiddling fingers.

Without even trying or wanting to, he'd made her feel like a freak. Armand realised anew how little he knew about this woman, despite all his best efforts.

'So you're one of the world's workers,' he said with that teasing gravity that seemed to relax her. 'Let me walk you through this difficult new process, step by step.' Sweeping a hand over the living room, he winked at her. 'Here we have popcorn, chocolate, wine and a DVD—there is a choice of comedy chick-flicks, just for you. We sit on the couch with our feet up on the ottomans, eat and drink and enjoy the movie. Now, do you think that's manageable?'

If anything, her blush grew. Her smile wavered, and instead of moving to the said couch she shifted her feet until they pointed in the direction of her room. 'You must think I'm such a weirdo.' Now her shoulders turned so all of her was facing her room. She was going to bolt.

Denying her half-accusation would only make her run. 'Well, yeah,' he continued to tease. 'But, as with snowboarding, it's my honour to be your very first chill-out partner.' Again, he swept his hand to the couch, the array of inviting foods.

She didn't even look. Her gaze was firmly on her feet. 'The T-shirt says it all.' Her hand swept vaguely over her shirt. *I'm not normal*, it said.

He swore beneath his breath, trying to control the rising anger, but the words came anyway. 'Would you like to tell me what's going on here, why you're acting as if popcorn and a movie is so wrong? This surely can't be one of your many state secrets.'

Now the blush melted down her throat and blended with her T-shirt. 'Trust me, you don't want to know.'

He laughed, but it was harsh. 'Trust, Rachel? I didn't realise that was a word in your vocabulary. I know it's only been two weeks, but frankly I'm tired of stumbling around in the dark with you. You question everything I do and say. I'm not the enemy, but I'm beginning to wonder if you see everyone as another continuation of your invisible battles. Or is it just me you treat this way?'

Her head drooped. 'Armand…'

'Don't apologise,' he interrupted her in a flat tone. 'You always do that, then you run and hide again or push me away. I'm not him, Rachel.'

A long stretch of quiet followed, and this time he refused

to fill it. She either trusted him now or she didn't, and he'd give up trying. Enough was enough.

At last she mumbled, 'No, you're not him. Or them.' Her feet shuffled, making an unobtrusive step towards the sanctuary of her room.

'Them?' he queried mildly, to make her stay. It was time.

'My family,' she muttered in a faltering tone. 'My parents and sister, Sara. I'm not like them. Nothing like them. Mama called me a changeling—you know? The child the fairies change for another at birth. I don't look like any of them, and I don't act like them. I'm—different.'

There seemed nothing he could say in answer to that, so he waited.

Eventually she sighed, as if shedding an enormous burden. 'You see, I was a smart child. *Very* smart.'

Armand was taken aback. How could she make being intelligent sound like she was confessing to murder? 'I see.'

'No, you don't,' she retorted, lifting her face at last, her anger bursting forth without warning. 'You were *born* one of the beautiful people, the son of a movie star and a multimillionaire. You were a movie star yourself until you retired. You were admired and loved from birth. I was a freak from the first moment I remember!'

Now wasn't the time to correct her presumptions, even if he wanted to relive his ugly childhood, picture-perfect only for the cameras. And at last she was opening up to him. 'Why?'

'I was diagnosed with an IQ of one hundred and eighty at the age of six. I finished high school at thirteen, and I had a double degree with a PhD by nineteen.'

'That's impressive,' he said, feeling his way with this, because she obviously was far from proud of her achievements.

'Oh, yes. Everyone was impressed with clever Rachel. The department came to Mama and Daddy when I was in first grade, telling them I needed special education. They put me in a special school. The boarding-school teachers loved me. The college I lived in was so proud.'

Armand frowned. 'And your parents?'

She shrugged. 'Dad was a travelling sales-manager. Mom was a doctor's receptionist. They didn't know what to make of me, where I'd got this ability from, or what to do with me when I came home. My sister Sara was pretty and popular. She liked to pretend she was an only child. Most of the time, she ignored me. I ended up spending my weekends and vacations studying at the school or at college. It was easier for everyone.'

She wasn't looking at him now, but was looking down at her feet. Shuffle-shuffle, toes stubbing against the carpet. Fingers twining around each other, or twiddling with her hair.

'When did that change?' he asked. Every question about her family seemed pregnant with tension.

She sighed. 'When I was thirteen, the teachers told them I could become a brain surgeon or a rocket scientist. I guess they thought I'd be able to support them when they retired. I did want to help people—but in a face to face way. Not with a microscope or a scalpel. I don't like blood or germs.'

'Not many people do,' he said, on a quizzical note. She sounded so ashamed of herself for that common weakness.

'Everyone said being a psychologist was a waste of my brains.' She frowned at the waiting food and drink in the living room as if it offended her. 'They only came around when…'

'When you met Dr Pete?' he prompted, sure he was right.

She sighed and nodded. 'He gave my career direction and focus. Before I met him I was working in a diner.'

'With a double doctorate and a PhD?' He was amazed.

'A PhD with a baby face,' she retorted with a shrug. 'Nobody wanted to hire me. They said no patient would take me seriously. I had to eat and pay the rent—and I wanted to study people, see what made them tick. I practised my skills on the people who wanted to talk. And then, after ten months, I met Pete—and he had enough dreams and direction for both of us.' Her voice softened. 'He took me to LA, gave me a home and a ring. He made me knock on the doors of every medical practice until I got a job. He's actually a screenwriter, you know, and has a degree in business and economics. He dreamed up the concept of the show, but we had to do a lot of study to get it exactly right. Before and after each show I had to study again, to find the right theme and make sure I had all my facts right. I—I didn't want to leave things like that to assistants.'

Repressing the urge to ask if Pete had worked at all while dreaming up the show, or if he'd used Rachel as his meal ticket until he found fame, Armand asked, 'How did he end up the front man of the show?'

Until now he'd been too stunned to think of how much information she was giving him. He had to get as much as he could from her now, before she clammed up again.

'I threw up on the first eight attempts to put me in front of a camera.' She said it so defiantly, as if daring him to laugh at her.

Holding in a flaring urge to pull her close, he curled his fingers into his palms. Both were itching to touch her, give her comfort. 'Some people don't want the limelight, Rachel. There's nothing wrong with that.'

After a momentary glance of puzzlement, she drew a breath, bit her lip. 'When I finally stopped throwing up, I just shook so much my words mangled. So Pete said he'd take the lead, if I'd play the supporting role. I'd be back stage and give him the answers.'

'I'm guessing that worked best for you,' he said, mentally chanting, *don't touch her or she'll run.* 'So how did you end up on the show?'

'Did you like the limelight? Why did you walk away?' she shot at him without warning, her eyes flashing.

He almost said, *this isn't about me*, but he held his tongue. If Rachel was asking, it wasn't from curiosity, but because she needed to know. 'No, I never liked it. It was a necessity at the time,' he said quietly. *Please don't ask any more.*

Those big, expressive eyes searched his for a moment, seeing too much. How she did it he didn't know, but he felt as if she looked into his eyes and down to his very soul. Eventually she nodded and moved away to sit at the couch. 'So what's the choice of movie for our chill-out night?' She grabbed a handful of the popcorn and shoved it all in her mouth at once.

It was a silent message given louder than anything Charlie Chaplin could have sent to his audience. 'I got us a range of classics. Take your pick, while I get the hot chocolate ready.'

Without looking at him she took up the three DVDs to read the blurbs at the back.

She was really good at dismissing him without a word— but, though he was willing to give her space, she'd opened the gate now. There was no shutting it again, no matter how she tried. Given what she'd said, he strongly doubted that her parents would have supported her leaving Dr Pete, even if he had been the one to break her wrist. Her sister didn't want to know her. It seemed she was an orphan adrift in the world. Someone had to let her know it was all right to be herself, that she could be liked and respected for the person she was.

And that closed the door on stupid thoughts, such as kissing her pain away.

The music of the opening credits was already running when he returned to the living room with two steaming cups. 'So, what movie did you pick?'

'*Notting Hill,*' she answered, her voice vague, humming along to the haunting sounds of She. 'It sounds lovely.'

'It— I believe it is,' he said, correcting himself just in time.

'It came highly recommended.' He sat beside her, closer to her than he'd been since the snowboarding lesson three days ago. Thigh just touched thigh as he stretched his legs over his ottoman. He didn't even know quite why he did it. It wasn't sexual provocation—even if she wanted that, he knew now he could never treat her as a casual playmate.

The truth was that he just wanted contact of some kind with her. Touching her gave him a sense of gladness in living he'd never known until now. Having a woman he desired so close but so elusive was as frustrating as it was refreshing. He couldn't seem to get enough of even the lightest contact with Rachel. The brush of his fingers against her skin when he moved a snowflake from her cheek moved him. The soft swish of her breath when she laughed intoxicated him. Inhaling her scent when she dashed by him after her morning shower was like a mint candy-cane, the ones he'd loved so much when he'd been a kid. And just holding her hand as they improved her snowboarding skills did something to him on a deeper level than he wanted to admit.

Rachel had inspired some crazy kind of yearning for the kind of relationship he'd never had before. He was yearning, waiting, but waiting less for the sexual act itself than for her to reveal her inner self to him. It felt unbearably sensual—at least for him. A situation that would no doubt end as soon as he'd…

*But you're not going to have her. That's it, keep telling yourself that.*

It was hard to remind himself every night when he awoke in a sweat, her face burning like a brand in his mind. Even her silly cat-pyjamas had begun to haunt him with longing.

He moved in just a millimetre, touching her more fully, and the bubbles of joy fizzled right through him. She was so close now, he could smell that wonderful candy-store peppermint scent in her hair…

She smiled up at him, but in her eyes was the slightest hint of the hunted deer, the confusion of a woman being given mixed signals. The look of a woman who doesn't want to know which signal was real: the back-off words or the touch-me body language.

He could have kicked himself again. What was he doing to her?

Forcing a smile from somewhere inside him that really didn't want to smile, he put a friendly arm around her. 'This is what friends do on chill-out nights,' he said without a quiver. With a hint of neither the laughter nor the consternation he felt in equal measure. And he hoped like hell she didn't look anywhere near his lap.

A light frown marred her brow. 'Okay,' she said, sounding only half-convinced. Then she turned her face forward to the TV screen. 'Oh, look, the movie's starting. I really like Hugh Grant.'

The words were a nervous babble. Now his smile was genuine; he couldn't help it, she just affected him that way. She made him feel as if he was one big smile, even when he ached to…

*You're asking to wake up again tonight*, he thought, resigned to his immediate fate. And he spent the next hundred minutes watching Rachel more than the movie.

'No. I am not going on that thing. There is no way you're getting me on that thing!'

Swathed in his ski-gear minus the goggles as the temperature was mild today, with no wind, Armand sat on the big, wide red sled. Holding the control with one hand, he extended the other to her. His legs were splayed in an invitation to sit there that she couldn't possibly miss. 'Come on, Rachel, try it. It really is fun, and I promise you won't fall. And, if you did, it's not like there's far to go,' he laughed.

She backed off another few inches, her trepidation far greater than when he taught her how to snowboard; he had absolutely no idea why. 'No.'

His face stilled. 'You said you were trying to trust me.'

The sudden coolness in his voice made Rachel's stomach clench a bit. 'I don't want to do this. Can't you just accept it, and not push me all the time? I feel as if I'm your dolly, or your science experiment. *Let's teach Rachel something new and watch her grow,*' she snapped, not sure why she was so angry, but she was.

She turned and stomped through the snow to a crevice at the end of the tree belt on 'their' slope, isolated from the resort, totally private—as if they were in their own world.

And maybe that was the problem. It was such a beautiful lie, she almost believed it.

'Do you want to talk about what happened just now?' The gentle voice came from behind her, about an inch too close, warming her shivering skin and smelling way too good. Woodsy, strong and dependable—another beautiful, believable lie.

She moved a touch closer to the crevice. 'Do you?' she retorted, but in the same tone as his. 'Do you want to tell me why you're doing all this, being so sweet with me, trying to heal me through fun and games? I get that you *know* about me, but you're so patronising, like I'm a little kid or your sister.'

She felt rather than saw him jerk back in reaction. Without looking at him, she murmured, 'Tell me about her.' Her hand reached out to his hair, fell an inch short. Wanting it so much couldn't be healthy for her.

After a long pause, he said, 'It's not just my story to tell.'

'Okay, then I'll tell it.' She drew in a cold, pine-scented breath—a counterpoint, a denial of the ugliness she had to speak now. 'What's her name, your little sister?'

'I have two sisters. Johanna and Carla.' It came out like a gunshot. Angry and accusative: *Don't ask. Don't say it.*

But she knew better. The people who want pushing the least need it the most. 'So who beat her, Armand?' She turned to face him as she asked the question that might just push him over the edge. 'Who hurt her, that you either didn't know or didn't do anything about it? Was it her husband, her boy-friend?'

The fury was white-hot in those stormy eyes. He didn't answer, but held himself rigid, ice-like in the sub-zero day. So frozen she thought he might shatter at a touch.

'Okay, you didn't know,' she said softly, as if an admission. 'She hid it from you, didn't she? You never saw her when she had the bruises. And when she had a cast on her arm or leg she always had such a reasonable explanation for it. She might even have laughed at herself. "I'm so clumsy, Armand, you know that".'

Waiting for an answer obviously wasn't going to bring it forth, so she kept telling the story. 'And then one day there was one accident too many, was there? Or she just stopped coming to visit and didn't answer your calls. You only heard from her when she called you, when she felt strong enough. When she could control the conversation. She knew you sus-pected, but you couldn't prove anything.'

Nothing. Not a word or a movement. He stood like a statue, not looking at her but out into the mountains behind them. Frozen, as if it would stop her words going into his ears.

'But then one day something happened. He went too far. He hurt her in a way she refused to accept—or she needed hospitalisation and the police became involved.'

Only the smoking heat in his eyes indicated he was alive. So pale and so cold, a beautiful statue, refusing to acknowl-edge anything she said.

'Is he in prison now?' she asked gently, but without remorse or pity. He had to say it. So often the victim got help but the family was left to suffer the endless guilt of not being perfect, not being able to protect the person they loved.

At last, perhaps because she just waited, watching him, he growled one word. 'Dead.'

'Good,' she said quietly. And, because it seemed right, she stripped off her glove, pulled his off too and cradled his hand in hers. It felt so right she didn't question the fact that she didn't let go after her customary thirty seconds. 'The questions don't help, you know. The what-ifs and should-have-beens never help anyone. But all you achieve by shoving them away in the back of your mind is driving yourself slowly mad with the guilt.'

He turned his face and she knew she'd hit home. 'Do you think I don't know that?'

With a silent breath of relief that he'd spoken at last, she answered what he hadn't asked. 'No, you'll never lose the questions—but you have to deal with them, Armand, or Johanna or Carla will never stop avoiding you.'

He pulled his hand out of hers. 'You don't know what you're talking about.'

She looked at him unblinking. Slowly she lifted her imperfectly healed wrist and rubbed it: truth revealed without a word. The silent sisterhood locked in identical chains of shame.

'It was my father.' He sounded driven, half-desperate, and she knew that if anything the half-lie between them was over. From now on he wouldn't treat her as he would a sister.

A surge of hot joy washed through her. The sweet deception that he didn't know anything about her abuse, and she didn't know about his secret, had grown harder and harder to maintain. 'You ask yourself the questions, Armand—or ask me. We can talk about it, what happened to your family,' she stressed, because despite what he thought she could take care of herself. 'Tell me, Armand. Ask me all the questions you can't ask them. You have to go through it to let go of it, Armand, because they see all your pain, the regret, and it stifles them, makes them feel weak—just as this overdose of fun does with me.'

'I just wanted to help.' The words were as cold as the ice around them.

'And you did.' The craving grew unbearable and she laid a hand on his hair. 'Don't ever doubt how much you've helped me just by being here, by letting me have my secrets. But I am not your sister.'

'I know that,' he snarled. 'I've never once seen you as my sister. As if that wasn't completely obvious to you, the way you back away from me whenever I get close.'

The anger inside those words startled her, because they seemed to come from a deeper place than wounded male ego. 'This isn't about my problem, Armand. This is about you.'

'I know that but, damn it, if she won't talk to me and won't come to me…'

'You go to her, Armand.' Oh, the stupid craving grabbed hold and wouldn't release her until she smoothed his hair, a flash of longing that only grew as she touched him. So intimate and yet it was never enough… 'You go to her after you've come to peace with the fact that you didn't stop your father. Then you accept her as she is—a survivor, even if she's damaged. Stop pretending it never happened. If you can accept her for the strong woman she is, then she can begin to feel normal at last.'

'Are you're saying I've made her feel like she isn't normal?' he demanded, leaning right over her in an open fury she'd never seen from him.

But she wasn't afraid of him. Armand would never hurt a woman physically; that she was certain about. 'If you never ask her, never talk about it, she senses that you're keeping her a victim in your mind. You unconsciously show her how much you want her to be something else by pretending the past never existed,' she said gently. 'She's been through a life-changing experience and survived it, no matter how much you or she want to forget. She isn't a victim now, Armand. She isn't a child either. She's survived suffering you can't imagine.'

He remained frozen, but the anguish in his eyes spoke for him and she began to dread that, yes, Armand could imagine it all too well, because he'd been there.

'Did you ever speak with her about it? Did you tell her how proud you are of her?'

He shook his head. 'We all just want to forget.'

'I want the moon, but that doesn't mean I'll ever have it.' When he frowned at her, so remote he might be on another planet, she tried to smile. 'We don't always want what's good for us, Armand. Talking about it doesn't just bring the monster out of the cupboard for you both—it will take your relationship to a deeper, adult level. Those horrible silences filled with fun events and determined blindness won't be needed any more.'

'I don't want to hear about her being degraded, hurt by that—' Without warning he turned and punched the tree behind him. It caused snow to fall all over them both in a tumble of freezing white, but somehow it wasn't funny. 'I don't want to know everything he did to her and I couldn't stop!'

'But you need to,' she said quietly. 'You need to take her out of that box you keep her in and allow her to be the woman she is. Until you do, you'll keep lying to each other.'

His fists clenched; slowly he turned back to her, but his eyes were closed. 'You don't know what you're saying.'

She took a breath, two, to calm herself. Then she said, 'If I don't know, who does? My parents don't want to hear. My sister refuses to believe it. Pete denies the whole abuse ever happened, and they prefer to believe I'm lying than that they could have let me down.'

The look he gave her was almost despairing, but he didn't speak.

She felt tears rush to her eyes and run down her face, cooling and making cold, salt tracks, but he'd turned away again. Instead of feeling safe, anger sizzled through her. 'I haven't pressed charges against Pete, not yet, so they *can* deny it. You have no such excuse. So let her tell you what she wants to, when she wants to, no matter how much it hurts you. *Ask her.* And you'll both heal.'

'Hell, no,' he muttered beneath his breath.

Normally at this point she'd pull back, let the person think about it before pressing her point. It was the right, the professional thing to do. She'd never later know why she lost it over the denial that was natural, human. 'Oh, for heaven's sake, Armand, *man up!*' she snarled, and then gasped at the audacity of those two insulting words. 'Otherwise you'll spend the rest of your life wishing you'd done something. Nothing is more useless than empty regret!'

Shaking off the snow, she marched past him, heading for the cabin. If he needed time to think, she'd give it to him in spades.

'Inflammatory words, Rachel.'

Before she was two steps past him he seized her, pulled her back. He moved in on her, his gaze on her mouth. His eyes were glittering, hard and dark like winter dusk. Still holding her so that she was bent backwards over his arm, his other hand pulled the hood from her head, making her hair fall around her face.

'No matter how gently I've behaved with you the past couple of weeks, you need to know I *am* a man, Rachel—and I have a man's needs.'

She gulped, staring up at him, but not in fear. Her tongue moved over her lips. 'Like what?' she whispered.

His eyes did that storm and lightning thing that made her insides flip and her femininity come to shimmering life. 'I want to know how it feels to kiss you. I've held back for your sake, but I advise you never to forget that I am a man—unless you want this kind of reaction,' he muttered against her mouth.

He really wanted to kiss her. Armand Bollinger, *noir* actor and one of the world's most beautiful people... Armand her friend—her kind, wonderful friend—actually wanted to kiss her, still wanted to kiss her despite the fact that she'd just pushed and pulled his world into pieces.

The thrill that ran through her was so strong, her knees almost gave way.

# CHAPTER EIGHT

'I'M STILL married, Armand.'

She was only half an inch from his mouth yet the words barely reached him, her whisper was so soft, so shaken. Her eyes were alight with heady, feminine yearning—but also with conflicted emotions. Her mouth said one thing, but her lips were speaking another language entirely. She wanted him, wanted this as much as he did.

But she'd still spoken, still said no. Although, she hadn't—she'd said *not yet*.

The thunder of his heart took a full minute to slow to something approaching normal, but his breathing was harder to rein in. His arms seized up, rebelling against his pride's need to release her immediately. 'Then don't challenge my masculinity again, Rachel Chase.'

It hurt to let go, but he did it, seconds later than he wanted to. His screaming body's need was having a hard time obeying a will fed only by his pride.

His eyes held hers, waiting for her answer. Would she be honest, or retreat into hiding again?

Her gaze dropped. 'Is that all it was to you, Armand? A challenge to your manhood—or a distraction from our conversation?' She sighed. 'I guess that makes sense, really.'

Astonished right out of his anger, he stared at her. 'You really don't know the answer to those questions?'

Her head drooped. Her eyes on her feet, she shook her head.

His hands curled into fists to stop himself from snatching her close. 'Talk to me, Rachel. Make me understand why you don't believe I could desire you.'

Her cheeks were almost scarlet, so hot they could melt snow. 'I'm not like them—the women you've been with.' Her hands lifted and fell in a hopeless gesture. 'Look at me.'

'I am looking at you. I like looking at you,' he growled, the fury flashing through him.

'Yeah, good old funny-face, like one of those big-eyed puppies in a toy store.' She shuffled her feet in a gesture he was beginning to know well.

He snatched her close again, his eyes blazing into hers. 'That's ridiculous. Damn it, Rachel, you can't be that stupid. Half the world loves you. Surely thousands of men have desired you before now?'

She gave another plaintive little sigh, wistful, wishing. 'My fan mail was all from needy people wanting advice, Armand. Pete got the love letters, the—the propositions.'

And it seemed Pete had taken a few women up on their offers, if he was reading her correctly. Damn it. No wonder she had so little faith in herself.

'You must have had boyfriends growing up?'

She shook her head, her cheeks scarlet. 'There was nobody before Pete. He was my first everything, my *only* everything.'

First kiss, first lover—first love. The quick hot blow of jealousy was unworthy of him, when he'd had too many casual lovers to want to count. 'What has that to do with whether or not I can desire you? I still don't understand.'

Bewildered eyes met his for a brief moment. 'Nobody else ever wanted me.' With a sad little shrug she turned away, her creamy skin flushed crimson, not with cold burn.

Armand restrained the curse, but he'd never wanted to yell

an obscenity more. In his entire life, he'd never had to come out of his place of emotional safety for the sake of a woman. He was always ten steps ahead of any woman he desired, ten steps nearer the door of goodbye. But sweet, damaged Rachel truly didn't understand. She truly thought herself undesirable—and if he didn't tell her now, if he headed for that door, he'd leave her for ever in that room, screaming *no man will ever want you.*

'I want you, Rachel,' he said quietly, struggling for every word. 'From the day we met, I've wanted to hold you, kiss you—and every night I fight the need to go to your room and make love to you.'

'Just proximity,' she murmured so softly he only just caught it.

The heat flaring through him loosened his stubborn tongue. 'No. Not proximity at all. It's you, only you. I've never said this to any woman before.' Unable to control it any longer, he snatched her close. The happiness that had spent a lifetime eluding him while he had tried and failed to protect his family returned in a moment's tantalising promise. It was there in the way she curved against him, in the wish so clear to read in those guileless eyes of hers. 'I've wanted you from the first, Rachel. Not because of your fame or your skills or the prospect of selling a story. You do things to me *no* woman ever has before.'

But she shook her head again. 'I can't believe this.'

Not 'don't'. *Can't.*

'It's impossible. It's a fairy tale. You might be a prince charming, but I'm no princess.'

Resisting every impulse that bid him to turn and walk now before he was in too deep, he repeated, 'Impossible, Rachel? It's impossible that I could find you beautiful, desirable? Who the hell did this to you?' Damn it, now he really *would* kill Rinaldi if he got within ten feet of the dirty jerk.

'I know what I am,' she said in a final tone, not asking for reassurance. 'Please, let me go, Armand.' She pushed at his chest.

He let her go. The pulsing beat of expectation faded to something hard and icy, leaving him feeling almost sick. 'Go on, run away,' he mocked as she stumbled past him. 'Is this my cue to say *man up*?'

She didn't even turn back. 'Probably,' she admitted sadly. 'And you'd be right.'

Frustration soared. Why did she have to be so honest all the time? 'How the hell am I supposed to answer that?'

A one-shouldered shrug showed her churning emotions. 'It wasn't a question. I'm not divorced yet. He might have cheated on me, but I won't sink to that. I won't betray myself.'

The words froze him, packed him in the kind of shame he'd never known before. He'd never touched a married woman in his life, and he could hardly believe his actions now. No matter that she was divorcing him, or that he'd abused her. Until Rachel felt free, she wouldn't be.

'Then you shouldn't have asked me, or provoked me,' he shot back, low and furious.

'I know.' She didn't apologise, didn't attempt to justify her actions, and that only made him feel lower.

This time when she kept walking, he didn't try to stop her.

*Three days later*

'My contract with the resort finally came through. I have to assess my new land and look at it again with my architectural designs. I'm flying in myself, over the Alps. I want you to come to the site with me and check out the progress.'

The words were stilted. He didn't want her to come. He was sticking to their bargain.

Pride warred with curiosity. She'd love to fly over the Alps.

She didn't want him to think she was some kind of pushover, but flying over the Alps… The lure was irresistible. And if he truly didn't want her to come why had he given her the one piece of information guaranteed to make her fall like a ripe plum into his hand?

That decided her. If he could be brave, so could she. 'I'd love to,' she replied with the cheerfulness she'd adopted since he'd grown so stiff and cold with her.

'Be ready in twenty minutes. Bring an overnight bag,' he said curtly, barely acknowledging her acceptance. 'Do you know where the hangar is?'

She nodded. 'Do I bring my ski suit or wear it?'

'Bring it—just wear your normal clothes. It will be warm enough in the plane. The forecast over there is for cool but clear weather.' With that, he stalked out of the cabin, the tension in him ready to snap.

*I want you. It's you, only you.*

The words still made her shiver three days after they'd last talked, three days since he'd voluntarily spent time with her apart from meals. The power remained because, no matter how cold and even harsh he'd become with her, he still wanted her. He wouldn't be cold and harsh if he'd overcome the pain of her necessary rejection, if he no longer desired her.

But he did. Every flickered look he gave her screamed the truth in neon letters. Even in her jeans, funny shirts, no make-up and house slippers he still wanted her. And that negated the loneliness of missing him. Almost.

Twenty minutes later they were strapped, bags stored in the cargo and Armand in the pilot's seat. 'Yes, I have my pilot's licence,' he said before she could ask. His face was still tense; for once he didn't look at her shirt with its funny logo, didn't ask. 'I'd like to visit my mother while we're there, if it suits you.'

'Of course,' she replied, hearing the wobble in her voice. He was visiting his mother only three days after their shattering scene, reliving his pain. 'I don't mind at all. But if you'd like private time with her you can leave me in the village or wherever, and I'll wander.'

There, she'd given him an out if he wanted it.

'If that's what I wanted, I'd have said so,' he replied, his whole bearing screaming 'back off, don't talk to me, don't ask'. 'I promised to care for you, never leave you alone. My mother won't mind if I bring a friend.'

For a moment she almost said the words hovering on her tongue: *am I your friend?* Right now she wasn't sure she wanted to hear the answer.

Then she frowned. 'Who's that watching us over there?'

Armand glanced in the direction of her finger. 'I don't know, but probably another guest. But don't worry; stop pointing and put these on.' He handed her a massive pair of dark lenses. 'With your shorter, lighter hair and these, let's hope whoever it is doesn't recognise you. At this distance even the best cameras would only give a grainy likeness anyway.'

'I thought I saw a flash before,' she murmured, looking at the weird sunglasses he'd given her. 'Whose are these?' Torn between amusement and indignation, she glared at him through the gold-rimmed sunglasses. 'Were these things made in the 70's?'

'Probably they were. They were my uncle's.' He shot her an inscrutable look for a few moments, then slowly a grin was born. 'You look like Fearless Fly—remember that cartoon?'

Realising he was trying to distract her, she retorted, 'I'm obviously too young to know.' When he chuckled, she poked her tongue out at him. 'You can be the Fearless Flier instead. Will you please take off?'

For answer, he checked in his flight path on the two-way, and moved the plane forward. The bright flashing light faded out as Armand lifted the small plane in the air. Was it just sunlight on somebody's glasses, or the sunlight bouncing off a camera lens or metallic edging?

She squeaked as the plane dipped and lifted. 'This is like a roller coaster. I've only flown in jumbos until now. Are the flip-flops always so bad in small planes?'

'The reactions are more intense in a small plane, because you feel every movement and bounce through every pocket of air.' As he got the plane level, he turned to her and frowned. 'Are you okay? You're looking a little green.'

Eggs and coffee were bad. Coffee and eggs were the enemy she didn't know she'd had until now. Her gaze clung to Armand's as if seeking salvation, but her breathing shook with every bounce of the little craft. Too many air pockets; eggs and coffee were burning in her stomach, rising to taunt her...

'Here.' With a terse word, an open bag was pushed into her hands and, grateful beyond words, she lurched forward.

A few minutes later, she finally emerged from the second air-sickness bag, trembling and with involuntary tears streaming down her cheeks. 'Just as well we're just friends. If I was one of your normal women wearing all that make-up, I'd look like a clown by now,' she joked, croaking.

He turned his face to hers, his expression gentle for the first time in three long, lonely days. He used a wet tissue to wipe her face, to clear the wetness on her cheeks. 'You're not like them in any way.'

He didn't say if it was a good thing or a bad thing, but she didn't want to ask. Her loud, undignified display had spoken for itself: she was nothing like them.

*I don't want to measure up to them. I knew all along that thinking of anything between us but friendship was a bad idea. I don't want anything else!*

And on that uplifting thought she sat huddled away from

him in miserable silence—unless turbulence would force her to croak, 'Bag,' again.

Eventually exhaustion claimed her. She drifted in and out of sleep, woken up only when she had to embarrass herself again. Apart from flying the plane and handing her ginger-mint tablets to help settle her stomach between bouts, Armand remained still and silent. No doubt he was counting his blessings that she'd rejected him every time he heard her retching again. *Please, God, let this torture soon be over!*

'Rachel.'

She jerked awake at the sound of his voice. 'Sorry,' she murmured through the fog clouding her mind.

'Don't be. I'm glad you slept,' he said quietly. 'I thought this might cheer you up.' He pointed just ahead of them, then down and all around. 'We're flying over the French Alps.'

She gazed over the window and a gasp escaped her lips. She'd been totally inspired, seeing the Swiss Alps coming in on the TGV train from Paris. But seeing the French Alps from above like this struck her with awe, with their unending, snow-capped magnificence. 'Oh…it's like a new world,' she breathed, just holding back from pressing her nose to the window as Armand turned the plane south. 'It's the most beautiful thing I've ever seen.'

'That's what I've always thought.' He smiled at her, the tense silence between them seeming to vanish along with her stomach contents. 'We just crossed the border. The airport is in France—we're about to land. We'll cross back into Switzerland to reach the land and my mother's house.' He handed her another bag. 'This will be the last time you'll need it, I hope. We'll be taking my Range Rover from here.'

'France,' she breathed again, feeling like the rawest *ingénue* and not caring. The romance, the magic of it grabbed hold of her sore and embarrassed heart, filling it with happiness. 'I'm in *France*.'

'I gather that thought makes all of your suffering worth-while?'

She nodded, her eyes shining. At this moment, it was worth everything. This was her first sight of France in daylight. She'd arrived in Paris the first time by night and, under the threat of someone recognising her at the time, had just bolted for her seat on the fast train to Zurich. But this was pure, up-lifting loveliness, one perfect, snow-capped peak after an-other filling her senses to overflowing.

'We're heading for the landing strip at the base of Chamonix. Hold on tight, we need to lose altitude quite quickly to land.'

He didn't have to tell her that. Her stomach had announced the descent with a brass band at the first drop in height. With a wretched groan, she forgot she was in magical France and the magnificent Alps, shoved her face in yet another clean air-sickness bag and kept it there until the plane was com-pletely still in a darkened hangar.

'We're here. Though it's only autumn, we're five-thousand feet above sea level, so it's quite cold outside even if it isn't snowing. You'll need your jacket and gloves.' His prosaic comment, without the patronising gentleness that had irked her before, soothed her frayed nerves. 'Take your time. I'll bring the car to you.'

She didn't move or answer even with a nod. The landing had been the worst, filled with sudden dips, and all she could think about was the reasons she'd never returned to any of the theme parks in LA after her first time.

Roller coasters and light planes were the pits.

Her mind remained venomously on that thought until the lovely, wonderful Range Rover with its smooth suspension and travel on blessed ground pulled up beside the plane. Only then did she move. Wary of every step, she hung on to anything she could as she headed towards the midsection where the stairs were.

Armand met her halfway up the stairs. 'You aren't wearing— Ah, I see. Let me,' he said, still crisp and practical, and put her trembling arms into the snug warmth. He zipped it up and put the hood over her head, encasing her in sweet heat. 'Come, I'll help you to the car.'

Just as well for, though her pride rebelled, her body had given up the ghost; she was so weak she could barely move alone. She leaned on him down one stair, two, then he swung her up into his arms and carried her to the open passenger seat. 'I've ordered a thermos of peppermint tea for you for the trip. You'll feel better soon.'

She couldn't even thank him, but her hand caught his and clung for a moment.

'You're welcome,' he said softly, with a smile that told her everything he'd done was no big deal and he wasn't at all disgusted by her weakness. Rachel sagged against the leather upholstery in relief. Having a man care for her needs without ridiculing her for it was such an amazing experience, she hardly dared believe Armand was real.

The psychologist in her had always understood why Pete had felt the need to put her down—he'd felt threatened by her intelligence and her superior knowledge of psychology, and then by her ratings. But the woman and wife had never quite managed to come to terms with it. She'd just felt unwanted, unloved, not pretty enough, too clever—always too much and not enough.

And that was why the man currently putting himself out to get her peppermint tea was so dangerous to her emotional well-being. A millionaire in shining armour. Maybe he was just superb at making all women feel special, beautiful and adored—she'd bet he was, given how women constantly fell at his feet. But that was her problem, not his. After so many years with someone who made her feel unworthy, every moment with Armand gave her a feeling of teetering at the edge of a precipice. She kept waiting to fall, only to smash to the ground when he moved on.

She started when he bent over her, pressing a thermos and cup into her hands. 'Pour only small amounts at a time and sip slowly. The honey will help you, but it could be too much if you gulp.' He poured a small measure of tea into the plastic cup. 'I think we should get your stomach settled a little before I drive.'

She stared at him in wonder over the rim of the cup as she sipped. 'Your mother's waiting for us.'

'Don't worry about that. She'll understand.' Then he smiled and pulled out his phone. 'Okay, I can see you're worried. I'll call her now, if that will reassure you.' He punched numbers into the phone and spoke in rapid French to his mother, in a dialect she couldn't quite grasp. Rachel sipped more tea and felt like the world's biggest nuisance. Why wasn't he ready to ditch her somewhere and get on with his high-flying, jet-setting life? Surely it was obvious by now she wasn't the kind to fly anywhere with him—literally.

'My mother wants to speak to you.' He handed her the phone.

In still greater wonder, Rachel prepared herself to talk to a woman any talk-show host would sell their grandmother to contact: the luminous, every-award-in-the-world winning, reclusive actress Claire Tessin-Bollinger. 'Hello, Mrs Bollinger?'

'Hello, Rachel, please call me Claire. Armand told me how you suffered on your first trip in a light plane. I well remember my first time. I think I went through seven air-sickness bags.' The warm, thrillingly accented voice that had haunted generations of movie-goers walked through a little crack in

Rachel's heart, and she loved the older woman instantly without having met her.

'Yes, I was pretty sick,' she managed to croak in reply, unable to believe the exquisitely beautiful Claire Tessin had ever been airsick. She was probably just reassuring her but, oh, she felt so much better, just hearing it. 'I'm so sorry to keep you waiting.'

'Please don't worry about it in the least. Time is in no way imperative for me. Go and see the land with Armand, and come here when you're done. A little time in the fresh air ought to revive you. And I look forward to meeting you, no matter what time you come.'

Rachel's heart totally melted at the comfort. 'Thank you,' she whispered, struggling against tears of overwrought relief. 'I'll see you soon.'

She handed the phone back to Armand. 'She's so lovely.'

'Feel better now?' he asked simply, as if that was his primary concern. She bit her lip and gulped. Too handsome, too kind, too perfect... Why did he care if she felt better?

'Yes,' she whispered, wishing he'd go away and leave her, wishing she'd never wake up from this lovely dream. This couldn't be her life. A man like Armand Bollinger could never have said, *I want you, only you.*

'Good.' He leaned over her, checking her seatbelt. His gaze met hers, so tense and dark it sent a hot thrill through her, negating the illness. 'We should go.'

No words came to her choked throat. She nodded.

After he clipped himself in the car, he said, 'Oh, I forgot, I have a present for you.' He tossed her another sickness bag, this one emblazoned with a sticker saying, 'Rachel'.

And just like that the shadows of tension and aching desire vanished. 'You can't tell me the shop had sick bags with stickers on them?'

He grinned at her and started the car. 'No, I had the bag

already. They sold the name stickers, though. It was my own invention.' His smile was full of too-innocent pride.

'Oh, you rat. You must've driven your sisters crazy,' she laughed, putting her Styrofoam cup in a holder. 'Where's the wolfish beast I met nearly three weeks ago?'

His grin grew, reminding her of the Cheshire Cat. 'Does it matter? What's important is that you're no longer wondering whether your breath smells of vomit or peppermint.' He winked at her when her mouth fell open in half-amused indignation. 'And I'll never tell.'

Rachel rolled her eyes. 'Oh, you were a holy terror as a boy, for sure. I'll bet your sisters hated you.' And as another shadow touched his face she added hastily, 'Let's go. I don't want to keep your mother waiting any longer than we need to.'

The road was steep and winding, but Armand drove with careful precision. It was obvious he knew the road well, and he warned her whenever they approached a bend. Rachel didn't talk the entire trip. Though the view was almost heartbreakingly beautiful, her stomach still burned and ached and the weakness was slow to leave.

But when they stood in the fresh, clear mountain air surrounding his proposed resort she soon forgot about feeling sick.

The land Armand had bought for his resort was on the far edge of a village. But, though the temperatures hovered just above freezing, the land was much further down on its mountain and there was no snow as yet. Winter hadn't arrived here, early or otherwise. It was sloping, mountainside land, unfit for farming, but covered with the heather-like flowers called Edelweiss, and other little flowers, red and blue. Deep square holes littered the slope, surrounding a natural rock pool, curling steam rising gently from its surface.

Armand turned to her, his expression too reserved to be real. 'What do you think?'

Understanding what her endorsement meant to him, she stuttered, 'It's—it's exquisite. But…the flowers…'

'They're indigenous plants, Rachel, and very hardy. What we dig up, we're going to replant—but because this resort will have hillside chalets on poles, it means there will be very little environmental impact. Given that this will be a wellness spa-resort rather than a ski resort, it has to be environmentally friendly to sustain the water source.' From the back seat of the Range Rover he pulled out rolled-up blueprints. 'This is what I have planned.'

Standing beside him, the unrolled blueprints in his long-fingered hands, she felt the intimacy of the situation. But that was ridiculous! This was part of his business contract, no more. *And no doubt I still smell of vomit!* She shook herself mentally, pushed wayward, wind-blown strands of hair from her face and forced herself to look.

'Oh, it's lovely,' she murmured, conscious not to breathe too hard.

True to his promise of exclusivity, there were only three-dozen chalets, all on poles for minimal environmental impact. They surrounded the spa, which would be rock-lined instead of tiled like a traditional pool. Above and around the pool would be the wellness centre, built again for minimal damage.

'As I hope you can see, there is no gym, no conference centre, not one building that will take away from the natural beauty of the place. That's why I fell in love with the land here.' He smiled. 'This is my mother's childhood village.'

Her brow crinkled. 'But doesn't your sort of clientele demand luxurious facilities?'

'Yes, they do. That's why there will be plenty of luxury transportation to the fully equipped facilities right on the furthest edge of the resort. It will be just over half a mile away so they can jog right down our own private road.' He pointed at the building near the proposed gate. 'This will be our wellness-fitness resort, so those who come here will presumably not be the kind to want a shuttle on hand to ride everywhere, but I will of course provide for such a request in case.' He glanced at her, then away. 'So, what do you think of it?'

Without hesitation and in total honesty she replied, 'I think you'll make everyone happy with this resort, Armand. It's a wonderful proposal—and, yes, it's definitely one I'd be happy to endorse. You've made it easy to love.' She grinned up at him. 'Can I be one of your first guests? Is there a waiting list yet?'

'Not yet, but I promise you, your name will be the first on it.' His smile was one she hadn't seen from him in days. No strain, no forced stretching of his lips, but genuineness, relief. No tension, no memory of her rejection. 'Thank you, Rachel.'

As they walked back to the car, he said, 'Maman has invited us to stay the night. I accepted on your behalf. I thought it best that you don't fly again until tomorrow.'

His voice was a shade too casual. The mask was back in place. He didn't know if she'd trust him, or would dig for deeper reasons why he'd answered for her. 'Thank you,' was all she could find to say that wouldn't take them back to a place where neither of them wanted to be. 'I think that would be best, as well, unless you have another dozen sickness-bags with my name on them.'

'No, not quite so many as that. I think I should stock up for tomorrow.' But his military-straight shoulders had relaxed a fraction, and he handed her back into the car with his customary courtesy.

Soon he pulled up in front of a picture-perfect, white house hundreds of years old that wasn't quite big enough to be a real château, but was warm and welcoming, with snow on the dark-red roof, window sills and hand-carved shutters with flower shapes at their heart. 'Oh, how lovely,' she breathed. 'I grew up in a nice house in the suburbs, all new, with straight picket-fences and laid-out gardens.'

'It is beautiful. This house has some pretty views of Chamonix, Mont Blanc and the valleys from the south windows. No, don't try to get out alone. You may not be steady yet.' He came round the Range Rover and helped her out of the car. He kept his arm around her as they headed up the thirty or so stairs to the front door. 'You're still shaking. I should have taken you to see the land after you'd had something warm to eat.'

'Food?' Rachel shuddered, trying to resist the urge to lean against him. When she left Switzerland, she needed to be strong, able to stand as she faced Pete, his barrage of lawyers and their agent. But for now Armand's care was a healing balm on years of raw wounds, and that much she would accept. 'I don't think so.'

'Don't worry. If I know Maman, she's made something your stomach can tolerate. She's suffered from air sickness all her life, especially in small aircraft.' When she faltered two-thirds of the way up, he lifted her into his arms and moved carefully up the final few stairs. He held her close after he put her down to press the bell. 'You're too shaky to stand for now. I'll go back for the bags once I've made certain you're comfortable.'

She looked down, but the mantra wouldn't come to her lips this time. She had to deal with this, cut her feelings off at the knees before she fell on them, literally. 'Please stop this.'

His finger was about to press the bell and he frowned at her. 'Stop what?'

He acted as if he really didn't know. Aiming for strength when she was already shaking, she said as steadily as she could, 'I've said I'll do the endorsement, okay? So stop doing all this—taking care of me. Making me feel as if I'm important to you. I know it's probably just what you do with women in general, but it—it isn't right.'

'What I do?' He released her. 'Would you care to explain that remark?'

He spoke quietly and she thought of his mother, who could be on the other side of the door. 'Isn't that why women fall at your feet, because of this? This ingrained courtesy you have? The wonderful manners? I'm sure your mother taught you, she seems a wonderful woman. You have younger sisters, one of whom...' She bit her lip. 'I remind you of her. I'm sure you want to—to redress the universal scales.'

His chuckle took her by surprise. 'Do I? Do I seem like some sort of new-age guru?'

Frustrated, she tried to square up to him—hard to do when she was shaking like a leaf and so very aware of his advantage of geography as well as height. 'Isn't it why one of your women called you the Wolf?' she demanded. 'You're strong, supportive, so very charming...but beneath all that you're a loner. There's always the door in front of you. It—it isn't right.'

'That isn't why I'm called that. Not at all.' The smile had faded during her mini-tirade; now there was nothing left of it, just those fathomless eyes in a face sculpted from cold stone. 'What isn't right, precisely?'

Rachel felt like a balloon with the air being slowly let out—deflating, making useless squeaking sounds. She looked at her feet and mumbled, 'You treat me like I'm a princess. I'm not used to it, Armand. I don't want to...become dependent. I'm leaving soon. I need to stand alone.'

A long silence ensued. 'You think I'm weakening you.' It was a flat statement, angry.

'I don't think you mean to.' She hesitated, looked up and

saw a perfect mirror for his tone in his eyes, and suddenly had no idea what she'd been going to say. 'It's just that you're so kind, so perfect…' Her words trailed away. She wanted to squirm.

Dragging in harsh, uneven breaths, he snarled, 'So I seem perfect to you? Well, perhaps you'd be more comfortable if I—' He shook his head and said no more but she knew: *if I treated you as Pete did…*

Jerking back without meaning to, she hit the doorbell with her elbow. With a tiny, mewing sound of pain, she felt his hand on her arm, helping her.

'Stop it!' she cried. 'I'm not a kitten stuck up a tree in your backyard, Armand. Don't try to rescue me unless I ask for it!'

'Oh, I beg your pardon,' a soft, musical voice said with a charming accent. Rachel started and pulled out of Armand's arms, feeling the blush burning her whole face and her heart free-falling to her feet. Could there be a more embarrassing way to meet a man's mother?

# CHAPTER NINE

RACHEL could barely look into the tall, white-haired, elegant beauty that was Claire Tessin. 'Oh, I'm so sorry, *Madame*. Um, I was just… We were…'

Claire broke into laughter, bright and golden. Slowly, Armand's deep laugh mingled with his mother's, mirth without malice, like distant bells tolling together. 'She knows what we were doing, Rachel.' He lifted his mother's hand in his and kissed it. 'Maman, it's good to see you,' he said in French. 'Obviously, this is Rachel. Rachel, this is my mother. Rachel's fluent in French, Maman.'

'Ah, but I don't practise my English enough,' Claire replied in English, smiling at a still-blushing Rachel. 'Please don't feel uncomfortable, Rachel. We all have our disagreements.' She ushered them inside the house and down a thin hallway lined with ancient doors to the living room at the back of the house. 'How are you feeling now?' The older woman looked at her face. 'I do not think you are always so pale. You did not eat yet?'

'I'm really not hungry, *madame*,' Rachel said with as much firmness as she could.

'Ah, but I have long experience with my enemy, *la maladie de l'air*. You will not feel better until you have eaten, I promise you. I've made a tomato and mint soup, with a hint of ginger. I always found it helpful after my ordeals in the air.'

'I knew I could count on you, Maman.' Armand hugged and kissed Claire. 'Rachel's had quite a bad time of it today.'

'I think she and I had much in common.' Claire turned back to Rachel, waving towards an old, pretty settee in faded pink and cream. A small mahogany table stood in front of it, laden with teapot, milk, sugar and cups. 'Pour the tea, Armand. Please make yourself at home here, Rachel. The tea will help you recover, so we can have a comfortable lunch on the settee where you can rest.'

Rachel sat, staring at the slim, upright figure as she left the room. 'She doesn't have servants to do this kind of thing?'

'Of course,' Armand replied simply. 'A housekeeper and gardener for the heavy housework that's beyond her now. But Maman prefers to cook and take care of herself whenever she can. She's always loved to cook, and her kitchen garden is her passion. The soup will be full of herbs she grew herself.'

After ten years in Tinsel Town, she could barely comprehend a woman of Claire's fame doing the cooking, gardening or any kind of cleaning. 'No wonder you're so…normal,' she finished, feeling idiotic saying it, but no other word came to mind. 'Your mother raised you to be just like other people, didn't she?'

'We *are* like other people,' he reminded her in a tone of steady gravity. 'I actually am a normal human being, as hard as that is to believe.'

'That's not what I meant.' But he passed her the tea he'd poured, unable to clarify what she had meant. She sipped at the cup; the tea was made with just a little milk and sugar, as she liked it.

He'd even noticed how she took tea.

'Maman did her first feature film when she was twenty,' he said when she continued drinking her tea, feeling the final residue of pain in her stomach and throat slowly subside. 'She saw the children of the other actors brought along with their nannies and tutors, children who either threw tantrums to get attention or were unnaturally well-behaved, and she decided that when she had children she would retire to raise them and give them as happy and normal an upbringing as possible. My father also did not want us to be brought up in the limelight.'

'I see,' she murmured, noting that Armand never once called his father anything but that—'my father'. Formal and cold.

'My father came from a very wealthy, upper-class family. They didn't want him to marry an actress. But instead of getting nannies and servants Maman left her career behind to raise us herself and to support my father's career. She'd spend days in the kitchen cooking when we had visitors. She only agreed to an au pair during the times when my father needed to take her on a business trip. So, while we are the children of wealthy parents, we've had what most people would consider a normal, if privileged, childhood.'

He had a strange look on his face—far away, as if he spoke of someone else's life. 'Was this your home?' she asked in a near-whisper, half-afraid to shatter the moment.

'Our holiday home, yes, for summers and ski week,' he answered, still wandering in the halls of happy memory. 'We lived most of the time in Geneva, though we lived two years in London, and we spent one memorable year in Manhattan where our accents and life made us exotic to the other kids. We were all pretty popular, but I think that was more because of Maman. There were a thousand cameras at the school every time Maman came for an event.'

'I'll bet there was. You've led such an international life,' she murmured with all the wistfulness in her heart. Again she noted that something missing—his father. 'It sounds so wonderful, so…sophisticated.'

'Yes and no,' he said, but jumped to his feet as his mother brought in a tray laden with soup and bread. 'Let me do that for you, Maman. Carrying all that weight can't be good for your arthritis.'

As Rachel quickly took the placemats from the tray Armand held and helped him set the table, she could see any explanation would have to wait for another time. Not that she'd believe the 'no' part. A childhood spent in Geneva, Chamonix, London and New York… What couldn't be wonderful about that? She felt like a backwoods provincial next to the Bollinger family.

'This soup is divine,' Rachel mumbled as she gulped her first mouthful. 'You're a gifted cook, *madame*—um, I mean, *Claire*,' she added in haste as Claire mock-frowned.

'Necessity is the mother of invention, isn't that what they say?' Claire rejoined, smiling. 'Not only did I need this soup after a flight anywhere, but I learned to cook in self-defence. On the set, there was a choice of ordering in, going to another restaurant with a high chance of being mobbed when you were exhausted after a long day's work, or I could eat in. So I bought cookbooks.'

'And discovered her true vocation,' Armand put in, deadpan, his eyes dancing. 'We never ate out anywhere as kids if she could help it.'

'I don't notice you turning the food down,' Rachel retorted. 'Or ordering in.'

He did that elegant shrug she always wished she could emulate. 'Would you, if your mother served you ambrosia?'

'My mama makes the best macaroni and cheese ever.'

His brows lifted in a mock-impressed expression. 'Would she consider living in Switzerland, catering to the American guests I hope to draw here?'

Rachel snorted. 'She's never been on a plane in her life, and every ship is potentially the *Titanic*. She's always been afraid of travel, except by train or car.' She tilted her head at him, with a challenging grin. 'But I know the recipe, I'm not a bad cook, and I need a new direction. Think there's a future for me with the Bollinger chain?'

'I'd have to do some serious taste-testing first,' he said with a straight face, but his gaze rested on her mouth for a moment and she felt heat scalding her cheeks.

Claire's eyes were gentle on them, one to the other. 'You're obviously recovering, Rachel.'

*Completely recovered, in fact,* she thought in wonder. 'It's this incredible soup—and all the tea I've been given in the past hour. Though I'd appreciate knowing where the bathroom is at this point,' she added, her blush intensifying, though why it did she had no idea. It felt ridiculous to think that a goddess like Claire Tessin would need a bathroom. She was one of the favoured few who probably did roll out of bed not only beautiful but elegant, perfect.

*I'll just bet Armand does, too*, she thought with an inner sigh.

'Rachel?'

She started and turned to see Claire on her feet. 'Come with me.' Feeling like an idiot, Rachel jumped to her feet and Claire led the way back down the hall and opened a door. 'Take your time.'

'Thank you. You've—you've been so kind to me,' Rachel faltered. It was strange to realise that when her sister, long-time friends and her husband had all let her down when she needed support, strangers from another continent had taken the role.

'You're welcome, *chérie*. You're good for my son,' Claire said softly. 'No wonder he brought you here to me.'

'No, no, that was to help me. It's just a business arrangement…' Rachel felt herself blushing again as she remembered how Claire had caught them arguing at the front door. 'I mean…' What did she mean? She'd gone blank as she'd discreetly hopped from one foot to the other, in pain but trying to be polite.

Claire smiled at her. 'What am I doing, keeping you here? We can discuss this later—but you should know, Armand has brought no other woman to meet me in the past fifteen years.'

'Um, okay, thank you.' Desperate now, she closed the door behind her.

It was only when she was washing her hands that the force of Claire's words struck her. Why had he brought her here? To gain time to think, she washed her face and rinsed her mouth but, try as she might, no reason came to mind…apart from the dreaded novelty-value.

Facing herself in the mirror, she knew it was that; it had to be the truth. No matter what euphemisms had been used to describe her puppy-dog eyes and way-too-big smile by the media during her brief brush with fame, sitting in a freckled face and plain brown hair, she looked exactly what she was: a dumb country girl with a growing crush on her smooth, sophisticated opposite.

Her mouth fell open when she realised what she'd just accepted, if only in her mind. She had a crush on Armand.

Oh, no. This had disaster written all over it. Calamity Jane meets Cary Grant; the prince enchants the Vegas ticket-booth girl; The sheikh hangs out with the checkout chick. A beautiful fantasy, but a happy end was never going to happen.

'Rachel, are you all right?' It was Armand, his voice filled with concern.

Pulling herself together with a final splash of very cold water on her face, she called, 'I'm fine.' She opened the door with a bright smile. 'I *really* had a lot of fluid, you know.'

He chuckled, apparently willing to forget their argument

for now. 'You lost a lot of fluid, too. I know, I had to dispose of it.'

Darn the man! It was when he was at his most ordinary that he took her breath away. 'I never promised you a rose garden,' she sang flippantly. 'I'm sure disposing of air-sickness bags was in the contract I signed.'

As she passed him, he took her hands in his and turned her to face him. His eyes were serious. 'Being with you is no hardship, Rachel. I haven't had this much fun in years—and that's the truth.'

Heart pounding and her blood racing like a go-kart downhill, she stammered, 'Sure—sure you have.' *Keep it cool, keep it together. He doesn't know what he's doing to me.*

'I told you not to challenge me, Rachel,' he said, soft with intent—and, before she could stop him, his mouth had brushed hers.

A moment's touch, but she'd suddenly lost the ability to speak. 'I...'

'I know,' he whispered against her mouth. 'It's all right. I wouldn't try anything in my mother's house. I brought you here because I knew she'd like you—and to show you how much I respect you. But I warned you before, don't challenge me, Rachel. It's asking for trouble.'

Her breath was stuck in her lungs and her knees were trembling. She nodded and forced herself to pull away. She kept her eyes closed for another moment. *Don't say it, not here in his mother's house. She actually thinks he cares about me.* 'No, definitely not kosher to do this in your mom's house, Bollinger,' she whispered, making herself smile up at him. *Like the kiss was no big deal for me. Like the sight of his face, my kiss still on his lips, doesn't make my knees weak and fill me with yearning for more.*

'Not gentlemanly of me at all, but I feel a little savage right now.' And he yanked her back to him. 'Believe in yourself, Rachel, or you'll force me to desperate measures.'

She felt more feeble by the moment, as her body cried out, *more, more.* Her battered heart grew little tentacles, wanting to hold him to her with unseen suction-cups. *Stay with me, please stay with me.*

That did it. She tore herself from his arms and shook all the way to the settee, which was blessedly empty. 'No more, Armand. It's been a hard few months. Please, give me space.'

The desire and need faded from his face and the thunder-cloud behind the sunshine that had taken her breath the first time they'd met returned in full force. 'Why don't you tell me what it is I'm doing that's so wrong?'

She shook her head. 'Not here, in your mother's house.'

'Maman knows we're both adults.'

She really didn't want to do this now, but he'd been the one to push her into it—and she had to say something now or regret it later. 'You've played the game for years with some of the world's most beautiful women. But I'm not one of them. I barely know the rules. I might be almost divorced, but I don't *feel* free yet. I still don't know what I want to do with my life, and I don't want to become the latest woman in a long line of Armand Bollinger's exes while I'm waiting to find out.'

The frown deepened between his brows. 'I've looked after you for over two weeks, shown you my hopes and plans—I even brought you to meet my mother—and you still think I treat you as if you're only a bit of transitory fun for me?'

He folded his arms, waiting for her answer, dark, angry, serious and beyond beautiful. She sat staring at him, enthralled, aching. Why did he *care*? 'I'm nobody's transitory fun,' she whispered. 'I don't know how to be.'

'Oh, I think you do. Don't play the country-girl card now. I've seen your show once or twice. I heard you give all your sage advice on healing through transitional people.' He stood over her, angry yet without threat. Even now, he wouldn't intimidate her to make his point. 'I'm beginning to wonder if you've been the one who's playing me all along, all alone and sweet and helpless to get your way.'

The truth of his words felt like being hit by a baseball bat for a home run. She felt shocked, appalled. But she said, 'You're right, I know what it is in theory, but I've never done it.'

'Oh, I think you have. I think you've been practising on me. What am I, your safe person because I don't have feelings? I don't get hurt, is that right?'

Again, he'd knocked it out of the park. Too handsome, too perfect—had she treated him as the Wolf, or as a real man?

She laced her fingers together tight. 'If I was doing that, I didn't know. I *was* alone, Armand. All I could think about in LA was escape, and I did—but when you arrived in your resort that day, I didn't know what to do. It was you that just took over.' Biting her lip, she drew in a breath and said simply, 'I understand if you want me to go.' Rising onto legs that still quivered, she walked to her bags, sitting against the back wall of the lovely, bright room. They felt like ton weights in her hands. 'Please thank your mother—and thank you, Armand. Thank you from the heart, for everything you've done for me,' she said quietly.

Armand swore in fluent French. 'Damn it, Rachel, you can't leave like this.' He strode over and pulled the bags from her. 'I'll see this through. I gave you my word.'

Trembling deep inside, she lifted her chin. 'I release you from your promise. And don't worry. I'll still endorse your resort.' Then she gulped. 'I didn't mean to—to use you, Armand, but you made it impossible to say no.'

'I suppose I did.' To her surprise, he gave her that rueful smile she couldn't resist. 'You're as confusing as hell, you know that? Every time I think I have a handle on you, you spin me around until I'm dizzy.'

A smile of pure relief curved her mouth. He wasn't angry any more and she shrugged. 'Sorry?' It came out as a hopeful question.

'All I wanted was to keep going as I was, making greater successes with my resorts, finding new ventures to build up from the ground,' he muttered. 'I was satisfied with my world. Then you came into it and turned everything upside down in minutes.'

'I seem to have a talent for that,' she admitted. It certainly resembled the shambles she'd created of her life. Calamity Jane had struck again.

Armand stopped the pacing he'd begun with his last pronouncement and threw her a searching glance. 'Stop it. Stop apologising. Stop blaming yourself for everything.' Suddenly he had her hands in his, refusing to let go even when she pulled and tugged. 'I could have walked away that first day, let you leave my resort and my life. You weren't trying to stop me. You've never asked a single thing of me. I've made all the moves.' He lifted her chin so he could look down into her eyes. 'I stopped you when you wanted to go it alone. I did all this, Rachel. It's my decision. I accept the consequences.'

Completely taken aback, she blinked at him but didn't find words. She blinked again, wondering if she was awake or dreaming.

He saw it, and his face softened even as he frowned. 'Has anyone ever said that to you before, Rachel? Just accepted the consequences for their own acts?'

'I don't think so,' she whispered. Somewhere deep inside a trembling began, the one that told her this was a big moment. Big. Life-changing. 'I mean, Mama and Daddy weren't like that, not really. Only once or twice, but those times were my fault…'

Softly, his fingers moved against her skin, sending tiny warm shivers through her. 'How long have you been accepting the blame for other people's decisions that turned bad?'

At first, all she could hear was the echoes of the past in the present: *am I Armand's decision gone bad?* Then she heard what he'd said. 'I don't know,' she mumbled.

'Months? Years? All your marriage—or all your life?' he pressed, his expression telling her he wouldn't let this go.

Rachel opened her mouth, and closed it. 'I don't know.' But it sounded horribly familiar, a song she'd been singing too long. *I'm sorry, I'm sorry...*

*I'm sorry, Mama and Daddy, but I don't want to be a doctor or a rocket scientist.*

*I'm sorry, Sara,* she'd said when all Sara's beautiful friends had laughed at her for having such a nerdy sister. And she'd run away, back to the college she'd been attending since she was fourteen, safe from ridicule, but so alone. She'd even apologised when Sara had said she had her bridesmaids picked out, and Rachel wasn't one of them. *I'm sorry I'm so plain and awkward.*

*I'm sorry, Pete doesn't want babies yet,* she'd said whenever her parents had nagged for Rinaldi grandchildren. *The show takes all our time. You have Sara's kids, right?*

*I'm sorry I'm not taller or prettier, Pete.*

*I'm sorry I'm smarter than you want me to be. I'm sorry I'm not as pretty as the women you meet at the studio. I'm sorry, you were wrong on what you said to that person in the audience—you'll need to retract it, I'm sorry...*

She'd even apologised to Pete when he had been in the wrong.

She'd apologised to Sara ten years later, apologised to already divorced, very rich Sara who'd complained bitterly when Pete had left her, Rachel, for Jessi… It was so embarrassing to have a famous sister that was such a loser.

*I'm sorry*, she'd cried wretchedly when Pete had said the least she could do for him was swallow the story he'd sold to the tabloids, and let him get on with his career. She didn't want to destroy the show, did she? Could she ruin a hundred and fifty families and shatter the million fans that depended on Dr Pete's continuance?

Armand had presented her with the big moment, the life-changing question—and she was a total failure as a psychologist because she had no answer. At least she had no answer she was prepared to give him, not to the smooth, confident, perfect Armand Bollinger. A wavering hand moved to her eyes. 'I—I think I need to sit down.'

'You've turned white. Come here.' But she couldn't make her knees work, so Armand came to her instead, lifted her into his arms and carried her back to the settee. 'Lie down with your feet up. No, let me,' he said, when she tried to pull her shoes off and performed the task for her. 'Just rest there until you feel better.'

Her eyes closed against the dizziness. Rachel opened her mouth to apologise and then closed it. It seemed there was one person in her life that neither needed nor wanted her apologies.

She had no idea how long she lay there, but eventually the spinning slowed enough to think. No, Armand had never needed her apologies from the first day.

She'd always known a crush on him was inevitable. But her feelings weren't based on his looks alone—though she'd never met a man more handsome—or his wealth, because he never flaunted it. It was just as he'd said to her: *I want you, only you.*

He expected nothing of her but for her to be who she was. He didn't want the Mrs Pete persona created by the Dr Pete phenomenon. He didn't want or need her to be the one to take the blame for him, because he was strong enough to accept his own consequences.

He just liked her. Just Rachel: no make-up, no glamorous clothing, no reed-thin figure or mahogany hair.

Her hand moved about until it found something warm, strong, human—his hand. She threaded her fingers through his, unable to talk, but suddenly her mind was clearer than it had ever been.

She was done—not just with apologising, but with accepting the criticisms levelled at her as fact for so long.

She turned her head, looking at him. He was crouched beside her, concern written all over his beautiful, intensely masculine face. She squeezed his hand and murmured, 'You really like me—just me?' She didn't mean to make it a question, but the habits of a lifetime took more than a lightning epiphany to change.

He nodded, a slow smile lighting his eyes, if not his mouth, warm and gentle—tender, almost. He murmured back, 'I like you…just you. And I want you. Just you.'

The little sigh seemed to come up from the deepest part of her heart. 'I need time to believe that, Armand. I need space.'

Those cloud-grey eyes were steady on hers, but without a hint of anger. 'Probably more than both of us knew.'

'Yes,' she sighed, and closed her eyes again.

'I think we should stay here a day or two,' he said quietly. 'Maman will be happy to put us up. She thinks you're wonderful.'

'I think she's wonderful too.' A little smile hovered around her mouth, but she didn't open her eyes.

'I think you're pretty wonderful too, Rachel,' he said softly. 'I've thought so from the hour we met.'

A lump formed in her throat and she couldn't answer—somehow even thanking him seemed fraught with dangerous belief. 'It's been a long day.'

'It's been a very long and hard day for you.' He pulled his hand from hers. She felt him rising, standing. 'Wait here a moment and don't think of anything.'

'Hmm,' she agreed, wishing she could stop thinking. In her lifetime, her inability to turn off her busy brain had been her life's bane—again, more than Armand knew. 'I'm so glad you like me,' she whispered. 'I like you too.'

'Rachel?'

She started a little; she must have fallen asleep, or half-drifted there. 'Hmm?'

'Drink this. I think you'll like it.'

Again she felt herself lifted, cradled against him until she was on his lap, half-sitting upright. Breathing in, she caught a fragrant, spicy scent, piquant and fruity. She sipped at the glass at her lips and sighed in happy contentment at the warm sweetly-spiced wine. 'Ooh, this is delicious. What is it?'

'It's called *glühwein*. It basically means "glowing wine", because it's served warm in winter. Maman makes it every winter, and keeps a dozen bottles in the cellar. She finds it reviving to her spirits.'

'I know why your mother loves it,' she murmured when she'd almost emptied two glasses of it. 'I can't even remember what had me so upset before. I like your mother's wine, Armand. I like your mother. She's amazing.' She took a final sip, licking her lips to savour the final dregs. 'Hmm. I like you too. Did I tell you I like you? I mean, really, I *like* you.' She smiled up at him, feeling all shiny and kind of fuzzy—like Armand's face right now. 'I do like you, and it's not just because you're so incredibly gorgeous, or because you feed me or give me airsick bags, or because you have the most gorgeous accent, or because you're a good kisser.'

'What is this "good kisser" rubbish? I'll have you know I'm a great kisser,' he retorted in mock indignation, but with a smile more tender than she'd ever seen before.

She giggled, finding it very funny. 'Well, not to challenge you, Armand, but I wouldn't really know.'

'Are you sure that's not another challenge?' he whispered in her ear. 'If it is, I wish you'd repeat it when you're not inebriated.'

She shivered with longing. 'Hmm.' She closed her eyes. 'Did I tell you how much I like it when you tease me and make me laugh even when I want to cry? I've never had so much fun before, Armand. I've never had a friend like you.'

'I thought you were enjoying my company, but thank you for telling me.' His lips brushed over her temple. She felt herself being lifted up into his arms. He was so strong, he never made her feel as if she was overweight… 'You need to sleep.'

She nestled into his shoulder and was asleep before he'd reached the top of the stairs leading to the bedrooms. Her last thought as she lay cocooned in masculine warmth and strength was that she'd finally met a man strong enough to show when he cared, to tease her out of the blues and never betray her confidence. But there had to be a hitch somewhere.

No man could be this perfect. If he was, then she'd have to go, to leave him to find her own sphere, because she was far too imperfect to reach for the stars.

# CHAPTER TEN

Sunlight filtered through the slits in the window shutters, enough to wake Rachel from a deep sleep. She blinked and rubbed her eyes, taking a moment to reorient herself.

The room was a pretty one painted a soft pink, with sheer curtains around the four-poster bed. It was obviously a girl's room. The double bed only had dints where she'd lain, she noted with relief.

A soft knock sounded at the door, and she realised that was what had woken her. 'Come in,' she said, rubbing her eyes again. She felt muddle-headed, groggy.

The door opened and a timelessly lovely face with pixie-cut silver hair peeked around it. 'Good morning, Rachel, I hope you slept well?'

'Yes, thank you, Claire.' She smiled without effort. It was ridiculous to feel intimidated by a woman as kind and gentle as she was beautiful and famous.

'Would you like to join us for breakfast, or have it here on a tray?'

To her surprise she felt very hungry. 'I'll join you, thank you.'

Claire smiled with genuine happiness. 'I'm glad, as we didn't get to know each other very well last night. The bath-room is two doors down the hall to your right, with every-thing you'll need.' She closed the door behind her.

As soon as she came downstairs to the bright winter-garden room—a glass construction at the back of the house, rather like a hot house with a dining table in the centre of the flowers—Rachel sensed something wasn't right. Quickly, she looked at Armand, who was setting the table with bright napkins and cutlery with an odd expression on his face, as if he was rehearsing words. 'What is it? What's wrong?'

Still holding the silverware, he looked at her. She read the hesitation in his eyes before he seemed to come to his decision. 'I had a call from the resort an hour ago. Your husband checked in last night, demanding a room and demanding to see you.'

She felt the blood drain from her face even as she nodded. 'I'm only surprised it took him this long,' she said with a calmness that felt like the prelude to a storm, totally false. 'Excuse me for a minute.' She ran back up the stairs to her room, and pulled her mobile phone from her handbag. For the first time in weeks, she turned it on.

Feeling Armand's presence standing behind her ten seconds later rather than hearing it, she handed him the phone. 'He's left over two-hundred messages. I've exceeded my phone capacity, but read the last one he sent.'

'Can he contest the divorce? Have you given him any grounds?' was all he said after reading the message.

'I'm not sure. I've never been divorced before.' She tried to laugh.

'Has he grounds for this action?' Armand pressed. 'Have you given him any reason to contest it?'

She shook her head. 'This has to be a bluff to intimidate me. Then he'll come to me and try to charm me into coming back. He wants me to save his show and his ratings. That's all he cares about. But I don't know what's in his counter claim.' She frowned. 'I'll call my lawyer as soon as it turns office hours on the West Coast.'

'He said he'd left you for a younger woman.' He didn't quite make it a question. He stood about five feet from her; either he was giving her space to maintain her silence, or he was keeping his distance from the married woman.

No matter what his reasons were for keeping away, it was time. She either trusted him by now or she ran, and she was done with running. 'He did—after I changed the locks. But he was already seeing her at that point, he had been for a few months.'

'When did he break your arm?'

'The day I changed the locks,' she murmured, feeling the relief of telling him flood through her. 'When he broke my ribs the first time, it was sudden fury. It couldn't have been an accident, as he claimed, but I decided to forgive him.'

'Because you loved him?'

His tone was reserved, withholding judgment or emotion. But she lifted her chin and turned to face him. 'Yes, because I loved him. He made me his world and I felt safe there for a long time—and happy. The first time he hit me, I forgave him because I couldn't face losing him…and also losing everything we'd worked twelve years to accomplish. But the second time I couldn't keep forgiving him because I had nowhere else to go.'

'Your family?' he asked, after a small silence where the question pulsed unspoken.

She shrugged, in a basic self-defence mechanism. 'They love him and the lifestyle he's given them. And Mama's forgiven Daddy a hundred times. Not for beating, but for infidelity.'

As if he sensed her anguished wish to leave that subject alone, he slowly nodded. 'Is forgiveness an option this time?'

'No.' A single word, but filled with resolution. 'It's over.'

He smiled at her then, and it was like rainbow shades of

joy coming after a long, dark rainy night. 'Let's go down to breakfast.'

Her fingers twisted around each other. 'Your mother...'

'She'll understand and want to help.' His smile faded, but when he spoke it wasn't what she expected. 'Women didn't press charges against their husbands back then. She had too much to lose—but she left him in the end.' His eyes turned cold, distant, but it wasn't aimed at her. 'He died a month later.'

Her humiliation fled in an instant. Her gaze flew to him, realising what he'd left unsaid, given the mysterious circumstances of his father's death. 'Oh, Armand...'

His eyes met hers, smoking dark with memory. 'My father sent us to boarding schools when I was twelve, the girls ten and eight—after I realised where Maman's bruises came from.'

Rachel opened her mouth and closed it, her mind racing. *That's why she quit acting until your father's death?* She didn't ask, didn't have to—the timeline was perfect. Every puzzle piece about this man who seemed anything but a wolf fit into place now.

She should have known. She'd thought he'd been talking about his sister when she'd challenged him to 'man up', but it had been his beloved mother he felt he'd failed to protect.

Her arms were around his waist before she knew she'd moved; her cheek lay against his heart. His chin rested on her hair as he held her. No movement, no words necessary. Empathy was best given in silence.

'I called Johanna and Carla,' he said quietly after a long minute. 'I think it's time we talked to Maman about our father.'

Rachel gulped down the sudden rush of tears. 'That was very brave of you.'

He didn't answer that. 'They'll be here this afternoon. You

can tell them anything about yourself, or nothing. We're all here for you, whatever you decide.'

Her throat ached and burned with gratitude, with wistfulness. 'You have a wonderful family, Armand. You're blessed.'

He lifted her chin. 'We are your family now, too, for as long as you need us.'

Even if she knew why he was doing this—he'd failed his family, and needed to save someone—she still wanted to cry. There was no pride that would fight this need, a need not for help or salvation but simply for someone to care. 'Thank you.'

'I've told Max to hold Rinaldi off as long as possible, until the family's here and you've worked out what the next move is.'

*You've* worked out *your* next move, he'd said. He wasn't taking control, only offering support. To him, she was no victim but a woman able to stand alone and make her own choices.

And that broke weeks of control. She went up on her tiptoes, her hand winding around his neck, pulling him down to her.

Their lips met. Such a simple thing, yet kissing Armand felt new and beautiful, like a sunlit pond, like drinking cool, sweet water after not knowing she'd been parched for years. He didn't pull her closer, since she was already against his heart; he didn't deepen the kiss, but he caressed her back and waist as they explored each other with the tentative discovery of a young child touching its first butterfly.

He knew, understood somehow, that she couldn't bear passion, not yet. Not until…

With a smothered gasp she moved back no more than an inch. 'Armand, I'm free,' she whispered, still holding him, her eyes huge as she realised the truth. 'He can come now for all I care. I can deal with him. I feel free of him at last.'

He didn't ask why, didn't joke or congratulate her, or even

try to kiss her again. If anyone could understand the significance of her words, it was Armand. 'Breakfast must be getting cold. Shall we go down?'

Once more he gave her the dignity and sense of control she so desperately needed, when she could so easily have fallen apart. She released him, put her hand in his and they walked down the stairs that way. Together.

'That's a fantastic idea, Rachel,' Armand's mother said a few hours later, her gaze dropping to the table. 'He's used to your being compliant, agreeing to everything he wants. He is also used to being the one in control in all matters. To face him this way will show him who you have become.' Her fingers tapped on the tabletop, and Rachel ached for the woman who hadn't stood up to her abuser until it was almost too late.

'But she can't face him alone!'

Sitting across from them at the dining table, Johanna frowned at her brother: a storm unleashed on a safe target. 'Pardon me, Armand, but when did this become your choice to make, or your judgment call on what she ought to do with her private life? Did she give you permission to become her conscience?'

'Johanna, Rachel is Armand's friend. He's merely worried, *tres cher.*'

Low and filled with loving reproof, Claire's voice stopped Johanna with her mouth still half-open. Her eyes darkened and grew stormy, strengthening her resemblance to Armand. Then she sighed. 'You're right, Maman.' With a sense of strain, she smiled at her brother. 'Go on with what you were saying, Rachel.'

Rachel deliberately didn't look at Armand as she repeated, 'I need to face him alone, to show him this isn't because of anyone's influence on me. He thinks he can still manipulate me by love, by coercion and the fear of what others think.

And if I show up with a support group, or even one—' she slanted a small, apologetic look at the man still holding her hand '—he won't have any reason to see the change in me. He'll deal with you, Armand, and not me.'

'Do you care what he thinks of you?' Armand's withdrawn tone in no way hid the anger, the fear. Fear for her.

Yet the apology in her eyes vanished. 'Everyone cares what others think of them, Armand, including you. As for Pete, perhaps I just care because I need him to see the woman I now am. If he doesn't, he'll never back down. He'll keep fighting the divorce.'

'He won't if you turn up with the police threatening to reinstate your restraining order—publicly this time!'

'He won't hurt me again, Armand,' she reassured him quietly. 'He won't have the courage to do that, not on my turf where he has no influence over anyone that sees us. If I choose the time and place, and he has to comply, it will weaken him. The meeting begins and ends with me. My choices. My way.'

'Did that work for you, Maman?' he snarled, swivelling to look at his mother in open challenge. 'If I recall, that was when our father packed us all away.'

Claire gaped for a moment. 'This is not about me, Armand, and this man is not your father.'

Claire was right, yet a cold knot of fear hit Rachel in the stomach and took up residence. Turning to Armand again, she took both his hands in hers. 'I know Pete. You don't.'

'I can't let you meet him alone,' he muttered beneath his breath. 'If he hurts you…'

The words touched her somewhere deep inside, a place she hadn't known existed, because until now nobody had ever fought to protect her. 'I'll meet him in a public restaurant, where you can be waiting nearby,' she said gently. Finally she accepted that compromise was possible for her, because someone really cared about her welfare.

'I want to be there. Someone has to protect you from him,' he protested, as if hearing her thoughts.

'I know you want to protect me.' Still holding his hands, she looked up at him, and suddenly it was as if only the two of them existed in the room. 'But I need you to respect my decision, Armand. For me, and my future. For my self-respect and well-being. For my healing, I need to have control of this.'

'I hate this.' With a low growl, he released her hands and paced around the table. Watching him, she noticed for the first time that the other women had discreetly vanished.

'I know,' she said, understanding because it would be how she'd feel. 'But this has to be my decision, my way. I have to face him with my own strength, not yours.'

He swore for the first time in her hearing, stalking from one end of the room to the other and back again. 'I don't know why you doubt your strength, when you've been pushing me from the first day.'

'I only had the courage for that because I knew you'd never hurt me.' She stood in his path, blocking his incessant pacing. 'Armand, you've given me a priceless gift these past weeks: faith in myself, finding my own strength. Don't ever think I don't appreciate it. But it's time I used those gifts now.'

She spoke with finality and, though he gave that harsh sigh and swore again, he gave the barest nod before walking around her and out the back door, vanishing into the brilliant late-autumn day, a spectre of perfection she'd found and lost.

Rachel watched him leave, aching to follow, but he needed time. He wouldn't let go of his fierce protective instincts—if he hadn't been born with them, his family experiences had cemented them inside his soul—but he had to accept his limits, with her or with any woman. If he didn't do it now, he'd probably burst into the meeting with Pete with sword drawn.

Where they would go later, when the intensity of this situation was done and he didn't have to be her knight any more, she didn't know. When he realised she could stand alone, she'd probably have her heart dented, maybe even broken. Men like Armand only came along once in a lifetime, a true knight in shining armour. A man who was everything she'd ever dreamed of but believed didn't exist outside of fairy tales.

'He almost killed Papa, you know. When Maman left and took us out of school, and Armand came from the set of his second movie to visit, Papa found us. Armand was seventeen then. When Papa tried to force Maman to come with him, Armand broke his nose and arm.'

Unsurprised by Johanna's presence behind her, she nodded. 'I thought he might have done something like that.'

'You're good for Armand,' Johanna said softly. 'He's stopped being the perfect gentleman and has become the Wolf with you. It's a really good sign.'

'The Wolf?' Forgetting all about her insecurities about the beautiful women he'd dated, Rachel spun around to face Armand's sister, burning with curiosity.

Johanna smiled with a touch of sadness. 'He's not the lone wolf he's been painted to be. I nicknamed him the Wolf years ago because he's so protective and faithful—he never leaves the people he loves in need of anything. As for all the women he's been with, he was kind and gentle with them, but never the Wolf. You see, wolves only mate once, and it's for ever. When he truly loves a woman, it will be for life.' The look Johanna gave her made a treacherous warmth bloom in her heart, its tender petals breaking open through her entire body.

'Oh,' was all she could think to say, in wonder. *And he's the Wolf with me...?* But she couldn't bring herself to ask it. She was almost afraid of the answer.

'Did he tell you about our father, and why he sent us to boarding schools?'

Dumbly, she shook her head, suddenly aware that there was much more to this story than she had first imagined. 'We'd rather be here to tell her, Johanna.'

Johanna stared at her mother and Carla as they entered the room, but Claire's hand landed on Rachel's shoulder. 'It's time, and Rachel is the person. Come, sit down, *cher*. Armand will be back soon enough, and we all need to say this, to be united before he joins in. He needs to see us strong—for, though you were both hurt, Armand was the one the most deeply injured.'

*Rachel is the person.* What had Claire meant by that?

Armand's youngest sister Carla started the conversation in a slow, halting voice. 'I think I was about eight when my father first hit me. He said it wasn't a female's place to argue with the man of the house.'

'Tell her why he hit you,' Claire murmured with an arm around her daughter. 'It's time we all talked of this. I should have made us all do it long ago.'

The lids of Carla's eyes, the sky-blue of her mother's, dropped. 'I woke up, needing water, and I saw him hit Maman. She was crying. I cried too. I told him he was hurting her, to stop it. So he—he backhanded me across the face.'

'You never told me!' Johanna cried.

Carla sighed. 'After Maman calmed me down, he put me to bed. He kissed me and said it never happened, that I had a bad dream...'

'And I told her the same the next day, when she asked me about it.' Claire nuzzled Carla's hair in loving apology. 'I wanted her to forget it, put it out of her mind. I didn't want her as damaged as I'd become.'

'He hit me twice,' Johanna mumbled. 'The second time, Maman left him. He said I was defiant.'

Claire nodded. 'I knew it would never end then,' she said, softly, sadly.

'And Armand?' Johanna asked, frowning. 'What did you tell Armand after he stopped him hitting you that time and he sent us all away?'

Claire looked down, her hands trembling. 'Your father never hit me again after that until after I left him, Johanna, nor did he hit Carla. I think Armand knocking him down shocked him. But he wasn't strong enough to stand your defiance without lashing back.'

'How often did he hit you?' Rachel asked, because Johanna couldn't bear to ask it, couldn't bear to not know.

'Not as much as you think, *chérie*,' Claire said to her oldest daughter, sitting like stone across the table. 'Most of the time he was a loving husband. But when things got stressful with work, if he drank too much or if he lost money and I said or did something to upset him...'

Rachel took Claire's hand in hers. 'You know that's not the truth, Claire. Weak people blame others for their mistakes and faults. Abusers never take responsibility until they've received help.'

Claire looked down. 'That is why I said you're the person to hear our stupid story, Rachel. Not because of your degree, but because of your experience and your empathy. But don't waste it on me—I have come to terms with the past.'

'Just not enough to talk to your children about it,' she said softly. 'I am not the person, Claire, because I clearly still have my own issues to fix. You're the one your children need to hear this from. Talk to them—talk to Johanna and Carla while I find Armand. And then talk to him too.' She touched the older woman's arm as she was trying to shake her head. 'You're too strong to let yourself off the hook, Claire. Talk to them. And I'll find Armand.'

# CHAPTER ELEVEN

ARMAND was walking back from the wild edge of the village, where the road led to the next town, when Rachel found him. By the abrupt stride and the preoccupied frown, he had yet to find peace about her decision, and he had more pain yet to come.

Aching for him, she waited for him to reach her. 'Hi.'

*How lame was that, Rachel?*

'Hi.' Now the intense look turned on her. 'Did you need to find me for some reason?'

*That's Armand*, she thought, a touch of tenderness shooting through her despite the unnerving expression he wore. *Straight to the point, needing a battle to concentrate on.*

When she hesitated, his eyes darkened. 'Is it Rinaldi? Does he know where you are?'

'No. Not yet, but I'll call him soon.' She reached out to him, twined her fingers through his as she tried to find the right words. 'Johanna told me about how you stopped your father from hitting your mother.'

His jaw tightened. 'Too little too late,' he muttered, pulling his hand away. 'Are you worried I'll hit Rinaldi now?'

Although she bit her lip, the smile came through the repressed cheek. 'More like reassured, Armand. You're bigger than he is.'

The chuckle was reluctant. 'So I can hover nearby, just in

case?' he asked with something approaching sarcasm. It told her more than she wanted to know.

She crossed her arms beneath her breasts and tried not to glare at him, but she was unable to stop the hurt from showing in her eyes. 'You really don't think I can handle him, do you?'

'Don't make this personal, Rachel. He broke your ribs, your wrist!'

She turned from the anger so clearly written all over his face, the protectiveness he refused to control. 'Yes, he did. And I handled it.'

'By running halfway across the world,' he shot back. 'You didn't even press charges.'

'I lodged the x-rays with my lawyer,' she said quietly. 'I needed time. Until I came to Switzerland, he was all I had. Everything and everyone else believed in him.'

'And now?'

The challenge in his tone was almost insulting, but with a strong effort she managed to hang onto her temper. 'Now I will do what I must to end his belief that I'll tolerate any more manipulation or abuse. But you need to think of your family.'

Like a shot he changed, moving around her to see her face, fierce concern in every line of him. 'Why, what's wrong?'

Gently now, she said, 'Your mother has things to tell you that all of you need to hear. She's waiting for you.'

He did that statue thing again, freezing in place. 'I don't want to hear it.'

'I know,' she whispered, closing her eyes, taking a step closer. Right now touching him was the last thing he wanted, and a risk she had to take. He jerked back when she caressed his face, but she opened her eyes, took another step and touched him again. 'But sometimes what we want isn't what we need the most. What we want doesn't help our loved ones. And sometimes what we fear the most isn't the worst thing we can go through.'

Armand swore savagely, pushing her off. 'Stop pushing me, Rachel. I said no.'

'So did I to your arguments, and yet I know you're right.' It hurt her physically to admit the truth, but it had to be said, for his sake as well as her own. 'Though part of me wants to face Pete totally alone and know I'm strong enough to do it without help, what I need is to know you're near me, just in case.'

He threw her a look brimming with suspicion. 'Why do I get the feeling that you just handed me a consolation prize?'

Her mouth twisted sideways in a rueful half-smile. 'Probably because you know that I want something in return. I want you to help your mother heal, and your sisters.'

He whitened. 'Damn you, Rachel,' he muttered in repressed fury. '*Damn* you.'

She watched him stride towards the house, tears stinging her eyes. The memory of the pain burning in his betrayed eyes would haunt her long after he'd forced himself to give his family what they needed.

Would the cost of the Bollinger family truth session be the fledgling trust between them? Had the Armand and Rachel story just become another blip in the life and times of the Wolf, not even worthy of an item in the news? Had it ended before it had truly begun?

It was almost two hours before Armand came out the same way he'd walked in—but either the world had changed or he wasn't the same man.

Though his life just might or might not have fallen to pieces, he could still look up and see the sunshine over the snow-capped peaks of the French Alps. He could breathe in and smell the scent of fallen leaves and drying grass.

And he could still smile at the sight of the wise, beautiful, strong-willed and temporary intrusion into his life hopping from foot to foot, clearly in pain, and in more than anxiety over his family session. 'Everything okay?' The worry in her voice was reflected in her eyes as she searched his face.

'Everything's fine, Rachel. Now, get to the bathroom before you explode,' he said, hiding the grin, not knowing yet if she deserved to have that reprieve.

With a swift, nervous look and bitten lip, she bolted into the house but, just as she'd done last night, she stopped politely when Maman called her. He watched through the window, an outsider, as his mother and sisters all hugged her and she hugged them back, looking the same yet somehow more peaceful.

Then she turned her face and gave him a swift, uncertain smile, including him even though he'd punished her.

He'd punished her for giving his family closure and serenity. The only cost was to the denial that had been his one self-indulgence, but it had hurt the people he loved most.

Once, he'd believed he'd done all he could to protect them, to make them happy and safe. Once upon a time—until Rachel had walked into his cabin, invaded every secret he'd thought well hidden from the world and showed him he'd done everything but the one thing they needed most: to listen, to heal them.

*No wonder you brought her to me. She's special, Armand.*

He waited until she'd run upstairs before coming back in. He wasn't ready for a group-hug session that included her. Right now he needed space from all these new emotions churning through him, and he needed time to work out what they were.

Right now only one stood out clearly: *I should never have kissed her.* He'd taken their friendship into a realm that neither of them was ready to explore.

Was it too late to go back?

Then he got the call that changed the direction of his thoughts entirely.

'Please leave me alone with Rachel,' he said to his family in a tone of courteous command when he'd disconnected, and they quietly vanished.

When Rachel came back down, he said baldly, 'He's worked out where we are from an interview he read about Maman. He's on his way here.'

He saw the colour drain from her face.

Despite her efforts at self-control, Rachel felt herself sway. 'Is it possible for an American citizen to take out a restraining order here?'

After a few moments, Armand said slowly, 'Since he's on his way here, I'd say no. I am certain he'd check on that law before he flew over.'

'That sounds like Pete. He wouldn't risk wrecking his career if it got out,' she replied with soft bitterness. 'Yes, you're right—and the temporary one I took out has lapsed.'

Armand took a step towards her and, after a hesitation, enfolded her in his arms, breathing together, just breathing, for a few precious moments. It was her turn to receive that empathy unspoken. 'So what do you want to do now?' he asked eventually.

'If I know him, he's sitting smugly in some aircraft, thinking I'm going to go back with him after a few nice words and kisses. And if that doesn't work…' She fingered her wrist for a moment before she pulled back to look up at Armand's face, tender and troubled.

His obvious concern steeled her spine.

'It's time to take control now, before he sees me.'

Before she could change her mind, she dialled the number of the man who'd once been her world.

* * *

Rachel was sitting in the restaurant alone when Pete walked in two hours later.

She watched Pete wind his way towards her, tall and well-built, so handsome and perfectly groomed. The movie-star quality he'd always had shone so brightly it lit the room. And he was smiling at her in the way that had never failed to make her want to do anything for him.

Watching him, she marvelled that his perfect face no longer made her insides flip. How had she never noticed the touch of sulkiness before, the charm that had such a spoiled-brat quality to it?

Or perhaps he was sulky now because she'd outmanoeuvred him even in this small matter. No doubt he'd expected to show up, stun her, smile at her and win her back.

Rachel lifted her chin, her mind racing. The plan was complete. She sat at the table in the centre of the restaurant where everyone could see them. Public opinion was everything to Pete; he'd do nothing to her here, where everyone could have a phone camera and Internet connection. He'd play the 'wooing lover' card, counting on her being lonely by now, and if that didn't work she knew he'd try to blackmail her somehow.

Despite her nerves, she had to hold in a smile. Pete didn't know what he was in for. A dozen other tables were taken—four of them by Bollinger family friends. Armand's sisters sat two tables away, pretending to chat as they drank too much coffee. Armand waited in the side room, where he could see them, but Pete couldn't see him. Because her famous face could alert Pete, Claire had elected to stay at home, but was anxiously waiting for news.

She wasn't alone—and that made all the difference.

'Hi, bunny. You look beautiful,' Pete said softly when he reached the table. He made no mention of her weight, hair colour or lack of extensions. 'But you always look beautiful to me.'

Yes, he was playing the Prince Charming card. What a shame for him that she'd met the real thing.

'The name's Rachel,' she said coolly. 'Please, sit down.'

'I love this place. Very rustic, ye olde world charm with all the carved tables and chairs and the ceiling beams. It's so fifteenth-century. No wonder you like it.' He came around the table, leaning in to kiss her.

Rachel kept her face stony without a hint of welcome. She didn't turn her face from him—he'd take it as fear of her re-action to him—but she didn't accept the kiss, no matter how he lingered on her lips. She counted three before she slowly moved back. 'I said, sit down.'

With a smile that seemed fixed, Pete caressed her shoulder for a few moments. *I'm the one in control*, his look said, even though the look of love was dominant. He had a plan—seduce her, make her want to come back—and he'd stick to it.

Pete never had a Plan B. He always had to win on his terms and, until today, she hadn't known it for the weakness it was.

'I knew you wouldn't abandon your T-shirts,' he said softly, allowing his fingers to trail over her shoulder before he finally moved to sit opposite her. He pointed at the shirt she wore. It was one of her favourites. 'It's how I found you. My PI took a shot of you standing outside your…cabin, wearing one. You looked just like the girl I met twelve years ago.'

She said nothing in reply. Anything she said now he'd take as capitulation.

'Did you order for us?' he asked, managing to make the question sound intimate.

She called over the waiter with a hand motion. 'This gentleman wishes to order,' she said in French.

The waiter asked Pete in French what he'd like. Pete frowned at Rachel. 'You know I don't speak French. Why don't you order for me, bunny? You know what I like.'

Once upon a time that tone would have melted her—but she wasn't that woman now, dependent on his affection. She smiled at the waiter. 'This gentleman doesn't speak French— do you speak English?'

The waiter handed Pete an English menu. 'What would you like, sir?' he asked in flawless English.

Rachel watched as Pete struggled with his temper. He'd always hated being at a disadvantage with anyone. Being faced with two people more knowledgeable than him at one time was too much for him to handle with equanimity. 'What are you having, bunny?' Pete asked at last, his gaze touching hers over the rim of the menu.

She handed the closed menu back to the waiter with another smile. 'Nothing for me, thank you. My *name*,' she enunciated with a distinct lack of warmth, 'Is Rachel.'

He tilted his head a little with a puzzled smile. So charming—yet she couldn't understand how she'd once been so charmed by it. 'You always loved being my bunny.'

She wasn't about to be drawn into a discussion of the past. 'Why are you contesting the divorce? What are your grounds?'

A flush touched his cheeks; his eyes flashed to the waiter and his jaw worked. 'I'll have a coffee to start, thanks,' he said briefly, handing back his menu. When he'd gone, Pete said coolly, 'It seems to me you've lost your manners, speaking so in front of a stranger.'

Instead of feeling chastened, she grinned. 'Only with people I feel no need to impress. My friends here think I have wonderful manners.'

His face darkened for a moment. He hated her having friends or anyone in her life that didn't have his loyalties at heart first—and the reference to not caring if she impressed him had got to him. 'Well, your family don't agree. When was the last time you called them?'

She blinked, and if the smile felt forced she accepted it. She knew her family would always have the power to wound her—especially because her family loved her enemy more than her. 'I believe just after you called and asked them to guilt-trip me into returning, or at least into discovering where I was,' she replied bluntly.

She watched his cheeks darken with colour and his jaw tighten before he remembered he needed to charm her. 'They love you, bunny. They want you to come home.'

'You mean they want me back on the show that gave them money and prestige,' she retorted. 'They love you. To them, I'm just the smart freak that got famous by accident.'

His jaw dropped a little at her blunt, accurate assessment of her family's feelings for her. 'Rachel, how dare…?' Then he seemed again to remember: *charm her.* 'I think you need to remember your own words on the show, bunny: *forgiveness is the key to finding peace, and the ability to move on.* They do love you. They just didn't know what to do with you all those years until I came along.' And his eyes filled with smugness for a moment before, again, he returned to his loving look.

Rachel frowned, watching his face change over and over, and realised his expressions were like masks he could take on and off at will.

The same masks he'd always used on her to get his way.

But now her blinders were gone. He didn't love her; he probably never had. He loved himself far too much and deeply to have room for anyone else—and all she felt was relief that, in walking away, she wouldn't hurt anything but his ego.

Funny; she'd thought the feeling of power, of controlling the situation, would be heady, or at least a good novelty, but instead she felt a twinge of pity for him. Fame and power was such a sad substitute for real happiness. And he didn't even know it.

So she dropped the game. 'Pete, I don't really care what pretext you used to stall the divorce. I want the divorce—from you, and from the show.'

He stilled with his hand halfway towards the water glass the waiter had brought him. 'And if I say I don't want it? What if I want you back, bunny—in my life and the show?'

She met his loving, pleading look squarely. 'You and I both know you wouldn't be here but for the ratings drop, and the offer I received—but that's not the issue. I don't want you, Pete. Not in any way.'

'So it's true,' he said very quietly, yet with the lightning change to venomous fury that used to make her shudder. 'You want your own show—after I *made* you.'

She didn't bother retaliating. People with self-delusions rarely let go of them. She knew she'd made him, and made the show, with her knowledge—and that was enough. 'I want the divorce. Make it happen—withdraw your counter claim.'

He lifted a brow, jutted his jaw. 'Or you'll do what?'

'Do you really need me to answer that?' She rubbed her wrist, and watched him whiten with the unspoken threat. 'I have the x-rays and copies of the restraining order lodged with three separate lawyers I've never used before. You can't reach them.'

He opened his mouth and closed it. His eyes moved as his mind raced, working out how to answer that.

Again she found herself taking pity on him. 'I can destroy you, but for the sake of all those years together I'd prefer not to. This divorce is happening no matter what, so let's make it as amicable as we can.'

'I told you I never meant to hurt you. You're my life, Rachel. Can't you forgive me and get past it?' His tone was pleading, the wooing lover again; his hands reached out to hers.

His wedding ring was firmly in place. *Nice touch*, she thought, and almost laughed.

Her hands remained on her lap as she gave up trying to use reason and went for the jugular. 'So the producers won't renew the show's contract without me on board, is that it?'

Abandoning the act faster than she could have hoped for, his face relaxed into naked anger and he nodded curtly. 'You know they won't—they want the double act or nothing. Carol has already told you, no doubt.'

He couldn't know that Rachel hadn't bothered to open any of her agent's texts yet. She'd wanted this situation sorted before she even considered the TV deal.

And it was then, only then, she realised she'd thought of Carol's texts before remembering what Pete had admitted— that he was only here for the show—and marvelled that it didn't hurt at all.

Scraping the chair back, she stood, all five-foot-one of her in her jeans and running shoes. 'It's over, Pete—the show and the marriage. Let the divorce go through, or I'll be forced to measures I don't want to take. But be assured I will—doctors' testimony, x-rays and all.'

He glanced around the room to see who had heard before he answered, low and hard with real venom. 'I should have known coming here wouldn't be worth it. Go, then, have your damned divorce, go back to your new man. You won't last a month with Bollinger—he's a serial philanderer, even with really beautiful women. You'll come crawling back after he's ditched you, and I'll laugh. I don't need you, anyway! I'll make it without you—I'll do better. I'll hit the Top Five in chat shows! See if I don't.'

'I hope you do,' she said sincerely.

He shot her a glance of loathing and walked out with careful dignity, smiling and nodding at everyone he passed, showing the world who'd won.

When he was gone, she released the breath she didn't know she'd been holding, whispered, 'I'm free,' and laughed and laughed. And she kept laughing when Carla and Johanna came to her and put their arms around her in celebration. They jumped together like cheerleaders in a victory dance, while the other restaurant patrons pretended nothing was happening, as they'd been instructed.

'Can I join in the fun?' Armand's amused and relieved tone came from behind her—and without stopping to think about it she turned and jumped into his open arms.

# CHAPTER TWELVE

Rachel jumped into Armand's waiting arms and his sisters, smiling, moved back to the table to wait.

'It's finally over, Armand,' she murmured, hugging him tight. 'I'm free at last.'

'You did it.' His arms closed around her, and he swung her around in circles until they were outside on the balcony overlooking the valley. 'You're free, Rachel, and you did it alone.'

'I really did. I can't quite believe it yet. It's like I've just woken up from a dream.' She hugged him again. 'He's gone, Armand. He's *gone.*'

He laughed and nodded, his forehead brushing her hair. 'Like bubonic plague. You swept that old rat's flea out of here.'

She burst out laughing at the analogy. 'I kind of pity him, you know? It's like control and success is all he has. Without it, he's nothing.'

He didn't look too compassionate as he said, 'Well, you might have started him on the road to reality, but now he can't ride back to fame on your coat tails.'

A massive smile filled her heart and radiated from her face. 'You really think so?'

'That makes a difference to you?' he asked, but it was a little too careless.

Why the question surprised her so much, she didn't know. That he cared for her was miracle enough—and he'd shown her too many times now for her to doubt it—but this…

*Was he jealous?*

Suddenly she was aware that this was the closest they'd ever been without a snowboard, a sled or any other pretext for touching. They were meshed together so tight she could feel his heart thumping hard against her chest, and she knew how worried he'd been for her.

*I want you, only you.*

Still hardly daring to believe in what her years of training told her must be true, she murmured, 'I'm a psychologist, Armand. It's what I've been trained to do, to read people, to heal people. But I'd failed with him for so long, I'd begun to think the problems had to be mine.'

With a low, growling sound almost of fury, he muttered, 'His problems were never your fault. You know about projection—how some people push the blame for their weaknesses onto the nearest object who'll accept it—but you don't apply it to those around you. When are you going to wake up, Rachel?' He hauled her up so they were equal, then he turned her face to his. 'You're free of him now. You said it.' And he kissed her, deep, hard and possessively.

For the first time he wasn't gentle with her, but she realised he knew what she hadn't known. That freedom had come, the choice to give him her passion or not, and she must have been looking at him with all the yearning in her body and heart.

And then her mind, heart and body were filled to overflowing, not just with passion and demand, but her own driving need for him. Her arms and lips were filled with Armand, and she loved it. The late autumn sun came out in sudden brilliance, shining on her back as she melted into him. Like a snowman in sunshine, she was melting in a kiss—something she'd believed only happened in the movies. Her arms were around his neck so tight she must have been cutting off his breathing, but he merely growled and heaved her even closer against him so there was nothing but beating hearts, uneven breathing and this deep, passionate kiss. This wonderful, perfect kiss that made a woman of her, a kiss that taught her the difference between existing and truly living. This kiss taught her the difference between a lonely girl's adoration of her rescuer, and a woman's lasting love, because it was Armand kissing her. Because it would probably always be Armand for her now…and knowing that didn't even frighten her any more.

Minutes or hours passed while they kissed; she didn't know or care, this glorious moment was all she craved. Then he trailed his lips over her face, murmuring endearments in French, and she was completely gone. 'Armand, oh Armand, I want you.' She turned her face, found his mouth with hers, and another brief eternity winged silently past as they stood locked together, totally absorbed in what was, to her, the kiss of a lifetime.

Much later, her face buried in his shoulder, she whispered, shaken, 'You were right.'

'Of course I was. About what?' he chuckled into her hair, kissing her temple.

'You are a *great* kisser.'

'*Oui?*' he murmured into her ear, lifting her chin. His smile was beautiful, honest and open, and it melted her anew. 'More?'

Her entire body was turning into a mess of heated honey pooling at his feet. 'Oh yes, yes, Armand… I want more, much more. I…' She kissed him, slow and lingering, while she gathered courage from his dark groan and his aroused body's rough movement against her. 'I want to drag you to the nearest bed and not leave it for a week.'

He drew in a breath. 'And you had to tell me this now, when

we're staying with my mother and sisters, not when we had the cabin to ourselves?'

Still a foot off the ground, she wound her hand through his hair and laughed, soft and rippling. 'I didn't know you were such a great kisser then.'

'Nor were you ready to know. And I did not know that you were capable of doing this to me, either, though I'd suspected it wasn't going to be like it was before.' He kissed her ear and she shivered with the power of his simplest touch. 'I have a feeling a week won't be enough. A month at least.'

A whole month of making love with Armand… Just thinking about it brought on another shiver. What was he *doing* to her? 'Maybe two months,' she dared to venture between kisses as heated as they were tender.

'Three or four,' he muttered, and groaned as she kissed his throat in near-shocked joy that he wanted her so badly. 'No. If you come to my bed, Rachel, don't plan on leaving that bed for at least a year. I'll stop you any way I can.'

*A year with Armand.* It was more than she'd dared to hope for. Another soft, lingering kiss near the base of his throat, where his pulse beat madly. Then she looked up and her eyes twinkled. 'I think we might have killed poor Frau Heffernan by that point.'

He chuckled between lingering kisses on her nose, eyes and mouth. 'They'd find her frozen on the *terrasse*.'

'She can be the new Ice Man. They'll call her the Peeking Woman.'

He looked into her eyes. 'I call you beautiful.'

She couldn't turn away when he looked at her like that; she *felt* beautiful and desired. With a will of its own, her hand slipped inside his jacket. She caressed his back through his thick shirt, and even touching him that much made a little strangled sound emerge from her throat. 'Armand, I want you so much it hurts.'

His eyes darkened with slumbering fire. 'We could fly home today. Or we could drive to an excellent bed and breakfast run by a friend of mine on this side of the Alps where we'd be totally spoiled without leaving the bed. Or I have a chalet an hour away that's totally private, with its own spa and sauna. It's fully stocked, and we can cook for ourselves.' His kiss left her in a mess of hot shivers. 'Your wish is my command.'

Now she understood the flash in his eyes when she'd said those words to him on their first week together. There was something almost unbearably sensual in hearing them, evoking images. 'Which one is closest?' she whispered urgently. 'How soon can we leave?'

Another kiss, rough and desperate with need. Then, holding her so tight she couldn't tell whether she felt her own heart beating or his, he muttered, 'We need to thank Maman and the girls. I need to say goodbye to my nieces and nephew.'

Something flattened inside her. 'Oh…of course, I'm sorry. I'm being so rude, after all they did…'

'Shh.' He laid a finger on her lips. 'No more apologies, remember? My family doesn't need them. I don't need them, either. I need you, just as you are.'

She felt her lips fall apart. 'Oh, Armand, what a *wonderful* thing to say.'

He nuzzled her mouth. 'I want this as much as you do. We'll be alone tonight.'

There were so many things she wanted to say, none of them appropriate. The end would come in its time. When he finished it and wanted to move on, she'd smile and not beg him to stay. But now was the beginning filled with wonders and possibilities. So she buried her face in his throat for a moment, just breathing him in, before wriggling a bit. 'Then let me down and don't touch me until we're alone again. I've got almost no hope of not embarrassing us both in front of your family as it is, but if you touch me…'

He let her feet touch the floor but, breaking her command immediately, he tipped up her face. When she met his gaze, the tenderness in his eyes melted her anew and made her forget everything but him. 'They already know about us, *mon doux*. Even if they hadn't seen the way I look at you, they'd know simply because I—'

Her phone buzzed at that moment. Agonised, she whispered, 'I'm sorry, I'll switch it off.' Then she looked at the caller and frowned. 'No, wait, it's my mother. If I don't take it, she'll just keep calling.'

'Family, eh?' He kissed her nose. 'Take it, *mon doux*.'

*My sweet.* The words almost made her switch the phone off again. But something made her hit the 'accept' button. 'Hi, Mama, how are you… *What?*' Within seconds she swayed where she stood. 'When?' she asked dully. 'I—I'm so sorry, Mama. I know, I'm so sorry…'

At first angered that her mother seemed to be demanding apologies within seconds of talking to her daughter for the first time in months, Armand saw the whiteness of Rachel's face, her eyes shining with tears about to spill over, felt her whole body shaking, and knew something was seriously wrong. He wrapped his arm around her shoulders, held her close and waited for her to tell him.

'I'll be home on the first available flight,' she murmured unsteadily. 'I know. I love you too, Mama.' She disconnected the call and looked up at him with the expression of a shot fawn. 'Daddy passed away ten minutes ago in the hospital. He—had a heart attack. He'd been sick for a week, but nobody knew where I was, and because I didn't check email and I had my—my stupid phone switched off, I wasn't there. *I wasn't there.*'

A few minutes before, Armand had noted that his friend

Patric had closed the balcony curtains. He was even more grateful for it now as he drew her into both his arms and let her cry out her first grief. He'd been where she was now, and knew she'd later hate it if anyone but he had seen her weeping. 'Ah, *mon doux, mon chérie*,' he whispered, holding her against his heart and aching for her. 'I know,' he murmured, rocking her slowly while her body jerked with the force of her choked tears. 'I know. I'm here.'

'But I c-couldn't say that,' she whispered, muffled against his shirt. His shirt was wet with her tears, a gift of her trust. 'I w-wasn't there, Armand. I should have checked my phone. W-why didn't I check m-my *stupid phone*?'

*Why hadn't I been there to stop him?* It was the question he'd been asking himself for eighteen years. Had his father died accidentally in that fire, or had he killed himself in shame for abusing his family? He'd asked that too for years without an answer, without healing. 'You thought you had good reason, *chérie*.'

She shook her head violently. 'Y-you know the w-worst thing? Pete was here. He knew how sick Daddy was and he d-didn't even tell me…'

He wasn't going to touch that; telling her he wanted to kill Rinaldi wouldn't help her now, only misdirect her grief into anger and blame that wouldn't help her get through this traumatic time. But if he saw Rinaldi at her mother's house, he'd take him outside and teach him to try bullying a *man*.

*Control it. Think of Rachel.* 'You'll be with your family by tonight, US time. I'll take you.'

'W-what?' Her eyes, drowned in tears, gazed up at him in wonder. 'You… You'd really do that f-for me?'

If he hadn't been almost sure before, looking into those beautiful drenched eyes that said, *'you're my prince, my hero'* did it. He'd never forget that look—and he'd never forget the moment he knew he was in love for the first and last time in his life. The Wolf had finally found his mate, when and where he'd least expected it—and he'd never felt so exhilarated or so terrified. 'Of course.' It was all he could say because everything else was entirely inappropriate, given her sadness.

'B-but… My fam— My mama…' Tears filled her eyes anew as she amended 'my family'. 'At home, at the…*funeral*,' she added, trying to sound strong. 'Mama will—will punish you for not being Pete, for being an outsider.' She sniffed again. 'Knowing Pete, he's running the whole thing like the show. He'll take centre stage. Can you handle it?'

He almost melted with tenderness. Without meaning to, she'd told him she wanted him beside her when she faced her hardest moments. If she needed him there, he'd be there. 'I can handle your mother and Rinaldi, Rachel. Don't worry.' With all the love filling him, he kissed her lips so gently, almost afraid of breaking her. 'I am considered rather charming in certain circles, you know.'

It was watery, filled with heart-wrenching sadness, but she managed a tiny chuckle. 'Yes, I—I've felt that once or twice.' Then she melted back into his arms, sobbing quietly, and he held her in aching silence, empathy and love that must remain unspoken—for now or for ever, right now he didn't know.

His entire life had been founded on one certainty: he'd always be alone. Protecting his family, being there for them and recreating everything his father had lost, had been a full-time preoccupation for so long. The fear that one day, when he was pushed too far, he'd end up like his father had sealed the deal. He'd never marry. But Rachel was a 'for ever' woman, and he'd never take that lifetime of security from her.

He didn't know what the future held, if he could even be the man Rachel deserved—or even if she could ever love him.

'When can we leave?' she whispered, startling him out of his reverie.

'We'll be on our way within three hours. All we need to do is book the jet and they'll do the rest.' He kissed her hair. 'Maman will want to see you to console you. Do you wish this from her? If not, I can call her.'

'It's all right. I'm okay now,' she whispered unsteadily, trying so hard to pull away from him, to stand alone. 'Let's go see her. I need to thank her for everything.'

But she trembled and against her will her body swayed. 'You're in shock, Rachel.' He lifted her into his arms, and made a heroic effort not to think of what could have been this night. 'Let me do this for you, *mon doux*. Let me help you.'

Like she'd done last night, she dropped her head onto his shoulder and sighed. 'You're too good to me.'

'You make it easy,' he whispered, pushing open the balcony door.

'I don't understand why.' She sounded plaintive, but also halfway towards sleep.

'I know, but one day you will,' he whispered. He walked inside the restaurant and saw the smiles vanish from his sisters' faces at the sight of Rachel in his arms.

'But what will I do when you have to leave me? I know you will one day.'

She'd said it so softly he wasn't quite sure he had heard the correct words, especially after the exquisite half-hour they'd had on the balcony. 'Why do you think I want to leave you?'

She didn't answer.

He looked down at her. Her lashes had fluttered shut, either from embarrassment or sheer exhaustion, but she was still hiccupping as she breathed. Her face was flushed with drying tear-tracks down both cheeks.

She'd had one hell of a day.

He looked up and saw the worried faces of both his sisters right in front of him. 'What happened, Armand?' Johanna demanded, pale and shaken, assuming the worst.

'Has there been bad news?' Carla asked, frowning at Rachel with obvious concern.

'The worst news,' he said very quietly, trying not to re-live the smug look on Rinaldi's face as he left the restaurant, knowing Rachel's jubilation would very soon turn to grief. 'I'll tell you at Maman's. Let's get her home where she can rest.'

# CHAPTER THIRTEEN

IT WASN'T quite how he'd imagined waking up beside Rachel for the first time.

When the captain announced they were ninety minutes from landing at Austin, Armand woke in the enormous double seats they'd turned into a bed by lifting up the mutual armrest. Rachel hadn't been sick this time—that was what ordering the best possible jet could do—but she was exhausted, lying in his arms beneath a thin pile of blankets, her head on his chest, her breathing deep and even. But they were both fully dressed and she was still pale, with dark smudges beneath her eyes.

She'd woken a few times during the night, and he'd held her while she'd wept.

'You know the saddest part? I never really knew him, Armand. He was my father, but he didn't understand me and I didn't understand him,' she'd told him during one session. 'He was handsome, charming—and a serial philanderer. His whole life was based on what people thought of him. I was the less-pretty daughter, a socially awkward geek, so I was an embarrassment—at least until Pete made me famous. Daddy tried then, but by then it seemed too late. I didn't trust him not to hurt me. But now I—I wish I had given him another chance.'

It had been so hard to remain silent at that point. She was

so beautiful to him—could no one else in her life see her as she really was? Were they all so blind that only fame made such an extraordinary woman acceptable to them? But he knew from bitter, silent experience that she had to lance this poison festering in her or it would warp her, change her from this incredible woman he loved, so he'd held her and let her speak without interruption.

'I remember some nights when I was little and he didn't come home all night. Mama would wait beside the front windows, waiting. She'd send me to bed, but when I'd get up to use the bathroom she'd still be there, watching for him. When he finally came home, usually in time for breakfast, she'd fuss over him, feed him and talk of something else, like nothing happened—like he hadn't spent the night with another woman. Like he didn't have her smell still on his skin. And when he went to work she'd go too, but she'd be wiping tears as she pulled out of the drive.'

Shuddering, she'd pulled away from him as she'd finished, but when she'd huddled into a ball by herself he'd dragged her back into his arms, rocking her until she sighed and gave in.

Her confidences had come to an end at that point, and he'd had more than enough to think about. Rachel was so beautiful, so loving and so wise, but she'd never been wise in her own life. Within a few hours of meeting her, she'd turned his world from hard and driven to the first true happiness he'd known since childhood. Something in him knew that, without his wealth or fame, she'd still think he was wonderful. Within a few hours of meeting his family, she'd healed decades of damage; they loved her as her own family didn't seem to.

Ah, was that it? Was that why she couldn't seem to heal her own hurts? Why she was so blind to everything he saw in her?

It was as if they stood on opposite sides of a slightly warped mirror, seeing the best and most beautiful in each other, but their own reflections were distorted.

He'd fallen asleep trying to work out what that meant.

As the captain announced breakfast, Rachel yawned and stretched so that he was obliged to release her. After the revelations in the night, he wondered if her movement had been deliberate, born of embarrassment or a need for distance from him. 'Are we almost there?'

It was odd. Just two days ago he'd have made a joke about that but now he felt unsure, as if he stood on shifting ground with her, even though she needed him here. 'The captain just said we're forty minutes out. We should get breakfast soon.'

'I really don't want to eat. My stomach....'

He smiled at her. 'I understand.'

'I'd better use the bathroom before we buckle up.' She slipped from the seat-bed and into the bathroom without looking at him.

She'd been doing that—avoiding his eyes—since telling him about her father's infidelities, and that she had been the unloved child. He frowned after her, but having no idea what to say or do to help her, he let it go. She had a hard day in front of her. His job was to smooth it as much as he could.

Armand was glad he'd organised a VIP private entrance to the States when he saw the media circus waiting for Rachel. From the customs stop to the limo was only a few steps and was so heavily guarded no one could approach her, only yell their questions from a distance—and as soon as they saw who was with her the questions doubled in noise and intensity.

'I never even thought about this, or that they'd know anything. I'm so sorry, Armand,' she sighed when they were inside the limo.

She was trembling again—and she hadn't faced the hardest part of the day yet. As the limo took off, followed by a varying assortment of vans, bikes and cars, he said, 'You didn't do any of this, Rachel. You have nothing to apologise for.'

'I should have known Pete would make a media announcement. Anything to gain a stupid sympathy bid with his fans.' Clenching and unclenching her fists, her gaze seemed fixed on her hands. 'I know you prefer privacy with—with your women—I mean, relationships. Just by your coming with me, I might as well have sold the story of being your latest squeeze to every magazine in America.'

Disturbed by the whiteness of her knuckles, he took her hands in his. 'Rachel, it isn't your fault. Let it go. You have more important things to deal with today.'

It was only when she sighed and nodded that he realised what she'd said.

*Your women. Your latest squeeze.*

Revolting words, yet it summed up his life until now with blunt vulgarity. And, combined with what she'd told him about her father, it was the most revealing thing she'd said since they'd first kissed. It switched on a light in his brain— but this wasn't the time or place to tell her that for all he cared the press could announce anything they liked if only she'd never say 'your women' or 'your latest squeeze' again, with that look of awkward embarrassment in her eyes. As if she expected nothing more than to be his latest lover, and be waved off like the others when he reached that exit door yet again.

Even their banter of yesterday took on new and dark connotations. She'd been putting a shelf-life on their time because of his past, and he'd played the game. He'd unconsciously confirmed that before long he'd want to leave her behind.

How was he going to make her recognise that she was special, precious to him—that he loved her—when everyone in her life had used the words to get what they wanted from her? How could he make her believe in him when he still didn't know if he could be the man she needed, and when she didn't believe anyone could love her?

Within seconds of the security people ushering them into the house, Rachel felt a sense of sick fatalism. As she'd expected, Pete had got back ahead of them, and was in the centre of the family circle like a benevolent god. He was sitting right between her mother and Sara on the white leather sofa. Each of them sobbed on one of his broad shoulders and he held them with the tender affection of a long-accepted family member.

It was a photo op that couldn't be missed, and she'd be willing to bet it hadn't been. A quick sweep of the large, creamy-white living room revealed no strangers as yet, but she had no doubt they'd be there. Somebody from their network had to have been given the exclusive.

'Just remember, don't let him provoke you. No matter what he says or does, it's to make himself look good at your expense,' Armand murmured in her ear.

She nodded, holding tight to his hand. Even if he was only doing this to get Pete off-balance, she was grateful for the support.

Then her mother looked up and her ravaged face made Rachel forget all about Pete, his petty strategies for popularity, or anything else. Tears filled her eyes and overflowed. 'Mama,' she whispered thickly, and opened her arms.

Mama got to her feet and took a step. 'Rachel…' The look of bewildered grief was more than Rachel could bear. She ran to her mother and rocked her as Armand had done for her. Her mama held her as if she'd never let go, the most affection she'd had from either of her parents, except in public, since her wedding day.

To her surprise, it didn't feel awkward or guilty; it felt good, like coming home. 'Rachel, he's gone, your daddy's gone,' her mother sobbed. Rachel nodded, held her just as tightly, and they cried together, cleansing tears.

Before long Sara was there too and, beyond surprise that her sister wanted to be with her, Rachel made room for her. Poor Sara had always been her daddy's favourite girl and, given her nasty divorce from her husband, she doubted Philip would be coming to pay his respects or even to comfort his sons.

Sara's boys, Danny and Seth, joined the circle, demanding their place with loud voices. Only five and six, they looked frightened at all this grief. The poor babies didn't understand why their mother cried so hard she couldn't talk, and Sara was too lost in her pain to give either of her sons comfort apart from vague pats on their heads.

Rachel resolved to go to them as soon as she could, but right now her arms were full of her mama and Sara. She was almost relieved when Pete squatted in front of the boys and took them in his arms, murmuring the platitudinous explanations the boys were still too young to take in, but letting them know they weren't alone.

For the first time in Rachel's memory, her mama was a mess. She wore no make-up, her eyes were puffy and red, and there was dried tears on her cheeks. Her clothing was crumpled—her immaculate mother who got out of bed an hour before everyone else to dress, do her hair and put on her face. Now she didn't care, but Rachel no longer wondered at her mother's unquestioning love for a man who'd cheated on her too many times to count. She knew now that, despite any precautions against loving the wrong man, the man who'd never stay faithful, the heart still wants what it wants.

The thought made her turn her head a little. Armand was standing about five feet behind her, his gaze steady and compassionate, and yet with something sweeter and deeper as it rested only on her. He sent her a little smile, and amid her tears her heart sang just a tiny bit.

Funny, she'd never thought of herself as like her mother in any way until now—but she was definitely her mother's daughter. She was touched by joy amid her grief, because Armand was here. He'd crossed the world for her. And her heart kept right on wanting what it wanted.

Pete waited until after the funeral, when everyone but closest family was gone, to put his ultimatums—or was it simple blackmail?—to her.

She'd been right and wrong about the press. Pete had granted an exclusive to their network, of course, but only a short press release the next morning. Pete promised he'd handle it all without letting them get near Rachel, Sara or her mother. He gave the eulogy with simple, moving affection, the son her father had never had. Every time he'd gone home with her, Pete and Daddy had had a grand old time, fishing, drinking beer and talking sports.

Despite knowing everything he'd done was to lift his public profile as a sensitive guy, when Pete came to her room later that evening, she said, 'Pete, it was a wonderful eulogy, thank you so much—'

His interruption was brutal. 'Lose the boyfriend, Rachel. The network and media are expecting us to give a formal statement tomorrow about our reuniting.'

Rachel blinked once, twice, unable to believe his gall. 'You're blackmailing me the night of my father's funeral?' she asked, blank with disbelief.

He shrugged. 'It's your fault. I wouldn't have needed to resort to tactics that are beneath my dignity if you'd known your duty and come back with me from Europe.'

'You didn't even tell me my father was sick.'

He sneered at her. 'Why should I? You didn't call your

mom to ask how they were. You didn't care about what I needed.'

Rachel gaped for a moment. 'You mean, I didn't fall for your lies again?'

He shrugged again. 'I said what women want to hear. It doesn't matter if you're nine or ninety, all you women want the same stuff: *oh, you're so beautiful. I love you, baby, you're the only one.*' He mimicked the words with a withering look at her. 'I bet your current boyfriend uses them on you, too. It's the fastest way to get a woman into bed.'

Something went cold in her then, that he could be so callous after the moving tribute he'd given her father today. 'There's no use in trying to pretend we're back together, Pete, it will never happen. And there were a load of reporters when I arrived with Armand at the airport.'

'So? Tell them you're just friends. He helped you through our temporary separation. I've already told the network we're back together—and if you want that job in LA, I suggest you take the smart path and ditch the pretty boy. They want the perfect couple, not the cheating, deserting wife, to give advice on failing marriages.'

Rachel took a few breaths to cool her fury before she spoke; payback was the kind of childish vendetta she abhorred. 'What you told the press or our producers is your problem. You chose this path. You chose to play the pride card. You told the world that you left me for Jessi.'

His jaw jutted. 'You made that bed for me when you changed the locks.'

She sighed. 'I'm not going to indulge in any childish squabbles with you, Pete. I'm here for my family, not you. I owe you nothing now. You ended any obligation I still felt for you when you refused to take me to the emergency room after you broke my wrist.' She said it deliberately. He'd always skipped around the point, like it had never happened. 'I should have changed the locks after you broke my ribs.'

He paled, but with fury. 'You say it like I *meant* to do it when you *know* it was an accident, and you provoked me into it.'

She put up her hand. 'Stop blaming me for your violence, Pete. I won't keep enabling you in your delusions. I don't owe you your career, or your fame, either. You've cheated on me and hurt me more than once. Come near me again and the world will get those x-rays.'

'You just want to scare me,' he sneered. 'You wouldn't know how to be so disloyal.'

'You're right. I don't want to be disloyal, despite knowing you've been completely disloyal to me for the past twelve years, both in bed and with the show.' As his face darkened with threat, she added, 'Go ahead, Pete, just try to hit me. Even if we weren't in my mother's house, do you want to take bets that my big, protective lover is behind the door just dying for you to make the wrong move?'

Within a second, a tap sounded on the door, very soft, one only—letting them both know she wasn't alone.

Rachel watched Pete's gaze swivel to the door for a moment. His fists loosened, and she saw him for the total coward he was. Any man who'd only hit a much smaller woman, and only when there was no chance of his being hurt, wasn't worth fighting. 'I don't need Armand to protect me from the likes of you. I don't need you now, Pete. You don't love me, and I don't love you. I don't even *like* you. You're a cheat, a liar and a bully. You were lucky to have me for as long as you did.'

'You wouldn't have dared say that to me if your boyfriend wasn't here to give you courage,' he spat, shaking with what she guessed was the desire to hit her—the only way he could prove his dominance now he'd lost emotional control over her.

'Probably not,' she admitted. 'But it felt pretty good to say it anyway.'

'I don't like my lady being insulted, Rinaldi. I like it even less when a coward like you tries to intimidate or threaten her.'

As Pete made an odd squeaking sound, Rachel glanced at the doorway. Armand filled it with his darkness, with flashing eyes and clenched fists, like an avenging angel. One step in, and he was towering over Pete, who suddenly seemed small. Was he cringing?

'You're a pathetic piece of work, to put this on Rachel while she's grieving.' Armand spoke slowly, almost glittering cold. 'You will not speak to Rachel again. You will not insult her, hurt her or make empty threats, Rinaldi, because mine are *not* empty. If you touch Rachel again I will break a lot more than your wrist. I'll make sure your face is no longer pretty enough for TV—and then I'll destroy you.'

The words seemed so much fiercer for their being quiet and controlled. After a long moment in which Pete neither moved nor spoke, Armand added with cool contempt, 'I'd leave now if you want any chance of resurrecting your career. You have ten seconds, Rinaldi. Close the door on your way out.'

Without even looking at Pete again, Armand glanced at his watch. Pete scuttled out without a word, squeezing past Armand with white face and terrified eyes. The door closed quietly behind him. The click felt definite. A door closed.

As he looked at her, Armand's eyes softened. 'Are you okay?'

She nodded, feeling awkward. 'I'm sorry about Mama being so cold with you today. She believes marriage is for ever, and to have two divorced daughters…'

She felt the sentence trailing into emptiness and opened her mouth to speak.

His hands touched her shoulders. He smiled down at her,

giving her space and comfort at once. 'Don't defend her, Rachel, there's no need. She needs to be angry at somebody right now. I don't mind it. My shoulders are broad enough.'

'That's so typical of you—you always say the right thing. How can you be so perfect all the time?' she burst out suddenly, losing it without warning. 'Don't you ever say stupid things, or get angry or shout, or want to hit…?' Then her foolish mouth stumbled to a halt when she saw the bleak look in his eyes.

'Yes, I do. But I have no urge to hit a woman, or a child,' he said with a calm too practised to be real.

She pulled away. 'What are you doing here with me? Was it just to be for me what you weren't for your mother, Carla and Johanna?'

His jaw worked for a moment but, though his fists clenched, he released them, slow and steady. He was pale, but his eyes burned as he looked at her. 'As I said, my shoulders are broad, Rachel. You need to yell at someone, here I am. Hit me if you need to. I can take it.'

'Of course you can, you're…' As fast as it came, her irrational anger dissipated—and far too late she finally understood. *Your father hit you long before you were twelve.*

She didn't need to ask. Of course his father had hit him. Small Armand, still a little boy, had taken the beatings so his mother and his sisters wouldn't have to be hurt—until he'd realised it had saved his family nothing. And, when he'd broken his father's nose in an attempt to stop the pain, he'd been sent away for his trouble.

Little Armand, only twelve years old, had been sent to a boarding school far from home for the crime of trying to save his family from being hurt.

No wonder he'd crossed the world for her. Small Armand had been helpless to stop the abuse; Armand the man would never allow it again. And, because she wanted more than she'd ever have with him, she'd repaid his unrelenting care and healing by sticking a knife into ancient, unhealed wounds he'd refused to show the world.

*Dysfunctional Rachel strikes again...*

'Armand,' she whispered. 'I...' She floundered, looking at those eyes, so cold, withdrawn. Devastated beneath. The protective wolf fought for everyone else, but was still a wounded cub inside. Curling over the pain, he refused to allow anyone to see it let alone touch it.

She closed her eyes. In her need to lash out, she'd hit the one person who'd shown her nothing but care and loyalty. 'Armand, I'm sorry. I should never have...'

He turned away. 'I think I'll go for a walk.'

Then it clicked, and she knew what she had to do. 'Are you afraid you'll hit me if you stay with me? If I make you angry enough, you'll take a swing at me like you did to your father? Is that it?'

She asked it in deliberate challenge, waiting, watching, to see how he'd react.

He neither moved nor spoke. The stiff back and half-curled fists answered for him.

'Because I don't believe it,' she stated, softly taunting. 'You were right before. I don't believe you'd hurt any woman or child, no matter what provocation they give you.' Though she was pushing him, his stillness hurt her heart; she had to reach out, to touch him. Her hand curled around his. 'You are not your father's son, not in the way you fear most. You are a good, strong, wonderful man, Armand Bollinger. The only person who doesn't believe in you *is you*.'

Her hand fell from his when he pulled his away. He didn't turn back; he was still stood looking at the door. 'I didn't ask for your faith,' he said quietly. 'From the start, I've asked

for nothing from you but an endorsement, Rachel.' And he
walked out the door—that wretched farewell door he'd been
watching constantly since the day they had met.

# CHAPTER FOURTEEN

IT WAS so hard to find sanctuary when you were in an unfamiliar place.

When you could walk away from the woman who made you feel too damned much, who never knew when to stop pushing your buttons, but you couldn't make yourself leave her entirely. When it was the night of her father's funeral, she needed support more than she knew and she was surrounded by people who cared but were weak and defensive, who didn't understand her at all.

*Go on, take it out on me. I can handle it.*

The words came back to taunt Armand as he strode the streets of this upscale Austin neighbourhood, seeking solace in solitude, but what had always come before with ease now eluded him like a child playing hide-and-seek. Because this time he couldn't handle it, couldn't take the blows. Rachel needed him to be strong, to take her grief on his shoulders—but, even though her life was shattered and her future uncertain, her hits had come at him like knife blades in his solar plexus. Because Rachel was the one woman who saw past the barriers in his eyes as if they were open doors to his soul…and still she found something to like there, to desire. To Rachel, he wasn't the weak and shivering child he'd always known was there. The boy who'd failed everyone he loved.

What the hell did she see in him?

He heard the heavy breathing, the running steps and high-pitched whining gasps, and knew it wasn't an evening jogger.

'Rachel, give me some space,' he growled, increasing his pace.

One whine, another and another as she caught her breath. 'I need you, Armand. Please.'

The words were guaranteed to stop him in his tracks and, damn her, she knew it. But the grief lacing her voice wasn't feigned, and he'd already turned back before he'd made the conscious decision. 'What is it?' he asked, tense.

'I can't stay here,' she panted. 'I have to get away.'

Even in the uncertain glow of the street lights, he saw she was trembling, could see the bewildered pain in her eyes. 'What did they do?'

'It's—it's so hard. I thought things might change after yesterday, but Mama's pressuring me to go back to Pete. She keeps talking about my vows before God being binding; Pete's playing the penitent-sinner card with her. And Sara...' She shook her head, looking at her feet, those shuffling feet. 'Sara resents me, because of you.'

Armand frowned. 'Me?'

'Don't pretend you don't know, Armand,' she said flatly. 'I saw the way she looked at you tonight, we all did.'

Yes, he knew. He'd seen the look in Rachel's sister's eyes tonight, after the wake had ended and the relatives and friends had gone home. It was as if Sara had noticed he was there for the first time—and she'd liked what she'd seen.

He met her gaze, shadowy with more than the night. 'And the famous psychologist would rather run away than deal with it?'

Her mouth pushed out before she spoke. 'That would depend on what you want in that area, wouldn't it?'

Something he'd eaten at dinner churned in his stomach.

'I am not your father—or your ex. I've never cheated on a woman in my life.'

'Even if you want to,' she whispered. It wasn't a question.

'You said you saw her looking at me. Did you see me looking back?' he demanded.

She lifted her face, her smile holding more than the shadows beyond the moon's soft light. 'You're such a gentleman. Even if you wanted to, I know you wouldn't do that, not in front of my family. And it's not like we were really together. A few kisses, a bit of talk, really doesn't mean a thing.'

The shrug she gave was the most eloquent piece of nothing he'd ever seen, a tiny movement. It told him a story of a girl, a woman who'd never known faith in someone else, a girl whose best had never been good enough. She expected him to go. Even if he could tell her how he felt, if he could convince himself he was the man to make her happy, she'd never believe it, or at least not for long.

Just then, some words of Rachel's to Rinaldi came back to him: *I will not enable your delusions.* And he knew what he had to do. Just as she'd set his family free of their chains of pain and shame, he had to let Rachel go to find what she truly wanted. If he didn't, he'd never be more than her emotional umbrella, her place of hiding.

'I'm heading back home tomorrow, Rachel. I need to get to work on the third resort. I suggest you go to Los Angeles,' he said quietly, moving a step back so she couldn't see his face and understand the exquisite pain ripping through him. The sacrifice he must make for her sake.

'What?' The bewildered pain on her face seemed to bounce off the moonlight and streetlight like twin accusations, and the anguish doubled. *Come with me, spend your life with me and I'll protect you from everything that could possibly hurt you, including me.* Wasn't that what he did best, what he'd always done? And it was only now, facing the woman he loved beyond life or breath, that he knew it wasn't enough. Not for Rachel, and not for him.

'You forced me out of hiding, Rachel. You made me face my past, my weaknesses, and give my family what they needed. Now you have to do the same for yourself and your family.' He forced himself to sound expressionless when his entire body was aching to scoop her up and hold her, to protect her from anything that could hurt or upset her.

Or make her grow into a fully-functioning adult.

'It's time to stop running and face your life. Find out what you want and then do it, no matter what everyone else tells you to do. Go to Los Angeles. Meet with your producers, your agent and whoever else has been pressuring you and tell them what *you* want.'

She shuddered. 'No, I won't. I can't.'

*Stand still. Don't touch her, or give her an excuse to hide.* 'You did it with Pete.'

'Because you were there!' she cried.

He put a finger over her mouth. 'It's always harder the first time, and even the second.'

Beseeching eyes looked up at him. 'Armand, please…not now, not this day.'

As the knife twisted in him, he realised something, something big: she was playing him. Yes, unconsciously, she was using every trick in her psychologist's bag again but this time to make him give in to his wolf's nature, the need to protect, wisely or unwisely. He had to stop it, or those he loved would never become the people they needed to be.

So he turned his back on her, and those beautiful, drenched eyes that said *I need you.* 'Psychologist, heal thyself,' he said, forcing his voice to sound brutal. 'I might have chosen the worst day for this, but on any other day it will still be what you need to do. Go to Los Angeles and sort out your life. I'll see you when you come to endorse the resorts—but don't come to me unless you're the woman I've always seen in you. I want to see you taking charge of your life, being the woman who knows I'd never want to cheat on her and is ready to commit to a functioning relationship. A relationship without a shelf-life.'

'Says he who's always run through the first open door he sees?' she snarled.

'Yes, says that man,' he said quietly. 'But I'm not that man tonight. This is the man you made me. You made me stop running and listen to all that I denied.'

'You ran tonight.'

'No. I tried, but it didn't work.' Truth rang in his every word because as he said it he believed it. 'You've changed me, Rachel. I might have walked away tonight, but I can't run from who I am. And neither can you. I won't let you use me to become someone you're not, weak and clinging to me because you're afraid to face the world.'

He didn't say it, but they both heard it: *I'm not Pete.*

'What if I don't know who I am?' she asked, her voice thick.

'The woman who changed my entire family within hours knows exactly who she is,' he said with finality. 'The woman who took over my home and changed my life was comfortable with herself before I met her, and after. She didn't change herself to impress me or meet the expectations of others, and I respected her for that. That's the woman I kissed, the woman I want a relationship with. The woman you lost within minutes of walking into your mother's house.'

Her voice was wobbling, drenched in misery. 'And you think I'll find her again in LA?'

She gave that adorable, vulnerable sniff. Armand had to curl his fists into hard balls to stop from turning to her, snatching her close and telling her he'd make everything all right. 'If not there, then somewhere else. Either way, I hope you do, Rachel—because, if you don't, I don't want you.' He sounded so damned harsh, but there was no choice but to say it, now he'd begun on this, the worst night he could possibly have chosen to attack her. 'I want to be with the woman I knew in Switzerland. Rachel Chase isn't a weak and dependent woman. She's as strong as she is fragile, as beautiful as she is self-deprecating, and she's as honest with herself as others. She doesn't need me to take on her fights while she hides. She can fight her battles and she won't doubt my fidelity. She'll know I'll be there for her when she's done, win or lose. She'll know she's the only woman I want. If you can't be that Rachel, then I release you from the endorsement; don't come back to me.'

In the sounds of her tiny snuffles, he recognised and accepted that he'd made her cry and he hated it. Longing to hold her, he stayed with his back to her. It was the only way.

Then there was a long silence, and he hoped she was thinking it through.

It took about two minutes to realise he was alone. She'd left without a sound.

Rachel had walked away from him this time, and he knew that by the time he found her mother's house again she'd be gone.

The wait was on. He just hoped he hadn't pushed her too far, that she'd come back to him—because he didn't know how many days or nights he'd be able to stand wandering in emotional darkness without her smile, her laughter and her touch to bring him to life.

*Six months later*

'So this is it, folks. I'm signing off from *Lifestyle Choices* on a weekly basis, though I will be hosting the occasional special.' Rachel smiled at the crowd of adoring fans' faces surrounding her and then at the camera. 'Look out for the first of my *Lifestyle Choices* later in the year. Good night, and remember—' she grinned as everyone in the audience chanted her mantra out loud '—if you don't love yourself as you are, nobody else will either!'

She laughed and waved as the camera went into fadeout. She spent another hour signing autographs and talking to members of the audience, many of whom were regulars begging her not to leave, that *Lifestyle Choices* was their favourite programme.

But she was done with fulfilling everyone's dreams but her own.

'Great show, Rachel,' Andy Sykes, the show's executive producer, walked her to her dressing room. 'I saw the preliminary specs. This one's gonna rate through the roof.'

'Then hopefully the first special will too, Andy. But if not, I won't cry.'

'You know, if you want…'

Rachel smiled. 'I don't want, Andy. No more contract talk. I'm happy with my decision.' Seeing his dejected face, she hugged him and kissed his cheek. Then she closed the door, and turned to finish the packing she'd begun before the show.

She had started packing long before the first *Lifestyle Choices* had aired. She'd lived the entire six months in LA half-packed. But the show was something she'd needed to do for herself, without her mama's approval, without Pete driving her on to success—and without Armand having her back.

Standing alone. *Psychologist, heal thyself.*

She'd done it, faced her life. She'd faced Sara even before she'd left Austin that night six months ago. 'Find your own man, Sara, and stop trying to take mine. I won't apologise for my life, or give up what I want to make you happy.'

And, in seeing Sara buckle and make a slightly resentful peace with her sister, Rachel had known herself for the first time—had known what she wanted and understood what she had to do. Armand was right. She'd had to be free to find herself, to know what she wanted, before she'd been able to make her own choices.

She'd flown to LA, and accepted a six-month contract for the show that became *Lifestyle Choices*, having three separate lawyers check the contract to make certain there was no clause to force her into staying. Despite unrelenting pressure from everyone around her, she'd made a calm announcement on the first show that she was divorcing Pete, that they'd never reconciled, and that they never would. If people wanted her advice, it would be from someone who wasn't perfect, who'd made mistakes and wrong choices in her life. But divorcing Pete wasn't one of them.

That show, as Andy had just said, had rated through the roof, and tickets to be in the live audience had sold out for the entire season within hours.

Throughout the six months, she'd ignored all questions regarding her relationship with Armand, and refused all demands for disclosure from the press and the network.

During the whole time, she'd utterly refused to see Pete. Rejected by the network, he'd had to settle for a cable show that had fizzled within weeks. When it had failed, he'd inundated her with flowers—but when his calls, compliments, insults, threats and demands had bored her, she'd changed her address and phone number. When he'd come to the studio, she'd had him thrown out. When he'd tried her family, she'd gone to court, facing him as she'd got a permanent restraining order. The x-rays and doctors' report had come to light, and Pete's name became mud in LA.

Last she'd heard, he'd been pounding the pavement trying to sell his latest idea for a sitcom.

She'd faced each of her mother's tearful calls with the dignity she'd never known in her family life. 'Mama, I never loved him as you loved Daddy. Pete broke his vows, not me. I have no desire to forgive him, and less to have him in my life. If you want a relationship with me, it will be on my terms.'

After three months, she'd got her divorce certificate, and had barely restrained herself from throwing a 'freedom party' on the show, but her glowing face had said it all. It hadn't even shocked her when her mother had had her to Sunday dinner with Sara and the boys that week.

The dinner had been surprisingly pleasant, no guilt trips, no demands. Sara had found a new man. Bill Manning wasn't a doctor, wasn't a rich man or famous in any way, but he made her happy—in fact, Sara was glowing. Bill had come in time for dessert, and Rachel had liked him immediately. His quiet sense of self would be good for Sara.

As she flew back over the lights of LA that night, she had a silent epiphany. Freeing herself from Pete and her sham of a marriage, from family expectation and the feeling of never being good enough, had set her free of the shadows of the past. Thanks to Armand. And she realised how much he'd denied his very nature to give her this priceless gift.

And she loved him more than ever, ached for those nights they'd never had.

But now, she was free of all her obligations. She'd done everything she'd set out to do, and she'd done it alone. It was time to go to Armand—and hope it wasn't too late.

# CHAPTER FIFTEEN

'THAT was very good, Rachel, but I really think that if we try just one more take we could make it perfect.'

Smiling that impish, sparkling happy grin, an immaculately dressed Rachel shook her head at the director and began pulling out the hair extensions that were so famous. 'Sorry, Manfred, but you see I don't do perfect.' Those shimmering eyes turned to Armand in cheeky challenge. 'What about you, Herr Bollinger? Do you want the perfect endorsement?'

What he wanted couldn't be expressed in public, but it must have been almost pathetically obvious that he was dying to get Rachel alone. Armand hadn't taken his eyes off her for a second since she'd arrived in Geneva by jet this morning, and everyone knew it.

Except maybe Rachel. If she'd noticed, there hadn't been a sign. She had been sweet, adorable, funny and professional all day. Her mind was on the endorsement.

'I think the last take was excellent, Manfred, thank you,' he said, striving to sound even. 'Ms Chase is right. We don't need perfection, and the light's beginning to fade.'

Here, Armand's word was law. Manfred sighed and muttered about edits, but accepted defeat. He called to pack up.

Armand strained to hold in his need as he walked over to her trailer. Inside, she stood pliant while the stylist removed the last of the hair extensions, scolding her for trying to do it alone, and the make-up artist removed the layers of paint needed for the cameras. Then she turned her face half an inch to be in his line of sight. She gave him that tongue-in-cheek smile and winked at him, and his body went into hyperdrive. He'd had to walk away before he snatched her into his arms and kissed her senseless.

All day she'd been the Rachel he wanted, the Rachel he'd demanded she become. It was driving him crazy to be so close, but never alone with her. Was she punishing him for asking too much? She didn't seem tense or angry; there was no yearning in her eyes, only sweet teasing.

Was she over him? Had she only come here for the damned endorsement?

Then, hours later it seemed to him, she emerged from her trailer, her pixie-cut hair back to normal wearing the jeans and trainers she preferred. She was *his* Rachel again—right down to the T-shirt that read, *sometimes your knight in shining armour is just a jerk in tin foil.*

He wanted to make a joke of it but then, wondering if it was a hint, he held it in.

'Shall we?' he asked quietly, pointing to his car, and she nodded.

They walked to the car in a silence that whispered 'awkward'.

'It's even more beautiful here than I remembered,' she said at last, her gaze on the valley, the Alps rising behind in spring-time beauty. 'How is your family? How is Claire? I'd love to see her. Is she at home?'

The warm tone made his heart pound. 'Everyone's fine. They all sent their love and want to see you too. Johanna and Carla came with their families when I said you'd be here. We can go see them now, if you like.' He added with difficulty, 'They're real fans of your show. They all watch it every week.'

'I'd love to see them.' They reached the Range Rover and,

though he moved to hand her in, she jumped up herself. 'I'm so glad they like the show—but they'll have to wait a long time for the next one. I've decided to go in a new direction.'

She pulled the door closed. Taking his cue with a heart filled with uncertainty, he walked around the car and got in. 'Care to share what that direction will be?' he asked far too casually as he drove down towards the gate of the almost-finished resort. 'You never mentioned it on the air.' He'd watched every damned show, drinking her in, jealous as hell of everyone who got to see her, to talk to her, to touch her. He wondered every show if she could give it all up, if she'd ever come to him or if he'd have to swallow his pride and demands and go to her. He'd wondered if he could ever tell her she'd set him free. He was *not* his father's son, and her speaking that fear aloud, telling him of her faith, had been like letting a non-existent monster out of the cupboard.

He'd been on the verge of booking a jet to go to her, with visions in his head of needing to beg her forgiveness or seduce her into coming home with him, when her agent had called to say Rachel wanted the endorsement set up. She'd be in Switzerland within a week.

'No. I didn't want the world to know.' Rachel stared out the window, drinking in the view, the alpine flowers dotting the landscape and lush grass. She spoke as if from a distance. 'I want to open a series of domestic-violence shelters and provide support for women and kids who feel they have nowhere to go, no one to listen to them or care. I was wondering if your mother or sisters would be interested in helping.' She turned to him, but her smile seemed remote. 'As fellow survivors, I think we'd have something valuable to give.'

It was like another hit to his solar plexus—but, as ever with Rachel, it was a correct hit, making him a better man. Sincerely, he said, 'I think they might do it. I think it's a wonderful way to use your best talents, Rachel. It's a brilliant idea—and I'd like to invest in it as much as you need.'

'Thank you,' she said quietly. 'But I was also hoping you might be interested in talking to the boys, the brothers and fathers? They'll need healing too.'

It was so tentative, that question, but without hesitation he answered, 'Yes, I would.' In fact, again it felt so damned right he wondered why he'd never thought of it.

It seemed he still had room to grow. He'd just needed Rachel to show him the way.

In the silence, he glanced over at her and saw the tears shimmering in her eyes: big as Texas, big as her heart—but was that heart his? He had to know. But he'd pushed her away, he'd made her do all these months of work, he'd set the demands in place. Now he had to wait for her to be ready to say what she felt.

'Thank you,' she said very softly, but as if she was thinking of something else.

'Are you okay?' he asked, feeling concerned. 'You've been working hard all day, and you must be so tired—jet lag is no joke. Do you want to rest?'

All of a sudden the unreal calm left her. 'No, I don't want to *rest*. I didn't cross the world for sleep. I want…wanted to tell you… Oh, darn it, Armand.'

This was it. Heart pounding like he'd run a race, he pulled over to the side of the road, just outside the village, and cut the engine. Looking at her, he saw her legs jumping up and down, her hands twisting around each other.

'Just say it, Rachel,' he said softly, lifting her chin, looking into eyes that weren't cheeky or challenging, but fragile, with wishes unuttered. 'Tell me what you want.'

Her gaze fell. 'Armand, I want… I hope that you still… Oh, drat it, I think I'm in love with you,' she blurted out, as if she hated every word.

As if she hadn't handed him the world all at once.

'You *think* you are in love with me?' he teased, his heart soaring. *She loves me.*

Her brow deepened in a frown. 'Look, I wanted to give you an out, if you only want a temporary thing with me.' She bit her lip, sniffed twice.

'I see,' he said gravely, holding in the laughter of pure joy. 'You *think* you are in love with me? It's really not good enough, *mon doux*. Either you are or you're not.'

At that gentle challenge ending with the endearment, her jaw jutted and her eyes flashed as they met his. 'You're not saying what you want,' she pointed out. 'You're not saying if you want it.'

'I know one thing. I don't want you to *think* you might love me.' He restrained the grin at the indignant look she shot at him. 'I want you to be brave, *mon coeur.*'

'All right, then.' With a determined look, she spilled out words. 'I'm crazy about you. I love you, I'll always love you, and I'm here for as long as you want me, all right? When you want me to go, I'll go, but I won't want to leave you ever. Okay? Did I say it right that time?'

She said it so fast, as if she was afraid she'd never say it at all unless she did it in a bunch. Armand didn't dare laugh yet, but the champagne bubbles of happiness were rising so fast he could barely contain it. As declarations of love went, it was the most aggressive, funny and ridiculous one he'd ever heard—but nothing had ever meant so much to him. 'It's all perfectly clear now,' he assured her with a quivering mouth. 'So you'll go when I say?' he added, pensive. 'But…what if I don't say it? What if I want…for ever?' As he spoke, he reached into his pocket, brought out a little box, and opened it.

Rachel gasped at the lovely, clean-cut diamond engagement ring and its mate nestled together. 'Armand…?'

'What if I say you're the most wonderful thing that ever happened to me?' he went on, taking the engagement ring out. 'What if I say you changed me and made me a happy man who's no longer afraid of commitment or of being his father's son? What if I say the last six months have been like a bleak wasteland without you and I never want to live another day, another hour, without you?'

Rachel sniffed again, but her eyes were twinkling. 'I'd say that all sounds lovely, but not quite romantic enough.'

At that, he burst out laughing. 'That's my Rachel. So, shall I say *I think I love you*?' he taunted, his eyes dancing.

She punched his arm. 'I'm waiting,' she said pugnaciously, but that adorable, big radiant smile was spreading across her face, lighting the car, lighting his life once again.

He couldn't help it; he kissed that inexpressibly kissable mouth and felt the rightness of it here in his mother's family village. History was repeating itself in the most beautiful way…a centuries-old tradition carried on and begun in the same moment.

Replete, and yet craving more, he pulled away an inch, kissed her again and then spoke. 'I've never said these words to any woman. I thought I never would—and then I met you. I'm crazy in love with you, Rachel Chase. I have been for months, and I always will be. I want you to be my wife, the mother of my children. I want to build a home here with you, raise our family and grow old—together; always together.' He held up the ring. 'Will you do all that with me?'

She was sobbing now, hiccupping breaths, but she stammered, 'Yes, yes, *yes*!' She only waited long enough for him to slide the ring on her finger before jumping at him, but she was restrained by her seat belt and fell back with a jerking movement. 'Oh, trust me to ruin my big romantic moment,' she grumbled.

Giddy, heady with the happiness only she had ever given

him, he laughed. 'Ah, my adorable Rachel, I've missed you like crazy. Don't ever change, and don't leave me again.' He undid her belt buckle and his, and she jumped a second time, landing with a breathless thump in his lap.

'I never thought I could trust a man again,' she whispered between frantic kisses. 'But then there was you, my knight.'

'Sometimes I'll just be that jerk in tin foil, you know,' he whispered back, laughing. 'But I will always be *your* jerk in tin foil.'

'Mine for always,' she agreed, her eyes shimmering with love, and kissed him again.

And, even though the entire Bollinger family was waiting to celebrate the greatly-hoped-for engagement, they waited for hours with their champagne slowly warming and their balloons slowly deflating. They didn't get their hugs and kisses, or to start the party for a very long time.

But they didn't mind at all.

\* \* \* \* \*

# DARING TO DATE
# THE BOSS

BY
BARBARA WALLACE

All the characters in this book have no existence outside the imagination of
the author, and have no relation whatsoever to anyone bearing the same name
or names. They are not even distantly inspired by any individual known or
unknown to the author, and all the incidents are pure invention.

First published in Great Britain 2012
by Mills & Boon, an imprint of Harlequin (UK) Limited,
Eton House, 18-24 Paradise Road, Richmond, Surrey TW9 1SR

© Barbara Wallace 2012

ISBN: 978 0 263 89397 7

23-0112

Harlequin (UK) policy is to use papers that are natural, renewable and
recyclable products and made from wood grown in sustainable forests. The
logging and manufacturing processes conform to the legal environmental
regulations of the country of origin.

Printed and bound in Spain
by Blackprint CPI, Barcelona

Dear Reader,

This book has a special place in my heart because it's the first time my heroine has a child. As a mother myself, I understand the desire to give your child all the opportunities life has to offer. So often we as parents sacrifice so our kids can live their dreams. We sit through sports practices, we invest in tutors, we worry about their futures, etc. This is the world my heroine, Liz Strauss, lives in. Only she has it far tougher. As a single mother, she is not only a parent, but the head of the household, which means dealing with all the day-to-day challenges that come with working and trying to maintain a home. On top of all that, she's carrying some pretty heavy baggage. No wonder she's ruled out romance!

Then there's Charles, my hero. There's something fun about taking a confident man and putting him in a world where he is completely out of his element. In this case, he's transplanted into wintery New England where hockey and slippery roads are the order of the day. Writing this story in the middle of a very snowy winter, I could totally identify with his desire to leave for warmer climates. Sometimes a little too much!

I loved taking these two characters, neither of whom is even thinking about falling in love, on a trip toward happily ever after. Deep down they are both such lonely souls. I was glad to play fictional matchmaker.

One other reason this book was so special: Liz's son Andrew. By the way, at this very moment the real-life Andrew will be waiting on his college admissions. It's not often a mother gets to capture her son's quirks and personality on the page. He was a good sport about the whole process.

As always, I love hearing from readers. Please contact me at Barbara@BarbaraWallace.com and tell me what you think!

Happy reading!

*Barbara Wallace*

**Barbara Wallace** has been a life-long romantic and daydreamer so it's not surprising she decided to become a writer at age eight. However, it wasn't until a co-worker handed her a romance novel that she knew where her stories belonged. For years she limited her dreams to nights, weekends and commuter train trips while working as a communications specialist, PR freelancer and full-time mom. At the urging of her family, she finally chucked the day job and pursued writing full time and couldn't be happier.

Barbara lives in Massachusetts with her husband, their teenage son, and two very spoiled, self-centered cats (as if there could be any other kind). Readers can visit her at www.barbarawallace.com and find her on Facebook. She'd love to hear from you.

To my family, as always, for all their love and support.
And to the real Andrew, Victoria, and Sammy.
Thanks for being such great kids.

# CHAPTER ONE

"Mom! Have you seen my history book?"

Liz Strauss let out a deep breath. She swore her son's baritone could be heard in the town house next door. "Where did you last use it?"

"If I knew that I wouldn't be asking."

Sure he would. Asking was so much easier than say, actually looking for the book. "Try next to the computer!" One of these days they would have to start communicating like normal people rather than hollering back and forth through rooms.

Today would not be that day. "Found it!" he called a moment later. "It was on the kitchen counter."

Near the food. Naturally. Crisis averted, for now, she returned to rehearsing her speech.

"Well, Mr. Bishop, as you know, my workload has increased since you arrived...."

Too whiny. She wanted to at least *sound* smart and sophisticated, since looking that way appeared out of the question. Staring at her reflection, she smoothed some imaginary wrinkles from the front of her turtleneck. Her chin length bob clung to her head like a limp brown helmet. In trying to stave off static electricity, she'd overdosed on conditioner again. She looked like a drab, helmet-wearing dud.

Taking a deep breath, she resumed rehearsing. "Seeing as how my responsibilities have increased, I was hoping… No, I believe…" *Believe* was a much better word. "I *believe* I deserve…"

Why was this so hard? She'd been practicing since the shower, and still had no idea what she was going to say.

If Ron Bishop were still president, she'd simply say "Hey, Ron, Andrew has a chance to attend Trenton Academy, I need a raise to cover tuition."

Unfortunately she no longer worked for Ron, God rest his soul. No, she worked for his son, a man she'd never knew existed until three months ago. What did he care about private school tuition or opportunities of a lifetime? He was too busy decimating everything his father stood for.

On the other hand, she really did deserve a raise. Since arriving, Bishop had run her ragged. Then there was the steady stream of complaints caused by his new policies. Not a day went by that an angry manager didn't stop her to vent their frustrations. If you asked her, she deserved hazard pay for playing gatekeeper alone.

Maybe that should be her argument, she thought with a wry smile.

A small television sat on the corner of her bureau. On screen, a perky weatherwoman chirped about potential snowfall. *Her* bob, Liz noticed with annoyance, shimmered and swung under the studio lights as she waved her perfectly manicured hand in front of the map. "Depending on the storm's timing, we could be looking at a very messy evening commute," she said, sounding practically giddy.

When weren't they looking at a messy commute these days? Liz switched off the woman and her annoyingly bouncy hair. It was getting late. Rehearsal would have to wait.

As she padded down the stairs to the main floor, Liz caught sight of the old juice stain marring the bottom step and did her best to quell her frustration. She had hoped to finally replace the old Berber carpeting this spring, but those plans would have to wait. She couldn't afford both home improvements and private school tuition. Heck, she could barely afford private school tuition alone unless she got this raise.

In the kitchen, her son, Andrew, was attempting to simultaneously stuff books in his backpack and half a bagel into his mouth. His six-foot-three frame and flailing arms took up most of the space, and she nearly had to duck to avoid being struck by a stray limb. He got his gangly height from her. Surprising their combined twelve feet could actually fit in the small space.

"One of these mornings you're going to choke," she remarked, grabbing a coffee mug from the open cupboard.

"Least then I wouldn't have to take my calculus exam," he shot back.

"Right, because death is always preferable to taking a test."

"This test, yes."

Calculus had been the bane of her son's existence all year long. "Why? You studied, didn't you?"

Although partially hidden by floppy brown bangs,

Liz caught his eye roll. "Like that matters. Mr. Rueben hates our entire class. He wants us to fail so he can have an excuse to yell at us."

Drama. Native language of the American teenager. Liz suppressed an eye roll of her own. "I'm sure he doesn't hate you. If you studied, you'll do fine."

Andrew took the coffee cup from her hand and washed down his bagel. "You always say that."

"And you always say you're going to fail. Score one for consistency." She snatched her coffee back. "Do you want me to pour you your own cup?"

"Don't have time. Vic's picking me up early so we can cram before school."

"Cram, huh?" A familiar lump dropped in the pit of her stomach. Victoria was a smart, sweet girl, she reminded herself. A nice girl.

A nice girl who had her own car and with whom her seventeen-year-old son was head over heels in love. Memories of backseats and misplaced teenage passion flashed before her eyes.

*He's not you, Liz.* So desperate to feel wanted, he'd toss the future away at the first sweet words of affection. From the moment she delivered him, she'd made sure Andrew never went a day feeling less than one hundred perfectly loved and wanted.

A car horn sounded outside.

"That's Vic," Andrew announced unnecessarily as he grabbed his bag. "See you after practice."

"Tell Victoria to drive carefully. The roads could get slippery later today."

"Yes, ma'am." Another eye roll. Wonder if he knew

when he was doing it, or if the gesture was automatic, like breathing.

"Hey, sue me for not wanting my only child hurt in a car accident," she told him.

"If it would get me out of this exam…"

"Don't even joke about it, mister." She silenced him with a wag of her index finger. "Good luck on your test. And be—"

He was out the door before she could finish the sentence.

Mug gripped between her hands, Liz fought the urge to watch and make sure they pulled out of her driveway safely. Andrew wasn't a little boy anymore. He didn't need his mother hovering like a helicopter, watching his every move. Knowing so, however, didn't make cutting the cord any easier.

Time moved way too fast. Seemed like only yesterday he was a seven-year-old clamoring to stay up past eight o'clock. Now here he was on the cusp of adulthood with a chance, if the Trenton hockey coach was to be believed, to earn a scholarship to a major university. Barring any stupid mistakes, her job was almost finished. She'd done good, she decided. Better than her parents. Then again, they hadn't set the bar all that high, had they?

Out of the corner of her eye, she caught her reflection in the microwave. How was it possible that her hair got flatter from the time she left the bedroom until now? Tipping her head upside down, she tried fluffing the strands with her fingers like they did at the hair salon. All that did was make her hair look like a static-laden mushroom.

Good thing she was banking on her efficiency and not her looks to charm her boss. As if the man could be charmed by anything but a spreadsheet anyway. Most of the employees were convinced he was some kind of walking computer.

Maybe that's what she should do. Lay out her arguments in a spreadsheet and shove the paper under his nose. Then she wouldn't have to worry about her hair or anything else.

Chuckling to herself, Liz sipped her coffee. If she thought the idea would actually work, she would. In the meantime, she'd better figure out what she was going to say to convince her boss to give her a raise. Andrew was going to Trenton Academy next year come hell or high water. He'd gone without enough in his short life. Her baby boy would have all the opportunities she never had, no matter what. Even if she had to beg, borrow or steal to do so. Today she planned on begging.

Hopefully Charles Bishop felt like giving.

Liz had planned on arriving at the office extra early to allow herself time to compose before making her request. Unfortunately she got stuck behind the middle-school bus and had to endure stopping every five minutes through downtown Gilmore and extra early didn't happen. In fact, plain old regular early barely happened. As she slipped out of her wool coat and fired up her computer, Liz wondered if she would even have time to catch her breath. She hoped to make her request first thing, before Bishop got engrossed in those spreadsheets he loved so much.

Maybe she'd luck out and he'd get stuck in traffic,

too. Although then he might be in a bad mood, and she didn't want that, either.

"Good morning, Elizabeth."

Drat. He'd arrived on time. Figures.

Flashing her best professional smile, she reached behind her and retrieved a sheet of paper from the printer. "Good morning. I was about to put today's itinerary on your desk."

As usual, the new CEO of Bishop Paper looked like a million dollars. Or multimillion, if Liz was to be accurate. Cashmere overcoat, designer wool suit, custom-cut shirt. He looked as natural standing in the no-nonsense offices as a marble sculpture at a flea market. His features, chiseled by anyone's standards, were dark and somber as he slipped the itinerary from her hand.

"Did Accounting deliver the revenue projections yet?" he asked, eyes scanning the schedule.

More spreadsheets. The man was definitely obsessed. "Not yet," she replied.

He raised his eyes to focus on her. Though she hated herself for it, Liz's breath caught. Framed by black lashes so lush it wasn't fair, her boss's cobalt eyes glistened like a pair of bright blue marbles. It wasn't fair that a man so cold and irritating in every other aspect had eyes like that. Why couldn't he have plain old boring eyes like normal people?

"Tell them I'd like the numbers emailed to me by ten o'clock," he told her. "I want to review them before our meeting this afternoon."

"Sure thing." She'd wait until he went into his office before delivering the bad news. Leanne, the VP's secretary, was going to have a fit, and her rants could get loud. Another reason she deserved a pay raise. To compensate for the potential hearing loss.

"I'm also expecting an overnight package from Xinhua Paper," he continued. "Bring it in as soon as it arrives."

With his business complete, her boss moved toward his office door. Liz's palms began to sweat. It was now or never. "I was wondering…" She began.

Hand already on his office door, he paused. His eyes turned in her direction again, causing another skip in her breath. "Yes?"

"Could I have a few moments of your time? I have something I'd like to discuss with you."

He frowned. "Something wrong?"

"No, nothing's wrong." Well, nothing but her salary. "I just wanted to ask you something. Job-related," she felt compelled to add.

"All right." Liz would have felt better if his response hadn't sounded put upon. "Let's go into my office."

His office. Three months and it still sounded strange to hear him refer to his father's domain that way. Yet every time Liz crossed the threshold, she got a hard reminder that Ron Bishop wasn't coming back. While alive, the former CEO filled his office shelves with photos from company events and fundraisers. Shots of him golfing in Bermuda with vendors. A picture of him grilling burgers at the company barbecue. Another of him cheering with staff members at a Boston baseball game.

There hadn't been a single picture of his son, however.

Charles removed the photos the day he arrived. His

idea of decorating consisted of bound data reports. The only vaguely personal item in the room was the super expensive coffeemaker on the corner credenza. The man could leave tomorrow and you'd never know he'd been there.

She waited while he hung up his coat. "What is it you wanted to discuss?"

Liz smoothed the front of her turtleneck, pausing to lay her palm flat against her stomach. "As you know, since you took over, my workload has increased. Not that I'm complaining," she quickly reassured him.

He'd crossed to the credenza and was measuring coffee beans into the built-in grinder. "Glad to hear it." There was a brief whirr and the coffeemaker started up. Liz had to raise her voice to continue.

"I realize when a company changes management, the transition brings a lot of additional work and that having been Ron's administrative assistant for ten years, I'm the best conduit between you and the rest of the company as far as information goes."

Good Lord, did that even make sense?

The grinding ceased making the room quiet once more. Charles pressed Brew. "And?"

Liz paused and took a deep breath. Go big or go home. Isn't that what Andrew and his hockey buddies always said? "And, given my extra workload, I was hoping you'd consider reexamining my salary."

"You want a raise."

"Yes, I do."

The room was silent except for the gurgling drip of the coffeemaker. Charles walked to his desk. With methodical precision, he removed his smart phone from his breast pocket, then slipped off his suit jacket and hung it over the back of his chair. Finally he rolled up his sleeves, smoothing each crisp fold. Liz felt like someone had started practicing slap shots in her stomach.

"You already make a pretty good salary," he finally replied, sitting down. "More than the other administrative assistants on staff."

"Yes, but I also do more than the other administrative assistants," she countered. "Not to mention I put in far more hours. I work late. I bring work home. I come in weekends. In fact, in many companies my position would be considered more than a simple administrative assistant." She was fudging that last part. But didn't Ron always say he couldn't run the company without her?

"No one's questioning your dedication, Elizabeth. Or your value to the company."

Good. Could it be she'd worried for nothing? Although the tiny voice in her head urged otherwise, a small seed of hope took root. She watched as Charles leaned back in his chair, the tips of his long fingers pressed together. "However, I'm in the process of cutting costs. There's a freeze on all reviews and pay increases."

"I know." She'd typed the memo. "I was hoping you would consider making an exception, given the circumstances."

"If I make an exception for you, I have to make an exception for everyone."

Her hope withered and died. "I'm not looking for a huge increase. It's just that my son—"

"Not at the present time, Elizabeth." He cut off her argument before she got started. "You can revisit the issue at your next performance review. In the meantime, I'm sorry."

Sorry, her foot. He wasn't sorry about anything except her wasting his precious time. For the first time since she started as a file clerk, Liz hated where she worked.

Correction. For the first time, she hated the man she worked for.

That same man was reaching for his phone, effectively dismissing her and her request like lint from his expensive slacks. "Make sure accounting gets me those numbers by ten," he said, without looking up.

Liz didn't respond. Why bother? He wouldn't listen anyway. The arrogant, numbers-obsessed, heartless, penny-pinching, arrogant...

She marched straight from the office to the ladies' room, running out of adjectives halfway there. Furious, she kicked the door open. Pain shot from her toe to her knee.

Good. Gave her an excuse for being teary-eyed should anyone ask. Because she absolutely refused to give her boss the satisfaction of seeing her upset. No, she would be strong and stoic and all those other great New England traits. Too bad stoic couldn't erase feeling like she'd been punched.

*No one's questioning your dedication or your workload.* The comment mockingly repeated itself in her head. That was her mistake, she realized, dabbing at her mascara. Getting her hopes up when she heard the compliment. When was she going to learn? Compliments, sweet-talk, promises—none of them meant a thing.

Now what was she going to do? Tell Andrew he

wouldn't be attending Trenton Academy after all? He'd been so excited about the opportunity. *Their players get recruited by Division I schools, Mom. Wouldn't that be cool if I could play for BU or Harvard?* Attending a school like Trenton could open so many doors for Andrew. Doors she never had the chance to even look at. She'd be darned if her son didn't get every opportunity.

Of course, thanks to her boss, she would have to find another way to open those doors. Maybe Bill... Right. She nixed that idea out of the box. Andrew's father hadn't come through in seventeen years. Why on earth would he come through now?

Like always, she was on her own.

Damn Charles Bishop and his belt tightening. She hoped he choked.

"First thing tomorrow morning, James. I'm not paying your firm a retainer to procrastinate." Hanging up, Charles swiveled around in his chair to face the window. Outside, a few stray flakes had begun to fall, their crystal shapes disappearing amidst the blanket of white covering the ground. Off in the distance, the White Mountains disappeared into the gray mist. Gray-white peaks crisscrossed with rock and ski trails.

He couldn't believe he was back in New Hampshire. After all these years, he'd thought the Granite State was forever in his past. A distant, unwelcome memory. Yet here he was, back in Gilmore, saddled with his father's beloved company. The lawyers suggested the inheritance was a final conciliatory gesture, a chance to fix in death what he left broken in life. "Consider it Ron's way of making amends," he'd said.

Charles couldn't care less what the reason was. His father hadn't wanted him; he didn't want his father's blasted company. Clearly, the old man chose the wrong legacy to hang his hat on. Far as he was concerned Bishop Paper was nothing more than another acquisition in a long line of acquisitions. Companies to be turned over as quickly and profitably as possible.

A soft knock sounded on his door. Turning, he saw Elizabeth in his doorway, looking like a beige turtleneck-wearing will-o'-the-wisp. She cleared her throat, the sound immediately calling attention to red-rimmed eyes, evidence of a ladies' room meltdown. No doubt she despised him. Or despised him more, as the case may be, since he was pretty sure he'd been abhorred by everyone since day one. Ice King. Wasn't that what they referred to him as behind his back? Fairly apropos, if you asked him. Certainly his insides felt numb enough.

To his assistant's credit, her reddened eyes were the only evidence of distress. She maintained a steely expression as she approached, her low-heeled pumps crossing neatly one ankle in front of the other.

"Your package from Xinhua," she clipped. A flash of veiled contempt passed across her features as she handed him the thick envelope. Definitely despised him. "Will there be anything else?" she asked.

"Not at the moment," he replied.

Turning on her heel, she strode from the room. Briefly Charles watched her depart, noting how her newly acquired stiffness gave her backside an attractive sway. She'd probably loathe him even more if she knew that's what he was thinking, he thought, corner of his mouth ticking upward.

Once the door clicked shut, he turned his attention to the package in his hands. Huang Bin was nothing if not prompt in his reply.

He'd known from day one, the key to unloading his albatross of an inheritance would lay in Asia. The heydays of New England paper manufacturing were over. For a medium-size manufacturer like Bishop to survive, it needed either an owner dedicated long-term to its success or a parent company large enough it didn't care about the location. And since Charles had zero interest in whether Bishop lived or died...

Fortunately for him, Xinhua Paper was interested in establishing a toehold in America. Soon as legally possible, he planned on selling. Closing the book on Bishop Paper once and for all.

By lunchtime, Liz felt moderately better. All, she conceded, was not lost. There were plenty of ways she could swing tuition. She could get a second job, look into a longer term loan. Or beg Trenton's financial aid office for more money. Their ears couldn't be any more deaf than the man she worked for.

"Who died?" asked Leanne Kenny. The accounting secretary walked into the break room. *Bustled* was a more apt word. Her square, stocky build made any other adjective inadequate.

"My credit score," Liz replied. "Think charging an entire year of school tuition would be a problem?"

"Still trying to get your son into Trenton, huh?" Reaching into the fridge, the older woman pulled out

a set of plastic storage containers filled with salad fix-
ings. "You know, going to public school is hardly the
end of the world."

"I know." Liz also knew Leanne thought her a snob
for wanting otherwise. Like most of the rank and file at
the company, her colleague sent her children to Gilmore
High and couldn't understand why Liz felt so strongly
about this. She didn't understand that for Liz, sending
Andrew to Trenton wasn't about the quality of education. Of course he would do just fine at the town high
school.

Of course, explaining her reasons would mean going
into the sordid details of her misspent youth, something
she wasn't about to do. Bad enough simple math told
part of the story for her.

She changed the subject instead. "Thanks for getting
those reports out this morning. Mr. Bishop was eager
to get them."

"He's always eager," Leanne grumbled. She poured
a container of creamy dressing over her bowl of lettuce.
"Man's definitely not his father. Ron believed in giving
people notice."

True, Liz thought to herself. She tore off a bite of
peanut butter sandwich. Interesting how they all referred to Ron by his first name while his son received
the more formal address. Then, they'd known Ron.
Most of them had worked for the man for years. Unlike
Charles, who they didn't know at all. Their new boss
went out of his way to keep his distance.

Like a king in his tower, she thought, this morning's
bitterness returning.

"What is his fascination with spreadsheets anyway?"

Leanne was asking. "I swear he demands a different report every day."

"The man does like his numbers." Probably looking for more costs to cut.

Leanne leaned forward, her eyes shining like a little girl with a secret. "Paul in Human Resources told me he's cutting the company barbecue. Said that if we wanted to 'play family'—" she framed the words with air quotes "—we could do so on our own time. Talk about harsh."

Harsh indeed. Obviously Charles Bishop was determined to eke out every penny of profit he could out of the company, employees' welfare be damned. How could a man be so different from his father? In this case, the apple hadn't just fallen far from the tree, it had rolled into the next state.

A noise in the doorway caused them both to jump. Since Charles took over, the entire company was on edge, with everyone waiting for the next big bombshell. As if Ron's death hadn't been big enough. To both their relief, Van Hancock and Doug Metcalf, two of the company's sales managers, walked in. Their down coats glistened with droplets of melting snow.

"You talking about the new boss?" Van asked, brushing dampness from his gray crew cut.

"Shh," Leanne said. "Not so loud."

"Sorry." He dropped his voice a notch. "So what did the Ice King do now?"

"Cut the employee barbecue."

"Not surprising," Van replied. "He's cut everything else."

"Wonder how long before he sells this place?" Doug wondered aloud. "I mean, isn't that what he does?"

"According to the articles online," said Leanne. "No reason to think this company will be any different."

Thinking of the overnight package from China, Liz stayed silent. Annoyed as she was with her boss, she had no intention of giving away proprietary information. Office gossip wasn't her style. Never had been. Though she might have indulged in a little Internet surfing when Charles came onboard. That was for research purposes however. One should know who she worked for, and seeing as how no one had ever heard Ron talk about his son before…

"Makes you wonder what Ron was thinking when he wrote up his will," the accounting secretary continued, stuffing a piece of lettuce in her mouth.

"Maybe he thought this time would be different," Doug offered. "Because it's a family business and all."

"Yeah right," she scoffed. "Did any of you even know Ron had a son?"

"I heard him mention something once," Van said in between bites of his cheeseburger.

Hearing the remark, Liz looked up. Like most of them, she'd had no clue Ron Bishop and Charles Bishop, corporate raider, were related until Charles arrived on their doorstep. "What did he say?"

"Not much," the salesman replied with a shrug. "It was when my eldest was looking at colleges a couple years ago. Said something about his son having gone to some technical school. I was surprised because I'd forgotten he'd been married. Had to have been twenty-five years or so since his divorce."

"I didn't even know that much," Doug replied.

Neither had Liz. She and Ron had worked side by side for a decade and he'd never mentioned anything. That stung. She'd thought they'd been close, especially since his heart attack. But then, it wouldn't be the first time she'd misjudged a relationship, would it? "Maybe the subject was too painful," she murmured, grasping for a reason.

"I bet," Leanne said as she stabbed another piece of lettuce. "Poor Ron. I miss him." The two men nodded in agreement. "This place will never be the same."

"No, it won't," a frosty baritone replied.

All four of them froze. You could hear a pin drop in the silence.

Liz looked up first, her eyes connecting with Charles's. He stood leaning against the door frame, shoulder propped, hands in pockets. He would have presented quite the nonchalant picture were it not for the sharp glint behind his blue stare. No idea how much Charles heard, but he'd clearly heard enough.

Guilty warmth crept into Liz's cheeks.

He didn't move a muscle. Not even a tick. "I'm sure the West Coast customers are open by now," he said to Van and Doug.

Bravado gone, both men, along with Leanne, quickly gathered their belongings. Liz moved to follow suit. She was halfway to the trash receptacle when his low voice halted her progress.

"A moment, Elizabeth."

Drat. Three sets of feet could be heard hustling away like rats deserting a ship. Leaving her and Charles alone.

Squaring her shoulders, she deliberately finished disposing of her leftovers before turning around, feeling Charles's gaze every inch of the way. "Yes?" she asked when she finished.

He pushed himself away from the wall. "I realize whenever there's a change in leadership, a company goes through growing pains and an amount of gossip is to be expected." His voice was soft, measured. "Particularly when the change is sudden and unexpected.

"However." He paused, leveling his blue gaze straight at her. Liz instinctively swallowed hard. "However," he repeated, "I expect a certain level of discretion—and loyalty—from my personal assistant. In the future, I'd appreciate if you refrain from watercooler gossip."

Liz's spine stiffened. In her palm, she held an apple, leftover from her lunch, and she squeezed the fruit tightly, her fingers crushing the pulp. Humiliation flushed through her, but she choked the feeling back. Tilting her chin, she met his stare head-on, for the first time grateful for her height as it forced her to look down her nose. "Is there anything else, Mr. Bishop?" she asked matching his measured tone.

An unidentifiable expression ghosted across his features. "No, that'll be all. For now."

"Then I'll get back to my desk." Palming her apple, she walked past, keeping her head high the entire time.

And pretending she couldn't feel his eyes watching her every step.

True to meteorologists' word, the storm peaked during the evening commute. What had been steady but light

snow all day had become a blanket of white, obliterat-
ing all but a few feet of visibility.

Downshifting for God knows what time, Charles
leaned back against the headrest and groaned. By this
point in the winter, shouldn't people know how to drive
in snow? Weren't New Englanders supposed to be of
sturdier stock? Steely backbone and all that?

More like his secretary, he thought, mood lifting
slightly. Elizabeth had surprised him today—twice
actually—with her shows of resolve. Looked like there
was a little mettle in that extra long spine of hers. Funny
how he'd never noticed before.

The discovery was the sole bright spot in what was
otherwise a very long day. His morning accounting
meeting turned into a daylong argument, filled with
defensive posturing and excuses. Each angry glare con-
veyed the same silent message. You are not your father.

Damn straight, he'd wanted to say. Better get used
to it.

Ahead, the road dipped and followed the trees lining the Androscoggin River. The car in front of him
stopped suddenly, forcing him to step on the brakes.
There was a sliding sensation as Charles's car fishtailed
toward a row of pines, and he quickly steered it back
under control. His two-seat Italian sports car wasn't
suited for winter driving. He should garage the thing
in favor of a sturdier vehicle with four-wheel drive, but
a stubborn part of him refused. Doing so would be like
giving in to his exile. Acknowledging he was settling
in New Hampshire for a long stay and that was decidedly not the case. Hell, he was already getting restless.
Unusually so. He'd felt unsettled, antsy, on edge since

getting the news about his father. Maybe it was being back in New Hampshire.

Or maybe it was simply all the cold and snow, he thought, watching the blades trek back and forth across his windshield. Hard to believe once upon a time, he saw the stuff as something almost magical.

*Look, Daddy! I built a snowman!*

*Not now, Charles. I'm busy.*

Charles closed off the memory. His snowman-making days were long gone. Now all he wanted was to get back to his condo, fix himself a martini and catch the evening stock report. Given the day, maybe even two martinis—

Son of a—! Brown flashed in front of his windshield. Charles slammed on the brakes, yanking his steering wheel harder to the right to avoid collision. His car began to spin. There was another flash of brown. A flailing of hooves against metal and glass followed by a jolt and a loud bang.

Then, nothing.

# CHAPTER TWO

THE more Liz thought about her little dress-down in the break room, the more irritated she became until by the drive home, her teeth hurt from grinding them. Fortunately the Ice King spent the bulk of the afternoon holed up in an accounting meeting, leaving her to work in peace. The nerve of him, singling her out. Then, worst of all, he had the audacity to flash her a condescending smile on his way out the door. *I expect a certain amount of discretion and loyalty...* Unbelievable.

Okay, so they shouldn't have been talking about him in the break room. But did he really think he could waltz in and turn the entire company on its ear without repercussion? That employees were going to simply sit back and say nothing during this—what did he call it? This difficult transition. What kind of person refers to his father's death as a transition anyway?

The kind who didn't have anything to do with him while he was alive, that's who.

She turned out of the parking lot. The narrow wooded road that led from the manufacturing facilities into downtown was unusually busy. Just her luck.

School bus this morning, snow backup tonight. No telling how long getting home would take.

Keeping her hands securely planted on the steering wheel at ten and two, she arched her back. Her shoulders and neck ached with tension as much as her jaw, and the notion that Andrew was home alone with Victoria didn't help. They were "doing homework" his text message said. She hoped that's all they were "doing."

If Ron were still alive, she'd have asked to take off early to avoid the traffic congestion, a concept his son would certainly reject, even though he departed before her. Did she ever miss her old boss. Ron had cared about his employees. Especially the last few years following his first heart attack. Bishop Paper is my family, he used to tell her. Knowing his biological family wanted nothing to do with him gave those words a whole new meaning, didn't it? Liz rubbed her neck, trying to shake off the disquieting prickle. Again, she thought to herself, why? Far as she could see, the fault had to lie with Charles. Clearly the man lacked the ability for human empathy.

Besides, she knew what neglectful parents looked like. They were tired and ignorant and forced their children to look for love in the backseat of a sedan, tossing them out when the search backfired. They weren't zesty and fun-loving and they didn't leave their children multimillion dollar companies.

Rounding the corner, the traffic changed from slow to a snail's pace. Squinting, Liz could just make out the bright flashing lights of emergency vehicles.

A few minutes later, as the traffic crawled closer, she saw the reason. A red sports car, nose-first in a snow-

bank. Only one person in town drove such an imprac-
tical and expensive car. Sure enough, Charles's dark
familiar figure stood glowering at a police officer while
a tow driver hooked a chain to the underside of his car.
Fortunately, he looked unscathed; the EMT was already
preparing to leave.

Liz couldn't help her satisfaction. Served him right
for driving the darn thing in the first place. With any
luck, he'd be stuck standing in the snow a good long
time, too. Till his outsides got as cold as his blood.

As she approached, Charles turned and looked in her
direction, almost as if he sensed her approach. Probably
her aging muffler. Either way, his eyes reached through
the windshield, catching hers and for a moment, everything else faded away except for their silvery-blue reflection in her headlights.

Aw, drat; he was her boss after all. Before she had
time to reconsider Liz had stopped and rolled down her
window.

"What happened?" she asked him.

"A blasted deer is what happened. Damn thing bolted
in front of my car."

Liz wished she could say she was surprised, but she
wasn't. Collisions with deer were fairly common on
these roads. Charles was lucky the accident hadn't been
worse. "Are you all right?"

"He hit his head, but refused medical treatment," the
officer said.

"The air bag hit me," Charles snapped in correction,
"and I'm fine." Despite his objections, Liz caught the
hint of a shake as his hand combed through his curls.
"Wish I could say the same for my car." A few feet

away, the tow crane started up. The sound of crunching metal could be heard above the wind, causing him to wince. "More so now," he muttered.

Meanwhile, the snow had begun falling even heavier. Flakes covered the shoulders of Charles's black coat. When they weren't raking through his hair, his hands were jammed deep in his pockets, and while his features were partially obscured by shadows, Liz suspected his cheeks were blown raw from standing in the harsh northeastern wind. To her surprise, she actually felt sympathetic. "Do you need a ride?"

Hearing the question, he looked as caught off guard as she did when asking. He looked to the police officer. "Do you need anything else?"

The man shook his head. "You can get a copy of the report from the station tomorrow for your insurance. And I'd reconsider having your doctor look you over. Whiplash doesn't always show its effects right away."

Charles nodded, but Liz could tell from experience, he was simply agreeing to end the conversation, that he had no intention of seeing a doctor. His father used to make the same expression.

Interesting. It was the first she'd seen a resemblance between the two men.

It wasn't until Charles retrieved his belongings and slid into the passenger seat that Liz questioned being a Good Samaritan. Normally she considered her SUV, chosen to accommodate her, Andrew and a ton of hockey equipment, to be quite comfortable. But somehow, with Charles riding shotgun, the space suddenly felt filled to capacity. She could feel every ounce of his presence buttressing her personal space. For someone who'd been standing out in the cold, he gave off a lot of body heat. The subtle scent of citrus and spice clung to the air, which had grown strangely close despite the large size cab. Gave her the overwhelming urge to shift in her seat. She wondered if Charles noticed the discomfort, too, because both his body and voice were stiff as he clipped his thank-you.

"You're welco— Oh my gosh, your cheek!" Under the illumination of the dome light, she could see the red slash of a friction burn marring his cheekbone. "You really did hit your head," she said, instinctively reaching to check closer. Her fingertips brushed across his stubble. "Maybe you should get that checked out."

"It's nothing." He shrugged off her touch, and Liz suddenly realized what she'd done. "Sorry," she replied, yanking her hand back. "Maternal habit. I'm forever checking my son's injuries."

Oh, drat, Andrew! She was going to be later than ever now. What had she been thinking? Quickly she reached for her pocketbook.

Charles eyed her. "What are you doing?"

"Texting my son."

"You have children?"

He sounded surprised. That would make him the only person at Bishop Paper who didn't know. "A son. He's almost… I want to let him know I'm delayed but will be home soon."

"Considerate of you."

Again, his voice sounded off, like he didn't quite believe her. "I don't want him to worry," she replied, pressing Send. On the other hand, now he'd realize he had extra time. Why if it were she and Bill and they had an extra fifteen minutes…

Andrew wasn't her. And Victoria wasn't Bill. She needed to remember that.

She must have frowned at her phone, though, because Charles immediately asked, "Is there a problem?"

"Signal's patchy. My message isn't going through." That'll teach her for going with the cheapest carrier. "It's all right. I'm sure he's heard on the radio about the bad commute. He'll be fine." He and Victoria.

"No offense, but your acting skills need a little work."

"It's fine." If he could snap, so could she. "Nothing I can't handle."

Out of the corner of her eye, she saw the tow truck pulling out into the traffic. She turned on her directional and pulled out behind it. Now that she'd gotten herself into driving him home, she might as well get to it. "Thirty-two Greengus Street, right?" She remembered Ron's address from company events.

"No. I'm staying at the Admiral Mill Complex."

Liz knew the place. The old textile facilities had been refurbished into condominiums last year. Still, she'd assumed he'd stay at his father's house. After all, he did own it now.

"I'm having the house renovated for resale," he replied, reading her mind. "And I prefer my own space," he added, turning toward the window.

"Well, from what I gather, the mill has a lot of it."

"Yes, it does."

They drove the next mile or so in silence. Liz did her best to watch the snow and the traffic, but the man next to her kept drawing her attention. She'd never realized how well sound carried when the radio wasn't blasting. In the stillness, every breath, every soft swish of his coat across his slacks echoed voluminously. Painfully aware of his proximity, she held her own space as close to her as possible, keeping her elbows tight to her body and willing her angles and limbs to stay narrow. Worse, he didn't seem to notice how much space he took up.

Not even when his sleeve brushed up against her side pocket, causing a shiver to course through her entire body.

"You can relax, you know. Despite what you all think, I'm not the devil incarnate. I won't bite."

Okay, maybe he was more aware than she realized. "I know."

"Is that so? Again, your acting skills, Elizabeth. You're a terrible liar."

No, he was a terrible passenger. "I'm giving you a ride home, aren't I? Why would I do that if I thought you were so evil?"

"You tell me."

Entering downtown Gilmore, they passed the town common and St. Mark's Episcopal Church whose tall white steeple rose up and disappeared in the snowy sky. A poster board sign on the lawn advertised the upcoming hockey pancake breakfast in Gilmore High blue and gold.

Liz felt Charles's eyes studying her. "You know," he said finally, "at least a dozen other employees passed by the accident site. None of them stopped."

"None of them are your secretary."

"Interesting. I didn't realize chauffeur was part of your job description."

"Guess I'm a woman of many hats." Not that she was being paid for them all, she noted silently.

"Appears so. Secretary. Chauffeur. Office confidante."

He meant the discussion he interrupted in the break room. Frustration flashed anew. "For your information, I take my position seriously." No matter how much she disliked her boss. "I do not share company secrets."

"Good to know. Because I need to trust the people who work directly for me."

"Runs both ways."

"Excuse me? Did you say something?"

She hadn't realized she'd spoken aloud. Her cheeks warmed. "Nothing," she replied, eyes staying glued to the road.

"'Nothing' sounded an awful lot like a complaint. If you have something on your mind, I'd like to know."

Liz heard the rustle of fabric. Without looking she knew he'd shifted in his seat and now sat regarding her closely. The scrutiny had her pinned to the spot. "Elizabeth? Your thoughts?"

If she didn't know better, she'd say there was a note of humor in the way he prodded her. Like he wanted her to argue with him. She shrugged, hoping her answer would come across as nonchalant. "I doubt anything I have to say will be of interest to you."

"Why don't you let me be the judge?"

Right. And then her opinions could come back and bite her. She'd been reprimanded and rejected enough for one day, thank you very much.

"If you don't mind, I'll pass."

"You're worried about repercussions."

"Do you blame me?" she asked, casting him another look.

"I give you my word."

"Yeah, well like you said, trust has to be earned."

Charles chuckled.

"I wasn't trying to be funny," she told him.

"I know. I was actually thinking your remark was..." He paused. "Well-aimed."

An odd choice of words. "Thank you." She guessed.

"I take it that's your way of saying the employees don't trust me."

"They don't know what to expect. First your father dies unexpectedly and then you show up. You have to understand, until a few months ago, no one even knew you existed."

"I know." Charles's voice was hard and flat and a tad too unaffected. She felt a stirring of sympathy, which disturbed her, because he was supposed to be the bad guy.

"People miss him," she said simply. "He was an integral part of our lives and now he's gone."

"Employers come and go all the time, Elizabeth. It's how the business works."

For Charles, sure. After all, he made his living rotating in and out company doors. Not Ron, though. "Your father considered the company family. That's how he treated us."

"I'm sure he did."

Once again Liz felt the unanticipated swirl of sympathy.

To her relief, a large black and silver sign rose into view, announcing the entrance to Admiral Mill. Liz took the turn like she was entering heaven. "Here you go. Safe and sound." And not a minute too soon, she added to herself. Today had been a roller coaster of a day, this drive being the last in a string of undesired and abnormal interactions with her boss. One second she's furious with him, the next she's feeling sympathy and fussing over the mark on his cheek. It was a schizophrenic mix and frankly she had a headache from all the different reactions he'd put her through. The sooner he stepped out of her car the better.

Which, from the way his hand was on the handle, looked to be imminent. "Thank you for your assistance," he told her.

"All in a day's work. Good night, Mr. Bishop."

"Good night, Elizabeth. I'll see you tomorrow morning. Shall we say, seven? I'd like to get an early start."

Liz blinked. Early start? "Um, sure?"

"Good. The gate will be unlocked so you'll have no trouble getting in. If I'm not out front, buzz the penthouse and I'll be right down."

"Buzz the penthouse," Liz repeated. She wanted to make sure she heard him right. "You expect me to drive you tomorrow?"

"I'm not sure how else I'm going to get to Concord. I have a meeting at the State House regarding the new environmental regs, remember?"

Of course she remembered. She'd set up the meeting. She hadn't expected to drive him there is all. When she opened her mouth to say so, he did something unexpected.

He smiled.

A damnably sexy off-kilter grin that arched his brow and, had it truly reached his eyes, would melt the insides of every woman in town. "Well, you did say chauffeur was in your job description."

The Charles Bishop roller-coaster ride was officially plummeting. His driver. He actually expected her to cart him to Concord tomorrow morning for a meeting.

*"Arrgh!"* Letting out a groan, Liz smashed her palm against the steering wheel. She didn't know what angered her more—her boss blithely assuming she'd do his bidding or her agreeing like some weak-kneed imbecile.

"Can't you rent a car?" she'd asked.

"The rental agency is two towns away, and I doubt very much it's open," he'd replied. "In case you didn't notice, it's snowing."

She'd noticed. The foolish snow was what got her into this predicament. She should have left him standing on the side of the road.

In the end, she'd had no choice but to concede. She liked getting a regular paycheck, no matter how small. And much as she hated to admit, he had a point about the businesses being closed until morning.

So she agreed to pick him up at seven o'clock. That didn't mean, however, she was happy about the task. Or that she was at all charmed by that sexy cockeyed smile he tried tossing in her direction.

Andrew and Victoria were curled up watching a movie when she unlocked the door. Her son barely looked up. "What happened? I thought you said fifteen minutes," he said. "You took forty-five. Your text said you'd be home in fifteen minutes."

"Mr. Bishop hit a deer and wrecked his car. I had to drive him home. I tried to send a text but the storm's messing with a signal. Were you worried?"

"No, I've been waiting to eat. I'm starved. Ow! What?" Rubbing his shoulder, he looked over at his girlfriend.

"Be nice to your mother," Victoria said.

"Listen to your girlfriend." Liz hung up her coat. "Do your parents know you're here?"

The young blonde nodded. "My dad said he'd come pick me up when he finished plowing out my grandmother's driveway. He didn't want me driving in the snow."

"Good idea." Though a better one might have been to have her go home straight after school. She studied the two teenagers sitting on the sofa. Victoria's long blond hair spilled over onto Andrew's shoulder. Did they have to invade each other's personal space constantly? Even when they weren't touching they were touching.

Kind of like driving in the car with Charles. The thought brought a warm unwelcome shiver.

"What's the new Mr. Bishop like?" Victoria asked. "One of my mom's customers said he was gorgeous. Hey!" This time she rubbed her shoulder.

"Andrew, don't poke your girlfriend. And yes, you could say he was good-looking." If lacking any kind of human feelings.

Unless you counted his smile. Or the wounded tone he tried to hide in his voice.

Kicking off her wet shoes, Liz padded her way toward the kitchen.

"I told Vic she could stay for dinner," Andrew called after her. "Is that all right?"

"Of course. She's always welcome. Have her call her father, though, so he knows."

"See," he said, poking his girlfriend with his elbow. "I told you she'd say yes."

That was her. Ms. Pushover. Word must have gotten around. "Hope spaghetti's all right with you two." She opened the cupboard and began pulling out the saucepans. "Do me a favor, Andrew. Check the freezer and see if we have any garlic bread, will you?" Nothing like garlic bread to keep the good-night kissing to a minimum. "How'd your calculus test go?"

"It went."

"Went good or bad?"

"It just went. By the way—" Andrew lumbered over to the fridge "—the furnace started making that weird noise again. Oh, and Mrs. Warren finished my recommendation for Trenton. You have no idea how badly I wanted to sneak a look, but she sealed the envelope. I put it in the folder with the application stuff. Oh, and Coach said he'd have something for me by the weekend."

Liz managed an acknowledging smile. Was it only this morning she asked for a raise? "Great, sweetie."

"I still can't believe you're going to Trenton," Victoria said. "You're not going to turn into some rich snob are you?"

"Of course I am. I'm going to be the star player.

Everyone's going to love me— Ow! She poked me again. How come you never yell at her?"

"Because I like her better," Liz replied by rote. She was busy pretending to draw water from the faucet. Soon as Andrew mentioned the furnace, she got a sick feeling in her stomach. It had been acting up all fall. She'd put off calling a repairman because she feared a big bill. Hopefully she could string things out a little longer. Thanks to today's rejection, she really couldn't afford any large expenses. Not if she wanted to pay Andrew's tuition to Trenton. And—she glanced at the two teenagers giggling a few feet away—she so wanted to give Andrew this chance.

Meanwhile, her head ached from going three rounds with Charles Bishop and she had to repeat the process tomorrow. Driving to Concord no less. Two hours down and two hours back, trapped in a car with his warm, space-consuming, citrus-scented, heartless presence. Oh, man, but she wasn't being paid enough.

Literally.

Across town, Charles stood in front of his living room window watching the snowflakes blow about in the dark. A deer. Talk about bad luck. Only in New England would a deer cause a car accident. There was a reason you didn't see Deer Crossing signs in downtown Los Angeles.

Sipping his martini, it dawned on him how lucky he was not to be hurt beyond a few sore muscles and bruises. Luckier still he didn't hit something larger, like a moose.

Maybe his good fortune explained why the fatigue

and tension he'd expected to feel at the end of such a long day never fully materialized. In fact, he felt remarkably… Licking the gin from his lips, he tried and failed to come up with a word. Certainly not relaxed; he hadn't been relaxed since childhood. Best definition he had was less tense. He was less tense.

And cold, he thought with a scowl. The mile-high penthouse ceilings did little to seal in warmth. Tearing himself away from the view—there wasn't much to see anyway—he stepped down into the pit area that took up much of his living room floor space. The gas fireplace didn't throw a ton of warmth, but it was better than nothing as he settled back against the leather sectional.

He'd been warm enough in Elizabeth's car, he thought, staring at the flames. Exceedingly warm actually. Her long, lean frame gave off a great deal of heat. He smiled recalling how, while driving, the gap of her wool coat fell open, offering him a glimpse of leg every time she raised her foot to brake. He'd always known she had long legs. Barefoot, the woman was an inch off his six feet, but he'd never appreciated how shapely they were until this afternoon when every brake light forced her skirt to creep up her thigh. For the first time in his life, he found himself not minding stop-and-go traffic.

He was a little disappointed Elizabeth hadn't shown more of her edge during their drive, the spark only igniting toward the end. Having witnessed it twice in one day, he found himself curious to see how steely that backbone would get when pushed. Then again, there was always tomorrow's drive to Concord.

Recalling the look on her face when he dropped that bombshell made him chuckle. Talk about utter disbelief. Then and there, any possible bad mood he had was erased by her wide brown eyes. Granted, making her drive when he could contact a rental car agency was heavy-handed but he couldn't help himself. Especially when she was so perturbed by the notion. Damned if he knew why, but he found sparring with his secretary incredibly entertaining.

Absentmindedly, he ran his hand across his sore cheek, mirroring Elizabeth's touch in the car. Normally he had no need for idle conversation, preferring to keep his relationships compartmentalized into one of two categories: business or personal and certainly never both together. But Elizabeth intrigued him. There seemed to be a number of layers to her he hadn't noticed before. Like the fact she had a son. Made him wonder what else lay beneath her lengthy surface.

After all, it wasn't as if he was interested in a romantic liaison with her. He was merely looking to make his stay in New Hampshire as palatable as possible while it lasted.

At last, a hint of warmth began spreading its way through his body. Stretching his legs, Charles drained the last of his martini and savored the sensation. Yes, he thought with a smile, tomorrow had potential to be very intriguing.

He couldn't wait.

# CHAPTER THREE

PART of Liz hoped to wake up and discover Charles's "request" to drive him had been a big misunderstanding. The other part hoped the storm reversed its sea-bound track and returned, leaving the entire state snowbound. Both parts woke up disappointed. The sky was gray but storm free when she pulled back the curtains to check. Unable to go back to sleep, Liz dressed and made her way to the kitchen only to find Andrew uncharacteristically awake and cooking frozen waffles.

"You're up early," she remarked. "There a problem?" Andrew never voluntarily dragged himself out of bed before two or three hits of the snooze button.

"Yeah, the furnace. It made too much noise."

Indeed. Liz had listened to the wheezes and grumbles all night long herself. That they were hearing the noises more often and for longer didn't bode well.

"Least you don't have to worry about being late." Grateful she couldn't see this morning's eye roll, she flipped the switch on the coffeemaker

"You're wearing that to work?" she heard Andrew ask as she was reaching for her coffee mug.

Liz glanced down at her lime-green fleece and jeans.

"It's casual Friday. What about you? You wearing that?" Though he was freshly showered, he wore sleep pants and no shirt. At the sight of her string bean's broadening shoulders, Liz felt a mixture of pride and anxiety. He was growing up fast.

Too fast.

"I didn't want to get food on my shirt." While talking, he slathered both waffles with peanut butter and jelly, then slapped them together like a sandwich. "Coach's got this thing about us looking clean at pep rallies." He took a bite. "You're coming tonight, right?"

"Of course." She'd missed no more than a handful of games since Pee Wee Hockey. Making sure Andrew had someone in the stands to cheer him on was a promise she'd made long ago. "I'll be there as soon as I drop off the boss."

"You really have to be his driver?"

"For today, yes. He has an important meeting in Concord."

"What a tool."

Tool was one word for him, thought Liz chewing the inside of her cheek. Although tools didn't usually provoke sympathy with the way they spoke. She was still trying to understand her unexpected reaction last night. Matter of fact, she was trying to understand the entire conversation. What did he care about what employees— or she—thought? "Regardless, he's also my boss. I don't have much choice. I'd like to stay on his good side."

"Then I'd definitely change the shirt."

"What's wrong with my shirt? I told you, today's casual Friday."

"Casual, Mom, not ugly."

All right, so it wasn't her best look. She didn't choose the outfit to be stylish anyway. While technically Fridays were casual dress days, most of the company dropped the practice after Ron's death. With Charles always dressed so formally, wearing jeans felt out of place. She was embracing the tradition today to prove a point. A passive aggressive way of saying "you're not the boss of me, even though you are" gesture. "I don't think it's that bad," she lied.

"If you say so, but don't expect me to acknowledge you at the game if you're still wearing it."

"You have to, wise guy. I'm your driver, too."

"I'll find another." Smirking, he polished off the last of his waffle sandwich in one bite. "I better get dressed. Vic's picking me up early. Sammy's going to show us how to do the calculus assignment before homeroom."

"Wait a sec!" She reached out and caught his arm as he passed by. "I thought you and Victoria did your homework together last night." Their heads had certainly been smushed close enough over their books.

"We did, but neither of us understood it."

"So why aren't you going to see Mr. Rueben? I thought he hosted help sessions in the mornings."

"Mr. Rueben hates me."

"Andrew—"

"Come on, Mom! He's awful. He talks in this monotone and I can't understand anything he's saying. Sam explains things better."

"Make sure he actually explains and doesn't do the homework for you." Liz had her misgivings. There seemed to be a lot of complaints about Mr. Rueben lately.

"Don't worry, I promise." He unhooked himself from her grasp and headed upstairs. "Oh, and Mom? The shirt's not that bad."

"Thanks." But as soon as she caught her reflection in the microwave, Liz knew her son was lying. The only flattering thing she could say about the lime-green fleece was that it did a nice job of bringing out her circles. Otherwise, the garment hung on her like a bright colored sack.

Liz sighed. Once upon a time she'd had potential. Tall and gawky, but attractive. Now she just looked tired. No one would look twice in her direction. Which was fine, really. After all, she had Andrew to raise now. She wasn't looking to attract or impress anybody. Besides, hadn't she dressed to impress yesterday? Look how well that turned out.

In the end, however, Liz changed. Or rather, she changed her sweater to a green and blue reindeer sweater and blue turtleneck. There was passive aggressive; then there was out and out foolish, and as much as she wanted to rebel, she also wanted to maintain some sense of professionalism. At least that was the story she sold herself. Her putting on a more flattering sweater or deciding to wear leather boots instead of quilted snow boots had everything to do with looking her best for work.

She arrived at Charles's complex five minutes to seven to find him already waiting in the doorway. Soon as she caught sight of his cashmere coat, her pulse picked up its pace. He looked, as always, amazing. It wasn't fair.

"Good morning, Elizabeth," he greeted upon opening the door.

Liz struggled to find her voice. Didn't help that he appeared to be slowly scanning the length of her while he spoke. "Good morning."

"Exercising casual Friday, I see."

"Is that a problem?"

She couldn't tell if the emotion crossing his features was disappointment or amusement or mixture of both. "Not really," he replied, shrugging off his coat to reveal an ash-gray suit perfectly cut to his broad shoulders and narrow hips that immediately made Liz glad she opted against the green fleece. "We're going to be in the car a good chunk of the day. Might as well do what you need to be comfortable."

"Well, if that's the case, would you mind if we grab a cup of coffee before getting on the highway? My first cup didn't quite cut the mustard and I could use a second." Not to mention, it would give her something to focus on besides the well-dressed man beside her.

The aftereffects of yesterday's accident showed as Charles settled stiffly into the passenger seat. Liz turned, intent on asking about his back and neck, only to forget how closely they were sitting. When he buckled his seat belt, the angle brought his face within inches. Not for the first time, Liz noticed how he gave the illusion of being far larger than he actually was. Even though she had a couple inches on him in the high heel boots, next to him, she felt strangely petite and delicate. She let her eyes travel to his cheek. Overnight, the reddened patch had darkened so it looked more like a scrape.

"Your cheek looks better."

Soon as she made the remark, the strangest expression filled his features. A bizarre combination of amazement and gratitude, as if she'd asked about something far more important than his cheek, it set off an equally strange fluttering feeling in Liz's chest. She looked to his eyes only to have him break away by settling back against the seat.

"If you want your coffee, you should get going," he said, eyes locking on the view beyond the windshield. "Otherwise, you won't have time."

They ended up stopping at the doughnut store near the exit. One of the few places Charles thought actually knew how to brew a halfway decent cup of coffee and even that was more serviceable than anything. The utter lack of decent beverages in the area was highly unacceptable, as far as he was concerned. If he was going to be stuck here awhile, he was going to have to rectify the situation. *If.* He chuckled to himself. As if sticking around would ever be an option. Better he light a fire under his lawyers.

He had to chuckle, too, at his secretary. Casual Friday, huh? Why didn't he quite buy that explanation?

Maybe because she hadn't worn jeans to work since he'd taken over the company? More likely, this was payback for his drafting her as a chauffeur. Looked like his secretary had a little control streak along with her backbone. He would miss the skirt, or rather the view that came with the skirt. Although, he thought stealing a peek, those jeans and leather boots weren't exactly hard to look at.

What did bother him, however, was his reaction when she asked about his cheek. It was a simple enough question, one any polite person would ask. And yet, when she mentioned it, his insides grew jumbled. He couldn't remember the last time someone wondered about his well-being, least not genuinely. He didn't know what to say. So he said nothing.

"Problem?" Elizabeth's question pulled him from his thoughts. Looking up, he saw concern etched on her profile. "You're frowning," she said.

Again, caught off guard by her observation, he lied. "Coffee's weak. I prefer a stronger brew."

"You are very picky about your coffee."

The understatement made him chuckle. "You've noticed, have you?"

"Hard to miss the personal coffeemaker set up in your office."

"Good point. What can I say? I have high standards."

"Must make life difficult," she replied.

"How so?"

She shrugged. "What do you do when things aren't up to snuff?"

"Then I don't waste my time. Why bother settling for second best?" He went to sip his coffee only to decide to follow his own advice and set the cup in the holder. "I learned a long time ago that what you get in this world is up to you." God knows, no one else gave a damn.

"True."

The edge to her tone caught his attention. Sounded like he'd touched a nerve. What hard lessons had life taught her? he wondered. Whatever they were, the scars didn't show on her face. Her profile was clear and youthful, lacking any of the ravages life could heap upon a person. Then again, as he well knew, scars didn't always show, either.

What were her scars?

Curious, he adjusted in his seat so he could view her better. As he learned yesterday, her face was remarkably readable, her thoughts and emotions playing out quite visibly. A horrendous trait in business, but utterly fascinating and refreshing to see. "How long have you worked for Bishop Paper?"

"Why do you want to know?"

Case in point. Mistrust colored every feature. "Curiosity," he replied. "We're going to spend the day together. Seems like a good time to get to know my assistant better."

"No offense, but I've been working for you for weeks. You never showed interest before."

That's because he hadn't realized how interesting she could be till now. "We've never had two solid hours with nothing to do but talk before."

"Suppose not."

And she sounded so thrilled to be in that position now, Charles thought with a smile. Obviously he was going to have to pull answers out of her. "So," he began again, "how long have you worked for Bishop?"

"Eighteen years in April."

"That long? You must have started young."

She frowned, as though he said something wrong. "Young enough."

"Do you like it?"

"I'd like to keep my job, if that's what you're asking."

"Don't worry, your head's not on the chopping

block." At least not during his short tenure. Hopefully Xinhua management would be smart enough to keep her as well. "Were you always my father's secretary?"

"No, I started as a file clerk. Your father promoted me about ten years ago, when Peggy Flockhart retired."

Peggy. He remembered the name. *You spend more time with Peggy than you do your own wife.* "Were you two—" he cleared his throat of the sudden frog that lodged in it "—close?"

"With Peggy?"

"With my father?"

Elizabeth touched the brakes. "What exactly are you asking?"

"You said yourself my father considered you all family. I'm simply curious how close."

"Not as close as you're implying, that's for certain."

Her answer was sharp-edged, and jabbed him in the gut. "Then how would you describe your relationship?"

"We were friendly. He was pleasant to work for. Made me—made everyone at the company—feel like we were helping him achieve something."

"It was all about the company then."

"It was about being part of the company," she replied. "There's a difference."

"Maybe," he replied. "Maybe not." Charles hadn't realized till she answered that he'd been looking to see whether somewhere along the line Ron found something—or someone—better. But he hadn't. In the end, it still amounted to his father putting the company first. Guess the lawyer was wrong. The old man hadn't changed.

He'd studied the cars in the next lane. Elizabeth was

a confident driver, he noticed. She navigated the high-way traffic with admirable ease. Although she'd been outraged at the suggestion, he wouldn't have blamed his father if he'd dallied with his assistant. She was definitely dalliance-worthy, if one were so inclined.

In the next seat, Elizabeth let out a long, frustrated-sounding sigh. "I enjoyed working for your father," she continued, explaining her comment further. "He made me feel…" She shrugged. "Appreciated."

"As opposed to me?" Charles asked.

"I didn't say that."

She didn't have to; the implication was obvious. "I assure you, Elizabeth, I appreciate your services very much."

"Of course you do," she replied, her smile closer to a smirk.

"You sound skeptical."

"Really?" She maneuvered the car into the next lane. "Whatever gave you that idea?"

"You don't believe I appreciate you?"

"What I think is that appreciating a person and appreciating their services are two very different things."

Charles sat back. "I get it. This is about my turning down your request for a raise. I already told you—"

"I know—" she cut him off "—you can't make exceptions."

"Precisely."

"And you're simply trying to cut costs. Nothing personal."

Again, correct. And yet hearing his words spit back at him rankled. Made him feel like he was the villain when he was simply practicing sound business.

Charles shifted in his seat. Since when did he care what employees thought of him anyway? He wasn't here to court favor or win friends. He was here to sell a company. So why then, did he have this inexplicable urge to argue his point till Elizabeth agreed with his logic?

Why, all of a sudden, did one secretary's negative opinion sit so uncomfortably in the pit of his stomach?

# CHAPTER FOUR

"You barely touched your lunch."

They stood in the coatroom of a local restaurant after having said their goodbyes to several key business leaders and the governor. "Was there a problem with your order?" Charles asked, his voice sounding attractively deep.

Liz ignored the way his breath tickled her ear as he held her jacket. He was lucky she couldn't dump the lettuce in his lap. When he insisted on her driving him today, she assumed that was all she'd be doing. She hadn't expected to be dragged into the meeting or to a fancy restaurant where even the waiters were dressed better than her.

"My salad was fine," she replied, shrugging the jacket out of his grasp.

"You certain? Because you could have ordered something different."

"I said it was fine. I simply wasn't hungry." Feeling self-conscious tended to kill her appetite. Everyone staring in their direction as they walked through the dining room.

All right, maybe they weren't staring just at her. They

could have been staring at the governor. Or Charles. He looked as out of place as her, only for the opposite reason. Even next to the state political leaders, he broadcast a genetic superiority over everyone else in the room. He didn't need the cashmere overcoat and expensive Italian shoes for people to know in a battle of the strongest, he would always come out the victor. If she weren't so annoyed with him, the female side of her would be flooded with appreciation.

But she was annoyed, so she stomped ahead of him out of the restaurant, moving fast enough that he had to jog to catch up.

Took him about a block. But he did. To her irritation, he wasn't even out of breath from the exertion.

"Are we in a rush to get someplace?" he asked.

"Home," she snapped. "If that's all right with you." On top of everything else today, the meeting and lunch had run long. At midafternoon, it was already starting to get dark. The streetlamps and headlights were on, and people had hit the streets, trying to beat the weekend traffic rush but in reality, causing one. The roads north would be jammed with cars from Massachusetts and south heading to ski country, Andrew's hockey game faced off in a couple hours, too. Dang.

"You could have given me a heads-up," she said. "Let me know that you expected me to join you in those meetings."

"I thought that was understood. After all, you have the best grasp of Bishop's green policies."

Bull. "Until yesterday, you planned to attend alone."

"Yes, but I didn't, so why not take advantage of the

resources available? The governor, by the way, looked very impressed."

"Sure he was. Right after he got over the fact I was wearing a reindeer sweater."

"You were the one recognizing casual Friday." He wore an amused smirk. So help her, if she didn't enjoy receiving a paycheck she'd smack him. "Besides," he continued, "didn't you attend meetings like this when you accompanied my father?"

"No. Ron was the people person. He didn't really need anyone's assistance."

"What a surprise."

"Excuse me?"

Charles's comment said he hadn't realized he'd spoken aloud. He had, though, and there was enough edge in his muttered words to make Liz forget she was supposed to be angry. "You said you weren't surprised."

"Are you?"

"No, I suppose not. Ron was always considered a bit of a maverick. So are you," she noted.

"Hardly" was his terse reply.

"That's not what the business magazines say."

"The business magazines exaggerate."

"How so?" She was curious. Understanding how he ticked might hold some clues to what the future held for her and the rest of the company.

"Well, for one thing, the term maverick implies recklessness. I do not believe in being brash. I prefer to base my decisions on economics and good fiscal sense, not my gut."

"You're saying your father didn't?"

"I have no idea what drove my father's decision-making, although it's clear looking at the numbers, it wasn't economics."

"Told you, he considered us family."

Charles's reply was a derisive snort.

They'd reached the parking garage lobby. As if on command, the elevator door opened the moment he pushed the button and Liz found herself ushered into the small steel space. The air smelled faintly of body wash. How did he do it? she wondered. How'd he manage to fill every room, every space he entered with his essence, dwarfing all around him? Needing space, she stepped to her left and leaned against the wall.

"You don't put much stock in sentimentality, do you?"

"I put stock in numbers," he replied. "Pluses, minuses, profits, losses. Those are things you can see and measure. Not some vague-sounding concept pulled out of thin air."

Like promises. Pretty words that didn't mean a hill of beans. Liz understood what Charles meant. Lord knows she wished she didn't, but she understood all too well. "Why put stock in something that will only fail you?" she agreed in a soft voice.

"Exactly," he replied, eyes meeting hers. A kind of sympathetic surprise shone in their blue depths. "All sentiment does is cloud your judgment. Better to avoid emotion altogether."

Such attitude didn't bode well for Bishop Paper, did it?

"You're right," she said. "You're not like your father at all."

"Told you."

Liz wasn't sure what to say. Instinct and experience told her to detest the man. Bishop Paper—or rather the fate of the company—meant nothing to him beyond the numbers on a balance sheet. And yet at the same time, something about the way he spoke held her back. His cavalier tone sounded too forced; his defense of the bottom line too emphatic. A part of her couldn't help feeling almost…sympathetic. Could it be, Charles's icy nature didn't run as deep as everyone thought?

Her suspicions grew when, as they reached their floor and the elevator doors slid closed behind them, Charles reached out and grabbed her elbow. "Hey!" His gentle grip stopped her immediately.

Turning, she found him firmly planted in her personal space, once more giving the illusion of being larger than everything else around him. "For what it's worth," he said, his blue eyes finding hers, "you did fine back at the meeting. It was good you were there."

She told herself the free-fall sensation his compliment sparked was her imagination.

Liz had been right about the traffic. This year's abundant snowfall made for terrific skiing. A boon for New Hampshire's economy, but bad for anyone driving the highway on a Friday afternoon. Particularly once it got dark. With each press of the brake light, Liz could feel the time inching closer to six-thirty. Drat. She was going to miss the opening face-off.

Next to her, Charles shifted in his seat, his frustrated sigh echoing her thoughts. Part of them anyway. She doubted very much he suffered from the internal confusion that had plagued her since leaving the parking garage. In the dark confines of her car, it was impossible to shake Charles's closeness. Every movement, every breath reminded her nerves he sat a slip of an arm away. Strangely enough, her elbow was still warm where he touched her, too. Odd that the touch of a man who prided himself on his cool detachment could radiate such heat.

At last, a sign announced their exit was only a few miles away. "About time," Charles said. "This traffic has been outrageous."

"Happens when you take too long to get out of the city," she replied. "Given how snowy it's been, we're lucky the traffic isn't worse."

"I'd hate to see how."

So would she, to be honest. She glanced at the dashboard clock. Six twenty-seven. By the time she got off the highway, took Charles back to his condominium, then drove out to the rink in Franklin she'd be lucky if she caught more than the final period. And that was if Charles didn't insist on stopping by the office first.

"What's the problem?" Charles asked.

"What makes you think there's a problem?"

"Well, the sigh you let out a second ago for starters. Plus you keep tapping the steering wheel and making little frustrated noises in the back of your throat. Do you have plans that you're late for?"

Why did that question sound probing? "Face-off," she replied. "Puck drops at six-thirty."

"Hockey?"

"Uh-uh. My son's high school team is playing their biggest rival tonight."

"And you're planning to attend. On a Friday night."

"Of course." As if she'd make any other choice.

Andrew was her son. "I attend as many home games as I can."

"Interesting."

"I don't know if it's that. In fact, if you ask Andrew, he'll tell you my presence is unnecessary."

"Why do you go, then?"

"Because. As his parent, I know he might not care right now, but when he looks back, he'll remember I was there."

"And be saved the sting looking up and discovering you weren't."

A full feeling stretched across Liz's chest. Yes, she thought, that was it exactly.

The traffic in front of her slowed to a stop. Terrific. In the back of her mind, Liz quickly calculated time and distance. Gilmore was fifteen minutes off the exit. It was another fifteen or twenty to Charles's complex, ten more to Franklin....

Screw it. She told Andrew she'd be at this game, and she wasn't about to renege, at least not because her boss made her play chauffeur. Besides, it served Charles right after making her attend those meetings today.

They inched their way up to the exit ramp. Stopping at the top, Liz took a moment to read the sign indicating Gilmore was to the right, before turning left, toward Franklin.

They arrived in Franklin shortly after the start of the second period.

"Let me get this straight," Charles said as they entered the lobby of the Franklin rink. "Your son plays for the Gilmore High School hockey team and you have to attend his home game two towns away. Why is that exactly?"

"The rink got struck by lightning last summer and caught fire. Coffee?"

"Good Lord, no." Charles scowled at the hot beverage vending machine in the ice rink lobby. "That's not coffee. It's lukewarm brown water."

"Suit yourself." She tapped her foot waiting for her hot cocoa to finish. "It gets cold near the ice."

"I'll survive. Trust me." He scowled again, his distaste obvious. "I'll definitely survive."

Liz imagined he would. Just as she imagined she was going to pay for this forced detour. Although Charles outwardly appeared calm, she wasn't fool enough to believe the façade for one second. After all, he'd appeared agreeable regarding her casual day rebellion this morning and look how that turned out. She wound up sitting in a meeting full of state leaders looking like a teenager in a reindeer sweater and faded jeans.

"Why doesn't Gilmore fix the rink?" he asked, his lips curling into a frown as he peeled his loafer from a patch of soda-encrusted rubber flooring.

A quick look at the scoreboard told her the game was still scoreless. Good, she hadn't missed much.

"The town plans to as soon as it appropriates the funds," she told him. "Until then, however, we're out of luck."

"You don't say."

She ignored the sarcasm. Part of the reason the town lacked funds was that they'd hoped to secure help from Ron Bishop, but he'd died before the request could be finalized.

No sooner did they enter the arena than the nudges and curious stares began passing from person to person. In her haste to make the game, she'd forgotten one-third of the team had parents who worked for Bishop Paper. Maybe this wasn't such a good idea after all.

With the burn of what felt like a hundred stares frying her skin, she pointed at a section of bleachers to the left of center ice. "I usually sit a few rows from the top," she told him.

"Looks cozy."

Liz was about to retort when it dawned on her his remark might be more than sarcasm. He had, after all, been in a car accident yesterday. "The top row would allow you to lean against the wall, if that would be more comfortable."

"Why would you…?" He looked taken aback.

"I didn't know how your back and neck felt after yesterday."

"Oh, right. Wherever you normally sit works fine." Confusion continued lining his face. Finally he seemed to recover, the lines smoothing and his face lighting with an expression she couldn't define. "Thank you for asking."

"You're welcome." His confusion transferred itself to her. It was a simple question. No reason for him to look at her so strangely. Or for butterflies to skitter across her stomach.

The crowd parted for them like the Red Sea. Liz suppressed the urge to hide her face as she climbed the bleachers. So she had arrived at the game with Charles Bishop. Big deal. Charles was the one who should feel out of place.

Except *he* was used to being scrutinized. He mounted the bleachers with the same imperial bearing he always had, nodding hello to employees and acting as if it was perfectly normal for him to be there.

To Liz's dismay, the crowd surged back as they sat down, forcing them to crowd together on the bench seat. Charles's leg ended up pressed against hers, the pressure stretching from hip to knee. Liz gripped her cocoa, thinking the liquid's temperature cold in comparison to the temperature spreading across her leg. What was that she said about it being cold near the ice?

"How are they doing?" she asked the mother sitting next to her. Might as well try to look unaffected. "I noticed no one's scored yet. Have there been many shots on goal?"

"A ton, but nothing's breaking our way," the woman replied.

"Sooner or later one will go in."

Just then, the Gilmore goalie made an amazing save, causing the crowd to erupt. Forgetting her self-consciousness, Liz cheered, too. It wasn't until she finished that she noticed Charles studying the ice with discernible confusion.

"Not a hockey fan, I take it?" she asked.

"Wouldn't know," he replied. "This is the first game I've ever watched. Which skater is your son?"

"Number thirty-two. The tall one. He's a right wing on the first line."

"First line?"

Oh, this was going to be interesting. "There are three lines of offense. They rotate in and out to keep from getting too winded. Andrew's on the first line. There he is now." She pointed as Andrew leaped over the wall and back onto the ice.

"Hey, Lizzie!" someone two rows down called over. "Did you see the coach from Trenton's here?"

"He is?" Scanning the crowd, she finally spotted the man by the Gilmore coaches' box.

"Any word about Andrew?"

"Not yet." Inside, the question made her wince. She hadn't wanted the subject brought up in front of Charles.

As she expected, he picked up on the reference right away. "Trenton Academy? You're thinking of sending your son there?"

She could imagine his number-oriented mind mentally recalculating her salary as he spoke.

"The coach is recruiting him," she replied. "But nothing's carved in stone."

"Interesting" was all he replied.

Out on the ice, Andrew received a pass. He brought the puck down the ice and at the last minute, passed to the center, who took a hard slapshot. A disappointed groan ripped through the crowd as the goalie made the save.

"Keep the pressure on, Sean!" a man hollered from the front of the bleachers.

Charles frowned. "Was that Van Hancock?"

"Uh-huh. His youngest son, Sean, plays center. The kid's only a sophomore, but he's having a terrific season." She winced as a player checked Andrew into the boards in a fight for the puck. As always, her heart waited until Andrew skated safely away before leaving her throat.

"Not a big fan of the hits, I see," Charles noted.

"I know checking's part of the game, but when it's your child getting nailed, it's hard to remember that. Once, when Andrew was really small, and believe it or not there was a time not so long ago, I yelled at the referee for not calling a penalty." Her cheeks grew warm remembering. "I was told to sit as far back in the bleachers as possible from then on."

"By the official?"

"By Andrew. He still says I have the loudest voice in the rink."

"At least you're here and cheering," Charles replied.

As if she would make any other choice. Andrew was her son. "I make it a point to attend as many games as I can. Work doesn't always make it possible."

"Does his father come to the games, as well?"

Bill? "Better luck getting it to snow in July." Too late she realized how embittered she sounded and she looked to her lap. "Sorry. Andrew's father is a sore topic."

"I take it he's not an active parent."

Active? More like absent. "Let's say he's not very interested in being a father."

"I understand."

There sounded like empathy in his voice. Curious, Liz looked in his direction, her breath catching as she caught the last of a shadow ghosting across his profile. She knew that shadow. She'd seen it in Andrew's expression when he didn't know she was looking, and in her own childhood reflection. For the second time that day, unexpected sympathy stirred in her heart.

"Did you play sports in high school?" She tried her best to picture a younger, carefree version of him running around an athletic field and failed.

Which was why she wasn't surprised when he shook his head. "Didn't have time. Too busy with school."

That she could picture. "Let me guess, you were top of your class."

"Actually at seventeen I was a freshman at Cal Tech. I opted to graduate early and take a scholarship."

Wow. "I'm impressed."

"Don't be," he said. "I had a lot of motivation."

What kind of motivation? Had he been looking to prove himself? Or prove something to his father? All of a sudden, her image of Ron Bishop as zesty and compassionate no longer seemed to line up quite as neatly as it once did.

"Funny how circumstances can fuel your resolve," she said.

"That's for sure."

Silent agreement wrapped itself around them.

For the next forty minutes, Liz found herself explaining the action on the ice. To his credit, Charles acted interested. She wasn't surprised to see him grasp the concepts quickly and by the end of the third period, he had a working knowledge of high school hockey.

As for the game itself, the score remained tied, with both goalies stopping shot after shot. Then, with a minute left to play, Andrew broke free. Once again, he brought the puck down the ice and passed off to Hancock, whose shot went wide. The puck ricocheted off the boards, and Andrew was there to pick it up.

Liz jumped to her feet along with the rest of the crowd. "Come on, buddy!" she screamed. "You can do it!"

She held her breath as Andrew's wrist shot careened

toward the upper left hand corner of the goal. At the
last minute, the goalie dove sideways, his arm raised
upward. The puck tipped off the top of his glove and
into the net. The crowd cheered wildly. Liz jumped up
and down, clapping and cheering. From the corner of
her eye, she saw Charles studying her. In her zeal, she'd
forgotten he was there. "Andrew's right," he said. "You
do have the loudest cheer in the stands." Liz's cheeks
grew hot.

"Not in a bad way, though," he added.

"Thank you, I guess."

"You're welcome." He smiled and Liz felt the most
uncharacteristic wave of shyness wash over her. It
forced her head to duck downward and catch her lip
between her teeth. Reaching up, she combed her fingers
through her hair, only to discover upon looking through
her lashes, that Charles was doing the same. That their
actions mimicked one another only made the shyness
more acute.

The buzzer sounded, breaking the exchange. Waking
from her daze, Liz sat down to gather her things.
Charles did the same, his hip brushing hers in the process. Quickly they both slid apart.

"How did you enjoy your first hockey game?" she
asked him.

"It was passable. Your son seems like a pretty good
player. Not that I'm in much of a position to judge."

"Thank you." She tucked her hair behind her ear.
"And thank you for letting me come straight from the
highway."

"If I recall, I didn't let you do anything. You were
driving and since I don't enjoy long walks—at least

not in these shoes…" To illustrate, he lifted his foot. "Anyway, you can repay my good nature by taking me to dinner."

"Dinner?" Liz repeated.

"Yes, dinner. I'm starving and I am not about to buy my dinner out of a vending machine. At least not during this lifetime. There's a restaurant in Gilmore. Nothing fancy, but I believe they serve a decent enough meal."

"You mean Mahoney's?"

"That's the place. We can stop there on the way to my complex."

Liz wasn't quite sure how to respond. Having shared one meal with the man already, she really hadn't been expecting to share a second. Worse, she wasn't expecting her stomach to grow all fluttery at the suggestion.

"I can't," she told him, surprised at how strongly she felt her regret. "I have to drive Andrew."

"Bring him along. Didn't you say he needed several meals a day?"

She did. But including Andrew didn't sound like the best idea. She hadn't been out with another man since Bill. When Andrew was younger she hadn't wanted him to feel threatened and now she didn't have the time nor energy to date.

*This isn't a date*, a voice reminded her.

"Unfortunately I can't," she told him again. "I have to give Andrew a ride home."

"Hey, Mom!" With impeccable timing, Andrew appeared at the rink's edge. "Vic and I are going to hang at Sam's for a little while to celebrate. She said she'd give me a ride home." His attention flickered to Charles and back. "That is, if you don't need me."

"I'm fine, sweetheart," Liz replied. "Be home by eleven."

Next to her, Charles's smile turned smug. "Will you look at that. Guess you're free to eat after all."

He offered her his arm. "Shall we?"

# CHAPTER FIVE

Charles had driven by Mahoney's a number of times since coming to Gilmore, but never gone inside. The brick-faced restaurant with an Irish flag by the door wasn't his usual style of restaurant. He preferred a sedate atmosphere where you could hear yourself think and get business done. However, since the parking lot filled night after night, he assumed it must have something to offer.

Standing in the doorway, brushing snowflakes from his curls, he was greeted by the sounds of laughter and Irish music. A blackboard on the wall listed homemade macaroni and cheese as one of the specials and suggested patrons try this month's local microbrew, an aptly named Twelve Weeks of Winter Dark Ale. The number of customers still occupying tables after the dinner rush was over appeared to confirm his assumption.

"Apparently this is the place to be," he mused.

"It's popular." Elizabeth's reply was as stiff as her spine. She was annoyed he'd insisted they stop, but couldn't say anything, having dragged him to a high school game.

As he examined the rustic decor, Charles realized

the situation was the opposite of today's lunch, this time with him the fish out of water. Except after a lifetime of being the outsider, the role no longer bothered him.

Looking back, the entire day had been a game of one-upmanship, hadn't it? Of course he didn't *need* her to attend his meeting with the governor—although her impressive knowledge of Bishop's research was useful—he'd simply wanted to see how she'd react. Her feistiness was fun to watch. And, if he were to be completely honest, part of him wanted to reassert his authority. It bothered him how much her approval seemed to matter. Like now. He shouldn't care about how annoyed she was; her job was to do as he asked. And yet, the frown on her face ate at him like a bad case of heartburn.

"No need to look like you're on the way to prison," he said. "Surely having dinner with me isn't so horrible, is it?"

"Let's just get a table." Unaware of his study, she sighed and combed the hair away from her face. The way the dark strands moved through her fingers reminded Charles of cascading brown satin. Did she have any idea how much attention the gesture drew to her? Or how many heads turned upon her entrance into a room? Heads that would turn regardless of who accompanied her. Mentally he shook his head. And she'd been concerned about looking out of place during today's meeting. Even in an out-of-date sweater and stony expression she presented one stunning sight. He was pretty sure the governor was smitten the minute he met her.

Gently he guided her by the elbow to a table near the bar. He'd been doing a lot of that today, touching her. Normally he avoided casual physical contact, particularly in business settings, preferring to reserve touching for meetings of a more intimate nature. But, like so many other instances today, Elizabeth had him deviating from the standard.

No sooner were they seated than a waitress came by, dropped a pair of menus on the table and promised to return shortly. Charles questioned that as he watched the woman disappear across the room. "So," he said, shrugging out of his coat, "is this where you hang out on Friday nights?"

"No" was her short reply.

"You mean there's a second town hot spot?"

"I mean I don't hang out in bars on Friday nights," she said, burying her head in the menu.

"Here I thought that uncomfortable look was all my doing."

"Don't assume it's not."

"Funny." He hooked his arm over the back of his chair. "You were fine with my company at the hockey game."

"That was different. You were already in the car and I didn't want to miss my son's game."

The picture of her proud smiling face popped into Charles's mind. He'd spent almost as much time watching her cheer on her child as he had the game. Her son was a lucky kid. What did it feel like to be the recipient of such sincere attention? To have someone who actually wanted you around. Who enjoyed your existence.

Returning his attention to the woman across from him, he shook off the hollow feeling threatening to break loose in his chest. "And now, evil boss that I am, I pay you back by buying you dinner."

"No, you're buying yourself dinner. I'm here because I had to drive you."

"You're eating as well. Should I ask for separate checks?"

She drew the menu closer. "If you want."

"Spoken like a real trouper." Behind his menu, Charles hid a grin. His good humor had returned. He'd been right to insist on her company. "I don't want. What I do want, however, is a drink. Think the bartender makes a proper martini?"

"I'm sure he knows how to mix drinks."

"Mix, sure. Anyone can mix gin and vermouth. It takes an artist to make a martini."

That made her set down the menu. "I didn't know bartending was an art."

"All drinks require skill to make them, if you want to drink something decent."

To his pleasure, he could see her fighting a smile. "That's right. You're a drink snob."

"To which I make no apologies." All the talk about drinks had made him impatient, and he signaled for the waitress. "Now, why don't you hang out here on Friday nights."

"I don't hang out anywhere. I have a child, remember."

"He's in high school, though. I didn't think they needed babysitters at that age."

"Are you kidding? High school is when they need the most supervision. Surely you remember."

"All too well."

"So do I." Though she tried to sound nonchalant, she

failed. Her voice was too regretful, her eyes a tad too evasive.

"Did something happen?" he had to ask.

He watched as she played with the edge of her menu, her downcast lashes casting half-moon shadows on her cheeks. "Andrew happened."

"Oh." *Oh*. Now he understood. "You're afraid Andrew and his girlfriend will…" Rather than say the word, he arched his brow.

"He's seventeen and in love. You know what that's like. You tend to believe forever is really possible."

A pipe dream if ever Charles heard one, though something about the way Elizabeth said it cut him to the quick. Earlier, she did say her ex was an absent father. He had a suspicion that bastard did far more.

"For what it's worth," he said, "not every teenager tries to have sex. And if he does, the odds of the same fate happening twice are fairly slim."

"In other words, I should relax because statistics tell me to."

"No, you should relax because your boss told you to."

"Oh, well in that case…"

The waitress appeared to take their order. Elizabeth ordered both specials. After a moment's contemplation, Charles did the same.

"What happened to the martini?" she asked him when they were alone again.

"I decided to play it safe. Odds are the items are featured because they're popular. Plus," he teased, "you ordered the same thing, so if it's unacceptable, I can blame you."

She laughed. Having never heard her do so, at least not in close proximity, he had no idea how pretty a sound her laugh could be. Or how pretty she looked when doing so. The corners of her eyes crinkled and two tiny dimples dented her cheeks. That he was responsible gave him a warm, satisfied feeling. "You should laugh more often," he said. "Looks good on you." So did the blush creeping into her cheeks.

"I laugh," she replied, playing with her fork.

"Not at work." Correction, not in the office. In *his* office.

"Crack a few more jokes and I might."

"That your way of saying I'm too serious?"

"I'm not sure serious is the word I'd use."

The waitress returned with their drinks. At the sight of thick foam floating atop dark brown liquid, Charles attempted to suppress his grimace. Across the table, Elizabeth coughed, a sign his attempt failed. "Let me guess," she said, "you know beer about as well as you know hockey."

"I was underage in college, remember." He took a sip. Just as he suspected. Heavy and bitter. Sort of like how he felt thinking about his past.

"What word would you use?" he asked, returning to the earlier conversation. "Or are you too much of a lady?"

He liked the smirk she tossed at him. "Scary. People are afraid of you, you know."

"I know." He paused. "You're not, though."

"No, I'm not. Not anymore."

"What changed?"

Leaning forward, she cupped her chin in her hand,

causing the neon bar lights to cast red highlights on the crown of her head. "To tell you the truth, I don't know."

Their eyes connected and Charles saw the flash of approval he'd been seeking all day. The sight struck him hard, arousing more than his body. He hadn't expected the sensation to be so compelling. All of a sudden he found himself seeing details in his companion he'd never noticed before. Like the crook at the bridge of her long nose, and the lines at the edge of her eyes that spoke of experience and smiles. The delicate curve of her lips. He imagined curves of a different type beneath her reindeer sweater. He must have been blind these past few months.

The corners of his mouth curled around his beer glass. "Well, whatever the reason, I'm glad."

Unless his girlfriend was hiding in the comforter wrapped around his shoulders, Andrew was home alone watching television when Liz walked through the door. "Thought you and Vic would be with your friends celebrating," she said. "And what's with the blanket."

"I'm cold, and Vic's got SAT class in the morning so she dropped me off early. How was your 'date'?"

"That wasn't my date. I told you, I had to drive Mr. Bishop today, remember?"

"I didn't know you were taking him to my game."

"Had to. We were running late and if I'd taken him home, I'd have missed your game-winning goal." She tossed a pillow in his direction, which he neatly ducked. "He was impressed, by the way."

"Must have been since he took you out to dinner."

"He was hungry. Really, Andrew, the man's my boss."

"So?"

So, she didn't appreciate the inference. "This was a one-time deal." Come Monday morning, everything would return to normal. Except she wouldn't be afraid of him anymore, she thought smiling to herself.

From his perch on the sofa, Andrew was giving her a look. "Did you get something to eat?" she asked him.

"Made grilled cheese when I got home."

"I'm guessing you left the dirty pan on the burner, too, hoping I'd wash it for you?"

The teenager gave her an exaggerated grin, mimicking a three-year-old in an attempt to look cute. Another night she would have told him to get off his duff and wash his own pan, but tonight she didn't feel like arguing.

"Oh, hey, Mr. Rueben wants you to call him next week," Andrew called out as she walked toward the kitchen.

"Did he say why?" Though the calculus teacher wanting to speak with her couldn't be a good thing.

"Nope. Just to call."

Intuition told her Andrew was holding back, but like the dishes, she decided to let the subject drop. It was late, and she was in too good a mood to press him for information.

She hated to admit it, but Charles made a pretty good dinner companion. Handsome, charming. More than once she'd found herself laughing. He'd told her she looked good when she laughed, she thought with a rush of heat. Been a long time since a man told her she looked good period. She'd almost forgotten what it felt like to have someone look at her as more than Andrew's mother. To be seen as a woman.

Will you listen to yourself? Now she was the one acting like tonight had been a date. As if that were possible. A man like Charles, rich, gorgeous…uninterested. He'd said so himself—he liked the best. She was pretty certain that standard applied to more than coffee and cocktails, same as she was certain a thirty-four-year-old secretary with a GED and teenage son didn't fit the bill.

Still… She turned on the faucet and grabbed a dish sponge. Tonight had been a nice change of pace. Even if it was a one-time thing.

A one-time thing. Charles's sparkling blue eyes danced in front of her, setting off an ache, big and cavernous in the hollow of her chest, and she suddenly remembered why she'd avoided dating all these years. Because the high from the encounter never lasted. You found yourself wanting another fix. And another. Craving the rush so badly you willingly believed all the false promises you were being fed. Eventually, though, reality broke the spell, leaving you alone and pregnant with no one to depend upon but yourself. She'd done the discarded and unwanted deal seventeen years ago. She had no desire to revisit those days again. Far better to stay on the wagon.

She shivered. Andrew was right; the town house was cold. Whatever warmth had carried her home had faded. Best she put Charles Bishop out of her mind, make herself a cup of tea and go watch television with her son. Where she belonged.

* * *

The next morning, the town house was still cold. Liz stared at the automatic thermostat sending a silent message for the temperature to increase at a faster rate.

"The water's not real hot, either," Andrew said from behind her.

"I know." Her own shower had been lukewarm at best, and only that temperature for a couple minutes.

"The furnace was making those weird noises again last night."

"I know that, too. Sorry," she quickly added, pinching the bridge of her nose. It wasn't Andrew's fault the furnace was acting up. Or that she was cold and hadn't slept well. All night long her king-size bed, normally her weekend sanctuary, had felt too big, the unused portion of the sheets too cold. "I'll turn up the thermostat. Maybe the house will warm up while we're out."

"Hope so. Cold showers suck."

"Thank you, Captain Obvious. Go get dressed. I promised your coach you'd be there to help set up tables."

She walked back to her bedroom kicking herself for not setting up the coffeemaker the night before. It was way to early on a Saturday morning to be up without a decent cup of coffee.

A decent cup. That's what Charles would call it, she realized with a shiver. So much for putting him out of her mind. She hadn't been awake a half hour and already he'd crossed her thoughts. Irritated even more, she grabbed her blow dryer. Maybe a rush of hot air would clear her head.

"Mom!"

Liz dropped her chin to her chest. If she got to dry her hair.

"Hey, Mom!"

"Check the kitchen counter," she hollered back. Whatever it was he was looking for, she was sure it would be there. She was beginning to think he never actually looked for anything in the first place.

Flicking the hair dryer on, she tipped her head upside down and started drying. The hot hair on her scalp only served to remind her how cold the rest of her body was. The church hall better have working heat, she thought to herself.

There was a knock on the door and Andrew's half dressed torso appeared. "You've got company," he said in a tight voice.

Company? "What are you talking about?" Must be one of the other hockey parents. And here she was still in her bathrobe with wet hair.

"And put a shirt on. It's too cold to be wandering around without one. Hey, where are you going?"

"To put a shirt on. You told me to."

"After you... Never mind." Teenagers. Tightening her belt, she headed downstairs. Three steps from the bottom, she almost tripped in shock.

"What are you...?" She was too surprised to finish the question.

Charles stood in her living room looking like a GQ model in a supple black leather jacket and faded jeans. He was peeling an equally supple pair of gloves from his fingers. When he saw her, he smiled. "Good morning to you, too."

A blush shot straight to her toes. "Sorry," she said,

brushing the wet hair from her face. "When Andrew said someone was here to see me, I wasn't expecting you."

"Obviously."

Dear Lord, but he looked amazing. Better than he had in her dreams.

The thought struck her sharply as she realized he had indeed been in her dreams. No wonder she couldn't shake him from her head this morning. "What are you doing here?"

"My smartphone," he replied. "I think I left it on your dashboard last night."

Of course. Why else would he come to her home except to retrieve something? "I'll go unlock my car and see."

"No need. If you give me your keys, I'll look myself. You're not really prepared for heading outside."

Liz looked down at the faded terry-cloth garment that barely skimmed her knees. In spite of her having pulled the belt as tight as possible, the front still gapped around her legs, revealing part of her thighs. She gave the belt another tug only to look up and find Charles's eyes watching her with cerulean intensity. All of a sudden the room halved in size. "Guess not," she managed to choke out.

"Not that the robe's a bad look. A little more casual than the reindeer sweater, but…"

Feeling her skin growing warmer, she turned away from his grin.

"And you give me a hard time for answering the door without a shirt on." Andrew ambled down the stairs, heavy-footed in his bare feet. "No one needs to see that robe."

"Manners, Andrew."

"Sorry," he replied, catching her tone.

"This is my son, Andrew," she said. "Andrew, this is my boss, Charles Bishop. Charles thinks he left his phone in my car."

Andrew tossed a head nod in Charles's direction; a greeting Charles, much to Liz's surprise, tossed right back. "Congratulations on the game last night."

"Thanks. Mom, we got to get going. I told Coach I'd be there at quarter to."

He was reminding her? That was different. "Andrew's team is hosting a pancake breakfast at the Episcopal Church this morning to raise money for the rink," she told him.

"Right, the new roof. I won't keep you then. Just let me know where you keep your car keys and I'll be on my way."

"Sure. I keep them on the kitchen count…" Halfway across the room a thought struck her, causing her to turn. "How'd you get here anyway?"

"Rental car. The agency dropped one off late last night."

"So you won't need my chauffeuring services any-more."

"No, you are no longer at the mercy of my schedule."

Lucky her, she thought as her fingers closed around the key ring. No more forced dinners.

An awkward silence settled between them. Liz looked down at the keys. Seemed silly to chase him off when he'd driven across town so early in the morning. The man probably hadn't even had his decent coffee yet. And, the fundraiser could use all the attendees it could muster. "If you haven't had breakfast yet, you're welcome to join us."

"You're inviting me to the pancake breakfast?"

Silly, she knew. He probably had a dozen other, better things to do. For that matter so did she. "If you're interested. Most of your employees will be there at one time or another."

"So attending would be good public relations."

"You could say that."

Charles stroked his jaw. As he thought, his eyes took on a strange, almost grateful expression. "Sounds like a good idea. I think I will join you."

In spite of herself, Liz's pulse skittered. "Great," she replied. "Let me finish getting ready and we'll go together."

Behind her, she heard Andrew march upstairs and loudly shut his bedroom door. "Don't mind him," she said. "He's mad he didn't get a hot shower. Our furnace is being temperamental."

"I see."

Yet again, they fell silent. Liz toed the carpeting with her bare foot, trying to think of something to do besides smile mutely. "I should get dressed, too," she said finally. "Do you mind waiting?"

"Not at all. I'll stay down here and warm up from the outside." To illustrate, he rubbed his hands together and blew on his fingers. "Maybe your furnace will start working better while I wait. Your son's right—it is chilly in here."

That's funny, Liz thought as she trotted back up-stairs. Soon as Charles walked in the house, the cold hadn't bothered her at all.

## CHAPTER SIX

"Your mother tells me you're thinking of going to Trenton Academy next year."

"Uh-huh."

"Good school."

"Yup."

This, thought Liz, was a mistake. Her son had been sullen and monosyllabic all morning.

"Trenton hockey plays in a bigger division than Gilmore High," she explained, setting her plastic fork down on her foam plate. "If Andrew goes, he'll have to repeat his junior year, but he'll also be seen by a lot more colleges, and have a much better shot at a scholarship to a Division I school."

"Impressive. You must be excited."

Andrew shrugged.

Oh, yeah, definitely having a refresher course in manners later.

In spite of the early hour, the tables in the basement of St. Mark's were full, mostly with families of team members. The players themselves milled about refilling the buffet pans with trays and pouring orange juice into plastic drink cups. The cool basement air smelled of bacon and maple syrup.

With a slight hint of citrus body wash. Liz wasn't sure she could truly smell Charles or if her imagination was teasing her senses, but each time he leaned back in his metal folding chair, she swore the aroma drifted past her. How could one man smell so good? Or look so good this early in the morning? Even after putting on makeup and her best turtleneck sweater Liz was pretty sure she still looked tired. Charles on the other hand, looked like he stepped out of a magazine.

And then there was Andrew. She could see this behavior if he was younger and Charles was a potential boyfriend, but neither could be further from reality.

"Of course, he has to keep his grades up to qualify. To play varsity sports, you need to maintain a C or better."

"Which I am," Andrew said, more to his pancakes to anything else.

"So far," she told him. "We haven't seen this semester's progress report yet." That reminded her; she needed to call Mr. Rueben on Monday. Hopefully it wasn't bad news. "He's doing great except for calculus. Math's always been a bad subject. Neither of us know what we're doing in it."

"Mom gave up freshman year when they started geometry."

"Excuse me for not remembering the Quadratic Equation."

"AX squared plus BX plus C equals zero."

Both she and Andrew looked up at Charles, who shrugged. "The Quadratic Equation." Out of the corner of her eye she caught Andrew's barely concealed eye roll.

"Anyway," she said, shooting her son a look, "Andrew decided to take advanced calculus instead of the easier level so this year's been a challenge. So far so good, though."

"That's terrific," Charles replied. "Better to take on the challenge than sit back and rest easy, right?"

"I agree." Annoyance forgotten, she smiled proudly at her boy. For all his sulky insolence this morning, he was a good, hardworking kid.

A tap on her shoulder pulled her out of her thoughts. Peeking over her shoulder she saw Leanne in her blue and gold Boosters' Club fleece. "Can I borrow you for a minute?" she asked Liz after saying hello to Charles.

"Well…" Both Andrew and Charles had taken their phones out and were actively ignoring one another. "Sure. What's up? Is there a problem with the pancakes?" Liz asked, knowing full well as soon as the older woman took her arm and dragged her toward the buffet line what this meeting was really about.

"What on earth is Mr. Bishop doing here?" Leanne asked.

"Having breakfast like everyone else in the room."

"With you and Andrew? What's going on? Van told me the two of you were at the hockey game together, and you went to Mahoney's afterward." Her dark red lips formed a large O. "He didn't…"

"What? No! Don't be ridiculous." What other wild rumors were out there? "He came by this morning to get his phone—which he left in the car," she added before her friend could comment, "and I told him about the breakfast. He thought it might be a good idea to mingle with his employees."

"He's only mingling with one."

"He's eating," Liz repeated. "What's the man supposed to do, travel from table to table with a foam plate in his hand mooching bacon?"

Back at the table, Charles and Andrew were still ignoring one another. As if sensing her scrutiny, Charles gave a quick nod in her direction. He then pointed to her empty coffee cup and gestured if she wanted more. Smiling, Liz shook her head.

The exchange didn't go unnoticed. "Are you sure you two aren't…?" Leanne waggled her eyebrows.

"No. No way." The happy, full feeling she had a moment earlier faded away, replaced by a hollowness in the middle of her chest. "He's our boss, Leanne. He wouldn't be interested in me in a million years."

Briefly she relayed the whole story, about Charles's accident to her driving him all day and how they ended up going straight to Andrew's game. "If I'd brought him home first, I would have missed everything, so I dragged him with me. Afterward, he wanted to get something to eat so we stopped on the way back. There's nothing else to it."

"And here I thought you'd crossed over to the dark side. Although to be honest—" the woman leaned forward "—I'm not sure I'd blame you if you did. Mr. Bishop might be a coldhearted bastard, but he's a gorgeous coldhearted bastard."

"He's not a bastard, period." Liz surprised herself with how easily the defense tripped off her tongue. "In fact, if you talk with him, you find he's an okay guy.

Interesting actually. Did you know he went to Cal Tech when he was seventeen?"

"Was this before or after he cut Ron out of his life?"

She didn't know how to answer. A week ago, a day even, she'd have readily agreed with the cutting comment. "I'm not sure the business with Ron is so cut-and-dried. Something tells me there's two sides to the story, and that maybe Ron's wasn't so innocent."

"I take it back…you have gone to the dark side."

"That's my point. I don't think Charles is as big an enemy as we made him out to be." Leanne would think so, too, if she'd heard the injured resignation in Charles's voice every time the subject of his father came up.

"Who's not the enemy? Bishop?" Van asked. He ambled toward the group, Doug Metcalf trailing a step behind. Wherever there was gossip, the pair was never far. "Morning, Lizzie. How was your night?" Innuendo dripped from his words.

Liz returned his smirk with a scowl of her own. "I don't know, Van, you tell me since you're so busy telling everyone my business."

The salesman threw up his hands. "Sorry. Didn't mean to touch a nerve."

"Well, you did." She refused to be fodder for watercooler gossip, especially when there was no realistic chance that what they were gossiping about could ever happen. She glared at all three of them before turning on her heel and marching away.

Charles sat alone when she arrived at their table, absently playing with his empty juice glass. Andrew had moved to the next table to talk with Victoria and her friend. When he saw her, he instantly straightened. "Problem?"

"Only that the office grapevine has been working overtime. Leanne wanted the details about our 'date.'"

Brow furrowing, he resumed fiddling with his cup. It was obvious the news didn't sit well with him. "What did you tell them?"

"The truth." Bitter as it sounded out loud. "I'm not sure they believed me, though."

"Why not?"

"Because I told them you weren't as big a bastard as everyone thought."

"Did you, now?" He sat back, arms folded across his chest and flashed her a smile. Liz felt her skin blush.

"Don't get too cocky," she told him. "They didn't believe that, either."

"No one ever does. I think, in fact, you're the first. Thank you."

His smile shifted and his expression grew serious. The sincerity in his voice traveled to her chest, settling directly over her heart.

"You're welcome," she said, and wondered if the ache she felt was hers or his. The pancake breakfast faded away, leaving them the only two people in the room. Like this morning, she felt the distance between them halve. And for a crazy second Liz caught herself wishing the rumors were true.

Charles broke the spell first. "I have to go," he said, although he made no effort to move. "I have a conference call with my attorney about a deal I'm working on. Would you like me to walk you to your car? I'll treat you to a real cup of coffee on the way."

"Thanks, but I promised I'd stay and help the committee clean up. Besides, I've got Andrew. He needs new work boots."

"Then I guess I'll see you Monday."

"At work." She added the words as much for herself as anything. Charles's deal comment reminded her exactly who the man sitting next to her was. A man far removed from Gilmore, Bishop Paper and everything else she could name, including her. A man who didn't believe in anything but balance sheets and figures. A man who, soon as he could, would leave for his next big deal. A man she had no business letting get under her skin.

First a high school hockey game, then a pancake breakfast. What next, running for town council? That'll be the day, Charles thought with a shake of his head. What would happen next was finalizing his deal with Xinhua, so he could rid himself of this company and get on with his life.

Alone in his office while he waited for his overseas call, Charles perched on his desk and stared at the White Mountains. He never realized how picturesque they truly were. Their snow-covered slopes glistened under the cloudless winter sky. If he squinted, he could make out tiny dots moving along their surface. Skiers. Good day for skiing, he imagined—if you were into the sport.

Did Elizabeth ski? Be a shame to risk breaking one of those long legs. Bet she ice skated, though. Charles could easily see her guiding her son around the rink when the boy was younger. Catching him when he fell.

She'd be smiling the whole time, too. A real smile. Not one reserved for public viewing.

*Come on, Charles, get yourself together.* His lack of focus these past sixteen hours astounded him. His mind insisted on wandering all over the place. In fact the only consistent thoughts in his head were about his secretary. Seemed like every five minutes her name would pop into his head or he'd get an image of her.

Like the way she looked this morning in that terry-cloth robe. Demure looking and yet the neckline spread open just enough he could tell she wasn't wearing anything underneath. The memory caused a sudden tightness in his body.

This was ridiculous. He'd had attractive secretaries before. Why did this one woman have him feeling so distracted and out of balance? He should be focused on the upcoming negotiations and how soon he'd be rid of this company. Wouldn't be long and he could finally close the book on his father, his childhood and every other bad memory for good.

On his desk, his phone vibrated, rattling loudly against the wood. Charles waited two rings before answering. "*Ni hao ma*, Mr. Huang. I've been expecting your call."

"All I'm saying is it wouldn't hurt for you to show the man a little courtesy. He is my boss," Liz said as she pulled into her driveway.

"I know. You've only told me six times since we got in the car."

"Maybe because I want to make sure you get the message." She looked over at the figure slumped in the passenger seat. Her refresher course started when she pulled out of St. Mark's parking lot, and as it progressed Andrew had sunk lower and lower in his seat till he sat with his knees wedged against the dashboard and his cheekbone resting on one fist. "What is wrong with you anyway?" she asked. "You've been surly since last night."

"Nothing."

Intuition said otherwise so she pressed. "You sure?"

"Don't worry about it."

Code for he wasn't going to share until he was ready. "Sorry, but I'm always going to worry. Comes with the job."

"You done?"

"For now."

She stepped out of the car and promptly shivered. Without a fan blowing hot air on her feet, the sunshine wasn't nearly as enjoyable. Thankfully she remembered to turn up the thermostat before leaving. With luck the town house was finally warm and toasty.

"I thought you thought Mr. Bishop was a tool," Andrew said as she fiddled with the door lock.

"I was wrong. Happens you know."

"So you like him."

Liz paused. Was that what his mood was all about? Because Charles joined them for breakfast? "Sweetheart, you know that Mr. Bishop only joined us because he wanted to mingle with his employees. Build up goodwill and all."

"He didn't mingle with anyone but you."

True, but she wasn't going to read anything into the

attention. No doubt Charles had his reasons. He wasn't a man who did anything without a reason.

Andrew pushed open the front door and they stepped inside. It was like stepping into an icebox. "Is it me, or is it colder than when we left?" Liz asked.

"Colder," Andrew replied. "Definitely colder."

Frowning, Liz knelt down and put her fingers to the baseboard heat. Given the temperature she programmed into the downstairs thermostat, hot air should have been coming out the vent. But the vent, along with the entire baseboard for that matter, was cold.

The morning's pancakes turned to lead in her stomach. This wasn't good.

By midafternoon she learned exactly how bad the situation she had on her hands was.

"I can fix it so you have heat," the plumber told her, "but bottom line is the furnace needs to be replaced."

Liz had known this day would come eventually. "How much?"

When he told her, her heart stuck in her throat. No way could she swing the amount. She was going to have to take a bigger home equity loan. If she had more equity to borrow against, that is after she budgeted for Trenton. Real estate prices in town weren't what they used to be.

Telling the plumber to go ahead and order the furnace and make the repair, she wrapped herself in a blanket and waited to warm up. Her stomach and her head hurt.

"Everything all right, Mom?" Andrew stood on the stairway wrapped in his comforter.

"Fine, sweetheart. The plumber says we're going to need a new furnace."

"Do we have the money?"

The stress must show on her face because he always asked when they were faced with a big expense. Charles was right; she did have a lousy poker face. "Don't worry about it," she told him, aware of how ironic the comment sounded coming from her.

"Because I don't have to go to Trenton or I can get a part-time job…"

"Don't be ridiculous. Furnaces break. It's a cost of homeownership. Why don't you text Sammy and see if you can hang out at his place for the rest of the afternoon? By the time you get back the furnace should be working."

"Okay."

She waited until he went back upstairs before laying her head on the armrest. Times like these the longing she kept buried in her heart rose up like a monster. A chenille throw was no substitute for a pair of strong arms and a shoulder to cry on. It wasn't that she couldn't handle problems on her own. She could and had since high school. But oh, to have someone to hold her close and tell her they'll take care of everything—even if the words were a lie… Sure would be nice.

She closed her eyes and imagined her throw was the aroma of citrus body wash.

Apparently headaches came in threes. Andrew failed his last two calculus exams. That's what Mr. Rueben wanted to talk about. "I'll work with him as much as I can, but I think he'd benefit from more intense one-on-one help as well," the teacher told her. "Someone who will sit with him a few hours a week and help with homework. He's lacking a number of basic skills he'll need to progress next year."

As well as succeed at Trenton, thought Liz.

Of course doing well at Trenton wouldn't matter if he couldn't play hockey, and unless he got his grades up, hockey wouldn't be in Andrew's future much longer.

Liz thanked the teacher and hung up, wondering where she would find a good tutor. Andrew would suggest his friend Sammy, but as good a student Sammy was, Andrew needed more. He needed an adult who would make sure he focused on his work. Later this morning she'd call the guidance office and ask for a few names. Right after she made an appointment with the loan officer at the bank. She was going to have to push up the loan process to pay for her new furnace. Which she had to arrange delivery for.

No wonder she still had her headache from Saturday. With a sigh, she lay her head on her desk. She knew something was up with Andrew's math grade. He was always making comments about the homework. Why didn't she press for more information?

The longing to be held struck again, stronger than ever.

"Need an aspirin?"

Lifting her head, she saw Charles watching her from the doorway of his office. He wore his standard work uniform, shirtsleeves and loose tie, but it wasn't his casual sex appeal that made her breath catch. It was his expression. He wore a look of concern that, focused on her, felt a lot like a hug.

"I came out to learn where you were on the notes from Friday's meetings and saw you had your head down on your desk," he explained. "Figured you had a headache."

"Headaches, plural," she corrected. "Unfortunately I don't think aspirin will help."

"What happened?"

"Nothing I can't handle." She sat up straighter and combed the hair from her eyes. "You said you were looking for something? My notes?"

"The notes can wait. Tell me what's wrong."

"I told you, it's nothing."

"Elizabeth." Squatting so that he was eye level, he grabbed both arms of her chair and turned her until they were face-to-face. "When are you going to accept the fact you aren't a very good liar? The fact you're upset is written all over your face. Did something happen with Andrew?"

Liz studied the man in front of her, amazed at the concern she saw in his eyes. "I—" She didn't know what to say. The very idea he offered to listen…it was a first for her. She wasn't used to having people offering support. Usually they ran the other way. The longing that had been twisting in her chest since Saturday suddenly exploded. She'd been handling everything on her own for so long now…

Before she realized, she was blinking away moisture from her eyes.

"Hey— Hey…" Charles moved closer, bringing his comforting warmth into her space. "It's okay. Is it Andrew?"

"I'm sorry," she said, dabbing at her eyes. "I'm being emotional for no reason. It's silly really."

"Why not let me be the judge of that," he said, his voice soft and gentle. "Tell me what's wrong."

Liz sniffed. "Where should I start? With the fact my furnace died and I have to take out a loan to pay for a new one? Which I'm already doing because I need to pay private school tuition..."

"Wait. I thought Andrew was recruited to play hockey for them."

"In a roundabout way. The school doesn't give out sports scholarships, and Andrew's grades don't qualify him for much in the way of academic merit money. We qualify for some breaks based on need, but it's not enough to cover everything. Though all of that won't matter if the kid can't pass math."

"He's not?"

"Spoke to his teacher about five minutes ago. He needs a tutor. Oh, and did I mention the kid told me this morning he needed new shoes and skates? Turns out he grew since last fall. Chances are he needs all new pants, too." She forced a wan smile. "Aren't you glad you asked?"

"You definitely have a few things on your plate."

"Fortunately I'm used to a full plate by now. As long as nothing else major breaks or Andrew gets himself in trouble, I'll be fine." Pain had settled behind her eyes, probably from sniffing back tears. She pinched the bridge of her nose. "Maybe I will take those aspirin," she said, reaching for the drawer.

"Here, let me." He reached across her to the top drawer where she kept a spare bottle of pain relievers.

Flipping off the top, he shook two capsules into her palm, then handed her the coffee cup by her keyboard. Liz watched everything with mute appreciation.

"You're welcome," Charles replied, reading her mind. He sat back on his haunches watching as she swallowed the pills. "Thursday, when you asked for the raise. Was that to pay for Trenton?"

"Sort of." She nodded. "I figured the extra money would help cover the loan payments."

"And I turned you down."

"I knew going in there was a good chance you would." Amazingly she felt the need to reassure him.

"But you asked anyway."

"Go big or go home, right?" Charles frowned so she explained. "It's something Andrew and his teammates say. Meaning go all out."

"Live or die trying, you mean."

"Exactly."

"A motto I always believed myself." He looked to his knees, but not before Liz caught an uncharacteristic look of regret. "I'm sorry," he said. "I didn't know what you needed the money for."

"Would it have made a difference?"

He didn't answer, because they both knew it wouldn't have. Charles lived by numbers, not emotion; he said so himself.

Yet, here he was listening to her complain. Go figure. "Now that I hear myself, I sound pretty whiny. I should be grateful for what I have instead of complaining. I mean, figuring out how to pay for private school is hardly a life or death situation."

"You want the best for your son. Nothing wrong with wanting the best, remember?"

His remark forced her mouth to curve upward. "You would believe that," she replied. "Andrew did without so much growing up. No father, no grandparents, and I want him to have all the opportunities and choices I missed on. It's that sometimes it feels like I'm swimming upstream to do so."

Nodding with understanding, Charles asked, "What if you had the raise?"

"What do you mean?" She tensed, refusing to listen to any implication in his words. No way she would be lulled into getting her hope up a second time.

"I mean, you can have the raise. I'll put in the paperwork this afternoon."

This couldn't be real. Charles Bishop did not just reverse his decision and give her a raise. Things like that did not happen. "Wha—what about not making exceptions?"

"I decided one time wouldn't hurt. I admire what you're trying to do with Andrew. Besides—" he pushed himself to his feet "—I look at it as an investment. Having a potential NHL star indebted to me could come in handy someday."

"I don't know what to say." Her heart was stuck in her throat along with a lump the size of Franconia Notch. Together they choked off her ability to do much more than smile and blink back a fresh round of tears.

"You don't have to say anything. You would have gotten the raise at your performance review anyway. You do earn your paycheck."

"Thank you." Her shoulders felt like they'd had a ten

ton weight taken off them. "Now I really have to make sure Andrew passes math."

"That's right. He's failing calculus."

"Hanging on by a thread. I have to call the high school and get a list of teachers who tutor. Of course, Andrew will no doubt complain about each one. When he's backed into a corner, he gets disagreeable."

"Wonder where that comes from?" Charles asked, with a smile that made Liz want to stick her tongue out. Certainly lightened the moment.

Only a moment, though. She sighed as her frustration rose again. "I blame myself for some of the problem. The way he complained about the class and his homework, I should have realized he was having trouble sooner. But he kept telling me he was going over the homework with Sammy."

"You need to cut yourself a little slack. You're doing the best you can."

"Thanks. Want to come by and tell Andrew that for me when he starts barking about his tutor?"

"I've got a better idea. How about I tutor?"

*What?* Her mouth dropped open. "You?"

"Sure. Last time I checked, I was pretty good with numbers. Cal Tech, remember? And, he won't be able to say I'm one of those 'boring old teachers.'"

True enough. But why? Why was he suddenly doing so much to help her when two days ago, he barely cared she existed? It didn't make sense.

"Because I want to," he replied when she asked him. He caught her chin between his thumb and forefinger, forcing her gaze upward until she met his eyes. Searching their depths, she looked for signs of motive

only to see nothing but deep blue. Suspicion warred
with gratitude.

As if sensing her hesitancy, he fanned his thumb
across the curve of her chin. "Because I want to."

It was only after he closed his office door that Charles
realized he'd never retrieved Elizabeth's notes. He'd get
them later. His head was still spinning over what he just
did. Had he really offered to tutor her son? And spon-
taneously reversed his decision on her raise? Because
she'd told him her problems?

Yes, he realized with a twisted feeling, he had.
Listening to her explain why Andrew going to Trenton
meant so much to her, the choked off emotion quivering
in her voice, cut him deep. Here was this woman trying
so hard to be both mother and father. She wasn't forgetting Andrew existed or shunting him aside in favor
of another, more important pursuit. She was trying to
give her son the world. And he impeded her efforts.

Would it have made a difference? Soon as she said
those words, and he'd looked into her shining hazelnut eyes, he felt three inches tall. For the first time in
his life he regretted a sound business decision. All of
a sudden he wanted nothing more than to make up for
his decision and prove to her he was more than some
profit-minded boss. All because the sheen in her eyes
kicked him so hard his chest ached. He wanted those
eyes to smile at him, goddammit, not look teary-eyed
and sad.

Letting out a long breath, he washed his hand across
his face and tried to regain focus. Negotiations with
Xinhua were going well. Mr. Huang Bin liked what

he'd seen so far. Meanwhile, Bishop Paper appeared to be bucking the trend as far as paper companies in New England. Last quarter reports showed profits up by three percent. Whatever flaws his father had as a parent, he knew how to run a company. Bishop Paper was in far more solid fiscal shape than he would have believed. And if the company implemented the greening initiatives they discussed Friday, like switching to hydropower, they would be in a strong position for the future.

*Not that you'll be here to see*, he reminded himself. Hydropower and chemical-free bleaching were items for Huang Bin to decide. He would be long gone by then.

For some reason the thought didn't give him as big a thrill as it usually did.

Must be he was tired. Too many late nights reviewing reports were catching up with him. Then again, what else was there to do around here besides work? Or hockey games and pancake breakfasts...

Dropping into his chair, he swiveled around to the window, marveling yet again at the beauty of his view. He had made Elizabeth's day with his spontaneity, he thought with a smile.

That, he realized, gave him a far bigger thrill than negotiations.

# CHAPTER SEVEN

"ANDREW, turn off the video games and get your math book out."

"To do what? Mr. Bishop's not even here yet. What am I supposed to do, stare at the problems I don't know how to do?"

"How about looking like you're trying?" she shot back.

Liz looked at the clock. Charles would be here any minute. The imminent arrival gave her barely enough time to straighten up. Her son could at least contribute by not sprawling across the sofa. "And put your empty soda can in the recycling while you're at it," she added, nudging his left leg.

"Now," she added when the teen didn't move.

"All right, all right. Stop freaking out."

"I am not freaking out. Charles was nice enough to offer his help."

*"Charles?"*

She shot her son a glare. "The least we can do is make sure the apartment isn't a pigsty when he arrives. Straighten out the couch pillows. And refold the afghan."

"Good thing you're not freaking out," Andrew muttered.

Maybe she was freaking out a little. It wasn't like Charles hadn't been here before. But yesterday's visit had been unexpected.

So was tonight's when she thought about it. Today's turn of events still had her head spinning. One minute she had the weight of the world pressing down on her shoulders, next Charles was giving her a raise and offering to tutor her kid. Like her very own Prince Charming.

Why? She figured the raise happened because he felt guilty. Having one's secretary break down could gnaw at your conscience. But tutoring Andrew? He claimed he offered because he wanted to, and she was trying very hard to take him at his word, something her experience made very hard to do. How many promises had Bill made and broken?

*Promise me you'll love me forever?*

*Baby, you know I will.*

This wasn't the same. Charles wasn't promising to love her. He wasn't even promising to stick around. He simply offered to help her son with his math homework. Maybe a guilty conscience was at play here, too. After all, he made both offers at the same time.

The doorbell rang. Liz jumped. Darn it, right on time. Nervously she glanced around the living room. Had the red sectional always looked so ratty? And that blue throw draped over the back. Could the room look more mismatched? She could only imagine what Charles thought. Probably ranked her decor right up with Mahoney's, the ice skating rink and the local coffee. Below his standards and lifestyle.

"You look a million miles away."

She jumped again. Charles stood behind her, shrugging off his overcoat. A coat that, she realized, was more expensive and luxurious than any of the furniture.

"Everything all right?" he asked.

"Everything's fine," she lied. *Giving myself a dose of reality, is all.* "I didn't hear you come in, is all."

"A voice hollered for me to let myself in."

Must have been Andrew. "We're still working on his manners."

"No worries," he said, draping his coat over the back of the sofa. "I'll get my revenge soon enough."

He'd come straight from the office because he still wore his charcoal suit and silk tie and as usual looked amazing. Sleek, sexy and yet—she realized with a quiver—strangely comfortable looking amid the worn furnishings.

"I told Andrew to set up at the table so you'll have plenty of room to work," she said, pointing to the butcher block table that doubled as a dining room and office. Andrew stood at the head chair rooting around his backpack.

"Hey, Mom, do you know where I put—"

"Front hall near the shoes. We're working on memory, too," she added.

"I heard that!"

"You were meant to," she shot back.

She and Charles shared a smile. The man might not offer smiles often, at least not unguarded ones, but when he did, the results could make your knees weak. Liz had to grab the back of the sofa. "I can't tell you how much I appreciate your helping him."

"I gathered as much from the five times you thanked me at work today." His smile turned warmer and for a second, he looked about to say something more. He didn't, though.

Instead, loosening his tie, he called over to Andrew, "What are we tackling tonight, anyhow?"

"First order derivatives." Andrew, who was in the process of crossing the room with his newly discovered math book, rolled his eyes. "Can't wait."

"Andrew!"

Charles laughed. Deep and rich and full, a sound made for turning insides into mush. "I'll change his mind."

Yeah, good luck with that, thought Liz. She had a feeling nothing would change her son's mind—about math or anything else for that matter.

Thankfully the "pep" talk she and Andrew had earlier about making an effort sunk in. Amazing what the threat of losing hockey could do for motivation because the kid actually paid attention to what Charles had to say. What's more, he was doing the work. After five or ten minutes of discomfort, the two of them managed to put their heads together. They were currently cruising through Andrew's homework assignment.

"Then you take the exponent, multiply by the front number, and subtract one from the exponent."

"That's it?"

"That's it. The key is not to memorize the equation, but to focus about the steps you need to get there. Your problem is you're trying to skip steps and that won't work. Math is all about breaking down big pieces of information into smaller pieces. The trick is not to try to do everything in your head or you get confused."

"I've been telling him that since he was eight," Liz remarked from her position at the kitchen counter.

"Mom!"

"What, a mother can't gloat when she's right?"

From over Andrew's bent head Charles flashed a grin in her direction that shot straight to her knees. It felt different having a man in the house. Back when she was a teenager, this is what she imagined happy homes were like, parents and children spending time together, sharing each others' lives. No stepfather with roaming eyes or mother complaining about having one too many mouths to feed. Tonight reminded her of the normalcy she'd strove to give Andrew his entire life. With a father figure to explain homework and a husband to lean on when times got tough. An old-fashioned and outdated fantasy? Sure, but what good was a fantasy if you couldn't create a perfect one, right?

Shaking off the rush of longing, she returned to chopping carrots. In the other room, Andrew grunted his understanding to something Charles was saying. She resisted the urge to look to the dining room table again. Her mind was already having difficulty staying focused.

What was it lately that had her thinking about fantasies anyway? Was it Andrew getting older? Or something else? Like a pair of concerned blue eyes that had been there to listen to her problems.

Remembering the touch of Charles's fingers against her chin, she smiled.

"Mom?"

Andrew stared at her with a look of embarrassment and frustration.

"I asked when we were having dinner," he said.

"Um… Twenty minutes." Unless she faded out again and burned the chicken.

"Smells delicious," Charles said. "I'm having trouble concentrating with my stomach growling."

"You're staying?"

"Why wouldn't he?" Liz cut in. Truthfully she was as surprised as Andrew. Sure, inviting a man to come by at dinnertime implied staying for dinner, but she'd assumed he wouldn't want to. "I'm afraid we're only having roast chicken breast and vegetables."

"Anything you serve sounds terrific as long as it's homemade. I haven't had a decently cooked meal in ages."

He hadn't? "You don't have someone to cook for you?"

"My housekeeper isn't what I'd call the best cook. She has an unhealthy fascination with ground beef."

"I have the feeling you'll be saying the same thing about me. When it comes to cooking, I'm all about the basics." Thank goodness she decided to take chicken out this morning instead of hamburger for meat loaf.

"I'm sure it'll be fine. Something tells me I'll enjoy anything you make."

*He's being polite.* Even so, her stomach did a somersault. "Just for that," she told him, "you get to have wine with dinner."

Not to mention that if he planned on joining them for dinner, she would need a drink or two herself.

* * *

Dinner was delicious. Granted, he wouldn't call the meal five-star cuisine. But sitting with Elizabeth and her son, sipping an okay glass of wine and listening to them talk about their days, Charles decided it was the best chicken he'd had in a long time. He told her as much after they finished and Andrew had retreated to his room.

Flashing a half smile, she pushed herself from the table. "It's all right, Andrew's out of earshot," she said, gathering the plates. "You can stop being polite."

That she couldn't take him for his word stung. "You don't believe me?"

"The man who called the chef at Mahoney's a philistine? No."

"Mahoney's is a different story."

"Oh, really, how so?"

She was heading into the kitchen so he grabbed some plates and followed. "The person who makes that concoction you called macaroni and cheese Friday night does not qualify to be called a chef. And besides, the chef at Mahoney's isn't…" *Isn't you.* The thought stopped him in his tracks.

Elizabeth glanced at him from over her shoulder. "The chef at Mahoney's isn't what?"

"Isn't going to make me do dishes," he lied. She'd never believe the true answer. He was having trouble believing he had the thought himself.

Didn't matter. His lie earned him one of those laughs he enjoyed hearing. "If you think that'll get you out of the chore, you're wrong."

"What about Andrew. Does he get the fun of helping, too?"

"Normally, yes, but I think I need a break. I'm sorry he's being so sullen."

"I didn't think he was being so bad."

"Let me guess, you were worse."

"I plead the fifth."

That earned him another laugh and Charles decided he'd scrub dishes all night so he could keep hearing the sound.

"He's really a pretty helpful kid. And friendly. I don't know what's going on with him these days."

"Maybe he's got girl problems or something."

"Nope. He and Victoria are still thick as thieves."

She turned to take the stack of plates from his hands and their fingertips brushed across each other. The contact, brief as it was, sent a surge of heat down inside him. She felt a reaction, too. If the color flushing her cheeks didn't say so, her barely audible gasp did.

"Wash or dry?" She moved to the sink, turning her back to him and her voice took on a higher pitch. "Since you're a novice, maybe you should stick to the easier of the two tasks and grab the dish towel. You can dry the pots and pans when I get to them."

"All right." What he truly wanted was to reach out and touch her again, to determine whether the spark was a one-time anomaly, but the skittishness in her voice warned him away.

He watched as she scraped the plates into the wastebasket, muttering some comment about a lack of a garbage disposal, before stacking them in the dishwasher. Then she turned on the faucet. Steam and apple-scented bubbles began to rise up from the stainless steel.

By now, the silence hanging between them had

grown thick and awkward, the lightheartedness from dinner vanquished by one accidental brush of their hands.

"Do you and Andrew eat dinner together every night?" he finally asked, trying to draw the moment back.

"As often as possible." Elizabeth plunged the saucepan into the suds and began swabbing the inside with a sponge. "I sort of insist. With me working, nights and weekends are the only family time we have. Although nowadays, between hockey and school and *Victoria*, we don't have as many meals together as we used to."

"I could count the number of meals my mother and I ate together on one finger," Charles replied. "I defined the term latch-key kid."

"Your mother worked?"

"Hardly." He reached for the pan she'd finished rinsing only to be disappointed when her fingers avoided his. "On second thought, maybe she did. Lord knows she put a lot of effort into keeping her boyfriends happy." Including ignoring her child. Charles had always believed if not for the child support Ron begrudgingly sent, she'd have checked out without him. "At any rate, I became very adept at reading a room service menu at a young age."

"Explains your obsession with high quality food." The comment was lighthearted, but there was empathy shimmering in her soft brown eyes. The way the emotion wormed through him took him by surprise. He hadn't expected to feel so...so *comforted*.

"I spent the better part of my childhood avoiding dinner with my family," she said as she submerged

another pot. "Wasn't too hard. My mom was more interested in my stepfather and her new family. Most of
the time I would make myself a sandwich and eat it in
Bill's car."

She offered a wry smile. "In retrospect, spending
time in the backseat of a car probably wasn't the best
plan. But I was a teenager and in love."

*And believed forever was possible.* Wasn't that
what she said the other night? He tried to reconcile a
young, love-struck Elizabeth sneaking off to be with
her boyfriend with the woman standing next to him.
He couldn't.

"Your family must be proud of how you're raising
Andrew," he remarked, trying to bring her back to more
positive subjects. When she got sad, the sparkle left her
eyes, and he didn't like the look.

Unfortunately he picked a bad topic for instead of
brightening, she grew a little sadder. "They've never
met him. I left home when I was pregnant and that was
it."

"Then they aren't in Gilmore."

"No, a few towns south," she answered. "I followed
Bill up here. He had a job lined up in Franklin. Then
when our relationship fell through, I stayed."

"And Bill?" He suspected he already knew the answer.

"He didn't. He's in Florida now."

Charles wanted to strangle them all. How could they
let her slip from their lives so easily? Then again, hadn't
he asked the same question of his own parents?

They were a lot alike, weren't they? Left to fend for

themselves, only she'd had it far, far tougher. His admiration for her grew.

"At least you can pride yourself on saying everything turned out well in the end," he said. "Raising Andrew on your own that is."

"I didn't have much choice once he was born. Don't get me wrong," she added hastily, finishing another pan and rinsing it under the water. "I love Andrew with all my heart…"

He interrupted the needless apology. "No need to explain. I understand."

"Thanks."

"You're welcome. For what it's worth, if I'd had a Bill with a car to eat in, I would have chosen that route, too. Well, maybe not exactly with a Bill, but maybe a Betsy or a Betty…"

His voice drifted off as their hands touched again. This time the spark burned stronger. Charles slid his fingers forward, letting their length align with hers, their slick, soap-covered skin caressing.

A small breath cut through the thickened air. Elizabeth was studying their hands with hooded eyes, her breath coming in ever shortening bursts. For a moment, neither of them moved. Charles's pulse raced. He felt like he stood on the edge of a great unknown not sure if he should step or not. This sensation, this heat, this whatever—he didn't know what word to use—was foreign to him.

Then, quick as it sparked, the moment shifted. "Last pan," Liz said. She pulled her hand away. "Your obligations for the evening are complete. I'll manage the rest on my own."

"You don't have to," he told her. Beneath the dish-cloth, he balled his hand into a fist and wondered if he was only talking about the dishes. "I can help."

"No need. You've already done more than enough."

Though she wore a smile, it couldn't mask the hint of brittleness in her words. Where connection had been, awkwardness rushed in to take its place. "Thank you again for helping with Andrew tonight."

She was backing off. Shoving distance between them, and Charles was pretty sure he knew why. She'd felt the same spark he did, and was turning cautious, unsure about what the connection meant. He knew because he felt the same way.

"You should probably get going," she told him. "I don't want to keep you here any longer than necessary."

"You're probably right. I have work to do." Plus, he wanted to process what happened. Figure out what he wanted to do with the attraction that was clearly flow-ing through him right now. At the moment the male part of him screamed for him to explore it further. He needed a step back to allow logic a say. "I'll see you in the office tomorrow."

"Thank you again for helping," she said.

Her soft smile begged to be tasted. "Please stop thanking me," he said. "I wanted to help." Then, be-cause the male part of him couldn't help itself, he paused at the door and let his eyes drift to her pink lips. "Good night, Elizabeth."

Liz was surprised her hands weren't trembling when she locked the door. Lord knows her insides were a complete jumble of anxious energy.

*You were imagining things, Liz.* His eyes did not zone in on her mouth just now. Those touches meant nothing. The accidental brushing of two hands doing dishes. Her insides ached for no reason. That had to be the explanation. She'd been fantasizing about how good a pair of arms would feel around her and she started projecting. Right? *Right?*

Or was it? In her heart she knew she hadn't imagined the way his eyes darkened as he said goodbye. But why would Charles want her? Was it because he figured, with the office grapevine already gossiping, why not take advantage of the situation? Because, after hearing her pathetic story, he figured she was an easy mark?

God, but she wished she knew which scenario was true. She wished she hadn't let her thoughts drift to fantasy. She wished she could tuck the need and awareness back into hibernation where they belonged.

But most of all, she wished she knew which scenario frightened her more: that she did imagine everything or that the desire she saw in Charles's eyes was real.

"Good morning, Elizabeth."

Charles's silky voice shot straight to the base of her spine, much to Liz's dismay. She'd spent the night in her cold empty bed battling images of blue eyes and soap-slicked hands. Now, having finally gotten her thoughts somewhat under control, he unlocked them again with three simple words.

She hated him.

"Good morning," she replied, keeping her eyes on her paperwork. She might not be able to keep her body from reacting, but she could pretend it wasn't. "Doug

Metcalf emailed you last month's sales figures. I printed out a copy and put the report on your desk."

"Thank you. And thank you also, again, for dinner."

"Thank you for helping Andrew and with the dishes."

She heard him chuckle. Since she still refused to look in his direction—doing so would only make her blush or give in to some other foolish reaction—she couldn't see his expression, but she could imagine the sexy twinkle in his eye. "Well, aren't we the grateful duo this morning," he said, his voice continuing to be a low, honeylike drawl. "How did you sleep?"

"Fine. The town manager's office called as well. He'd like to schedule a meeting with you for next week." She began sifting through the papers on her desk. "I told him I would get back to him with some potential dates…."

His hand reached out and stilled hers. "Are you planning to avoid eye contact all day?"

No, only till she regained a sense of reality. She stared at the hand resting on top of hers. Like so many of their physical encounters, it was hardly a touch at all. A quick pull of her hand would break all contact. Problem was she didn't want to pull away. *She wanted more.*

"I was simply reaching for the hard copy of your desk calendar is all," she replied, shoving the traitorous thoughts away.

"I see. Then you won't mind looking up."

She did. Mind. And she looked up. Only because not doing so would be childish. Soon as she made eye contact, however, she realized childish might have been the better alternative. Especially upon seeing the intense dark blue looking back.

"Much better," he said. "I'd like to speak with you in my office if you don't mind."

"About what?" She wasn't sure she wanted to know.

"My office, Elizabeth."

Feeling suddenly meek, she followed him in, taking up position in front of his desk while he hung up his coat. Another mistake, since the posture put her back to him.

"There's no firing squad," he said in her ear. His warm breath tickled her skin, causing goose bumps to erupt down her neck.

"Do you always have to do that?" she asked, swiping at her skin.

"Do what?"

"Sneak up on people."

"I don't 'sneak up' on people ever."

"Then you're a naturally stealthy walker."

"I'll take that as a compliment," he said, coming around her to the front of his desk.

"Take it however you'd like," she replied.

Standing face-to-face wasn't much better than having her back to him. Now her personal space not only had to contend with his citrusy scent but with the sight of his dark curls and freshly shaven skin. Her only saving grace was the pair of high heels she chose to wear this morning, that allowed her extra height. And even then, he still managed to make her feel petite and under his gaze.

She made one last effort to regain professional decorum. "You said you wanted to speak with me. What about?"

"This."

He kissed her.

The kiss wasn't passionate or hard and demanding. Quite the opposite. It was a quiet, gentle touch of the lips. By the time Liz could register what happened and react, the moment was over. Leaving her off balance. "What…?" Dazed, the words wouldn't form.

Charles smiled. "That's more like it," he said, the back of his hand reaching out to brush her cheek. "I thought about doing that all night long."

"You did?"

"Uh-huh."

A thousand butterflies chose that moment to take flight in her stomach. She pressed her palm flat against her abdomen to quell them. Suddenly fascinated by the artwork hanging over his credenza, Liz walked toward it. "Do you always feel the need to kiss your secretaries?"

"Only the tall, feisty ones."

"I see."

"You don't believe me."

She could feel Charles studying her and imagined the narrowing of his blue eyes as he tried to decipher the problem. She didn't know what she believed. She was relieved to know the attraction she'd felt passing between them was neither imagined nor one-sided. But knowing the attraction was mutual couldn't quell her uneasiness.

"Oh, I believe you. I'm wondering what made you think the desire was mutual."

"Because I know it is. Or would you prefer to keep pretending we're not attracted to one another." Once again, he'd found his way directly behind her.

"Dammit, I'm going to buy you some tap shoes," she whispered.

"I'm not the one who's tap dancing around the obvious," he said with a chuckle. His hands came to rest on her shoulders. "We're attracted to each other, Elizabeth," he murmured. "I didn't press the issue last night, but seeing you this morning, well…a part of me couldn't help itself."

Liz bit her lip, choking back the sigh that threatened to escape. Charles's touch was strong and comforting. The closeness of his body invited her to lean back against his broad chest. Offering support. Offering *more*.

"Couldn't help yourself, huh?" she heard herself saying.

"This wasn't planned, if that's what you mean. Nor was last night. I didn't come to your house last night with an ulterior motive."

"How did you—?"

"Your poker face. I could see the mistrust a mile away last night. I'm sure if I could see your face, I'd spy it again now. And I get why, too."

"You do?"

"Life is unfair. A person needs to protect himself."

Exactly. Relief began to wash over her, only to wash away. He understood because of experience. At the realization, a tightness wound its way around her chest and for a moment she wished she could let go and lean into his arms.

"You know those silly team building exercises?" she asked. "The ones where you fall backward and the other person has to catch you?"

"Trust falls?" She could tell he was confused by the reference.

"Can't do them to save my life. I wuss out every time."

"Hmm." Leaning forward, he managed to encroach on the little personal space she had left. "Tell you what," he said, his voice so silky and soft the words felt like a caress. "You let me know when you're ready to try."

# CHAPTER EIGHT

Over the next three weeks Charles became a fixture in the Strauss household. On Monday and Wednesday he would arrive at six o'clock sharp to help Andrew with his homework. He always stayed for dinner, insisting he enjoyed Liz's no-frills cooking. Liz was pretty certain the compliments were more out of politeness since no one could possibly enjoy meat loaf as much as he claimed. For his part, Andrew appeared to be shedding some of his sullenness. The other night, he and Charles actually watched part of the hockey broadcast together.

On nights that Andrew played hockey, Charles found his way to the games, bearing cups from the doughnut shop to "rescue" her from the vending machine coffee, which he called a travesty to coffee growers everywhere. His enthusiasm for high school hockey wouldn't win any medals—but he did cheer at the appropriate times, and made a point to speak to parents who worked for him. With each game he attended his corporate approval rating increased. Liz wasn't surprised. When he wanted to, he could turn on the charm better than anyone, a fact she knew all too well. His silky voice was incredibly hard to resist.

A lot of things about the man were hard to resist, she thought with a guilty smile. She sat at her desk staring at her computer screen. Charles said he had a breakfast meeting so she was completely alone. She should be using the time to catch up on work, but her mind kept wandering over the past three weeks.

Although he made no bones about his attraction to her, Charles had been the perfect gentleman. At work and when tutoring Andrew, he kept his distance. But when Andrew left the room, he would steal sweet, semi-chaste kisses that would linger with just enough promise to make her insides melt with need. He never pushed for more; always letting her set the pace.

They were playing things safe. Correction, *she* was playing things safe. The growing sense of normal that surrounded seeing Charles at her dinner table or next to her on the bleachers told her she had to. Things were too good to trust they would last and far as she was concerned, life was hard enough. No need asking it to kick you in the teeth. Protect your heart; save yourself the fall.

"This overnight package arrived for Mr. Bishop. I told reception I'd give it to you." Leanne bustled into the outer office still in her red pea coat and boots. She read off the label. "Confidential. Interesting."

"Thanks." Liz took the package without comment. Her colleague was fishing for gossip again.

"Glad to help. By the way…" Lifting herself up, she rested her bottom on the corner of Liz's desk. Her boot heel tapped against the wood, the soft *thump* keeping time with the tapping of her index finger on her knee. "I wanted to tell you that whatever you're doing to your boyfriend, please keep doing it. Did you know he actually told the VP there was no rush to get him the next round of reports? *No rush.*"

"I told you, Leanne, I'm not *doing* anything."

"Right. Well, keep 'not doing anything,' because I like this new mood of his."

If Andrew were here, he would roll his eyes. Liz did the job for him. Leanne would believe what she wanted to believe, but Liz… Whatever was going on between her and Charles, she wouldn't presume to have any kind of power over him. The man would do what he wanted. If he told accounting there wasn't a rush, he no doubt had a very good reason.

Like the fact he wouldn't be here much longer. Her gaze flickered to the overnight package. Score one for playing it safe.

"Earth to Lizzie." A manicured hand waved in front of her face. "Is Andrew excited for tonight's game?"

Blinking, she nodded. "Can't wait." For the first time in years, Gilmore High School looked to win the state title. Tonight was the semifinal game. Fortunately, thanks to Charles, his grades had improved enough so he no longer had to worry about being benched. "Should be a good game."

"I'd love to see the kids win. They've played hard this year. Do you want me to save you and Mr. Bishop a seat?"

Again with the gossip. Liz shook her head. "You can save me one. I have no idea if Charles plans to go or not."

"Plans to go where?" The topic of their conversation walked into his office. Liz couldn't help but notice he had unusually bright eyes for so early in the morning. Whatever meeting he had must have gone well. Again, her gaze dropped to the package on the desk.

Leanne, on the other hand, jumped immediately to her feet. "Mr. Bishop! I was just delivering a package to Liz for you on the way to my office."

Silently Charles began to remove his gloves, one finger at a time. His eyes focused like lasers on the accounting secretary, their blueness probing as he waited for her to say something. Leanne smoothed the front of her coat. Then smoothed it again. "Which I've delivered," she said finally. "So I'll be on my way."

"Good idea."

"Was that really necessary?" Liz asked once they were alone.

"Good morning, Elizabeth, and yes. I like to keep people on their toes."

"Yes, we wouldn't want them to know you're a nice guy." She couldn't help her smile. Leanne's fluster was amusing.

He smiled back. "No, we definitely wouldn't want people to think I'm nice, would we?" he drawled, leaning in so close she could feel his mint-scented breath on her lips. Her mouth ran dry. Would he kiss her here? In her office where anyone could walk in?

Instead he teased her by running the tip of his glove along her nose. "Now where is it Leanne is saving me a seat?" he asked, eyes sparkling.

"Tonight's Gilmore hockey game. The semifinals."

A shadow crossed his face, dimming the brightness. "I can't. I have a conference call this evening."

"Oh." Liz hated that her heart sank with the news.

She had no reason to be disappointed. Just because he'd come to games in the past didn't mean he was obligated to come to every single one, or clue her in on his plans if he wasn't.

"I'm sorry," he said. As if he owed her an apology.

"No need." She thought she did a pretty good job of sounding unaffected. "I'll let you know how they do."

Playoff games were always more popular than those during the regular season. Arriving at the Franklin rink, Liz couldn't find a parking place. She was forced to drive around the block several times and even after that, ended up snagging a space two streets over. Fortunately the weather gods had decided to bestow a midwinter thaw on the area, making walking the extra distance bearable.

Arriving at the crowded arena, she realized every student in all four grades from both schools had to be in attendance. The bleachers were jam-packed. Out of habit, she scanned the crowd for a familiar head of dark curls, getting halfway around before she caught herself. *He's not coming, remember?* He was back at the office waiting on an overseas call.

Leanne stood near the training room door. "Thought you were saving me a seat," she greeted the older woman. "What happened?"

"Playoffs happened. Apparently the opposing team has a very active booster club. It's standing room only. Best I can do is offer you a space here by the door. I can't see much, but since you're taller, you might have better luck. Where's your other half?"

"On the ice," Liz replied. Standing on her tiptoes, Liz

spotted Andrew coming off the ice. He already looked sweaty and tired.

"I mean your boss. Is he parking the car?"

Dear Lord, but the woman didn't stop. "Contrary to what everyone thinks, we aren't a matched set," Liz told her. "We don't do everything together. In fact, Mr. Bishop is still at the office."

"He is?" Amazingly, even after what Liz told her, Leanne looked genuinely surprised. "I thought for sure he'd come tonight. Especially after—" The rest of her sentence got lost as two players smashed into the glass, causing the crowd around them to cheer. Liz quickly checked the numbers, saw that it wasn't Andrew and continued. "Especially after what?"

"Van and Doug told me he— Come on, Jimmy!" Looking to the ice, Liz saw Leanne's son make a terrific defensive play to save a goal. No sense pressing the woman any further. The names Van and Doug told her all she needed to know. There was some kind of new office gossip about Charles floating around, and as usual, those two were right in the thick of it.

Best she just watch the game and put all thoughts other than hockey out of her head.

She'd succeeded at the task pretty well, until the beginning of the third period when her senses began to tingle as though she were being watched. Scanning the crowd she saw no one. Then a familiar baritone whispered close in her ear, "Have I missed much?"

Liz jumped. Seeing Charles standing there, silly foam coffee cups in his hand, made her heart jump. "What are you doing here?"

"Hopefully watching Gilmore High School win,"

he replied. "I stopped at the doughnut shop on the way here. Would you believe there was a line?

"I think the truth about the vending machines has gotten out," he added in a low voice.

What she couldn't believe was the fact he was there. "What about your overseas call?"

"I rescheduled."

Liz coughed away the frog in her throat. Silly that his change of mind should get to her like this. It was only a high school hockey game for goodness' sake. So what if no one had ever rearranged plans for her in what felt like forever. "I didn't…"

"I know," he replied, not letting her finish. The understanding in his eyes shot all the way to her toes. "Drink your coffee before it gets cold."

Liz did as she was told and was mid sip when Leanne turned around to notice Charles had joined them. "Mr. Bishop!" she exclaimed. "You came after all. Lizzie said you couldn't make it."

"I had a change of plans."

The other secretary nodded with so much enthusiasm, her gold earrings slapped her jaw. Liz could imagine what kind of speculation was running through her head. "I'm so glad," Leanne was replying. "I wanted to say thank you in person. Van and Doug told me about your offer."

Charles waved her off. "It was the least I could do."

What offer? Liz listened with curiosity hoping the conversation would provide an answer but before Charles and Leanne could continue, a cheer erupted from the crowd drawing everyone's attention back to the few minutes of the game.

Gilmore won six to four. As the crowd filtered past them on the way out of the rink, Liz felt Charles's hand on her arm, his gentle grip pulling her close. "I don't want you to get trampled," he whispered in her ear.

"Seeing how I've got a good two inches or more on half the people here, I don't think that's a problem."

"Better safe than sorry." Though outwardly she rolled her eyes, the idea he was looking out for her secretly thrilled her. She felt delicate and feminine and dare she say, desirable? That notion thrilled her even more.

The crowd took a while to depart. Liz allowed herself the luxury of leaning back against his broad chest ever so slightly, not completely leaning on him but enough so she could feel his shoulder nudging between her shoulder blades. His temple hovered next to hers and while she nodded greetings to people passing by, the proximity allowed her to pretend the breath fanning her cheek was caused by a far more intimate embrace. When at last the crowd thinned, he released her, but the memory of his touch remained, along with the sensations it stirred inside her.

She looked over and, from the dark blue of his eyes, saw the closeness had affected him, too. "Did you really reschedule your call?" She needed to know he wasn't handing her a line. "Why?"

Charles shrugged. "It was a play-off game. I realized if the team lost, it would be the last time I'd have to watch them play."

The last time. Liz tried not to think about how those words settled so heavily. "I had no idea you'd become such a high school hockey fan."

"I like watching the crowd. Their passion is addictive." His eyes bore into her as he answered, the silent message unmistakable. The air in their tiny corner grew thick and clingy adding fuel to heat already running through her limbs.

Seeking to break the moment, she looked to the empty cup in her hand. "Well, the crowd is heading home now," she murmured.

"So it is." She felt the gentle pressure of a hand on the small of her back as he bid her to move. "Come on," he said, his voice husky. "I'll walk you to your car."

He led her outside, past a handful of fans sneaking cigarettes by the entrance and through to the rear of the parking lot. While they were inside, the sky had gone from starry to mottled gray and black clouds, taking away much of the warmth. Liz hardly noticed. The hand splayed against her back spread a warmth she could feel throughout her body. She combed her hair from her face, letting the night air wash the skating rink's staleness off her cheeks.

"Feels good, doesn't it?" Charles noted.

She nodded. "Though I'm sure the cold will catch up with me soon enough. Who knew a room with an ice floor cold get so warm?"

"Pack a couple hundred people inside and anything will get warm."

The ice rink was in a quiet part of town, near the high school and old town cemetery. As they walked in comfortable silence along the oak-lined sidewalk, past century old tombstones and family vaults, Liz was reminded of the old wives' tale. "Think we should whistle to ward off evil spirits?" she asked.

He drew her closer. "Don't worry. If anything bad is out there, I'll keep you safe."

The way he said the words, slow and deep, knocked on the walls around her heart and for a moment, she almost believed him.

A shiver invaded her thoughts.

"Cold's caught up with you," he said.

"Guess so." She didn't dare tell him the real reason she shivered was the way he made her feel.

"Hold on then." Stepping in front of her, he took the lapels of her overcoat and pulled them tight. A simple gesture, but it left Liz feeling cocooned in warmth and security.

"There," he said, his hands lingering, "we wouldn't want you to catch cold."

"Do you take this good care of all your assistants?"

"Only the ones I've kissed. Which, by the way," he added, letting his finger slip down the slope of her nose, "is a very, *very* short list."

"Good to know." Again, she almost—almost—believed she was special. Lord knows that right now, with the night air swirling around them and the heat of his body gliding against hers, she wanted to.

Switching gears, she returned to a question that had been nagging her since he arrived. "What offer was Leanne thanking you for?"

"I told Van and Doug I'd contribute the remainder of the funds needed to rebuild the ice rink."

"But that's…" Liz nearly tripped, she was so surprised. Fundraising efforts had only recently begun; last she heard, the balance needed was a sizable one.

Charles shrugged. "Makes for good public relations."

Except he looked almost embarrassed to have been found out. Hardly the reaction of a man seeking publicity for his good work.

Though she knew he wasn't looking for her approval, she gave it anyway. "I'm impressed."

If it was possible for a man's lashes to sweep over his eyes, Charles's accomplished the task. When he looked back at her, their color was softer, cobalt with a gratitude he need not feel as far as she was concerned. "Thank you, Miss Strauss. Your approval means a lot."

He was sincere and the fact her opinion actually mattered to him caused her entire body to fill with a warm glow. Suddenly everything about the night felt different. She felt different. Something had shifted inside her chest. A crack had formed in the wall, and her heart, so long protected, opened up.

Fingers trembling, she reached out and brushed them against his. Charles sucked in his breath at the contact, then a second later, she felt his fingers entwine with hers. "Do you need to give Andrew a ride home?" he asked.

She shook her head. "He has a date with Victoria. Why?"

A smile crossed Charles's features. A tentative, hopeful expression. "How would you like to taste a really good martini? Just a drink," he hastened to add. "No pressure."

This time the shiver passing through her was hot and left a trail of awareness in its wake. "I'd like that."

Charles's penthouse was located in a condominium complex on the banks of the Androscoggin River.

Originally a textile mill, the cluster of buildings had been converted into residences a year before. She looked around with amazement. Sleek and modern, with ceilings at least fifteen feet high, the place was a designer's dream. The exposed brick walls blended seamlessly with hardwood and granite fixtures. Floor-to-ceiling windows, black as the night outside, reflected the furnishings like giant mirrors. Liz stepped off the foyer and found herself in a submerged pitlike area filled with an oversize sectional sofa. The focal point was a gas fireplace. A fireplace Charles lit by flicking a small switch on the wall.

"Wow. This is incredible." She was too blown over to say much more. Put her two-bedroom town home to shame, that's for sure.

And yet for all its gloss and opulence, the apartment felt empty. Like Charles's office, there were no photos or homey touches. No souvenirs from day trips. No clay handprints propped on bookcases. No books for that matter. The painting above the fireplace wasn't even hung; it sat propped on the mantel. An artsy way of displaying the work, but Liz couldn't help thinking the style had more to do with expediency. Charles could move tomorrow and it would take less than a day to pack his belongings. And most of that time would be for his wardrobe.

Liz's amazement dimmed a little.

"I keep the liquor in the kitchen," Charles told her.

He led her round the corner to a gourmet kitchen, which could house two of hers. "I certainly wouldn't trip over Andrew in this place," she joked only to realize how the comment sounded.

However, if Charles heard any presumption in her words, he didn't say anything. He was busy opening the oven door. "Shepherd's pie," he remarked, closing it again. "Told you my housekeeper had a fixation with ground beef."

Leaving the casserole in the oven, he crossed to the giant granite island. There he took out two glasses and a cocktail shaker from the cupboard beneath. "I'm pretty sure they had a basketball team in mind when they designed this place," he replied. "Too bad the average height in New Hampshire isn't six foot seven. Now, remember, I said it takes an artist to make a proper martini."

There was a bottle of gin on the counter. Not surprisingly Liz saw the brand was extremely expensive. "And are you an artist?"

"Not in the least," he replied with a straight face. "But I have practiced enough that I'm getting very close. First thing you have to remember is the mixing."

"Let me guess. Shaken, not stirred." The teasing note in her voice surprised her. She felt playful and it wasn't like her.

"Never." His eyes widened as if she suggested sacrilege. "Shaking bruises the gin."

"Oh," Liz replied. "We wouldn't want that."

"No, we wouldn't. I was referring however to the gin-vermouth ratio. The key is balance. You want just enough vermouth to bring out the gin's flavor but not so much as to overpower it."

Cupping her chin in her hand, Liz watched with fascination as he measured the duet of alcohol into the shaker. "I had no idea mixology was such a complicated science. Here I thought bartenders just poured liquor into a glass."

"And you would be wrong." He poured the drinks, dropped a toothpick-speared olive in each glass, and handed one to her. "Taste."

She did as she was told. Icy cold gin set her tongue on fire.

"This is where you say it's perfect, by the way."

"Okay," she said, taking another swallow. "It's perfect. Mahoney's can't come close."

"Told you so." He grinned, and Liz's insides did a little tumble.

Reminding herself the evening had no pressure, and needing to add a little space, Liz took her drink and headed toward the living room. In the pit area, the fire crackled invitingly. She stood before it and studied the glaringly bare mantel.

Charles walked up behind her. "Penny for your thoughts."

She had a dollar's worth. "Ever notice you can tell a lot about a person by their surroundings?" she asked him. "How they decorate. The items they leave lying around."

"Sure."

"I was thinking how I couldn't see any traces of your personality in this room. It's gorgeous, but it looks like something out of a decorating magazine. I don't see… well, *you* anywhere."

"Are you suggesting I'm hiding something?"

She shrugged, unsure what she meant. All she knew was that as beautiful as the room was, it made her sad. "Are you hiding something?" she asked.

"No. I simply believe in traveling light. No sense in dragging a lot with you."

If you didn't plan on staying. Made sense, but she wondered if there was more than just short-term living involved. This was, after all, a man who grew up in hotels. "What's your regular home like?"

"My regular home?"

"The one on the West Coast."

He stared up at the painting. "Pretty much the same. A little more furniture maybe."

But few personal touches. Same as this place. Quite a contrast from her, who'd saved every Popsicle stick decoration and souvenir from the last seventeen years. But then, he wasn't a man who valued intangibles, so keepsakes would hold little value.

"Makes for easy cleaning for sure," she mused. "Your housekeeper must be grateful...makes up for those windows."

She thought she kept a light note to her comment, but apparently not because he didn't smile the way she expected. In fact, he regarded her with a strange kind of seriousness.

"Let me show you something," he said after a moment.

Taking her by the hand, he led her across the room. Seeing he intended to lead her upstairs, Liz hesitated. Charles gave her arm a gentle tug. "It's not what you think. Come on."

Slowly she followed up, up and around the twisting stairs to the loft above the kitchen. Stepping up into the room, she gasped. It was like flipping a switch. Where downstairs was a pristine showplace, the loft was a paper-laden disaster. Reports, balls of discarded paper, newspapers, Sticky Notes, etc. littered the surfaces like some exploded office paper bomb. A pair of ties lay draped over the back of his desk chair, which was occupied by a stack of books so it couldn't be sat on anyway. In fact, the only thing not littered with paper was a large leather easy chair in the corner.

"Oh. My. Lord." Liz stifled a laugh. "You're a slob."

"Closet slob," Charles corrected.

"Still a slob."

A half full legal pad lay on the corner of the desk. Picking it up, she saw that an array of shapes and scribbles covered the margins. "Doodles?"

Charles blushed. She loved it. Seeing the mess made her think the man who came to her house, the one who liked meat loaf and chicken dinners, was real.

That he was willing to share this room with her made her heart skip.

Setting the notepad down, she moved over to the other side of the desk, only to pause at the object in the corner. A scuffed baseball. It looked out of place among everything else. Running her fingers across the stitching, she looked at Charles questioningly.

"When I was around eight or nine, my father came out to San Francisco for an extended business trip. Somehow my mother heard he was in town, so she dumped me off at his hotel for the week. I forget where she and her boyfriend were going at the time.

"Anyway, most of the week I was stuck in the hotel room while he made sales calls."

"By yourself?" Didn't he say he was only eight?

"I was under strict orders not to leave the room under

any circumstances. I was used to it by then so no big deal."

Sounded like one to her. Liz's respect for her former boss began to slip. This was a facet of Ron Bishop's personality she'd never known, yet it was strangely believable.

"What does that have to do with the baseball?"

"Apparently he told one of his potential customers about me, because the guy wanted to go on a father-son baseball outing."

"Ron was a sports nut."

"Yeah, and he had the misfortune of having a son who knew less than nothing about them. Still, I was excited to go and I caught a foul ball."

He took the ball from her and tossed it in the air with his free hand. "We had a good time that day. A real good time. Ron told me we'd go to another one next time he was in town."

"Did you?" She was afraid she already knew the answer.

The ball landed in Charles's palm with a soft plop. "Didn't have the time. Building a business takes work. I didn't really expect him to keep the promise anyway. My mother had already explained having me wasn't exactly in my father's plans. More like a failed gambit on her part."

"I'm sorry," Liz whispered. She didn't know what else to say.

"Don't be. I wrote both my parents off as lost causes a long time ago. The day I was accepted into Cal Tech, I said goodbye and never looked back."

Had he really? She studied the ball in Charles's

hand. The lone souvenir carried along in a lifetime spent jumping from place to place. Thinking of a young Charles, holding on to the memory of one perfect afternoon, a piece of her heart broke away. His talisman wasn't so unlike what she'd been chasing in the backseat of Bill's car.

"Did you know your father had a heart attack?" she asked him. "I mean besides the one that killed him. Happened a few years ago. He had to have a quadruple bypass."

He was staring in the depths of his martini glass. "That's too bad."

"Afterward, he began acting a little differently. Company outings got more elaborate. We got better benefit packages. He took up golf. A lot of people figured his newfound zest was his way of cramming in as much life as possible after all those years building a business. That he regretted not enjoying his success earlier in life."

"What's your point?"

"I don't know. I wonder now if maybe he regretted more than working too much."

"You sound like his lawyer. He suggested the same thing. Then again he could also have simply wanted a person named Bishop at the helm of his legacy." Draining his drink, Charles set both the glass and the baseball back where it lay among the papers. "We'll never know what Ron was really thinking, though, will we?"

There was so much quiet bitterness in his voice, the last of Liz's walls crumbled away. Setting down her glass, she moved closer to him. Her fingers touched his cheek, stroking the faint stubble that lay beneath them. When she looked at his face, she saw eyes that were hooded and dark, the pupils blown so wide the blue was barely visible. His mouth moved to hers.

"No pressure," he whispered in a voice already low and thick.

"I know."

All their other kisses had been foreplay for this one. Liz moaned as Charles's mouth took hers. His lips were demanding, unyielding. He tasted of gin and coolness and heat. The woman in her cried out at being awoken at last, and she wrapped her arms around his neck drawing him closer. It was like throwing a match on a pile of dried kindling. Having ignited, there was no putting out the fire. This, she thought as Charles lowered her on to the floor, papers crinkling beneath their bodies, this was what she'd been missing for so long.

A few hours later Liz found herself back in her car, her body still burning. "Stay," Charles had asked as they lay together. The feathery touch of his hands on her thighs had almost made her say yes.

But she couldn't. She had a son to go home to. So she'd gotten dressed and kissed Charles good-night at the door. On the way out she spied a stack of papers on the entranceway table she hadn't noticed before. Documents from Xinhua Paper reminding her how Charles made his fortune. A cricket on her shoulder suggested she regret what happened, but she couldn't. She knew better than to expect promises or declarations of love from Charles and that was fine. And truth be known, she didn't want promises. She didn't expect

love. Promises broke your heart. Love left you vulnerable.

No, she wouldn't be foolish enough to believe tonight
had anything to do with love. The emotions lurking in
the corner of her heart wouldn't take control. She would
make tonight about pleasure. About allowing herself to
be a woman for the first time in years.

She pulled into her driveway. The town house was
dark except for a dim light in the living room. Odd.
Andrew usually left every light on in the house, even
when he went to bed. The kid was single-handedly
keeping the power company employed. Looking in the
rearview mirror, she checked her hair and makeup, hoping she didn't look too disheveled. Hopefully Andrew
was in bed so she wouldn't have to come up with an
explanation.

Dear God, she was sneaking around on her kid! What
was she doing? The memory of Charles's firelight face
hovering above hers quickly dissolved her rebuke.

Suddenly something caught the corner of her eye,
and the moment was ripped away. No… It couldn't be…
Sure enough, there was Victoria's compact parked by
the curb.

Her stomach sank. They weren't… They wouldn't…

In a flash she was out of the car and flooding the
room with light before the front door had a chance to
shut. Andrew leaped to his feet, his eyes bugged. His
shirt was undone.

"Mom! You're home! I didn't hear your car."

"Obviously." Amazingly her voice remained calm.
Looking to the sofa, she saw Victoria struggling to sit

up and fix her blouse at the same time. Difficult with
your bra unhooked.

Seeing where she was looking, Andrew stepped away
from the sofa, presumably to draw her attention away.
"Vic and I…"

"Were saying good-night," Liz answered for him.
"You were saying good-night."

"Right." He held out a hand to assist his girlfriend.
If she hadn't been ready to kill him, Liz might have
considered the behavior gallant.

Silence engulfed the town house, the kids too mor-
tified to talk in her presence. Good. Body stiff, Liz
made her way to the kitchen. Glaring at the cabinets,
she waited till Andrew returned before speaking.

"Mom—"

"Don't." She cut him off. "Do you have any idea how
furious I am with you right now? What were you thinking? Here? In our living room?"

"We weren't having sex."

"Oh, well then…" She yanked open the cupboard.
"I thought I raised you to be more respectful—to be
smarter."

"We are being smart. I told you, we weren't having—"

"Close enough," she shot back. "And maybe not this
time, but what about next time, huh? Or the time after
that! I'm not stupid, Andrew. How can you be so…"
Dammit! She was so angry she couldn't talk straight.
"For God's sake, you're only seventeen years old. What
were you thinking?"

"You should talk," she heard him mutter.

Bad answer. Her stomach churned. She couldn't deal

with this. Not right now. "Just go to your room," she told him. Her jaw hurt from gritting her teeth. "I don't want to see you till tomorrow.

"And leave the cell phone behind," she added. No way was he going to sit in there texting.

Andrew immediately let out a disgusted groan. Acting as if he was a victim. "Oh, come on!"

"Now!"

"Fine." Thankfully he knew better than to argue. At least she had that going for her.

As soon as she heard the bedroom door slam, she grabbed a wine bottle from the cupboard. Her stomach felt as if someone had kicked a hole in the middle of it. Her baby boy…

*We weren't having sex.* She shook her head. The temptation was always one incredible kiss away. She knew all too well.

After all, Charles's scent was still on her skin.

# CHAPTER NINE

UNBELIEVABLE. It was snowing again. Did the stuff ever go away? He'd thought for sure last night's thaw was a sign of improving conditions. That was New England for you. Wait five minutes and the weather would change.

Charles stared out his office window. It wasn't snowing hard, but the clouds had closed in over the mountains. He missed them. The view had become part of his routine.

Didn't matter. He was still in a good mood.

Something had shifted inside him overnight.

He didn't have a name for it, but his chest was full with the feeling. As if he'd gone to the edge of the precipice and taken a plunge. He felt amazing. Exhilarated.

Of course that might have more to do with Elizabeth. Sweet, *passionate* Elizabeth. He'd been with women before, but…wow. There weren't words to describe the experience. He couldn't get enough of her. Couldn't get close enough to her. It was like he wanted to crawl inside her skin and become a part of her.

God, listen to him. Eight-thirty in the morning and he was rarin' to go. Might as well be a teenager.

The ringing of his cell phone broke his thoughts. When he saw the number, he counted two rings and answered.

"*Ni hao ma*, Mr. Huang Bin."

On the other end of the phone, Huang Bin laughed. "Greetings to you. You sound quite energetic this morning. I take it your business crisis resolved itself satisfactorily."

"Yes, it did. Thank you for agreeing to reschedule." Charles blamed his canceling on a business emergency. He didn't dare jeopardize negotiations by saying the emergency was a hockey game.

Even if his attending yielded amazing results.

"Not a problem," the man on the other end replied. "This hour allows me to talk without interruption. I received your latest batch of financial information, and I must say we at Xinhua are quite impressed."

"I'm honored. Thank you."

"We believe it is time to move forward. I would like to take a tour of your facilities. To see for myself if your company is what we are looking for."

"Naturally."

"I will be in Boston at the end of the week for a symposium on Asian Trade. I would like to visit then."

Charles paused. "Did you say the end of this week?"

"Yes. Given how smoothly negotiations are going, I see no reason to delay, do you?"

"No, I don't." His good mood deflated slightly. He hadn't expected Huang to want to move this quickly. It meant he wouldn't have as much time with Elizabeth as he'd hoped.

Huang's voice sounded in his ear. "Charles? Are you there?"

"Yes," he said, recovering. "I'm sorry, you were saying?"

"I said that I would call you when I arrive in Boston. We can work out the time and date then."

"Sounds good. I'll talk to you at the end of the week."

They spoke for a few more moments, mostly small talk about family and weather and then Charles hung up. They were closing in on the final stage. If Huang liked what he saw it wouldn't be long before they hammered out the sale.

Immediately his mind traveled back to last night, and the experience he'd hoped to repeat as many times as possible. Damn. He washed a hand over his face. He didn't realize his time in New Hampshire would be ending so soon.

He wasn't sure he was quite ready to leave.

Standing in the doorway of Charles's office, Liz felt the heat from last night flare back to life. From the day he took over as her boss, she'd noticed how seriously he concentrated on his work, to the point that everything around him seemed to fade away. Back then she'd attributed the immersion to a form of tunnel vision, an inability to see beyond the numbers on the spreadsheet. She knew better now. She knew he channeled the same degree of attention to every task he sought to accomplish. Watching him clack away at his keyboard, she smiled remembering exactly how dexterous those hands could be.

Her smile faded. Memories were all she'd be experiencing from now on.

"Hey."

Her greeting came out so softly, she was surprised her voice was even audible. And in a way she half hoped he hadn't. This was not a conversation she looked forward to.

Unfortunately he looked up and smiled. "Good morning." To her dismay, his eyes held the same warm sparkle as they did last night. The gentle way he spoke, the way one was supposed to greet a lover, did not help, either. Both went straight to her chest, making her heart skip.

"How are you this morning?"

*Simply marvelous.* After Andrew stomped off to bed, she downed a glass of red wine, spent the night tossing and turning and woke up with a headache. Plus thanks in large part to the headache, not only did this morning's attempt at "talking" with Andrew fail, but her carefully made vows of maintaining perspective flew out the window when Victoria drove up. What's more, she didn't know what had her more worked up, catching Andrew or the fact that a mere hour before, she herself had lain in her boss's arms having what was, quite possibly, the most amazing night of her life.

"Fine," she lied in answer to his question. "You?"

"Perfect." Again with the lover's voice. All thick and lazy, it made Liz squeeze the door for support. He wasn't playing fair. A voice like that would make any woman weak in the knees.

He turned his attention back to the screen. "Do you know if Finance sent over the capital investment summary I asked for? I didn't see it in my inbox. I specifically told them to submit numbers to me today."

Good. He'd returned the focus to business. Business she could handle. "I'll call over this morning and remind them you're waiting."

"Remind them why, too." Closing his laptop, he rose from his desk. "Now," he said, zeroing his attention on her, "let us turn to more important matters."

Rising from his seat, he crossed the room, those eyes boring into her every step of the way. Liz's mouth ran dry. She'd forgotten the downside of his focus. You couldn't escape once caught in its sights. Eyes still locked with hers, Charles leaned forward and reached slowly behind her, his sleeve brushing the waistband of her skirt.

The office door clicked shut, closing the rest of the world out. "Good morning," he repeated. This time, he punctuated the greeting by pulling her in for a kiss. Much to her chagrin a tiny mewling noise escaped her mouth as she melted into him.

When he finished, they were both left breathless. Charles fanned his thumbs across her cheeks. "That's more like it," he rasped. "Much better than a boring old financial report." He pulled her close again.

Somehow Liz found the ability to back away. "We can't," she told him.

"Why not? If you're worried about getting in trouble at work, you needn't. I know the boss. And I promise I won't be filing an EEO complaint anytime soon, either."

She broke free from his embrace. It killed her leaving the warmth behind. "It has nothing to do with work," she told him.

"Then what is it?"

"I was thinking about last night…"

Charles leaned in a little closer. "So was I."

He wasn't playing fair. How was she supposed to put the brakes on anything when he insisted on talking like they were back lying in each other's arms? *Just spit it out, Liz,* she told herself. Go big or go home.

Crossing the room, she regained her personal space. "Look, I'm sure we both agree that what happened last night was…nice."

"Nice." His expression faltered a second, before re-affixing itself. "I would choose a different word."

They both knew she would, too. Like explosive or otherworldly. Squaring her shoulders, she pressed on, recalling the words she prepared earlier. "Regardless, given the circumstances, I think it would be best if what happened between us didn't happen again. We should keep things professional."

"I see." Crossing his arms, he leaned against the door. A dark, lean, unreadable pillar. "I hate to break it to you, Elizabeth," he said, "but that boat sailed a long time ago. Right around the time I first kissed you."

Liz blushed. He had a point.

Charles was studying her with confusion. "Has something changed that I don't know about? Because last time we saw each other, we were on the same page."

"I had some time to think, is all," she said, combing her hair back. "I'm not sure it's the best idea for me to be having an affair with you. I mean we have to work together."

"True. Although last time I looked, we also weren't

the first people in the world to mix business and pleasure."

Did he have to draw out the word *pleasure*, giving
it all sorts of connotations she'd rather not picture? "I
mean I work *for* you."

"Again, we aren't the first so why don't you tell me
the real reason for this sudden change of mind."

"Fine. It's Andrew." With that, she marched across
the room, to his desk, purposely keeping her back to
him for once, so she wouldn't be further distracted by
his gaze. Breaking things off was a lot harder than she
thought. Last night had opened a Pandora's box of feelings she was having trouble keeping under control. The
minute she stepped into the office, every touch, every
kiss had pooled hot and aching at the base of her spine.

Still, if she expected Andrew to keep his libido in
check, then she should do the same. "I need to think
about what kind of example I provide him."

"If you ask me, you're providing him with a fantastic example."

"Not anymore," she whispered.

"Excuse me?"

"I said, not anymore." She sighed. "I walked in on
Andrew and Victoria last night."

"Oh."

"Oh, indeed."

"Were they…?"

"He claims they weren't planning to go further than
what I saw, but you and I both know in the heat of the
moment, the best of plans mean squat." *After all, look
at us last night*.

"I'm sorry. I know how worried you were something

like this would happen." His hands suddenly appeared on her shoulders. Heaven help her, but they felt so comforting there. "Did you talk to him?"

"Sure, but it was a little hard making a strong argument when I'm wearing this." Turning around, she tugged at the collar of her shirt to expose the bruise in the hollow of her neck. "Now he sees me as a big hypocrite."

"Why, because you and I…? Elizabeth—" he reached for her again "—he's seventeen years old. Surely he knows the difference between what a teenager does and two consenting adults who—"

"Who are having a short-term fling?" She yanked herself away before he could touch her and sabotage her resolve. "I'm sure he's going to see the logic in that sort of thinking."

"What makes you think this is short-term?"

He did not just say that. Did he think she was that big an idiot? "I know about Xinhua Paper, Charles. Are you really going to stand there and tell me you, America's most famous corporate flipper, are not negotiating to sell this company?"

His silence was enough of an answer. "I didn't think so. And if I get involved with you, all I'm doing is giving him permission to do the same. He's going to take one look and say 'Mom's having fun, why shouldn't I sleep with the girl I'm in love with?'"

She took a moment to calm down, hating for how badly she wished she could lean on him. "Look, I don't want him repeating my mistakes. I don't want to see him ruin his future."

"Like you did yours."

She nodded. "Yes. Last night was great but we both know it's not going anywhere, and I'm still raising my son. He may be in high school, but he still needs guidance. I can't afford to screw up. Please tell me you understand."

For several moments, Charles said nothing. Finally, however, he nodded. "I don't like it, but I understand. From now on we'll keep everything on a strictly professional level."

"Thank you." His acquiescence was exactly what she wanted, and yet disappointment he didn't argue the point stabbed her anyway. She suddenly felt quite hollow and alone. With the taste of regret in her mouth, she walked back to her desk. In the opposite direction she wanted to walk in. Behind her, she heard Charles taking a seat. "I'll go find out why Finance hasn't submitted those investment figures yet."

She closed the door to his office so she wouldn't change her mind and turn around.

"I'd like to propose a toast. Here's to Gilmore High School Hockey, runner-up in the Division Three State Championships!"

The crowd gave a lukewarm cheer, the sting of the afternoon's loss still hurt.

"Hey, what kind of attitude is that?" Van asked when his toast fell flat. "You guys made it all the way to the finals."

"Yeah and got smoked six to one," his son Sean replied.

"So you'll get them next year."

"Great, and since Andrew won't be there we can lose six-zip," another player said.

Watching from his seat across from Van, Charles took in the exchange with mild amusement. When Van asked him if he would join them after the game, his first inclination was to say no. With Huang coming tomorrow, he had a lot of work to do. Plus there was a business in Tucson he wanted his lawyers to look at. He really should call Jim Cavalier and get them to work. A hockey game dinner wasn't a priority.

But here he was for the same reason he rescheduled his conference call the other day. He couldn't pass up the chance to watch Elizabeth. Sure, he saw her every day at the office, but since their "breakup," their interactions had been kept on a strictly professional basis. Tonight was a chance to watch her while she cheered on Andrew. The way her face looked lit up with enthusiasm was too beautiful to pass up.

Of course, this evening wouldn't end quite as spectacularly as the last one because he was "respecting" her wishes and keeping his distance.

The effort was killing him. One night of lovemaking—not even one night—with Elizabeth was akin to one dose of drugs. Not nearly enough to knock her out of his system. His body craved more.

Then there was the fact he couldn't shake the feeling this thing with Andrew was only part of the problem. He couldn't stop wondering if she'd frightened herself by letting go and was using her son as an excuse.

Van tried again to get the team into the party spirit. "One more time, guys. Here's to Gilmore Hockey!"

At the other end of the table, Charles watched

Elizabeth raise her soda and cheer with the best of them. "Mr. Hancock's right," she said. "You all should be very proud of yourselves for getting this far." She wore that sincere encouraging smile of hers, the one that when turned in your direction, made you feel like you could scale buildings. Seeing it, Charles realized it wasn't just the sex he missed. It was that smile, and the way she made him feel like smiling back. He missed sitting next to her.

He missed *her*.

At the table, Doug, Van and a few other people had started discussing what they considered a bad refereeing call in the first period. While they debated, Charles saw Elizabeth slip away to the bar with a pair of empty soda pitchers.

To hell with it, he decided. He wanted to talk to her. Grabbing a nearby empty tray, he pushed himself to his feet.

Elizabeth looked engrossed in the basketball game playing on TV when he approached, but her quick side-long glance in his direction told him otherwise.

"I'm pretty sure those kids have eaten every boneless chicken in New England." The joke earned him a wan smile. It was a start.

"Great game," he continued. "Too bad they lost."

"Can't win all of them," she replied, eyes still glued to the set.

Was she talking about the game or them? He wasn't always sure with her. "No, you can't. Doesn't mean you shouldn't try."

Studying her profile, he noticed for the first time

how dark the circles were beneath her eyes. "You look tired."

"Busy couple of days. My boss is expecting an important visitor."

That wasn't why she was tired, though, was it? "I'm worried you're not getting enough sleep. I know I haven't been." His voice dropped so only she could hear what he said next. "My bed has been too empty."

"Charles…"

He took a mental step back. Hard as it was, he did promise. They fell silent. Forced to wait while the bartender filled her order, they both pretended to watch the basketball game. All he noticed were two teams running back and forth across a parquet floor. His attention was far too distracted by the woman next to him to attempt and learn what was going on.

Eventually he tired of the pretense and plucked a cardboard coaster from a nearby stack. "Lovebirds look like they're behaving," he noted, rolling the coaster square over end across the bar.

"So far anyway."

"How's that battle going?"

Liz shrugged. "The usual. I'm horrible because I insist on knowing his whereabouts and activities. I'm horrible because I won't allow him to hang out at Victoria's after school. I'm horrible because I exist. The usual."

Sounded harsh. "You okay with the attitude?"

"He thinks if he's obnoxious I'll feel bad and cut him slack. Things will blow over in a week or so."

"I wish there was something I could do to speed things along." Besides staying away.

He rolled the coaster up to her hand, letting the edge

rest against the tip of her index finger. Touching her but not touching her. His hand twitched to trade places with the cardboard.

As if sensing his thoughts, she pulled her hand back. "Thanks, I'll be all right on my own."

"Alone being your favorite state of being and all."

She glared at him. "That's not fair."

No, it wasn't, but he only partly regretted the remark. "Life's too short, Elizabeth."

"And you're going to be leaving town in a few weeks. Let's call it a draw." With a rough shove, she pushed the coaster back in his direction, a silent reminder she wasn't interested.

Realizing he wasn't going to get anywhere, Charles chose to take the hint and head back to the table. When he got there, he noticed one extra person. "Tim?"

Town manager Tim Callahan stood and shook his hand. "Glad to see you, Charles."

"Good to see you, too. What are you doing here?" He realized town hockey was a big deal, but showing up at a consolation dinner seemed a little excessive, and far as he knew Tim didn't know any of the families personally.

"I came by so the whole team could hear my announcement," the town manager replied. "Take a seat."

Still unsure what was going on, Charles sat down while the town manager stood up.

"May I have your attention, please," he called. "As you know, last summer the ice skating rink was struck by lightning and destroyed. We've been working on a replacement, but town funds have been limited.

Fortunately, a private donor has stepped up and generously offered to pay for repairs and renovations."

The table cheered. "No more practicing in Franklin," Andrew said, fist pumping the kid next to him.

Charles looked to his plate and ground his teeth. So this is why Van insisted he be here. He didn't want them to make a big deal.

"Shortly after the donation was made, the fundraising committee came to the town with a request. The Board of Selectman voted in favor of it earlier this week and I'm here to announce that the new rink will be officially named the Charles Bishop Arena."

Again, the table cheered. Charles was stunned. "I don't know what to say." They were naming the rink after him? Him. Not his father. Warmth found its way to the center of his chest, melting the cold that had been there for so long and he felt like his chest would need to expand twice its size to accommodate the sensation.

"Thank you." He didn't trust himself to say anything more in case he choked on the uncharacteristic lump in his throat. "Thank you."

From her place at the bar, Elizabeth could see the back of Charles's head bow and issued a prayer of gratitude that she couldn't see his face. As it was, knowing he was no doubt struggling to maintain composure had her fighting her own battle. She wanted nothing more than to run to his side, to hold him as he rode out his emotions.

Seeing him today had been so difficult. She barely got through the workdays, and to be reminded of their time outside the office… Just knowing he was in the bleachers a few feet away was killing her. As much as she dreaded his departure, part of her was counting the days. Maybe then she could get rid of the longing that kept her up at night. These feelings he'd awakened were harder to put back in hibernation than she thought.

At least she could say she gave Charles some closure. He'd never know she'd been the one who suggested the name change from Ron Bishop to Charles. After hearing his story the other night, the change felt only fitting. Charles Bishop might not stay around, but he'd always know someone in Gilmore cared he was here.

# CHAPTER TEN

"GREETINGS, my friend! It is good to finally meet you face-to-face." Entering the main entrance, Huang Bin clasped Charles's hand in a very Western handshake. "I am looking forward to touring your fine facilities."

"I think you'll be pleased with what you see," Charles replied. He took a good look at the man who would be the next CEO of Bishop Paper. The eldest son of a successful business dynasty, Bin was a handsome man with short black hair and a fit physique. He had a quiet arrogance about him that implied confidence and success. He was ruthless, unfailingly polite and, if rumors were to be true, exceedingly charming, especially when it came to the opposite sex. It was this last part that didn't sit well with Charles. He wasn't sure he liked the idea of Elizabeth's new boss being such a playboy.

"I must admit," Huang said as they walked to Charles's office. "When I first heard you were selling a paper company in New England, I was quite surprised. Based on your reputation, I did not expect to find you attached to an operation this small. But then I realized the connection. Your father started this company?"

"He did. About thirty-five years ago."

"A very admirable achievement. And now, following his death, you wish to capitalize on the fruits of his labor."

"I wouldn't exactly say capitalize." The word left a bad taste in his mouth.

"Do not fear," Huang replied, holding up a tanned hand. "I understand the desire to break free from one's father. I, too, inherited a company."

"I think you'll find Bishop Paper to be different from Xinhua in some respects."

"I have no doubt."

He pushed open the door to his outer office, allowing his guest to enter in front of him. Hardly surprising, Huang noticed Elizabeth at her desk straight away and smiled. She smiled back. Charles stepped in the space between them before opening his door. "You will find our company is small and quite family oriented. It's something we pride ourselves on." What was he saying, *we*? He couldn't care less.

"The company's size is one of the reasons we are interested," Huang replied. "We would prefer our first foray into North America to be a small scale."

Their conversation was interrupted by Elizabeth, who entered with a cup of steaming tea. Again Huang smiled. A little too brightly if you asked Charles.

An hour later Huang Bin was still in his office and still smiling. By now Charles had a headache. Huang had insisted Elizabeth join them on the tour—"To take notes," Huang claimed. He spent the entire tour forcing himself to remain cordial while convinced Huang was stealing glimpses at Elizabeth's long legs when he wasn't looking.

This deal, he thought, better be worth the effort.

"I am even more impressed than I was when I arrived," Huang said with enthusiasm. "You have a fine facility here. I can see what you mean about it having a family atmosphere. I was most impressed with the way you knew many of the employees personally."

"That is a byproduct of small town business. You find you cross paths with employees at a lot of events."

"How—" he searched for the word "—quaint. Do all the employees attend these 'events'?"

You mean *Elizabeth*, Charles wanted to ask. He wasn't sure he liked Huang Bin. The man was too much like an Asian version of himself.

"Depends upon the event, and the employee," he replied.

"I see. I look forward to learning the various activities."

"Then you would like to move forward?"

"Very much. With a few changes, I believe Bishop Paper will make a good acquisition and a good start to our North American venture."

"I beg your pardon?"

"Xinhua prefers a more streamlined production approach than you do in America. However, I believe we will be able to transition in time and keep most of the employees."

Most of the employees? "You're planning on layoffs."

"Some. It is inevitable I am afraid."

"But Gilmore is a one employer town. If you lay

people off in this economy, they will have trouble finding new work."

"I sympathize with your loyalty and we will do our best to retrain. However, in the long run, a small work force will be required."

Layoffs. And after they'd named a damn ice skating rink for him. He felt sick to his stomach. "What am I supposed to tell my employees?" he asked to no one in particular.

"With all due respect, Charles," he heard Huang reply, "they will not be your employees for much longer."

*They won't be your employees much longer.*

Charles settled onto a bar stool at Mahoney's with a sigh. He couldn't bring himself to go home. As long a day as he had, he really didn't need to spend the evening in the apartment Elizabeth said had no personality. Layoffs. Damn. He knew the Huang family could be ruthless, but cutting jobs in Gilmore would be disastrous for the town's economy.

*Layoffs never bothered you at any of your other companies.*

They bothered him now. At other companies he didn't know employees' names. Last thing he wanted to see was people like Van Hancock out of work.

Elizabeth would be safe. Huang seemed more than interested in keeping her on board. Him and his unctuous smile.

He signaled for the bartender.

A pudgy man with salt and pepper hair and an armful of menus wandered over. "Welcome to Mahoney's, what can I get you?"

Charles ordered the ale. He was in a Twelve Weeks of Winter mood.

"Sure thing," the man replied. "Do you mind if we work around you while you drink? We got new specials to insert." He pointed to a stack of white paper.

"Knock yourself out," Charles replied. He wasn't in the mood to talk anyway. Not after an afternoon of being cordial to Huang.

This time he noticed the beer didn't taste quite so bitter. Either they'd tapped a new keg, and the heaviest flavor had sunk to the bottom, or he was acquiring a taste. Either way, the beer wasn't as bad as he remembered. Though hard to believe anything would be tasty without Elizabeth's company. She had turned out to be New Hampshire's brightest spot.

He slipped a page from the stack, wondering if the specials might be better, too. Out of habit, he ran a thumb across the stock, recognizing the grain immediately. "BishopLite," he said softly.

"What's that, mate?" the bartender asked.

Charles shook his head. "Quoting the paper stock, is all. It's BishopLite, fifty pound."

"You can tell from feeling it?"

Surprisingly he could. He'd been studying samples all week in preparation for his meeting. Nothing else to do since he couldn't study Elizabeth. "We manufacture it."

"Now I recognize you. You own the paper company."

"Did anyway. I made a deal to sell the place this afternoon."

"You don't sound too enthusiastic."

"Long day."

"Well, congratulations nonetheless." The man went back to changing out the menu folders, only to pause a second later. "Going to be weird not having a Bishop own the paper mill."

"Yeah," Charles caught himself saying. "It will."

The bartender was right. He didn't sound enthusiastic. By all rights he should be thrilled. He was finally rid of the albatross his father left him.

So why did he feel like he was leaving town with unfinished business?

Later he walked from the pub to downtown, partly to clear his head and partly because he was too restless to drive. Gilmore was a good-looking town. He'd been too young to notice when he lived here. The town common reminded him a little of a Christmas card with its walkways and snow-covered pavilion. If you stood at the far left corner, you saw a different view of his White Mountains. Funny, how he'd started thinking of them that way. That's what happens when you stare at something every morning. Or maybe he was simply developing fond feelings for the town. These past few weeks were the closest he felt to having a permanent home.

A short walk farther took him past St. Mark's where he attended probably his first and only pancake breakfast. His first, no second breakfast with Elizabeth. Terrible food, worst coffee. But it raised money for the ice rink.

The rink. He still couldn't believe they were going to name the blasted thing after him. He was going to insist if it bore his name it provide decent coffee. Maybe he'd make an additional donation to make certain. How ironic that he'd never have known about the rink—or Gilmore hockey for that matter—if not for Elizabeth wanting to watch Andrew, and the kid would never play there. He'd be off at Trenton next year. Kicking a block of snow that had broken onto the sidewalk, he watched as it broke into pieces. Least he'd helped Elizabeth fund that dream. Too bad their affair got snuffed before they had the chance to experience it fully. Instead he'd driven a wedge between mother and son and cost them all.

He stopped in his tracks. If he was going to leave Gilmore, the least he could do was fix what he broke.

Elizabeth's car wasn't in the driveway when he arrived at her town house. His chest felt a little hollow at not seeing it. He'd come to expect her smiling face to answer when he knocked.

This time, however, he hadn't come to see Elizabeth. The person he came to see was the young man who opened the door. "Mom's not here," Andrew said in a flat, tight voice.

"I know," Charles replied. "I came to see you."

"Me?" The kid flipped his hair from his eyes. When visible, you could see the resemblance to his mother's. "Why?"

"Because I think it's time you and I talked man-to-man, don't you?"

"About what?"

"Your mother."

Without waiting for an invitation, Charles let himself in.

*  *  *

News of the upcoming acquisition spread like wild-fire. Charles had barely left the building when rumors started flying. By midafternoon Liz had received a dozen visitors all wanting to know the same things: when was Charles leaving and what did the change mean for Bishop Paper. Liz answered as best she could, but the truth was she didn't know any more than they did. That Charles was selling the company and Huang Bin was her new boss. She didn't like her new boss.

Leanne was among the first to come by looking for information. Not having seen them yet, Liz half expected the buzz birds to be close behind, but no. "I just heard the news. Does this mean you're leaving us?"

Making a production out of changing the toner in the copier machine so her colleague wouldn't spot her sudden mistiness, she was forced to pause when Leanne asked her question. That was one she hadn't expected. "Why would I be leaving?"

"When Mr. Bishop leaves of course. Are you going to be going with him?"

"No." She shoved the paper drawer closed as hard as she could. "I'm not going anywhere."

"Oh, sweetie, I'm so sorry. I know you were crazy about him."

She *liked* him, Liz wanted to correct, ignoring the warning bells the thought set off. They'd had a few good weeks spending time together and one really great night of sex. Nothing more. She was decidedly *not* crazy about the man.

Although she would like to know when he was leaving so she could be prepared. That is, so she could give people notice. All the speculation had left a gaping hole in her chest. On the plus side, the pain reminded her she'd done the right thing to break it off. If it hurt this badly now, imagine what she'd feel like if she'd truly had time to fall. Thank goodness she protected her heart.

By four o'clock, Liz had had enough and drove home. If Charles could take off early without word, so could she.

Immediately upon seeing the familiar car in the driveway, Liz's heart stopped. What was he doing here? She marched her way to the house curious to find out. The front door was left open. She was halfway through the opening when she caught Charles and Andrew's conversation.

"So you see why she's going a little overboard, don't you?"

Dear God. She pressed her palm to her mouth so they wouldn't hear her gasp. Was he talking to Andrew about what happened?

"Yeah," she heard Andrew say, "but does she have to be so crazy?"

"Can you blame her after what she walked in on? Your mother wants you to have the best possible future. It's what makes her special."

"I know."

"Trust me. Your mom's awesome. My parents didn't give two squats about me."

Liz's palm curled into a fist, which she jammed to her lips. For some reason Charles decided to take it upon himself to talk with Andrew. Why would he go and do something like that? An emotion shook itself loose.

A scary, powerful emotion she didn't want to feel. He shouldn't have done this. She had the situation handled.

Squeezing her eyes shut, she packed the reaction away before shutting the door as loudly as possible. "I'm home," she called, faking an upbeat greeting.

"Hey, Mom!" Andrew called back.

Wearing her best faux smile, she made her way into the living room. "Charles, what are you doing here?"

"Talking to Andrew," he replied.

"Is that so?" She looked at them both, waiting for further details. Instead she witnessed a conspiratorial look passing between them.

"He wanted to talk about calculus," Andrew told her. "To make sure I'm okay now that he's not tutoring and all."

"How nice of him."

"Yeah, it was really helpful."

It took all her effort to nod and pretend her son wasn't lying to her. "Do you mind if I talk to Mr. Bishop alone?"

"No." The teenager unfolded himself from the sofa. "I'll see you later, Mr. Bishop."

To her amazement, Charles held out his hand. "I'm glad we sorted things out, Andrew."

"Me, too." Grabbing his cell phone from the coffee table, he pounded his way upstairs. A few seconds later, his bedroom door shut.

Liz opened her mouth to speak, but Charles beat her to it. "How much did you hear?" he asked, sauntering toward her.

"Enough to know you weren't talking about calculus. What were you doing?"

"I wanted to clear the air with your son." He coughed. "Since I'm partially to blame for this cold war you're having."

"You shouldn't have," she replied.

"I wanted to."

"I mean, you shouldn't have."

"And now you're upset." Ignoring the arms she'd folded across her chest as a blockage, he leaned forward and caught her chin with his thumb and forefinger. "Why?"

"Because I don't need you to come running in to my rescue just because he and I are having a disagreement." She broke away from his touch, hating how her body instantly melted at his touch. Even now, her skin burned where he touched her. "I can handle this on my own." In the back of her mind, a tiny voice questioned her real reason for being stubborn after accepting all of Charles's other help. She was afraid to answer. Afraid to admit the truth.

"I know you don't need my help with this issue," Charles told her. "But I don't like leaving loose ends."

"Is that what I am, a loose end?" Sounded about right.

There was no mistaking the regret in his eyes as he traced the back of his hand along her cheek. He studied her face for a long time until the regret became muddled with a new and different emotion. One that Liz couldn't name or rather was afraid to, because seeing it made her heart start to race uncontrollably. For a moment, he looked about ready to speak, but his lips moved without words. It was as if he were trying to form the thoughts and failing.

In the end, he simply stroked her cheek a second time, drawing out the contact for as long as possible while his brow furrowed in confusion. "Goodbye, Elizabeth."

He left her standing alone in her foyer.

That night, Charles sat in his study staring at the ball on his desk. The loft reminded him of Elizabeth these days. Hell, everything reminded him of Elizabeth, even the baseball. From now on he'd forever associate it with the night the two of them shared. The most incredible experience of his life.

The first time he shared part of his past with someone.

He still didn't know what prompted him to open up like that. For all intents and purposes, sharing personal information with someone was illogical and poor business practice. But Elizabeth made him act out of character. Hell, he actually had a heart-to-heart with a teenager because of her. Which didn't go all that bad, once they got started. He'd never qualify as a fifties sitcom father, but he did all right.

With a long sigh he set down the ball and picked up the report he'd been searching for. The original green initiatives proposal. He smiled, thinking of how easily Elizabeth rattled off facts and figures at the meeting in Concord. Sitting there in that ugly reindeer sweater, looking like a damn cover model. Looking back, he'd been a goner the minute she lectured him outside the restaurant.

A goner. His heart stilled. Was it possible? Elizabeth's face danced before him. He pictured her eyes. How they could be soft and light like hazelnut one moment and dark like chocolate the next. How they could turn black with desire or flash white-hot with determination.

How they could make you feel ten feet tall with their sparkle.

An ache locked itself in his chest. He finally understood why this sale bothered him. He hated the idea of leaving Elizabeth behind. He hated the idea of leaving her at all.

*Of losing her.*

The emotion that had plagued him for days finally had a name. Breaking free, it spread through his limbs and into his heart, filling him with a certainty like never before. He wanted Elizabeth. He wanted home cooked meals and high school hockey games and calculus homework. He wanted martinis and doughnut shop coffee and risking his life hitting deer. What he didn't want was to leave Elizabeth.

He was in love with his secretary.

The next morning Liz was sitting at her desk trying to pretend yesterday never happened. That Charles had not stopped by her house to talk with Andrew. Try as she might, she couldn't get the look on his face out of her mind. Something about his expression wouldn't let go and the power frightened her. She wanted nothing more than to bury herself in work for the next few weeks.

"Good morning, Elizabeth."

Would she ever hear Charles's greeting and not feel a reaction? Looking up she saw him standing in front of her with a smile brighter than any she'd ever seen.

Rather than speaking, he pulled her into his arms and

kissed her. A hard, passionate kiss that left her shaking and clinging to his coat. When she finally had the strength to move her forehead from his, she wished she hadn't.

What had been a hint of vague emotion in his eyes yesterday was now brilliant and certain. Its vibrancy called to her very core, wrapping around her heart and filling it with promise.

It scared the hell out of her.

"What if I told you I've decided not to sell Bishop Paper?" he asked her.

"I don't understand…."

Smiling, he brushed the hair from her cheek. His fingers were cold from the weather, and yet she was certain the temperature wasn't the cause of her shiver. "I've decided to stay in Gilmore."

Stay? He was staying? She'd been so certain his existence in her life would be temporary.

"But…"

He pressed an index finger to her lips. "I did a lot of thinking last night. I couldn't figure out why this sale didn't feel the same as the others. Normally by now I'd be ready to move on, knee deep in my next business acquisition. But I haven't even looked. I hadn't even thought about looking. You know why?"

Too stunned to speak, Liz shook her head.

He cradled her face in his hands so she had to look in his eyes. "The past month has been the most amazing month of my life. For the first time, I felt like I was a real part of something. That I had a place I belonged. I want to hold on to that feeling."

"By staying here at Bishop." Her head started to

swim. The air wouldn't go into her lungs, making her dizzy.

And still Charles kept smiling, his eyes resplendent in their blueness. "No, I mean staying with you. That's what I realized last night. Every good memory I have of this place involves you. You are the reason I want to stay, Elizabeth. I love you."

*I love you.* Liz's insides froze. She should be thrilled. This is what she was supposed to want, what she told herself not to hope for, and here it was happening. Why wasn't she overjoyed? Why did her entire body feel numb? Her heart began slamming against her rib cage. The room started to close in on her.

She pushed her way from his arms, to the other side the room where she could think.

"Elizabeth?" He came up behind her. "What's wrong?"

What was wrong was he'd said he loved her! "You can't love me," she told him, staring at the wall.

"Why not?"

"Because." God, what she would have done to hear those words once upon a time. What she did do to hear them. "I used to dream those words meant forever."

"They still can," he said, trying to draw her into his embrace.

"No," she said, fighting him. "That dream died a long time ago. I'm not sixteen and a half anymore. Dreams don't have the same appeal. Even if you get them, they fall through. Companies get sold. People leave. And believing they won't only leaves you worse off than before." That was the real bottom line. She'd loved and been stomped on enough in this world. She wasn't going to be stupid enough to try again.

"So, what?" he asked her. "Better to be alone than risk love and lose?"

"Why not?"

"Because it's a load of bull crap, that's why."

Liz blinked at the word. "Bad things happen all the time, Elizabeth. Life can kick you in the teeth. That's no excuse to not live."

"I live."

"No, you live through your son. That's not a life. That's existing."

She whirled around. "Don't you dare judge my decisions. I'm not the person who came here intending to obliterate his father's legacy."

"You're right." He met her toe-to-toe, his jaw tight with emotion. "I came here and I hated the man. I wanted to wipe his stupid company off the face of the map. And I'm not going to deny that I'm still angry, either. But you know something?" His nostrils flared. "I also figured out that getting rid of my father's memory wasn't going to fill the emptiness in my chest. That could only be filled by being part of something."

"For how long?" Liz countered.

"What?"

"How long will you be a part of this great something? I turned you down. There's no reason for you to stay. How long before you find a new buyer?"

Choking back what sounded like a groan, Charles jammed his fingers through his hair. "Why can't you believe I simply want to be here for you?"

"Because no one has before!"

The confession tore through her, coming out like a shot. She stood, fists at her sides, waiting for his reaction. For the inevitable admission she was right again. For him to back away from her like Bill and her mother.

But to her surprise, he didn't. "I'm not like the others," he said in a quiet voice. "The only one running is you."

# CHAPTER ELEVEN

Liz sat in her car in the darkened driveway telling herself she did not run away. She protected herself.

It was a lie.

*I love you.* What was wrong with her? An incredible man tells her he loves her, and what does she do? She should have thrown herself into his arms and told him the truth. That she was in love with him, too. Because she was. Much as she wanted to deny the truth, her heart knew otherwise. And yet instead of running toward him, her feet sent her the other way.

She was an idiot.

Andrew was already home and playing video games when she finally found the energy to walk into the house. Soon as he saw her, he dropped the controller. "Did you get my text?"

"What?"

"My text? I sent you one about an hour ago. My acceptance to Trenton came today."

Though hard, she managed an enthusiastic smile. "That's great, honey."

"They sent a whole bunch of financial aid stuff, too. I left the papers on the dining room table."

"Thanks. I'll look at them after dinner. Do you want to invite Victoria over to celebrate?"

"Sure. Do you, um…" He worried his bottom lip in his teeth. "Do you want to invite Mr. Bishop?"

Liz winced. "I don't think so."

"Why not? I thought you guys were having a, you know, a thing." With nonchalance she could only wish for, he retrieved the controller and returned to his game.

"Not…" Might as well be honest with the kid. "Not anymore."

"Is it because of me?"

"No."

"Mom…" He turned off the game. "Charles came by and talked with me. He told me you were worried that you'd give me the wrong impression and how upset you were with me and Vic."

"I know. I overheard part of the conversation."

"Figured you did."

She really didn't fool anybody, did she? "So, you want to tell me what he said?"

"I already told you," Andrew said with a shrug. "We talked about Victoria and how much you wanted me to have all the opportunities you missed out on, and how his parents pretty much ignored him growing up. Said he wanted me to appreciate how lucky I am. I do, you know."

She ruffled his hair, getting an annoyed head jerk. "Thanks," she said with a smile.

"He's not a bad guy really. I mean, he's a little stiff and he likes math a little too much, but just so you know, I'm cool with you dating him."

"I appreciate the permission." More than he'd know. "But I don't think that's going to happen."

"How come? It's clear he likes you."

"Yeah, he does," Liz replied, looking at her hands.

"And you like him, so why not hook up?"

"It's complicated."

Her son looked at her with a seriousness that made her realize her little boy wasn't so little anymore. "Not really. Not if you're into each other."

Later that night, Liz sat in the dark and thought about what her son said. Was it really as simple as allowing Charles into her heart? She was too old to rebuild her life again if it fell apart.

*But what if it didn't fall apart?*

A stupid question. Things always fell apart. Was whatever happiness you eked out worth the pain of eventually losing everything?

Rolling onto her side, she listened as Andrew got ready for bed. She was so proud of him for getting into Trenton. Her baby boy. He'd grown into such a great young man. She wouldn't trade him for the world.

*Even though he's going to leave you?*

Her insides stilled as the double standard smacked her square over the head. She loved Andrew with all her heart and soul, and though she knew he would leave her someday, she didn't regret one minute of having him. Far as she was concerned, the only person who lost out was his father. Her son had been worth every ounce of pain, sacrifice and fear.

*You're living through him. That's not living. That's existing.*

Rolling onto her back, Liz stared at the ceiling.

So maybe grabbing a little personal happiness would be worth the risk?

*What if it fell apart?*

*What if it didn't?*

Liz sighed. She wished she knew for sure.

Staring out into the parking lot, Charles couldn't help feel a tiny grain of relief. For the first time in what felt like months, Charles could see grass. Granted it was brown, but the promise of green and rebirth existed.

He wished he could say the same for his relationship with Elizabeth. They were still at a frozen impasse. Originally he'd hoped, after talking to her, she might see things differently, but as the night stretched out into morning, that hope began to fade.

Maybe she was right. Maybe forever was a big fat fantasy.

Go big or go home. Liz pressed a palm to her abdomen and knocked softly on the door.

"Come in."

Charles stood with his back to her, watching out the window. She wished she knew what he found so fascinating about the parking lot, but no matter. He looked so perfect standing there, her heart automatically flip-flopped.

"Hey," she greeted in a soft voice. "Can I have a word with you?"

He turned, and her breath caught. Wasn't fair a man could have such beautiful eyes. Nor was it fair they looked so sad.

*Because of her.*

"What can I do for you?"

Where did she start? "About yesterday. What you said…"

He waved her off. "I was out of line. Forget it."

"No. I can't. You were right."

He stared at her. "What?"

Now or never. "I'm scared."

There. She'd said it. "I'm scared that I'll finally be happy and life will pull the rug out from under me. That I'll end up lost and alone and worse off than ever. I wasn't sure I could survive losing something really wonderful. And you are the most wonderful thing that has happened to me in a long, long time. So I buried my heart as deep as I could and told myself I could fall. Because if I did, I'd crash and burn."

She paused. Charles didn't say a word so she plunged onward.

"Even now I'm afraid I'm making a mistake. I mean, I thought I'd be fine if I stayed alone. That I wouldn't get hurt, but…but…" Voice cracking, she sniffed away the emotion. "I'm pretty darn unhappy right now. So maybe the excuses are just as bad. Maybe I wasn't protecting my heart after all."

Again, Charles said nothing. Liz's heart sank. *So much for taking a chance.* She'd waited too long. She'd pushed him away one too many times.

Dejected, she turned to leave. "That's all I had to say. I just wanted you to know that when I said no, it wasn't because of you. And I'm sorry if I made you think it was."

"No one ever said life came with guarantees."

She stopped. "I know."

"I can't promise you a lifetime of never ending happiness, Elizabeth, or that there won't be problems and bumps in the road. I don't know what tomorrow will bring.

"The best I can do," he said, coming up from behind her, "is promise to try my damnedest to see that the ride is as wonderful and smooth as possible. The rest, you simply have to take on faith."

She let his words wash over her. Amazingly they were the most reassuring promises she'd ever received. "Faith, huh? I think I could try."

"Really?"

Starting now. Squeezing her eyes tight, Liz relaxed. And fell backward.

"Whoa! What the—"

She tumbled into Charles's waiting arms. Opening her eyes, she smiled at the man gazing down. His eyes bright with more emotion than she thought possible.

"You caught me," she said, touching his cheek.

He kissed her palm. "And I will every time. I love you, Elizabeth."

At that moment, Liz knew that no matter what happened in her future, this moment was worth every chance she took. "I love you, too," she told him, pulling him down for a kiss. "I love you, too."

# EPILOGUE

"MOM!"

At last. The salon promised the mousse would give the style lift, and for once in her life, her hair was volumized and behaving.

"Mom!"

The door to the ready room burst open. Liz smiled at the young man in the doorway. Dressed in his black tuxedo, the Trenton alum and new college freshman looked like a million dollars. Tears of pride sprang to her eyes. "You look so handsome," she told him, smoothing his lapels.

He brushed away her aggravation. "Mom, hurry up."

"Just a minute. I need to catch my breath." About a thousand butterflies had just taken flight in her stomach.

"Now, Mom. Everyone's waiting."

"Fine," she replied, sighing. She'd remember this next time he asked for a little more time. "Do you know where—"

"On the table by the door."

"Oh, right. Thanks."

Hands shaking, she hooked her arm through his and let him lead her out. "How do I…?"

"Great, Mom." Andrew paused and smiled, giving a glimpse of the man he would someday be. "You look beautiful. Now, let's get this show going."

The doors opened, and a hundred faces turned to look at her. Liz didn't notice. Her eyes were focused on the man standing at the front of the church. Charles wore a smile brighter than any light.

Instantly the butterflies in her stomach stopped. This risk, she thought, would be a piece of cake.

On the arm of her son, she headed down the aisle toward her future husband. The man who would always catch her when she fell.

\* \* \* \* \*